John McCabe is the author of four other acclaimed novels, *Stickleback*, *Paper*, *Snakeskin* and *Big Spender*. He lives in Birmingham and works as a geneticist.

Acclaim for

BIG SPENDER

'One of the ten men making the novel worth reading again'
Arena

'Riotously funny . . . One of the funniest novels you're ever likely to read'
Birmingham Post

'McCabe's writing is original, entertaining and compelling'
The Times

'Witty and incisive about the preoccupations of modern life'
Observer

SNAKESKIN

'Coincidence is just another tool of fate. And John McCabe uses this tool like a master craftsman, creating a thoroughly enjoyable comedy of errors . . . Every twist and turn of *Snakeskin* makes you wonder just how many sub-plots McCabe can introduce into one book and it's a pleasure to watch the whole story unfurl'
Punch

'McCabe's madcap third novel is Carl Hiaasen meets John O'Farrell by way of Leslie Neilsen. Hi-octane hi-jinx'
Mirror

Also by John McCabe

STICKLEBACK
PAPER
SNAKESKIN
BIG SPENDER

and published by Black Swan

HERDING CATS

John McCabe

BLACK SWAN

HERDING CATS
A BLACK SWAN BOOK : 0 552 77090 6

Originally published in Great Britain by Doubleday,
a division of Transworld Publishers

PRINTING HISTORY
Doubleday edition published 2003
Black Swan edition published 2004

1 3 5 7 9 10 8 6 4 2

The author and publishers are grateful for permission to reprint lines from
'The Best' by Tina Turner © 1988 Knighty Knight Music (administered by
Wixen Music Publishing, Inc.) and Mike Chapman Enterprises (c/o Zomba
Music).

Set in 11/13pt Melior by
Kestrel Data, Exeter, Devon

Black Swan Books are published by Transworld Publishers,
61–63 Uxbridge Road, London W5 5SA,
a division of The Random House Group Ltd,
in Australia by Random House Australia (Pty) Ltd,
20 Alfred Street, Milsons Point, Sydney, NSW 2061, Australia,
in New Zealand by Random House New Zealand Ltd,
18 Poland Road, Glenfield, Auckland 10, New Zealand
and in South Africa by Random House (Pty) Ltd,
Endulini, 5a Jubilee Road, Parktown 2193, South Africa.

Printed and bound in Great Britain by
Cox & Wyman Ltd, Reading, Berkshire.

Papers used by Transworld Publishers are natural, recyclable products
made from wood grown in sustainable forests. The manufacturing
processes conform to the environmental regulations of the country of origin.

For the next generation:
Baby Jones, babies Gibson, baby Gayle, baby Bellamy, baby Travis, baby McMullen, baby Gittoes, baby Bulman, baby Hagan, baby Moore and, of course, baby McCabe.

HERDING CATS

An End to Peace

A stack of pallets blazed in the corner of a dying industrial building. Two men stood and faced the same direction, flames alternately lighting and shading their features, a greasy sweat oozing from their pores. The slimmer of the two tucked a baseball bat through the belt of his grubby jeans. 'I want . . . a bigger share,' he snarled.

'No way,' the other answered. 'We carved it up fair and square.'

'That was' – a piece of wood crackled and sent a spark fizzing through the air – 'seven years ago.'

'So?'

'You were strong then. Now you're dying . . . on your arse. I've heard the rumours. So I want more . . . of what's going.'

The silence was broken by another violent crack in front of them. 'Taunsley is a small town, and I'm a big player. There's no way you can reach me.'

'No fucker is out . . . of reach. Not even you.' When riled, the leaner man talked in short volleys, his machine-gun delivery hitting home in prickly bursts. Behind a second stack of broken pallets, a pair of eyes watched proceedings intently.

'You can't touch me. And you know it.'

'Maybe I don't . . . know it any more.'

'You've got your ten per cent. Be thankful for that. The town is quiet and there's been no trouble for a long time. So let's just leave it there. Now unless there's anything else, I—'

'I know how to . . . ruin you.'

'I am a rich man,' he replied irritably, as a pallet infested with flames succumbed to the attack and collapsed, bleeding sparks across the floor towards another pile of timber. 'I employ a lot of people. You won't be able to ruin me.'

'That all depends . . . on your definition,' the man answered.

'Meaning?'

'Finances don't even . . . come into it. Your definition of ruination . . . is not my definition.'

There was a lengthy pause, punctuated only by a mild whimpering noise as flames took hold in the adjacent wood. Both men gazed into their own fire, too enraged to look at one another.

'Spell it out for me.'

'I'm saying that . . . in this age of image and communication . . . of commerce and advertising . . . ruination has taken on another meaning.'

'Which is?'

'Now the mayor is dead . . . things are set to change . . . in Taunsley. A lot of his by-laws . . . have been overturned.'

The eyes that had been observing the scene widened considerably as the fire really got going.

'So what are you proposing – using local by-laws to damage me?'

'Or lack of. And then,' the slimmer of the two said, removing the bat and scratching his newly cropped hair with it, 'I'm coming to get you.'

As his companion slipped back into the darkness, the portly man savoured the last of his cigar. He licked his dry lips. Fear and anticipation surged through his body. It was time to go to war again. He tossed the spent butt into the fire and watched the flames slowly eat it up. Seconds after he had walked away, the roofless building was filled with commotion. A large, scruffy man tore through the increasingly alight pile of timber concealing him. Taking out his member, he treated his shoes, which were on the verge of melting, to a prolonged river of urine. While he doused himself, he opened a can of warm lager and swallowed it gratefully. Being burned alive didn't, as far as he could recall, feature among the duties of his job. Squelching away from the scene, the tramp-like man took out a notepad and scribbled down the details he had been able to discern between moments of blind panic. On reaching his car, which had been hidden at the back of the building, he sprayed himself liberally with a can marked Toilet Freshener. The pubs were still open, and he was willing to bet that a combined odour of singed hair, molten shoes, urine, cigarettes, lager and poor hygiene was not going to get him served. Still, one more piece of evidence had been collected. The Big Story was about to enter its final and bloody phase.

Simply the Best

Inside the office of Tim Power Advertising plc, Taunsley, Avonshire, Tim Power sat at his desk, appreciating that Taunsley was a small town with a big problem. Its 30,000 residents, almost without exception, were oblivious to the outside world. There was an insularity about the place that unnerved people who passed through. The gene pool was more of a puddle, most visitors not staying long enough to muddy its waters with their genetic material.

But what made the town's isolation all the more remarkable in an age of cheap and fast transport was its geography. It lay in the middle of a flat expanse of arable land, close to motorways, railway lines and even an airport. On still summer evenings the continuous rumble of other people's progress could clearly be heard above the town's torpor. Taunsley could barely have been more accessible. The whole world was available to its residents at the turn of a car key. But no one, aside from his girlfriend, chose to leave. Few journeyed in the opposite direction either. Those who did weren't exactly given a civic reception. And as a recent new arrival, Tim still felt more like an intruder than an incomer.

Glancing up at his sole client of the day, Taunsley's

first and only advertising executive tried to remain calm. Without really listening, he appreciated that it was about to happen again.

'So what I really want is something, how shall I put it?' Mr Fellows of Fellows and Sons Motors, Taunsley, paused.

Tim did all he could to speed the painful process to its inexorable conclusion. 'Direct?'

'Direct!'

'I see.'

'Now we're getting somewhere,' Mr Fellows beamed. He was lean, fair, and always dressed in linen suits as if on the perpetual verge of a safari. He scratched his scalp, not in the usual way, but by keeping his hand still and nodding his head. 'Above everything else, it's directness I'm after,' he continued.

'And you want me to come up with a campaign, some slogans, that sort of thing?'

'Yeeesss,' he replied. 'Only I've already come up with a slogan.'

Tim entertained the mental image of Mr Fellows being run over by one of his own cars. 'Which is?' he asked, knowing full well what it was. Seventeen clients, and twelve of them had the same lousy slogan.

Mr Fellows cleared his throat and puffed himself up, as if he was pitching a huge new concept. '**Simply the Best!**'

In his reversed role, Tim summoned his best impression of surprise and admiration. '**Simply the Best!**' he echoed.

'What do you think?'

Please kill me. Someone, drop something heavy on me from a large height. Put me out of my misery. A big London ad firm, expenses, clever campaigns, receptive clients, for this. What the hell was I thinking? And if I ever meet Tina Turner there's going to be trouble. Tim tried to disguise his bitter regret. He steadied himself. This was the fourth **Simply the Best** since Monday. It was going to be a long week. 'What do I think?' Again, images of an easy death and a quick exit from being the sole advertiser in a small town seduced him in sharp monochrome and tasteful slow-motion footage. 'Fucking,' please death come now, 'fucking,' he looked hopefully up towards the ceiling, 'fucking,' he shook his head and made a pact to try and last until lunchtime without cursing his change in fortune, 'fantastic!' he said, finally. 'Love it! Let's go for it!'

Mr Fellows sat back in his chair and grinned. '**Fellows Motors. Simply the Best!**'

Tim ran an irritable finger down the bridge of his nose. What was it with this town? Surely there had to be a compromise. To try to appease his client and yet move things forward, he decided to propose a daring move up the evolutionary ladder of creative advertising. 'OK, it's good,' he said, resting forwards on the palms of his hands, his expensive watch clinking against the glass of the table, 'but it's slightly . . . well, overused. So how about this? Just a slight shift in emphasis.' Tim took a deep breath. '**Fellow's Motors – Better Than All The Rest.**'

While Mr Fellows mouthed the new words to himself, Tim's assistant Dave coughed portentously. Tim glanced over at the other side of the office. On Dave's desk, a small sign read, 'David Manners, Assistant Advertising Executive, Power Advertising'. A few weeks ago, Tim had been severely outfoxed by a work experience girl, who hadn't wanted the work and certainly didn't need the experience. At sixteen, she had run rings around him. He smiled, before realizing that his assistant was about to say something.

'What tag line are you going to use then, eh?' Dave asked. **'Better than anyone, anyone I've ever met**? Doesn't quite scan, does it?'

Tim glared at him. Technically it wasn't Dave's job to assassinate his ideas in front of mediocre clients. 'No, but it's something different.'

'There isn't anything different. Those are the lyrics, that's how it goes.'

'But—'

'You can't muck about with a classic. Look,' Dave explained, heading for the CD player, 'I'll put the song on again.'

Tim stood up. 'No you fucking won't,' he said with menace.

Mr Fellows cleared his throat. 'I don't really want to take sides,' he muttered, removing a small fleck of something from his suit, 'but I think Dave's got a point. "Simply the Best" is an all-time great. And if it ain't broke, don't fix it.'

Tim sat back down and reclined his chair with a forced smile, an expression of benevolence painted across his displeasure. Before he had come to Taunsley, everything had been right. What had struck him the very first time he visited was the lack of marketing in the place. It was like a blank canvas. Journeying from London to Taunsley was a weekly culture shock. The tube had ads on the escalators, ads on the trains, even ads on the ads. Every available chunk of the city was being eaten by a visible essence which spewed catchy slogans and half-amusing puns. Nothing escaped its clutches. The clothes you wore, the phone you carried, the watch you checked. Objects had become self-promoting, their logos large enough for everyone to see, the disposable consumer durable becoming the new hoarding. It had you by the balls, and this is what Tim loved. It didn't matter how rational you were about the whole thing, it still sucked you in. It was that powerful. No one was immune. Not even advertising executives.

Taunsley, however, was different.

The reason the town was so untouched by the hand of advertising was down to its recently deceased mayor. For motives unclear both to Tim and to Taunsley, the town had remained virtually free from the evils of word-play slogans and soft-focus pictures for nearly two decades. As a result, local businesses went unpromoted except by word of mouth. Supermarkets were forced to compete solely through offering the best prices. Companies had to plough money otherwise wasted on marketing back into research and development. There were no products that promised to change your life, just parochial 'Thompson's Bicycles' kind of stuff. This was what advertising used to be. Direct. Straight from manufacturer to consumer. Where everything did exactly what it said on the tin, and where the advertiser wasn't Satan in a posh suit, just a necessary source of information. And the town, while not actually thriving, was at least getting by.

However, things were beginning to change. The previous year, the mayor had perished in an industrial accident and the council had quietly overturned his ruling. So the situation had appeared ripe for the picking. Tim was an advertiser in seemingly the only population in the country which wasn't surrounded by brand names and logos staring out from huge overwhelming billboards, on lamp posts, on the sides of buses, at train stations, in taxis, or on unfortunate souls strapped into sandwich boards. He would, he had hoped, bring the joys of commercial promotion to those previously deprived of it outside their living rooms. And yet the only catchphrase the town was interested in pursuing came from a single song inflicted on the world in the mid-1980s. He glanced up at Mr Fellows, his smile fading. Endless conceptual possibilities were increasingly boiling down to just one message. And the fact that Millhouse Motors, Granger's Garage and Renault of Taunsley were all also **Simply the Best** didn't appear to bother him in the slightest.

Mr Fellows went away distinctly happy, and Tim sat and watched his head bob along the sparse pavement below. Momentarily, he imagined putting a hole through it with a sniper's rifle. Business was verging on the disastrous. Hour by hour, all the money he had ever saved was leaking from his bank account. And with clients like Mr Fellows insisting on the same cheap and dismal slogan the situation was unlikely to change. In fact, quite why most of his clients bothered to use his services was beyond him. Still, in a town like Taunsley, he was rapidly discovering, a lot of things didn't make much sense.

CoHABITation

After work, Tim swung off the heavily used bypass and headed for home. He lived in St Paul's Square, a small area where four of Taunsley's streets banded together to create an enclave of relative sanity within the town. Large terraced properties that bordered the central park were so sought after they fetched the same price as cramped one-bedroom flats in Clapham. Their owners drove German cars rather than the Japanese, French or even, rarely, British vehicles favoured by the rest of Taunsley. Gardens were frighteningly well taken care of, and even the pavements appeared unusually hygienic, with the town's dogs respectfully taking their business elsewhere.

Tim drew up outside his house and sighed as he approached the front door. He was suffering from an unusual domestic situation. Generally, the lowest number of people needed for successful cohabitation is two. Tim and his girlfriend Zoe, however, had whittled this requirement down to one. It was a minimalist arrangement which seemed to suit Zoe substantially more than Tim. While she made her way around the circumference of the world with a rucksack on her back and a Lonely Planet guide in her hand, Tim paid the bills and kept the place more or less tidy. He closed the door behind him and let his briefcase sink into the thick carpet. On the floor was a postcard with a distinctly un-British beach on the front. He slid the card into his trouser pocket without reading the blue biro on the back, and hung his jacket on the banister.

The timing had been less than ideal. Just as Tim had ditched a perfectly acceptable life in London, Zoe had received the offer of a lifetime – a cheap round-the-world trip with her best friend. She had seized the joint opportunity of adventure and boyfriend evaluation with the alacrity of one stuck in a small town and an uncertain relationship.

'This will be the ultimate test,' Zoe had said, as they struggled towards the coach station with luggage enough to fill a plane.

'Of what?' he'd asked.

'Of our commitment. If we can manage for a year, we must be right for each other.'

'But we are right for each other,' Tim had pleaded. 'You don't have to test me to discover that.'

'Look, you'll be able to throw yourself into your business venture. And by the time I get back, you'll be a millionaire and we'll know how strong our feelings truly are.'

'I know how strong my feelings are,' Tim said, continuing to dispute the logic of his girlfriend's actions, 'or I wouldn't have moved here to be with you.'

Zoe put one of her bags down and hugged her boyfriend, the airport coach appearing over his shoulder. 'Don't fail the test,' she said, kissing him goodbye.

Tim had stood and watched silently as his girlfriend boarded the bus, leaving the driver to strain her rucksacks into the luggage compartment. When the vehicle pulled out of Taunsley's coach station, she waved enthusiastically. Tim waved back, but with less

21

eagerness. For the second time in his life, he had been abandoned. First his father had left, a week before his twelfth birthday, with barely a word of explanation, swearing to one day come back for him. Now his girlfriend had repeated the trick. And judging from his father's form, there was no guarantee he would ever see her again. He had walked disconsolately back to St Paul's Square to begin a minimum twelve months' lonely celibacy.

Checking the empty answering machine, the irony of Zoe's behaviour didn't elude him. While she travelled halfway round the world to find herself, he had journeyed less than a hundred miles to discover himself entirely lost. While she was coping with foreign languages and strange customs, Tim was struggling to penetrate the thick vowel sounds and bizarre conventions of Taunsley. And while she undoubtedly found the natives interesting and open, Tim had been welcomed into the region with nothing more hospitable than an indifferent shrug. After months of planning, they had managed to live together for just five weeks. Two and a half years of long-distance love, and here they were again, now more remote than ever.

Tim trudged up to his room to change out of his work clothes. Glancing around the place, he smiled a little, pleased with the progress he was making. Five months ago, when he'd taken over responsibility for what was supposed to be their joint home, he'd immediately set about de-feminizing the place, to reinforce the fact that she had left and that he would now be living alone. Out had gone cushions, throws, rugs, coasters and place mats. Exotic spices, interesting herbs and all fruit and veg had been purged from the kitchen. Her fifty-two bottles of various bathroom nonsense had been replaced by toothpaste, soap, shampoo and deodorant, which sat rather sadly on a shelf used to groaning under an excessive weight of preening material. Anti-ageing, anti-wrinkle and anti-sag creams from the bedroom had been confined to the back of a drawer. (The anti-ageing creams came with a sell-by date, which didn't seem a good sign.) Roughly 4 stone of coats had been extracted from their hiding place in the bedroom wardrobe. Twenty-eight pairs of very similar shoes had been frog-marched up to the loft. Eleven pairs of variously faded jeans and fourteen tops were similarly ejected. In their place, Tim had triumphantly hung his three work suits, five shirts and four pairs of shoes.

Unfastening his trousers, Tim remembered the postcard in his pocket. He examined the front, which held a greeting from New Zealand. He flipped it over and squinted at the round, even handwriting on the back.

'Have been thinking about your business,' Zoe wrote. 'Phone my uncle, Barry Dinsdale. Time and Motion expert. Number in book. Knows what you need to know. Barry will sort you out. Missing you greatly. Only seven more months. Hang on in there, love Zoe.'

Driving to the Bottle Bank

Barry Dinsdale, Time and Motion expert, sat on his sofa and watched the second hand of the large living-room clock stutter round in slow circles. It was 20:24:52, 20:24:53, 20:24:54. In six seconds, it would be 20:25 exactly. The children were already bathed, fed and sent to bed. His wife was getting ready to leave for the gym. The washing-up was being processed by the dishwasher. The kitchen had been wiped, and the living room tidied after the onslaught of his offspring. He sat up and straightened the shoes he had just kicked off, before opening the TV listings. Barry used a marker pen to identify programmes of possible interest. He then jotted down times and channels in a notebook he kept on a nearby table, and set his watch alarm for one minute before the beginning of the first programme. Despite an awkward gap of twenty minutes around 9:30, the evening was laid out before him in fluorescent pen and watch beeps. And then he noticed that the remote control was on top of the TV. As he stood up, he glimpsed an image of his wife through the double doors rounding up her sports stuff, and cursed. Although he could see the benefit of exercise, this particular activity rankled with him. It wasn't the fact that she kept in shape, and fantastic shape at that, more the way she went about it. He had tried arguing with her but to little avail. Confrontation merely brought out her mile-wide anarchic streak. However, for the sake of something to do before the first programme began, he decided to have another go as she entered the room.

'You seen the car keys?' Cathy asked.

Barry seized the opportunity. 'So you're driving there?'

'Uh-huh.'

'Look,' he said as she spotted the keys, 'I know I've mentioned this before, but what *is* the point in driving to the gym to use a running machine?'

'Not this again.'

'But where the hell does it get you?'

Cathy Dinsdale, recently slim, trim and toned, remained defiant, sports bag in one hand, keys in the other. 'Out of the house, for a start.'

'But surely it would be much more efficient to run around the park a couple of times? No need to use the car.'

'You drive the car all the time.'

'That's not the point.' Barry ran a bad-tempered hand through his short bushy hair and adjusted his glasses. 'I don't use it to go to a gym to operate a machine that serves absolutely no purpose.'

Cathy's eyes widened. 'It serves the purpose of helping me run,' she enunciated slowly.

'You've got legs for that. And the council have generously paved most of the town to provide a surface for you. I mean, what is the point of a running machine?'

'It measures how far I've run.'

'You could do that in the car.'

'You said I shouldn't use the car,' she answered tersely.

'I only said . . . Look, how far is it to this gym?'

'A mile each way.'

'And how far do you run when you get there?'

Cathy adjusted her disturbingly short dress. 'Couple of miles.'

Barry appeared to swell. 'And you *pay* for this?'

'Forty-two pounds.'

'A year?'

'A month.'

'Christ.' Barry rubbed his face and tried to remain composed.

'You'll be telling me next that the exercise bike I've ordered is a waste of time.'

'*Well* . . .'

'Or that our rowing machine is useless and I should simply get a boat and trawl around the local duck pond.'

Barry inhaled a long, calming breath. 'Let me explain.' He placed his hands on Cathy's shoulders to ram his message home. 'Darling, it's like when you drive to the bottle bank to recycle a few bottles. The energy you use doing it, and the harm you do the environment starting your car, travelling there and parking, is far greater than the net benefit of salvaging a couple of pieces of glass. It's all wasted energy. Driving to the gym to fake running or cycling is lunacy, when you could simply run or cycle.'

'Finished?' Cathy asked, shrugging his hands away.

Barry remained silent. He'd only just got started.

'Before I go,' she mouthed slowly and deliberately, 'I'm doing all this for you. I want you to remember that. And as you sit there on your arse while I put myself through gruelling exercise after gruelling exercise, think to yourself, this is for my benefit.'

Chance would be a fine thing, Barry muttered.

Cathy walked out of the room, past her husband, making vicious eye contact. From the kitchen came the sound of bottles clinking. She returned. 'And I think I'll recycle these bottles while I'm out,' she summed up. 'That's unless you want them inserting somewhere painful.'

The phone rang and Barry took the welcome opportunity to limp back to the sofa, away from further attack. Picking up the receiver, he resolved in future not to antagonize his wife until he had rehearsed his arguments more fully.

Tim and Motion

On the telephone, Barry Dinsdale sounded unusually pent-up for a resident of Taunsley. In a slightly nasal voice, Barry said he knew a lot about the commercial world, particularly with regard to efficiency, and suggested that they meet at Tim's premises the following afternoon. That way, he added ominously, they could mix business with pleasure. On the other end of the line, standing alone in the kitchen, Tim Power couldn't see it himself. Neither his girlfriend's distant relatives nor an ergonomics expert were likely to bring any joy to his life. And as a combined event, misery was almost guaranteed.

Business was slacker than ever, and Tim spent a good deal of the following morning examining the items that littered his desk. As well as an impressive array of products he had advertised in his career, his bureau groaned under the mass of several largely redundant executive toys. Tim had bought these under the impression that he might need occasional distraction from the high-powered activity at hand. Fat chance, he sighed, rearranging them in alphabetical order in readiness for the afternoon meeting. As he did so, his set of clackers collapsed, sending ballbearings with attached wires scurrying across the desk. During the forty-five minutes he devoted to rounding them up, swearing and sellotaping the 1970s contraption back together, he pondered the nature of his current venture. This was the first, and hopefully last, time he would ever be self-employed. Previously Tim had always worked for other people. It was easier that way – there was someone to dislike, someone to secretly blame when it all went wrong. Now, scanning the office, he appreciated that things were different. And although his workforce technically constituted only one person, who was more a sullen presence than an actual force, Tim still now came under the dreaded and despised category of 'boss'. It was, he readily conceded, an uncomfortable position, and barely an improvement on not being in charge.

When finally his clackers had been stitched back together – a medical complaint he was sincerely desperate to avoid – he tried them out. If anything, they were slightly disappointing, and didn't so much clack as thud wearily. Noticing that lunchtime was approaching, Tim left the office with Dave silently in tow. Taunsley's sole Creative Advertising Team drank a combined effort of five pints, scoffed four sandwiches, one bag of crisps and a Mars bar, drew heavily on eleven cigarettes, visited the toilet four times, invested one pound fifty in the jukebox, lost (Tim) or won (Dave) three games of pool, and, satisfied with such multitasking, staggered back to work.

From first impressions, when he eventually arrived almost three-quarters of an hour late, Barry was not going to make Tim's existence any more fun. He shook his right hand with enough force to spill the coffee Tim was holding in his left. There was a vague air of authority about him which reminded Tim of a teacher trying to regain control of an unruly class.

After introductory pleasantries, Barry nosed around the office of Power Advertising, holding a clipboard in front of him and occasionally tutting. Tim sat back and watched him mistrustfully, his bladder slowly filling. Barry completed his tour and perched on a chair opposite.

'So,' Tim asked, 'do you think you can save my business? Get me heading in the right direction?'

'Quite possibly.'

'Great.'

'But first things first. If I've got one immediate observation,' he said, 'it's that your office set-up is holding you back.'

'Really?'

'Give me a few days, though, and I'll have it running like a well-oiled machine.'

Tim examined a collection of cigarette butts in his ashtray. They looked like fat maggots that had run into brick walls. He knew that his business was so inefficient it made local government look ruthless, and that while he wasn't actually bankrupt yet the tide of money was flowing firmly against him. Maybe, he conceded, it was time for expert intervention. 'How?' he asked hopefully.

'I'd check how you sit.'

'I slump, mainly.'

'How your filing system was arranged.'

'What filing system?'

'Where your employees are located in relation to you.'

'Dave usually sits four hundred yards down the road, in the pub.'

'How you log your calls.'

'Back of an envelope.'

'Your means of employee communication.'

'I shout, generally.'

'How you spend the majority of your day.'

'Seat tilted back. Feet on desk. Multitasking.'

'You know, that sort of thing.'

'Right.'

Barry tried to appear serious. 'But I think from what I've seen already there are some serious issues here.'

'You do?'

'I'm afraid so. It's my job to spot these things. I'm an Ergonomics Engineer.'

'So you've trained in engineering?' Tim asked.

'No. Ergonomics.'

'And what has that got to do with engineering?'

Barry wiped his glasses clean using his tie. 'It's a technical thing.'

Tim monitored the comings and goings of the car park below. Although something obviously needed to be done, having a stranger poke around his business was unsettling. 'Look, Barry,' he said, 'I called you last night because Zoe said you might be able to help me. Things aren't going well. But I would have thought I needed firm business advice above everything else.'

'Let's get your office right for starters, and we'll take it from there. What I want to do initially is to bring my electrogoniometer in and set it up.'

'Sounds painful. What does it do?'

'It measures and records the amount of bending or twisting of a joint and determines how active you are.'

'So?'

'To be successful, you first have to work correctly.'

'And then what?'

'I'm going to spend a day with you. Determine how much effort you put into each sector of work, see how you assign tasks, that sort of thing.'

'Tasks?' Barry really had no idea what he was letting himself in for. The office received an average of three phone calls a week. 'Well, it's your funeral,' Tim replied, shaking his head. 'Your funeral completely.'

Threatening Behaviour

Derek Gribben scanned through the Employment Required section of the newspaper in front of him, through his old address book, through the personal details of all his employees, but drew a blank. Where, he wondered quietly, do you get that sort of person? Who do you contact to find that calibre of man?

The skills he was seeking rarely showed up on CVs. If anything, the expertise he was after generally kept itself to itself, and certainly didn't advertise. In fact, the higher the level of qualification, the less you knew about it. And it wasn't as if you could phone anyone. As far as he knew, 'Breaking and Entering', 'Threatening Behaviour' and 'Aggravated Assault' weren't listed in the *Yellow Pages*. Just to make sure, he checked anyway. When the inevitable result had been confirmed, he shouted at his secretary to get him a coffee. Awaiting caffeine stimulation, Derek flicked idly through one or two of the employment records in the open file he had been perusing. These men had given him short-lived hope. Knowing them as he did, he was amazed to read that none reported criminal activity among their hobbies. Even Kevin Connolly, who had virtually been born in Borstal and was, Derek firmly believed, stealing from him on an hourly basis, listed his Other Interests as 'Reading, Charity and Travel'. Believe the job applications of half of his staff, and he seemed to be running some sort of literary club for perpetual do-gooders.

Derek looked out at his workforce, and a grim sight it proved to be. Any one of them, the women included, might be able to help him. But how did you find out? To ask would be to show his hand. And while Kevin Connolly certainly didn't spend his evenings reading and hadn't travelled further than a series of detention centres, he was unlikely to own up to wrongdoing, especially to the man who paid his wages. One of his workers entered the office and apprehensively asked for the afternoon off, which Derek declined. The man slunk hurriedly away, petrified of his boss, a situation Derek did nothing to rectify. He liked it that way. It was, he felt, best that as many people in Taunsley were scared of him as possible. Certainly, local rumour had it that he was not a man to fuck with, and this brought him a large measure of satisfaction. It had been a hard-won reputation, and losing an arm in the process had only increased the fearful respect which most people showed him. With a single exception, however. Derek's secretary dropped a cup of coffee on his desk, the saucer collecting a fair proportion of the liquid.

'Cathy,' Derek barked, 'you've spilled some. Go and get me a cloth.'

Cathy Dinsdale, wife of Barry, ignored the instruction. 'Get one yourself,' she answered, sauntering back to her seat. These were the four hours of the day when she wasn't cooking, cleaning or tending to the needs of her household, and she was buggered if she was going to be running around mopping up hot beverages at work as well. And although she had recently noted a

34

large shotgun in her boss's filing cabinet, Cathy doubted he would shoot her over such a small matter. Besides, dealing with an obvious psycho like Derek Gribben was fantastic practice for putting her husband in his place.

Derek scratched the back of his head irritably and returned his thoughts to the scheme at hand. Maybe, he thought, scalding his tongue on the coffee, there was logic in keeping this business removed from his place of work. People in small towns talked. Secrets were few and far between. Which brought him back to his original dilemma. How did you ask someone if they were willing to break the law for you, without the whole population finding out?

Derek touched his tongue with the index finger of his only hand. The tongue felt numb and tingly, just like the stump of his arm did from time to time. He slammed his fist onto the table, summoning forth another flood of coffee. Cursing, he moved his newspaper out of the way. As he did so, and on the point of admitting defeat, his attention was grabbed by a headline. Perhaps that was it, he whispered to himself. Perhaps that was it. In the Court News section of the local paper, a few stories held potential. There were several neighbourly disputes and the odd domestic. Not exactly what he was after, but the idea was there. Reading on, he quickly came to see that it was just a matter of picking the right story. He would monitor the *Taunsley Mercury* for the next few days. Some time soon someone was going to slip up badly. And when they did, Derek Gribben would be onto them before they could say, 'Suspended sentence pending psychiatric reports.'

Assessment

Two days later, and Tim was apprehensive. Barry's arrival was imminent and he had a bad feeling about what he was going to say. Time and Motion people, he imagined, rarely brought good news. He carefully opened the leaflet Barry had given him, entitled 'How to Stop Procrastinating and Get Your Business Back on Track'. As far as he could see, the trick was to stop wasting time on peripheral activities and to simply focus on the main issue at hand. Prioritize. Organize. Focus. He reread the leaflet. Tim noticed a spelling mistake, and drew round it with a biro, before highlighting it with his marker pen. He entered 'Mention spelling mistake to Barry' in his list of things to do. Then he worried that the pamphlet's grammar wasn't too good and had a go at rewriting it himself. Twenty minutes later, Tim heard a car door slam outside and peered through the window. It was Barry, and he knew it was time to face the music.

When he finally entered the office, Barry appeared flustered. 'Bloody traffic,' he said, as Dave grappled with his coat, like he was trying to remove it without his permission. 'And those flaming kids.'

'You've got children?' Tim asked.

'Don't ask,' Barry replied seriously. 'I mean it. As

a general rule, please never ask me about my off-spring.'

'Right,' Tim nodded, mildly curious.

'Or my wife.'

'Fine.'

'Well, here it is,' Barry beamed, his agitation subsiding. He held a slim brown file up in front of him.

'Great. Sit down. Give me the news.'

'Are you ready?'

'As I'll ever be.'

'Sure?'

'Please don't drag this out. If you've got something bad to say, let's have it.'

Barry paused and squinted at Tim with his bloodshot blue eyes. 'OK, here we go. This is a breakdown of your day's activities.' He cleared his throat. 'So, to start off with, you spend 14 per cent of the day actually working.'

'How much?'

'14 per cent.' Barry peered at Tim over his glasses. 'This equates to roughly sixty minutes.'

'And the rest?'

'The rest – well, in no particular order, 8 per cent scratching, 3 per cent moving your bowels, 8.5 per cent using the computer to send and receive dubious emails, 2 per cent examining your watch and sighing, 2 per cent puffing out your cheeks and making a popping noise, 9 per cent talking on the phone, 2 per cent checking for non-existent phone messages, 2.5 per cent removing papers from your in-tray, 2.5 per cent putting the same papers back in your in-tray, 2 per cent slurping cups of tea, 1.5 per cent eating, 1 per cent sniffing various office items, 1.5 per cent yawning, 1 per cent chewing your pen and appearing thoughtful, 1 per cent biting your fingernails, 0.5 per cent complaining about a migraine, 2 per cent reading the packets of various headache cures, 6 per cent drawing on a piece of paper which you then threw in the bin, 1.5 per cent staring blankly out of the window, 1 per cent swearing at your assistant . . .'

'*Executive* assistant,' Dave interjected from the far side of the office.

'4 per cent unsuccessfully trying to steal other people's slogans from the internet, 3 per cent rocking back on your chair and attempting to balance, 2 per cent telling your *executive* assistant to get busy with things, 1 per cent flicking idly through magazines, seemingly without absorbing anything, 1.5 per cent reading the *Taunsley Mercury* and guffawing, 0.5 per cent cutting headlines out of the *Taunsley Mercury*, 0.5 per cent humming a tune which appeared to be – although I might be mistaken . . .'

'What?'

'"Simply The Best" by Tina Turner.'

'No fucking way.'

'2 per cent playing Solitaire on your PC.'

'I was *thinking* . . .'

'0.5 per cent taking your computer mouse to pieces, 3 per cent trying to put it back together, 1 per cent ordering a new mouse, and – and this is the important one . . .'

'Yes?'

Barry furrowed his brow and glanced up from his clipboard. '14 per cent rushing through your single meeting of the day, complaining about being busy.'

Tim shrugged. 'It was an important client – Brenda Davies of Jenkins Meat Products.'

'But they're the town's largest employer. Why, on such a slack day, did you mess them about?'

'To give the impression that I was snowed under and

38

was doing them a favour. You know how these things work.'

Barry didn't appear convinced. 'Not really,' he answered.

Tim placed the biro he was chewing back on his desk, and took a sip of tea, scratching his arm, thinking things through. 'So, overall, what you're saying is that I'm wasting most of my time?' he asked.

'Yes. In terms of corporate efficiency—'

'No, I mean wasting my time coming to work.' Tim stood up excitedly. 'You're saying I could just pop in for an hour a day and get every bit as much done?'

'I suppose that's one way of looking—'

'Right, from now on . . .' Tim scanned the figures he'd scribbled down. He pondered for a second. 'Hang on, that's only 91 per cent,' he said. 'What about the other 9 per cent?'

Barry cleared his throat. 'I couldn't, in all good faith,' he said, 'give you 100 per cent.'

'I see.'

'And I also took the liberty of performing a similar assessment of Dave yesterday.'

'God help us,' Tim muttered quietly.

'Your assistant—'

'Execut—'

'Whatever, spends his day in a remarkably similar way to you, except for the following points: he spends 4 per cent less of his time scratching, but 3 per cent more in the toilet. He plays Minesweeper instead of Solitaire on his computer, but devotes roughly the same proportion of his time to it. In addition, he does nothing but shrug for fifteen minutes of the day, picks his ears for about ten, makes a frankly irritating clicking sound—'

'You've noticed that? I told you, Dave, but you wouldn't believe—'

'Glares at you for around 2 per cent of his day, makes and answers what appear to be fake phone calls, and passes about an hour so inactively I couldn't even categorize it.'

Tim sat down again. 'Anything else?' he asked.

'There is some more information. I'll tell you what the conductive polymer sensors attached to your muscles told me.' Barry paused ominously.

'Go on,' Tim sighed.

'That you exerted virtually no muscular forces throughout the whole day.'

'Is that unusual?'

'Only among the living. You basically – and I hate to say this so bluntly to a kind-of relative – did nothing yesterday.'

Tim didn't like to tell Barry that the previous day had been one of his more active ones. What shocked him was not the amount of time he was wasting at work, but the amount of time he could be spending elsewhere doing something constructive. His activities had expanded to fill the available space, even to the extent of spending three-quarters of an hour each day scratching. 'All of this is fascinating, Barry, really it is,' Tim said, 'but I don't see how it's going to help me get out of the situation I'm in.'

'Efficiency is always a good starting point for improvement,' Barry answered, putting his clipboard down. 'After all, you can't run before you can walk.'

'But it's the cash side of things that's really killing me. I mean, I can live with being inefficient, as long as I have enough money coming in. But I don't. I'm in danger of going under.'

Barry was quiet for a second. 'Business takes time to

change. We'll get there, but it might take a few weeks. Meanwhile, you need something quick. I have an idea.'

'Yes?'

'From what Zoe tells me, your house must be costing a lot to run.'

'Small fortune.'

'OK, what about this. Get a lodger in. Half the bills and half the rent paid – that's going to save you a few hundred a month for a start. And while you're easing your domestic situation, we'll begin to get Power Advertising firmly back on track.'

Tim looked out of the window. A bamboo blind hung uselessly in front of the glass. It didn't so much block the light as inconvenience it slightly. Tens and tens of bamboo plants all chopped down to make an object which achieved nothing. The sky was grey and turning greyer. A minuscule plane made unhurried progress above, vapour trails pointing firmly away from Taunsley. A lodger. Two or three hundred a month. That wasn't the worst idea he had ever heard. Copy lines began to scream through his mind. **Rent is Money Well Spent**. **Home A-loan Makes You Moan**. And now Power Advertising had a mission for the afternoon. The *Taunsley Mercury* had a daily 'Accommodation Available' slot. He glanced over at Dave. He would get his best man on the job.

The *Taunsley Mercury*

The *Taunsley Mercury* was wedged into the first floor
of a characterless two-storey development near the
centre of Taunsley called Quayside Landings. In truth,
there was no quay, just a dirty tract of water, but this
proved the general principle that companies would
build offices next to a fucking puddle if it would
make them sound more exotic. The *Mercury* was the
longest-surviving non-free newspaper of the town and
its offices almost entirely surrounded those of Power
Advertising. On the floor below lay an administrative
centre for local government, as well as other various
work units and bureaus. All in all, it was a jumble of
public and private slothful enterprise.

Before he had committed himself to the disaster of
setting up business in Taunsley, Tim had envisaged
getting to know the ad department of the *Mercury*. He
imagined negotiating cheap space, doing favours for
favours and building his client base through the wide
readership of the newspaper. He had been badly mistaken. Sitting at his desk and flicking through it, he
could now see that there was a very good reason
nothing was happening. The newspaper was crap. The
front page screamed the unpromising headline **Local
Owl Makes Good** (an owl raised in the Taunsley area had

been used in the making of a new film). A second revelation came in the form of the equally thrilling **Man Walks To Church**. (A pensioner had apparently walked four miles to church. When asked why, Eric Cartright, 76, said, 'Because I wanted to.') And it was downhill from there on in.

'For fuck's sake,' Tim muttered to himself. Most of its journalistic efforts were so dire that he had recently become obsessed with the low level of reporting. He cut the two headlines out and pinned them on a board above his desk. They joined a rogues' gallery of similarly talented stories, including: **New Bus Stop For Gravely Street?**, **Wheelchair Puncture Fear** and **Kwiksave Opens Branch**. What really upset Tim was the fact that interesting things must surely be occurring in the town. Taunsley couldn't be that dull. And besides, it was always small towns, rather than cities, in which all the really scandalous events occur. Tim had tried modest populations and excessive ones, and knew for a fact that the former saw more than its share of dodgy activities. In fact, scale the average rural town up to the size of a city and it would make Bogotá appear calm and uninteresting.

He based this assumption on good evidence. When he was fifteen, growing up in a village numbering fewer than two thousand people, an 85-year-old spinster had been raped and murdered. The police interviewed every male over fourteen, but failed to turn up a culprit. What their investigation did uncover, however, was a series of goings-on which would have embarrassed the Roman Empire. There was a porn ring, a wife-swapping group, badger baiting, drug dealing, illegal stills, gun clubs, bare-knuckle fighting, counterfeiters and even an arson society. And all because every member of the village had to account for their actions on a single weekend night or face a potential murder probe. The nefarious activities of this one small community had made page three of the *Daily Mail*, a fact that still warmed its inhabitants to this day. Amplify those activities to a city of two million people – Birmingham, for example – and the government would finally have a good excuse to annex the West Midlands.

Tim flicked to the 'Accommodation Available' section, shot a menacing scowl at his deputy and stubbed his cigarette out violently.

'And what the fuck is this?' he demanded, holding the paper open at the relevant section.

'An advert,' Dave replied helpfully. 'For your lodger.'

Tim let it pass. There was one section of the *Taunsley Mercury* that was always lively, and he turned to it hoping for better things. The Court News was an extended fools' gallery of stupidity. Any ill-conceived act perpetrated by people not genetically cut out for crime found its way there. Tim scanned the relevant pages with some enthusiasm. Things began promisingly.

Taxi Runaway Runs Into Own House

The court heard today that Trevor Yardley, 26, of Arden Road, Taunsley, ran out of a taxi to avoid paying the fare, while it was parked outside his own house. The taxi driver, Mr Philip Mantle, telephoned the police, who promptly arrested Mr Yardley when they arrived and rang his doorbell. Mr Yardley initially claimed he had been asleep at the time of the incident, but was unable to explain why he was wearing shoes in bed, and why 7 witnesses at the town centre taxi rank had identified him as a man repeatedly asking for spare change.

Mr Yardley was released on probation pending psychiatric evaluation.

Further down and the standard was still high.

Newsagent Robbers Recognized From CCTV

Two men – Richard Grimes (24) and Anthony Stoker (27) – have pleaded guilty to robbing a newsagent 5 weeks ago. The court heard that both men, who are presently unemployed, wore balaclavas with closed eyeholes during the raid. After banging into each other repeatedly, they were forced to remove their disguises to find the cigarettes they had intended to steal, and were later recognized from CCTV footage. In answer to the magistrate's enquiry as to why the men had so hampered their activities by sewing the apertures of their headwear virtually shut, Mr Grimes explained that they didn't want to be identified from the colour of their eyes.

Both men will be sentenced later this month.

The disasters continued.

Auto-Car Theft Pair Discharged

The court heard that two drunken youths were apprehended whilst attempting to steal their own car. Martin Reas, 18, and Alan Davison, 19, had locked themselves out of the vehicle after an evening of heavy drinking last month. The publican of the White Swan Inn called the police when he saw the men smashing the window of a blue Ford Orion, which the pair claimed joint ownership of. Summing up, the judge thought it inappropriate to force the defendants to pay themselves damages, and bound them over to keep the peace.

Mr Reas and Mr Davison were given conditional discharges.

Beneath, lurking ominously in the corner was the encouraging:

Man Runs Himself Over

A paramedic who attended the scene described to the magistrates the unusual set of circumstances which had resulted in the accident. Mr Appleby, 63, a carpenter from Moss Lane, Taunsley, had pulled up outside his garage to park his car. Accidentally leaving the handbrake off, the automatic vehicle proceeded slowly forwards, knocking Mr Appleby over and pinning his leg under a wheel. He cried out for help, and his neighbour, Janine Saunders, 37, who was looking after her child of 10, answered his plea. The court heard that against her wishes, Miss Saunders, who cannot drive, was persuaded to reverse the car. With Mr Appleby's advice she successfully backed the car off his leg, but unfortunately ran over her own daughter. Hearing the child's screams, she then drove rapidly forwards, crashing the car into a wall. All three were subsequently admitted to Casualty.

The court learned that Mr Appleby, who is banned from driving, will not be prosecuted over the incident, since the ruling magistrate was unable to determine whether running yourself over on your own land actually represents an illegal act.

The final disaster of the Taunsley Court News put the others in the shade. As with its companions, it was penned by the enigmatic Gary Shrubble, seemingly the *Mercury*'s only journalist. Tim read the report again with growing admiration.

Burglar Begs Police Protection From Poodle

The magistrates were today told that a burglar who called for help whilst breaking and entering a residence in Wormley tried to persuade the arresting officers that it was his own house. Alistaire Smythe, 33, from 187, Smelton Crescent, Taunsley, had gained access to the property by smashing the front door in. Once inside, he had evidently collected a pile of valuables to take with him. It appears that the owner's dog had then gained access to the house and had set about attacking Mr Smythe, who phoned the police for help. When the local constabulary arrived, Mr Smythe, who is well known to the police, claimed that his own dog had turned against him and asked them to put it down. He also alleged that the front door had been damaged as a result of the dog attack, and that he had piled his valuables in the hallway to protect them from the savage poodle.

Mr Alistaire Smythe was bound over to keep the peace, and placed on probation for 18 months.

As he cut the article out and pinned it in the centre of his gallery of criminal incompetence, Tim wondered about the standard of punter who would call the police during a burglary. He glanced out of the window and smiled to himself. What sort of man could be so stupid?

Meeting Alistaire Smythe

Alistaire Smythe strutted down the high street, red steel-toecapped Dr Martens slapping the pavement with enthusiastic menace. As Taunsley's sole surviving skinhead, Alistaire carried with him a pride that more than filled his impressive six-foot-four frame. While others had moved on, sold out or settled down, he had remained true to the cause of cheerful racism. Nothing gave him greater delight than harassing anyone of a creed which was any less than the purest white. As he caught sight of himself in a shop window, he cursed. First, it was May, and the coming summer months as always filled his heart with dread. It was almost time to steal another bulk supply of sunblock to see him through to autumn, when he would be safe again. Second, his hair was growing disturbingly quickly. It was nearing grade three, and bitter experience told him that anything longer than grade two could get him into very unwanted trouble. He made a mental note, which he almost instantly lost, to have normal grade-one status reinstated as soon as he had some money, and to lift some sunblock next time he was in Boots.

Alistaire narrowly avoided a large dog turd on the pavement, which jogged a recent memory. Fucking dogs, he swore to himself. If he never had to see another bastard canine it would be too soon. And as for the *Taunsley Mercury*, the journalist who wrote the piece about him was going to be very sorry. He was a laughing stock. Blatant misrepresentation, that's what it was. The cunt of a reporter Gary Shrubble got the facts wrong, and there was nothing he could do about it now. It hadn't been a poodle. He spat out a string of phlegm. It was a fucking dachshund, which was different. There was a name for that sort of thing as well. Defecation of character. That was it. He'd been well and truly defecated. As he thought about it though, he remembered that the dog had a hell of a bite for a rat-sized mutt. Maybe he ought to try and steal one, he shrugged, wondering where dachshunds could be obtained at short notice.

Reliving the events of the break-in, he again recalled how out of order the coppers had been.

'For fuck's sake, Ali,' they'd said when they arrived, 'we *know* you don't live here. We've arrested you four times this year already. We drive you home when you're too pissed to walk. And your mum's always having us round to talk to you.'

'But this is my new gaff,' he had replied, trying to control the situation.

'So what's the address?' a young-looking copper-bastard asked.

That had been the cruncher. He had no idea. It just looked like a good property to burgle. What with the rat-dog tearing at his jeans and the filth standing there as calm as anything, he appreciated that trouble was brewing. And then the dog had sunk its teeth into his flesh, and things had really become difficult. 'Please, drag this thing off me,' he had been forced to scream, hopping round the living room of someone else's house.

The cops had merely stood there, watching with interest. He winced, recalling that as he began to lose a lot of blood one of the fuckers had piped up, 'Sorry, Ali, we can't come between a man and his dog. That's a domestic, in our book.'

Ali had to spell it out once and for all. 'It's not my fucking dog! It's not my fucking house!'

Again, the pigs had been slow to react. Eventually, one of them had hit the dog with a truncheon and the thing whimpered away with a couple of inches of bloody denim in its mouth. Ali limped slightly as he recalled the events, and ejected another measure of phlegm. He turned into the town's miniature shopping centre, and wondered whether he ought to intimidate any of the security guards today. He quickly decided against it. The only visible guards would have difficulty keeping order in a crèche. Picking on them would be distinctly unfair, he judged. Besides, they were all white. Which was the problem with a small town like Taunsley – it wasn't in the least bit multi-cultural, and hence the number of harassment opportunities were severely limited. Moving to a larger town with more non-whites, however, would clearly defeat the object of his white supremacy. This para-dox had tormented Ali for several years, and he had never been able to quite square it. The closest he had managed was deciding that a sabbatical at her majesty's pleasure might provide an entertaining change for a few months. Ali had recently started to come round to the idea that, rather than trying to evade capture in the future, he should actively seek it. Although it was true to say that he had never actually evaded capture for any crime he had attempted, the legal system had been curiously reluctant to have him locked up. Maybe it was time to raise the stakes. A longer criminal record would mean more respect on the streets. He could make some useful contacts. His board and lodging would be taken care of. And, above all else, jails were full up with more than their fair share of ethnic minorities to persecute. It wasn't as if they could run very far either, incarcerated as they were. In fact, as he came to think about it, catching the eye of an anxious security guard, maybe prison was indeed the best place to be.

Events had recently taken a step in the right direction. The only thing he had been able to salvage from 'Burglar Begs Police Protection From Poodle' was that, by having his name in the paper, some unexpected work had fallen his way. And when the phone call had come through, from a man even he was scared of, Ali had been delighted to accept the mission. This could be the one which pushed him into the promised land of jail. True, it was a step up from his usual endeavours. This would involve going in armed, ready to fight, maybe break a few bones. He would need to be cold, disciplined, hard, aware of the dangers, prepared to inflict a monumental beating if it came down to it. Ali picked up his pace. First things first. Preparations had to be made. He entered a hardware shop and bought a pair of bolt cutters, a large hammer and a razor-sharp chisel. Cutting himself slightly on the implement, Ali reached for his mobile to receive another call from the man who was masterminding the attack. The details were finalized. In just over forty-eight hours, it would be time to go to work.

Life Style

Tim Power perched on the edge of his sofa, thumbing through lifestyle magazines. He glanced around his front room at the cluttered interior and looked back at the glossy pages in front of him, showing bored models sitting uncomfortably in minimalist settings. It was becoming increasingly obvious to him that what little style he did have was being chipped away by Taunsley, and that the less said about the life side of things the better. While he appreciated that the entire point of lifestyle magazines was to make you thoroughly miserable, he couldn't help thinking that they had begun to actively mock him. They were no longer saying, 'Look, this could all be yours if you buy the right things.' Now it was closer to, 'None of this will ever be yours. But to cheer you up, here's a picture of a girl's arse.'

He lit a cigarette and pondered the recent changes in his life. From the rush and thrust of corporate life in a big city to a failing business in a small town. From brief cohabitation to virtual singledom, with none of the fringe benefits. From three years of relationship trust to one year of relationship test. From perpetual activity to effective stagnation. From never even having a headache to frequent, throbbing, defeating migraines. This was a vicious circle inside a downward spiral of decline. In between bouts of lifestyle-inspired antagonism, he monitored his watch. Three consecutive days of Accommodation Available adverts in the *Taunsley Mercury* had amassed one solitary phone call of interest. The potential lodger was due any minute.

He had a final flick through a topless/gadget/fashion/sport/home-furnishings magazine and stood up as the bell rang. At the door was a pale and slightly edgy woman who entered the front room with trepidation. After a quick scan of the property's finer points, Tim made her a cup of tea and they chatted.

'I was a bit curious about the ad,' she said, pulling a strand of brown hair away from her mouth.

Tim took a deep breath. The massive lack of interest in his house was due to mistakenly entrusting the advert to his executive assistant. It was increasingly clear that Dave couldn't even advertise for a lodger. He had approached the thing like he was mounting a major campaign. Dave placed a teaser ad in the *Mercury* two days before – **It Is, Are You? Call Tim and Talk Freedom** – which had confused the fuck out of a lot of people and resulted in eleven abusive calls. The following ad had been marginally more straight-forward, but was still causing problems. **The Des Res Address That Says Yes!** was his banner line in the tiny accommodation box. 'Really?' Tim asked slowly.

'When you say **The Freedom to Live Wherever You Choose to Live, Whenever You Choose to Live.**'

'Yes,' Tim replied reluctantly.

'Well, this *is* the place, isn't it? There isn't anywhere else as well? And it's available now?'

'The ad was placed by a fu— friend of mine, who got a little carried away. It's just a simple house-share,

53

nothing more, nothing less, and certainly not, as implied, a lifestyle choice.'

'I see.'

Tim was distracted by the woman's long slender fingers, which ended abruptly with ferociously chewed nails. 'I'm sorry,' he said, 'what was your name again?'

'Ann Hillyard.'

'Right. And should I call you Ann, or *Miss* Hillyard, or what?'

'Actually, Doctor Hillyard would do fine.'

'You're a doctor?'

Time stood still and Dr Ann Hillyard listened to her thoughts, loitering in the front room of a stranger's house. The relationship is over as far as I'm concerned, her thoughts told her. If it goes on any longer my belongings will be repossessed. I have been trying to escape him for months. Here is the perfect opportunity. Best just to up and leave. This is a very nice place, close to the hospital. Tim is a reasonable man who lives alone. Unlike most of the people I encounter all day, he doesn't have anything obviously wrong with him. The rent is on the low side. Short-term accommodation in Taunsley is awful. Vacancies in St Paul's Square are a rarity. I have to move quickly. Don't appear too desperate, but do try to come across as a good tenant. Nod slowly. Smile. Say, 'Yes.'

'Of medicine?'

'Yes.'

'And you work at the hospital?'

'Yes.'

'Do you work long hours?'

'No.' There was a brief silence. Ann changed the subject. 'So you've had lots of other people round?' she asked.

54

'Lots,' Tim lied, quietly cursing his assistant. 'Twenty or thirty, at a rough guess.'

'Good.'

'And you've seen some other places?'

'Several,' Ann also lied, glancing at her watch. 'In fact I've got to be on my way. You know, houses to see . . .'

'Fine.' Tim got up and walked towards the front door. 'Well, I'll let you know.'

'When?'

'As soon as I can. I'm making a final decision on all the people I've seen either today or tomorrow.'

'OK.'

Tim and Ann stood in the hallway, silent, Ann wanting to move in and Tim wanting her to take the room. After a few more seconds, Tim said, 'Actually, do you want the room?'

Ann looked at him. He seemed vaguely trustable. 'Yes,' she replied.

'It's yours.'

'But what about all the others who've been round?'

'I'll get my assistant Dave to say it's already let.' He ambled back into the living room with Ann in tow. 'That should confuse a few of them.'

Patience

Dr Ann Hillyard's second patient of the next day was by far her most interesting current case. Simon Jasper was Taunsley's only flasher. He was probably the first one as well, for as Simon often said in his more lucid moments, there was bugger all worth taking your trousers down for in the town. Ann opened a scientific journal and allowed her mind to wander. Things were looking up. She had a new place to move into. She was finally about to leave her boyfriend. Two years of bleeding her dry and he would once again be on his own. Let him fend for himself now, she smiled. There was a sense of victory about the whole move and she congratulated herself. Her new landlord obviously had a plethora of people around to see the house, and she was the one who had swung it. One small lie, and it was hers. Ann tried not to feel too bad about it. After all, she was frequently getting mistaken for a proper doctor, so why not turn it to her advantage? As long as there were no major catastrophes, she would be fine. And given her training in psychology, if things did go wrong, she was reasonably confident that she could summon some cognitive strategy or other to defend herself.

When he eventually arrived, Simon Jasper appeared

flustered. Ann noted with relief that all his clothes were still on. Maybe they were making progress. She closed the journal she had been attempting to make sense of and placed it on a shelf suffering under the weight of a number of such periodicals. It had been a while since she had published anything. She was lagging behind and badly needed to catalogue some minor insanity as soon as possible. After completing her DClinPsych at Brisdle University, her second hospital attachment was Taunsley. The first, in nearby Bridgton, had given her a thorough grounding but had been low in behavioural extremes. The inhabitants of Bridgton, she had soon determined, represented a disappointingly narrow spectrum of dementia. Taunsley, in stark contrast, offered a wealth of opportunity on this front. And Simon, in particular, was her most promising project. His rigorous application of flashing standards presented Ann with a good place to begin the session. 'You recently told me that you only expose yourself to good-looking women,' she said, as he sat down and made himself comfortable.

'Given a choice, yes,' he replied, scratching his neck.

'Because most flashers don't discriminate.' Ann toyed with her bracelet and blushed slightly, remembering her first session with Simon. 'Classically, they tend to be seeking shock value.'

Simon was uncharacteristically quiet for a few moments, while considering the point. 'I guess I'm just a higher quality pervert than most,' he responded finally.

Ann tried to lose her mental image of a semi-naked Simon. She silently reread some of the copious notes she had made in her previous meetings with him. 'Mr Jasper suffers from an almost paralysing insecurity. To overcome this, he has been on a three-month course of Antevidolone. As such, this treatment represents a pharmo-psychological experiment, given that Antevidolone is only at the Phase Two clinical trial stage. Paradoxically, the drug has, if anything, been too effective, and has resulted in a near total loss of personal self-consciousness. Intrinsically, we are trying to inhibit his inhibitions. However, we may have been a little too successful.' Ann thought for a second. Christ, it must be liberating. It was what people paid for on Saturday nights in pubs and night clubs. Only whatever alcohol or pills they swallowed they never quite attained the level of emancipation that he managed. Essentially, being Simon Jasper was now very much like being permanently inebriated in a room full of people who love every action you undertake. You never think twice about doing whatever you feel like doing. And for a man who had previously lived most of his life with crippling timidity, the transformation was a revelation.

The single drawback, however, was his sexual deviancy, which was beginning to get him into trouble. Hence her involvement with his case. 'So how are the drugs working out?' she asked.

Simon twitched slightly. 'The drugs? Fine.'

'And what do you feel about the lower dose?'

'It's all right.'

'But is it lessening your urges?'

'A bit. From time to time.'

Ann made some more notes. Maybe she should suggest an even lower dose. It was a balancing act though. Too little of the medication, and he would revert to permanent anxiety. Too much and it was lock up your mothers, daughters, sisters and aunties time. 'And the side effects?'

'Difficult to tell . . .'

58

'Do you think the new dosage has reduced them?'

'Maybe.' Simon was particularly uncommunicative, and Ann worried that he was relapsing into anxiety. In truth, Simon was battling the urge to wave his penis at her.

'I guess we might think about altering your medication again,' she said.

'S'pose,' Simon answered, mentally unzipping his flies.

'You know I'm not a proper doctor, and I can't prescribe you anything. You should see your GP, who might change your intake. I'm simply a psychologist studying the effect of this new drug on your interesting behaviours.'

'Yeah.'

Ann scanned her notes. 'And tell me how your new project is coming along.'

'Good.' Simon sat upright, suddenly animated, as if he'd been awaiting this one question. 'I've been reading about it. I'm going to start the process any day.'

'Process?'

'You know' – he waved his arms around – 'the big change. The transformation.'

Ann was particularly interested in Simon's project. There was mileage in this man. He had hidden depths and deeply suppressed motives. Soon she was hoping to write him up as a novel case of behavioural switching in response to a drug side effect. Currently there was an almost feverish academic interest in Antevidolone, the first pharmaceutical to directly target insecurity. She finished the notes she was scribbling. 'Right. Well, that'll do for today,' she smiled. 'Thanks for coming in.' She stood up and extended her hand, signalling that the short consultation session was over.

'Cheers,' Simon replied. He stretched, twitched slightly and headed for the door. On his way out, he glanced out of the window. Banging on the glass, he shouted, 'Tim!'

Ann shuffled out from behind her desk and joined him. Together, they watched the smartly dressed man below meandering through the hospital site. 'You know him, do you?' she asked, her breath hazing the glass.

'Oh yeah,' he replied, before shouting 'Tim!' again. Outside, Tim Power glanced blindly around, before entering a building marked 'ENT'.

'So what's he like?' Ann continued.

'Top guy. Taunsley's only advertiser, you know. Used to be almost famous – adverts on the telly and everything. Then I think something went wrong and he ended up here.'

'Really? What happened?'

'I heard a rumour from my mate Dave. He reckons that Tim managed to bankrupt a multinational company with a single advert.'

'One advert?'

'So they say. But he doesn't tell me much. I only see him when he's on his way home. I just guard his office.'

'Just his?'

'Well, the building. Quayside Landings.'

'How long have you known him?'

'Ages. We go way back. Three months at least.' Simon turned from the window. 'Why?'

'Only wondering,' Ann answered, wiping the glass in front of her face, 'because I'm about to move in with him as a lodger.'

'Are you?'

'I'm afraid so.'

'Probably needs someone to share the bills since his girlfriend went travelling.'

'What's he doing in the hospital?'

'No idea,' Simon answered with a shrug. 'Short cut maybe.'

'To where?'

An unusually attractive nurse made her way across the street below, and Simon got sidetracked. 'Dunno,' he mumbled, in imminent danger of dribbling down the glass. 'Wherever he needs to go.'

Kettle First

Barry Dinsdale, beleaguered Time and Motion expert, tutted as his wife dished out the evening meal. He watched as a plate was filled, slapped onto the table in front of one of their six unruly children, before another was similarly extracted from the draining board and taken to the cooker.

No, no, no, no, no, he said to himself. The plates should be laid out and the food served at the table in one go, avoiding the need for repeated trips back to the cooker. Experience had taught him that it was better to think than utter such words. He was, after all, hungry, and would rather eat from a plate than from the floor.

'Tea?' Cathy asked in a voice equally hassled and uninterested.

'Please,' Barry replied, watching her slide a couple of mugs off the draining board, retrieve the milk from the fridge and drop a teabag into each cup. While he monitored her, he marvelled that the human body, which was built for such efficiency, should be overruled by the human mind, which could be so thoroughly inefficient. Again, his brain screamed a long sentence of Nos. **Kettle first to quench your thirst**, he recited. While the water boils, you have all the time you need to put a teabag in, find the milk, select a spoon, whatever makes you happy. He sat and twitched as Cathy filled the kettle to the 'Full' level, indicated by a symbol showing eight mugs, a good six more than they were likely to drink. He wondered whether he could surreptitiously reach for the stop-watch that always lurked in his coat pocket, but again decided against it. A strong cup of tea, no matter how wastefully made, was better than a slap in the face.

'How was work?' Barry asked.

'Fine,' Cathy grunted. 'If you like spending half a day with a sociopath.'

The kitchen was in its general state of bedlam, and while the kettle struggled to heat enough water for a small bath, Cathy scurried around attending to the multitudinous needs of the room's occupants. Now that the youngest child was two, things were slightly easier, in that everyone could eat the same food. But still, chaos reigned untamed. Children shouted, cried, laughed, copied, repeated and screamed. Foodstuffs winged their way through the air with alarming regularity. Utensils dropped to the floor every couple of seconds. Spillages plagued the kitchen table from six sets of clumsy hands. Cathy was frenetic, one step behind each successive disaster. Barry muttered to himself under his breath. There were obvious rules of domestic efficiency, which his wife ignored on an hourly basis. He had tried to implement a number of common-sense approaches to living on several separate occasions, but his wife hadn't shared his enthusiasm. After a heavy bout of criticism one week-end, she had turned to him and asked, 'So what exactly is *your* role in this relationship?'

He had been caught slightly off-guard, but managed to summon a few responsibilities at short notice. 'I'll tell you. I turn off lights. I unblock sinks. I drive the family taxi. I fix things that break. I do the garden. I carry heavy items. I mow the lawn. I take rubbish to the tip. And, on top of that, I work forty-five hours a week so that we can all live together.' While this had pacified his wife for a short period of time, the truce had been an uneasy one.

Barry mumbled a thank-you as Cathy plunged his tea onto the counter, spilling a fair proportion of it. He sponged up the mess with his tie and risked a look at his offspring, wondering how fussy adoption agencies were these days. Did they require a minimum level of discipline in the kids they took? As he finished his meal, vainly dodging flying items of food, he made a mental note to look into it.

And then, glancing around and ducking an airborne missile, an idea hit him squarely in the face. It was a revelation! He could save Tim Power's business! More than this, he could change the entire commerce of the town. His family was, essentially, a small population of consumers. The room was littered with a multitude of basic and uninspiring products, purchased to meet specific needs. All he had to do was to extrapolate the consumer needs of his household to the Taunsley situation. Then, the only remaining problem would be to convince Tim Power of the genius of his twisted logic. He strode out of the room and picked up the phone, almost breathless with excitement.

Tangential

Tim spent an unusually large number of minutes staring at his watch. Barry Dinsdale's time and not-much-motion studies had discovered that he devoted almost quarter of an hour a day to this activity. Even by this dizzy level of achievement, today was exceptional. And the reason wasn't just the usual clock-watching, but a growing suspicion that his timepiece was no longer working. The watch, a disturbingly expensive Guccimarni, didn't have a second hand. He dreaded to think how much it might have cost with one. But the minutes seemed to pass so slow in Taunsley that it was difficult to tell for sure if the thing had stopped. In the watch's static hands he saw Ronnie Power, his errant father, who had left a young family frozen in time and never returned. A man whose creation was famous throughout the land, a constant mocking reminder of his absence, and the real reason Tim had entered the world of advertising. Thank fuck he can't see me now; Tim sighed. As he dejectedly slotted the Guccimarni into one of his drawers, Barry arrived at the office. He had called the previous evening in a state of some agitation and scheduled a hasty meeting. What he needed, Barry suggested, sitting down opposite him, was a strategy.

And, he explained in an unusually animated way, he had come up with the perfect solution. Tim listened suspiciously. 'Let's face it, Tim,' he began, 'business isn't good.'

'So tell me something I don't know.'

'You need to drum up some work.'

'How?' Tim asked, glancing across his cluttered desk. 'Nobody actually seems to want anything.'

'There is one obvious cure.'

'What?'

Barry cleared his throat ominously. 'Advertise,' he said.

'Advertise?'

'Advertise.'

'But . . .'

'I've been holding back from saying this because you're almost family.'

'Almost? She's 12,000 miles away.'

'Look, the single thing you don't do for yourself is the very thing you're supposed to be doing for everybody else. Who's going to want to give you their money if they don't see any evidence of what you can do?' Barry straightened his tie, which appeared to be stained with some sort of baby food. 'If you don't advertise yourself, how can you advertise other people?'

Tim sat in an uncomfortable silence, feeling a migrainous vein throb across his temple. It seemed to be beating 'He's-right, he's-right, he's-right'.

'Here's a business paradigm for you,' Barry continued. 'A man in an evil black eighty-grand Porsche pulls up outside a factory. Makes sure the workers see him arrive. The factory is in danger of going under. Wages are low, morale non-existent. So what do the employees think?'

'Here's a wanker in a Porsche?'

'No. They think, We're saved. Because the ad-man has sold *himself* to them. He's a big enough player to afford a highly expensive motor. That's the first job of any advertiser.'

'You're saying I should buy a Porsche? I couldn't even buy a fucking Proton at the moment. Look, Barry, I appreciate all your help, but I do understand the advertising business. Success breeds success. I know that. I've been there. Ads on the telly.'

'One ad.'

'OK, one ad.'

'And the campaign which bankrupted a company.'

'But it's just not that easy in a small town,' Tim said, moving the subject along. 'I seem to have drastically overestimated both the amount and complexity of advertising required here.'

Barry was silent. He had to sell his idea to Tim in a more direct way. He wasn't really getting his point across. Staring glumly out of the window and thinking, Barry's mood entered a moment of harmony with the drizzle. This seemed to have become his natural state of being. Grey and drizzly. He glanced down at his tie. With occasional damp patches. While he always knew he would end up a miserable bugger at some stage, he just hadn't anticipated it being this soon. Barry realized that, much as certain people envisaged being nurses or firemen, he had foreseen nothing but whingeing. This was reflected in his choice of job. Grouchiness should have gatecrashed his fifties or sixties when his useful life was ending and a whole new era of moaning could open up before him. But no, Barry was thirty-seven, and was already expending most of his energy disparaging the conduct of strangers. He scratched his omnipresent stubble and risked a quick peek at Tim. Aside from driving taxis, very few spheres of gainful employment encouraged you to pass more time openly criticizing the actions of others. And the beauty of being an ergonomics consultant, he had recently become aware, was that people actually thanked him for doing so. With the sole exception of his wife, no one ever returned the favour either. None of the workers he appraised suggested that his efficiency advice was inefficiently delivered. Even Tim, as he looked across at him, was taking on board what he had said as if it was the unquestionable truth. In short, his job was one-way traffic, the purest form of moaning available to man.

'Look, Tim,' he said, returning to the point and stretching, 'what did you notice about Taunsley when you decided to set up business here?'

'There was virtually no advertising.'

'Exactly. And there still isn't. It is – as you've said before – a blank canvas, which you've got to soil with your slogans. But first you have to make people aware of your product.'

'As you've mentioned. So how do I—'

'Simple. Put some billboards up. Design some posters. Catchy tag lines, great images. And in a prominent place – "Tim Power Advertising", phone number, etc.'

Tim scratched his face irritably. 'But that's the very problem, Barry. We can put up hoardings and posters wherever we want now that the mayor has gone—'

'Philip Blunt – poor cunt.' Barry smiled, shaking his head in memory. 'What a way to go.'

'We can even book out whole pages in the *Mercury*, but we don't have any products to advertise. No one seems interested in getting us to sell their stuff. It's catch-22. And unfortunately Taunsley's crazy system of no advertising seems to work perfectly well.'

'I think you're missing my point. There's no catch-22 if, and this is the cruncher, there's no product.'

'How do you mean?'

Barry cleared his throat impressively. 'Advertise something that doesn't exist,' he replied.

Tim ceased his doodling mid-stroke. 'What?' he asked.

'I had the idea last night while I ate my tea. It's brilliant, if I say so myself. The reason you're stuck is that none of the local businesses think they need to advertise. But if they can see you handling a new, incredible consumer durable with great efficiency, they'll be queuing up to use you.'

'But if they don't feel the need to advertise anyway . . .'

'So here's the clever bit. The fictitious product must appear like it's going to compete with every existing product in Taunsley – cars, housing, sportswear, sausages, orthopaedic shoes, the whole lot. It's got to make every manufacturer nervous, strike the fear of God into them. Just like in the real world. And every retailer has to be desperate for it, shops crying out left, right and centre.'

'And then let the manufacturers soil their underwear,' Tim enthused as he caught on to the possibilities.

'Exactly. The spell will be broken. Taunsley will no longer be a cosy conspiracy between local businessmen. They'll suddenly be forced to compete with each other again. All you and your – ' Barry coughed – 'executive assistant have to do is to come up with the product itself.'

Tim glanced doubtfully over at Dave. 'A product whose name and image is vague enough to be anything? So that everyone thinks they've suddenly got competition?'

'That's the idea.'

'Boss. Boss. I've had a brainwave,' Dave shouted from the far end of the office, his arm raised as if he was still at school.

'Go on.'

'It's like a gadget, but with buttons and a screen, and it does stuff, and you can't live without it.'

'And?'

'Well, that's it.'

'Right.'

'Or – get this. A phone which takes pictures and plays mini-discs. While surfing the net. A photo-pixo-disc-net-man.'

'I think you're barking up the wrong tree, Dave. You don't need an actual item as such, just a name, an image and a slogan,' Barry explained. 'Something that will scare the pants off your average local business-man.'

'OK. What about a fridge with a TV built into it?'

'Dave.'

'Yes?'

'Shut the fuck up.'

'But it's like you keep telling me,' he complained. 'Become Your Product. That's what you always say. Look, I've got it written down.'

'Well, this is an exception to my rule. We don't need a product. Just a marketing idea.'

'Exactly,' Barry exclaimed. 'Because ads are so tangential these days, you don't know if you're being sold a soap powder or a whole new way of life. All we need are fuzzy shots, ambiguous phrases, beautiful people. Let the punters make up their own minds.'

And with that, a decision was made, and one which would for ever change the course of commerce in Taunsley.

Bewildered Herd

Mayor Philip Blunt was a man who had aspired to a single condition – happiness. And since he hadn't achieved it in this life, he fully expected to see a lot of it in the next. The main reason his life hadn't been happy was that he had tried to do everything possible to ensure he qualified for lasting contentment in heaven. Because doing what made you cheerful on earth, he readily appreciated, was an almost sure-fire guarantee that you wouldn't get to lounge around on clouds all day strumming heavy instruments.

As such, Philip Blunt's existence had been a massive gamble. Should he discover too late that there was no God, no lazing around in paradise to be had, no afterlife, then he was, he freely recognized, well and truly buggered. So Philip Blunt had spent a great deal of time weighing up the two options. An eternity of joy with God, versus sixty or seventy years of good times with his fellow man. Since he didn't like many of the people he knew, God had won the day, and Philip had devoted his life to a ruthlessly miserable existence on earth. And he had been nothing if not successful. In fact, he had gone further, and deprived a very large number of people of their happiness as well. As the longest-serving mayor the town of Taunsley had ever known, Philip Blunt had managed to inflict a tangible amount of depression on its inhabitants. Why should they enjoy themselves, he reasoned, if he wasn't going to?

Things had started well for Mayor Blunt. Born into a wealthy family, he had been doted upon. As a baby, but certainly not as an adult, he had been blessed with extraordinary looks. His face at nine months of age was as chubby, round and snub-nosed as any infant. More than this, Philip had a maturity to his face which made him look like a shrunken adult. In short, he had character and cuteness in ample supply. His mother, besotted by her only child, had sought the opinion of others, who had all been in agreement – he was exceptional. To this end, she entered Philip into several competitions, sending commissioned photos wherever appropriate. Philip's big break came quickly. Apples Soap, which had a tradition of plastering baby pictures over its packaging, shortlisted and finally accepted Philip as the face of Apples for 1948. For nearly two years he was dressed, undressed, faffed with, coaxed, prodded, smiled at and photographed with zealous abandon. And when his looks matured to the extent that post-menopausal women no longer went weak at the surgical stocking, Apples dropped him. His mother set about reviving his modelling career and signed the toddler up with an agency, which was where things really took off. Until he was nine, Philip Blunt regularly appeared in faked wholesome family photographs with unrelated models. The fledgling advertising industry set its stall out for the decades to come with its images of grinning children, doting mothers and stern-but-genial fathers. Philip and his pretend siblings and parents promoted everything from Ovaltine to Mother's Pride bread with a

73

rosy-cheeked contentment that unnerved real families the land over.

By the mature age of ten, however, the offers had begun to dry up. Philip's features were changing. Too much attention, exposure and bribery were conspiring to make him plump. Younger, fresher children started to take over, and bit by bit, he slipped into obscurity. Philip's following years were marred by both increasing bitterness and a longing for salvation. He had been dragged out of the limelight kicking and fighting.

Like many people with a grudge, Philip decided to exact his revenge on society by representing it through the local council. None of his early fame was known to the residents of Taunsley. Philip Blunt had grown up some thirty miles away in the bustling market town of Burnbridge. Although his infant face had adorned many of Taunsley's advertising hoardings, by the time he moved to the town he was unrecognizable. His rise to mayor was slavish and puritanical. And by his forty-second birthday, Philip Blunt had achieved his single aim. He had banned adverts in his town. As a consequence, whereas the average American was exposed to around 3,000 advertising images each day, the average Taunslian saw about three.

The mayor was astute, and even in the seventies had seen what was happening. A need culture was becoming a desire culture. Advertising, which had its roots in propaganda, was leading the charge to link irrelevant products to uncontrollable longings. After all, he had been one of its first victims, his cherubic face adorning lightbulb boxes that middle-aged women bought to satisfy vague but insatiable feelings of a need for children. What, he had come to question later in life, did the image of a baby have to do with purchasing lightbulbs?

Of course, there was no way he could censor TV adverts. At the height of his powers, in the mid nineties, he calculated that if the average person watched four hours of TV a day, half of it on ITV or Channel 4 where ads rolled over at about twenty-five an hour, they sat through roughly fifty commercials. When he compared this with the sheer bulk of product placement facing people from the outside of buses, the inside of buses, the back of bus tickets, the outside of taxis, the inside of taxis, on trains, on train tickets, on train platforms, from billboards, in bus shelters, on local radio, in toilets, at the cinema, through the post, on vans, lorries and cars, at point-of-purchase displays, on football hoardings, in match programmes, at checkouts, on fliers, hanging off the sides of buildings, printed on T-shirts, on kiosks, via the phone, on garage forecourts, towed behind bi-planes, on key rings, pens and baseball caps, through computers and in shop windows, this seemed almost insignificant.

The other area which distressed him greatly was newspaper advertising. However, through his connections with the *Taunsley Mercury*, he had been able to exert pressure in this area as well. Unwritten rules had been agreed in exchange for a generous subsidy of office space in the once-prestigious Quayside Landings. Adverts were permitted as long as they didn't exploit the hidden and instinctive longings of the bewildered herd known as man. Fat chance, given the nature of most of the *Taunsley Mercury*'s offerings. But during his reign, Philip Blunt had managed to put a stop to virtually all local advertising.

That is, until an industrial inspection went painfully wrong.

Bad Medicine

Dr Ann Hillyard moved in almost instantly. One minute Tim had been strutting around in his underpants with impunity. The next he was hiding in his bedroom listening in dismay as the house was refeminized. He had expected Ann to give a month's notice at her previous residence, but three or four days after first viewing the house she had turned up with a rented van full of junk, nervously glancing up and down the road each time they carried another box inside. She was never specific about where she had come from, but Tim guessed she was eager to leave.

Braving the outside of his room one evening after work, several changes were quickly apparent. The bathroom had returned from its state of minimalist functionality to resemble some sort of storage home for used cosmetics. The kitchen, once a wasteland of half-clean dishes and empty pesto jars, had filled with dubious utensils of uncertain function. The living room, with its cushion exclusion zone, was painstakingly re-padded. And lifestyle magazines for men were joined by similar publications for women, unobtainable ways of living for both sexes intermingling on the cold dark coffee table.

Ann's recent invasion of the house had made Tim's

craving of Zoe all the more acute. Suddenly, reminded of the short, happy weeks they had cohabited, he panicked that she would never come back to him. He pictured Zoe on a beach somewhere and he ached to be with her, warm sand running between their toes. In the absence of such a possibility, Tim padded along the deep carpet of the upstairs landing and stood nervous and silent outside Ann's bedroom. Music seeped under the door with Ann's voice vainly harmonizing along. He had let the place go downhill since Zoe left, but now things seemed to be picking up. He surmised that, as long as you can bear the clutter, just having a female about a house somehow transforms it into a pleasant environment. And there was one other obvious benefit as well. He took a small step closer, trying to pluck up courage.

Like many men, Tim believed that going to the doctor's was tantamount to compromising his masculinity. Bothering a medic with anything less than decapitation really meant 'I'm a bit of a wuss who doesn't deserve to have a Y chromosome'. To restrict GP visits to the bare minimum, he therefore saved up health niggles until he'd accumulated a decent number, which, taken together, amounted to a respectable level of infirmity. If not quality of illness, Tim aspired towards quantity. On the several occasions he had actually been seen by a doctor, he had been able to reel off a long and impressive list of continued ailments dating back many months, from a blackened toenail through a chesty cough to an itchy scalp. He would leave the surgery with a wad of prescriptions so impressive that people would hold doors open for him.

Tim was well aware that he wouldn't have treated his car with such a profound lack of respect. In fact, he wouldn't even have treated his pushbike as badly as he did his body. But now that he had a doctor in his house, maybe he didn't have to be quite so ill before requesting medical attention. As he loitered by Ann's door, he nevertheless counted eleven well-being issues, and decided that if she wasn't impressed by their nature, she might well be bowled over by their cumulative mass. And that was neglecting to mention the actual bona fide problems that specialists at the Taunsley District Hospital were clearly failing to fix. He quickly focused on his ailments in turn before making the final decision whether he was ill enough to bother her. Yes, he had become prone to the sort of migraines that stop you seeing straight. No, he couldn't flex his left index finger as well as he used to. Also, his skin felt unnaturally dry. A small rash was just about visible on his torso, if he squinted. His right eye continued to flicker sporadically. The intermittent throbbing in his temple kicked back into life. Toenail fungus appeared to be attacking him again. Given that he wasn't in the least bit flatulent, he must, he firmly believed, be suffering from trapped wind. There was an ache in his groin, though this may have been less medical than sexual in origin. His legs felt like they were swelling up. His neck cricked if he moved it too quickly. And to make matters worse, most of his complaints came with a readymade TV slogan, which seemed to perpetually echo around inside his brain. **Tense nervous headache? Itchy flaky scalp? Dry peeling skin? Painful trapped wind? Irritating water retention?** He rapped on the door, his left index finger bearing the brunt of the attack. A few seconds later, the door opened and Ann stood before him.

'Anything wrong?' she asked.

Tim was silent for a second. Eleven things were

wrong. It was just a question of where to start. 'I'm not very well,' he answered.

'Nothing serious, I hope?'

'Individually, no. Collectively, I'm probably on my way out.'

'Oh dear,' Ann said, taken aback. 'If there's anything I can do . . .'

'Well, actually, I think there is.'

'And what might that be?' Ann asked, with what she would later realize to be breathtaking naivety.

'Look, you're a doctor. We live together. If you ever need advice on brand recognition or product placement, you only need ask. So I know this might be a bit out of order, but I just wondered whether you could check me over?'

Ann looked him up and down. To her untrained eye he appeared in rude health. However, she was beginning to show clinical symptoms herself. Her palms were sweating, her heart was thumping, her stomach had tightened and her face was blushing. 'You want me to examine you?'

'If it's not too much trouble.'

'Yes, about that doctor thing . . .'

'What about it?'

'It's just the sort of doctor I am . . . I'm what they would call a . . .'

'What?' Tim asked almost desperately, the dull ache of a fresh headache beginning to pound his sinuses. 'I thought you said you were a medical doctor.'

She was trapped and knew it. Ann wiped her palms discreetly on her skirt. She would either have to admit to the falsehood or perpetuate it. Either way was less than ideal. Since she had moved in only a matter of days previously, it seemed a bad idea to own up already. She needed this room. There was no way she

79

could possibly go back to her boyfriend. She made a policy decision to bluff her way through for the time being, and then to address the issue further down the line. 'I am. I meant that I'm what you might call a specialist.'

'A specialist in what?'

'Um . . .' Fuck knows. 'Look,' Ann said, biting the bullet, 'what's wrong?'

Tim began to reel off his list of maladies, and with each symptom her heart sank a little further. After he had finished, some ten minutes later, he stood expectantly in front of his housemate, still outside her room. 'Well,' he enquired half seriously, 'am I dying?'

Ann flicked a strand of hair out of her eyes and interlocked her fingers under her chin. Although there was no need for immediate panic, she was beginning to see that pretending to be a doctor in order to move into decent accommodation might not have been her best idea ever. Especially if your landlord was a borderline hypochondriac. Luckily, there was a way out of the potential catastrophe lurking in her landlord's alleged ailments. On her bookshelf lay a hefty textbook of medicine. And then she remembered something else. 'ENT,' she said.

'What?' Tim asked.

'I saw you heading into the ENT department of the hospital a few days ago. So something's obviously wrong with your ears, nose or throat.'

'Must've been someone else,' he replied quickly.

Ann examined his face in surprise. 'Someone else? It was you. I saw you.'

'There's nothing wrong with my ears, nose or throat,' he said flatly. 'But what about my symptoms?'

'Right,' she answered, a single eyebrow mutinying upwards.

'The rash, for example. Do I have,' he took a deep breath which felt potentially asthmatic, 'meningitis?'

Ann held her own breath, hoping that this would diffuse the new blush inevitably racing across her face. Tim was rooted to the spot, staring expectantly into her eyes, trust breaking out across his features.

'Well?' he enquired, after an uncomfortable lull. 'I mean, I'm sorry to ask, but it *would* save me a trip to Casualty.'

Think. Say something. Appear clinical. Buy some time. 'Let me have another look.'

Tim raised his T-shirt again, and Ann noted the pleasing definition of his torso. And then she saw the rash and panic began to set in. 'It's not my area of expertise,' she blurted.

'But is it meningitis?'

'You'd need a dermatologist to be certain.'

'Surely you could take a guess.'

'It's strictly against medical ethics to guess. You must understand that.'

'But there's a way of telling, isn't there? Using a glass, or something.'

'Ah yes. The glass test. Right, we'll need a glass and, um, some tonic water. And bring the gin.'

'Gin?'

'It's an important part of the test.'

'Right.'

'And some ice.'

'OK. And you're sure this isn't just a gin and tonic you're getting me to fetch you?'

Chance would be a fine thing, Ann sighed. No, these items should keep him busy for a couple of minutes while she retreated into her room, found the relevant section in her medical textbook, and discovered what the fuck she could do to detect meningitis.

81

The Customizer is Always Right

Simon Jasper had never actively sought the security profession. Rather, it had found him. In fairness, few people actively set their sights on becoming shopping-centre guards or car-park attendants. Career advisers rarely nudge even their keenest under-achievers in such a direction. Instead, they recommend a failed police career with dishonourable discharge first before aspiring to walk up and down parking lots looking miserable. Security, then, was generally one of those occupations you drifted into if you were skilled at nothing, had been shamefully fired from a position of authority, or were generally unsuitable for the job of guarding people's welfare.

Simon's route in had therefore been atypical. He simply found himself one day with an almost pathological longing to wear a uniform with 'Security' written in large letters across the back, and was drawn in like a rabbit to oncoming headlights. This, Dr Ann Hillyard had later told him, reflected his almost suffocating insecurity. At the age of twenty-two, Simon had been mildly less anxious than a particularly nervous humming bird.

The career fix had been quick and easy. There had been a brief interview. He had filled in a form which had an ominously large space for previous convictions. A senior guard had gently tried to put him off on account of the four GCSEs Simon had accumulated at school. And that was it. Days later he was an insecure sentry plodding around with the word 'Security' daubed across half of his body, substantially more at peace with himself.

Two years into his occupational therapy, the chance to watch over the Quayside Landings building, home of the *Taunsley Mercury*, had come as a major promotion for Simon. No longer would he have to chase shoplifting whippet-youths out of supermarkets, or try to appear menacing in dingy multi-storeys late at night. And although the new job meant a virtually nocturnal lifestyle, this too had its perks. As the only person allowed on the premises after 11 p.m., there was little risk of being disturbed and hence a good chance of a few hours' sleep. Also, given his all-consuming insecurity, the opportunity to hide from normal society for most of the day was one he had seized with the greedy hands of desperation. Soon Simon settled into a pattern of very bearable work. During the night, when people slept and burglars broke into unguarded buildings on the other side of town, he nosed about, kipped intermittently and masturbated over custom car publications. For between bouts of flashing, car customization had become Simon's new goal.

What first attracted him was the magazines. They were sensational. There was a beautiful parallel between the pneumatic blondes draped over bonnets and the cars themselves. Almost without exception, the girls also appeared to have been customized, with their own enlarged headlights and lipo-reduced bumpers. But more than a flimsy excuse for softcore pornography, the magazines represented the dream of improvement. It was all about taking what you had and making it better, and this is what appealed to Simon.

At first, and as a novice, he had been confused. Simon couldn't help wondering why people didn't customize cars that already had potential. Beginning with a fifty-quid Ford Fiesta seemed to be asking for trouble. Wasn't this, he wondered, simply an extended bout of masochism? Admittedly, seeing an old banger with a four-foot spoiler nailed on the back can cheer a lot of people up. But soon Simon came to realize that this was the very point, and it touched him profoundly. Cars you wouldn't drive if you were paid to became glistening monuments to the quest for perfection. Junkyard write-offs, discarded by ungrateful owners, were lovingly restored. It didn't matter how lowly, worthless or neglected you were, nothing was beyond transformation. Even insecure security guards. Rather than improve himself, however, the object of Simon's attentions became a rusting Vauxhall Nova with a leaking floor-pan and an engine that didn't so much smoke as regularly catch fire. And so, when he should have been mooching around Quayside Landings in the early hours of a moist Wednesday morning in May, he was sitting outside in his car, devouring a dubious publication and dreaming of upgrading his Nova into something worth having. And tonight, he decided, having already told Dr Ann Hillyard about it, the time for transformation had arrived.

Simon started the negligible motor and pulled out of the shadow of the building. He had read and masturbated so much that his eyesight was failing in the gloom. Regardless, he was going to remove the standard Nova exhaust silencer and fit a racing one. Bringing the car to a halt under a light in the car park, he killed the already struggling engine and caught sight of himself in the rear-view mirror. His front teeth turned slightly inwards, like a partially opened double gate, and his ears, as if to compensate, protruded alarmingly through his increasingly lank hair. While he was in little danger of landing a modelling contract in the near future, the rest of his features were pleasantly non-descript. He paused to squeeze a blackhead before sliding out of the car. In the boot was the Sports Silencer, which sounded like an unsettling contradiction in terms. However, he quickly appreciated that he had left his set of spanners at home. Clenching his crooked teeth, he left the car park again, picked up his tool box and coaxed his one-litre machine through the silent streets of Taunsley. He gripped the steering wheel in nervous anticipation. In a few short minutes, along a small number of empty roads, his work would begin, one component at a time, until perfection was his.

Buzzing with excitement at the job ahead, Simon pulled once more into Quayside Landings. He did so at speed, attempting a handbrake turn to mark his entrance. As he screeched to a halt, something caught his attention. The rear door of the building was gaping open. Worse, there was a movement on the first floor. For a second, he forgot he was a security guard. Then the reality kicked in. This was his office block. Someone was encroaching on territory he was paid to defend. Simon jumped out of the car. He locked his jaw and bunched his fists. It was time for action. He grabbed a spanner and ran towards the door.

Matador

Alistaire Smythe had paced around the weed-strewn car park of Quayside Landings several times over the last few days, summing up the level of security and scouting for potential entry points. This was a professional job that required planning and discipline. The scary man on the phone had said so. 'Do it thoroughly . . . do it well,' he had demanded. 'And, Ali, don't fuck it up.'

And Ali had been uncharacteristically thorough. Whereas his breaking and entering experience was confined mainly to breaking, with only occasional success in the field of entering, this operation was going to be different. Also, and with any luck, he wouldn't be calling the police to come and rescue him from the ravages of a dachshund this time. So far, his surveillance had failed to detect any dogs. So the job was achievable. The real problem, he had come to realize, was in what happened afterwards. Ali's notion that being locked up could only be an improvement on his current situation had withered as quickly as it had come. All it had taken was a documentary he'd been forced to watch with his mother the previous evening. Some of the guards in the featured prison were black. *Black*. And free to come and go, while white prisoners remained locked up like slaves. Ali had come close to attacking the TV. So prison now didn't seem such a good idea. Which raised an important issue. Ali was nothing if not recognizable. Every line-up the police had ever forced him into had been a personal disaster on account of being six foot four, habitually dressed in combat clothes, heavily tattooed and with substantially more skin than head.

Camouflage had therefore become a necessity. On one of his recent reconnaissance missions, he had spotted several CCTV cameras overlooking the grounds. For this reason, Ali skulked into the car park wearing a colourful scarf that obscured most of his features, some badly fitting clothes from the local Oxfam and a pair of dangerously fluorescent trainers. He hoped to fuck that none of his cider-guzzling fighting friends saw him. While not exactly a slave to fashion, Ali imagined his everyday look expressed a certain violent dignity. Also, his normal ensemble was, he felt, ideal for making people tend towards the nervous. In his present state, Ali was painfully aware, he would have difficulty scaring an edgy pensioner with an overactive thyroid.

It was 3 a.m. and the air was wet. Ali approached a rear door and glanced around. The security guard had gone, so it didn't matter if he made a little noise. The entry point was lit, and he wasted no time hammering his chisel through the lock. A couple of minutes later and he was in. He switched his torch on and crept along the ground-floor corridor towards the stairs. Through the frosted glass of office windows, computer screens glowed in the gloom. Ali made a mental note to take a couple of them with him on his way out. The stairs were carpeted and silent. The building groaned occasionally, and his stomach grumbled along with it.

On the first floor, he removed a small piece of paper from the dreadful jacket he was sporting. Using it as a guide, he crept along a corridor, before stopping in front of an unmarked door. He scanned the map a second time. This was definitely it. He used the chisel again and similarly violated the lock. Ali smiled. There were five or six laptops all within easy reach. Result. He picked them up and stacked them outside the door. And then he paused. He had to focus. He was being paid a decent sum of money to do a specific job. The computers were just a performance bonus. Ali tiptoed through the large office until he found a metal filing cupboard marked 'Accounts'. Pulling a robust drawer out, he withdrew a handful of papers and ran his torch over them. A puzzled look spread across his thick features. Each was headed with the words 'Taunsley Mercury'. Realization was slow to come. 'Wrong fucking office,' he cursed eventually. 'Useless mother-fucking map.'

Leaving the *Taunsley Mercury* light of a few laptops, Ali made his way back down the main corridor. Having turned the map through ninety degrees, the building plan was beginning to make more sense. The large blue and white checked scarf he was wearing slipped down and obscured his eyes. What he'd really wanted was a balaclava but he'd been unable to find one at short notice. He readjusted the headwear and soon found himself outside a door marked 'Tim Power Advertising'. Again, the entrance was breached and he headed towards a filing system. There he extracted the entire paperwork and was about to examine it when a noise grabbed his attention. Through the window, a vehicle had screeched into the car park and a security guard was climbing out. The fucker was back. This meant trouble. Ali snatched the wad of papers and as many of the laptops as he could manage, and sprinted for the door. He loped down the stairs three at a time. The rear exit was still open, and he charged through it with a momentum that would have unsettled a matador. There was a crash and a shout, and as he looked back he saw the guard lying sprawled on the floor. Ali continued to dash across the tarmac, but as he did so the scarf started slipping over his eyes again. With his hands full, he began to run blind. He raised an arm to adjust his elaborate headwear and shed a couple of laptops. Then the file of papers fell open and its contents dispersed themselves through the night. He stopped, picked up a few relevant ones and tucked them inside his jacket, before once again sprinting for all he was worth. Further down the road, the problem recurred and he lost another computer. By the time Ali had cleared the site, he was reduced to just two computers and an ill-fitting disguise. The guard had climbed back in his car and was speeding his way. Ali left the road and jumped over a gate, heading off across a stretch of gardens. The man's words echoed around the large space between his ears. 'Do it thoroughly . . . do it well. And, Ali, don't fuck . . . it up.' Slowing and looking back, Ali removed his camouflage. The guard was nowhere in sight. He cut down a couple of alleys and began the long walk home. A4 pieces of paper blew down the road like anaemic tumbleweed. This was going to take some inspired lying.

In the Mood

Dave tossed a fresh batch of soiled papers onto Tim's desk and asked if he should try to find some more. Tim surveyed the crinkled and stained pages, each with Power Advertising emblazoned across the top. For some unknown reason, the client details of several Taunsley businesses that had entrusted him with their marketing had been strewn around the car park and along a nearby road. A few sheets were relatively sensitive, in that they detailed company account numbers, annual turnover and commercial strategies, but Tim struggled to understand why someone had been interested in stealing them. Especially if only for the purpose of littering the town. He told Dave not to bother. Besides, thanks to Barry's recent initiative, they had backed up most of the records on a computer. As he sorted through the bundle, there was a knock at the door and a dishevelled character apparently fresh out of the pub staggered into the office.

'Gary Shrubble,' he said, offering a tobacco-stained hand. '*Taunsley Mercury*.'

'I'm a big admirer of your work,' Tim replied, looking guiltily past the journalist at his rogues' gallery of useless news reports.

'Right,' Gary Shrubble answered slowly. 'Anyway, I

understand you got broken into as well.' He placed a grubby Dictaphone on Tim's desk and pressed 'Record'. The device looked like it had absorbed the grime of a thousand small-town stories and was none too inspired by what it had heard.

'As well?'

'We got done. Four laptops. Insured, of course, but that's not the point. Just thought I'd get your side of it, if you don't mind.'

'Not at all. How come they burgled both of us?'

'Ah. That's the thing. We don't know. The fuzz are in their usual state of bafflement.'

'Yeah, they weren't a lot of help for us either.'

'Between you and me,' he wheezed, 'I've got some inside knowledge. Turns out a place by the ring road was robbed last week. And, by the shape of it,' he said, glancing surreptitiously around the room, 'by a foreign-looking gang.'

'Mmm,' Tim replied, raising his eyebrows.

'The security guard here . . .' Gary Shrubble tried to read something biroed on the back of his hand.

'Simon Jasper.'

'That's it, says he got some CCTV footage he can let us have. Think we'll run with the story. Certainly beats the usual rubbish we print. Anyway,' he continued, scratching himself liberally, 'I just wanted to know what they stole.'

'Only a few files.'

'Files? What kind of files?'

'Advertising data.'

The reporter peered doubtfully at Tim. 'Must have been out of his head on drugs.'

'The intruder was on drugs?'

Gary Shrubble straightened slightly. 'My hearing's not so good. Could you say that again, loud and clear?'

he asked, nudging his recording device closer.

'I said, "The intruder was on drugs?"'

As Gary Shrubble etched the word 'Drugs' on his hand, Tim wondered momentarily whether he was sleeping rough. By the look of his clothes, and especially his shoes, he obviously didn't spend a lot of time grooming. Also, his hair appeared to have been recently singed, and his overcoat was peppered with burn holes. The journalist finally clicked the Off button of his tired Dictaphone before slurring goodbye and leaving the office.

Tim tried to return his attention to Barry Dinsdale's inspired campaign for a non-existent product, but quickly found he was getting distracted. Almost every slogan he doodled or image that flickered seemed to revolve around sex. Had it always been this way, he wondered, or was his hormonally soaked brain beginning to drown in self-denial? The issue of not copulating, with anybody, for a year was wearing him down. Love was undoubtedly important, vital even. Sex, on the other hand, and he certainly would have to use the other hand, was much more essential than this. While it was true that his love for Zoe was as strong as ever, he was beginning to run into problems. He craved her when he was alone, and when he flicked through photographs of her. But rather than satiating his desire, remembering Zoe only served to add to his yearnings. Tim discovered that absence, which undoubtedly made the heart grow fonder, also made other anatomical regions keener as well.

It was now almost six months into Zoe's test of faith, and Tim was beginning to fall ill. Side-effects of his enforced abstinence were becoming increasingly apparent. Women who previously wouldn't have roused even a flicker of interest now became veritable goddesses. Cleavage graduated from being a bum-shaped region of mild interest to a land of golden opportunity. Driving past the local girls' sixth-form college on a sunny day was becoming a hazardous occupation. Even the sound of Tina Turner was affecting him in ways previously only evident in his father. And now there was another problem, the worst thing to beset a man suffering in a sexual vacuum. Suddenly Tim had found himself sharing a house with an alluring single woman.

In many ways, it wasn't the sex but the maths of the situation that was to blame. Zoe, if her last reported sighting was accurate, currently resided some 12,000 miles away in an Antipodean youth hostel with narrow bunk beds and scratchy sheets. Ann, however, slept in the room next to his, in a comfortable double bed with an invitingly silky bedspread. It was almost impossible to have a greater discrepancy between the distance of a loved one and the proximity of a fancied one. In fact, as he thought about it, the distance between himself and his housemate was tiny. Their mattresses abutted different sides of the same wall. They were virtually in bed with each other anyway. All that was needed was the removal of a thin layer of bricks which sat between them. And at this rate, one ill-judged turn in the middle of the night and Tim's permanent erection would do the job.

Dave cleared his throat and Tim glanced up. Unusually, his assistant's presence almost felt like a relief.

'I've got some new advertising ideas, boss,' he said. During the last couple of days, Dave had been spending a considerable amount of time working up some slogans of his own.

'Go on, then,' Tim said, scratching his scalp.

Dave walked over and stood alarmingly close. 'This one's for Rhyl.'

'What the fuck is Rhyl?' Tim asked.

'A place. In Wales.'

'But we're not selling small coastal towns.'

'I'm just saying if we were, you know, if Rhyl wanted to mount a campaign to get tourists in.' Dave paused, trying to build some dramatic tension, which Tim sought to pre-empt.

'Go on,' he said wearily.

'OK. A young trendy couple are on a beach. Black and white photography. Behind them, slo-mo waves crashing in. He looks into her eyes. The soundtrack bursts in. It's U2. **You're the Rhyl thing, even better than the Rhyl thing . . .**'

'What?'

'You know, the *Rhyl* thing . . .'

Tim blurted out the most positive thing he could muster. 'Next.'

'Danzig.'

'What?'

'In Poland. Say if they wanted us to promote their town. Young couple strolling along some streets. Black and white footage. The soundtrack . . .' Again, Dave allowed the non-existent tension not to mount.

Tim was one step away from banging his head on the desk. 'Yes,' he answered impatiently.

'You know that song by the Nolans, "I'm In The Mood For Dancing"?'

'I wouldn't own up to it in public.'

'Well, we rerecord it – **I'm in the mood for *Danzig*, romance-*zig* . . .**' he sang. 'What do you think?'

'Next.'

'Right. Swansea.'

'Oh no.'

94

'A young couple on a beach . . .'

'Dave – you're still missing the point. You're trying to fit the product to meet the tag line. Technically it should be the other way round. Besides, as Barry and I kept telling you, we don't need a product at the moment, we need a name and a slogan. I appreciate you telling me your ideas, but we want a simple poster image.'

'OK. Got it. Let's call the thing RhylZig. We'll have a poster of a couple holding hands on a beach . . .'

'What is it with you and beaches?'

Dave made an unusual clicking sound with his mouth. He closed his eyes and swayed slightly. Then he said, 'I just like them, I suppose. It's a freedom thing.'

'So why is RhylZig a name people are going to aspire to?' Tim asked him.

'Dunno really.'

'Is it by any chance because you're trying to adapt your frankly unappealing tourist ideas to meet the needs of our mystery item?'

'Suppose so. You see, it's where Rhyl and Danzig meet,' he said, pointing out the obvious.

'Well, we need something unusual around here. We need fresh thinking. Put your other campaigns on hold, Dave. Let's brainstorm something entirely new.'

Tim and Dave sat in silence for several minutes, Dave furiously scribbling away, Tim staring out of the window. Barry's plan was a potential way out. And despite being a little unconventional, to say the least, desperate situations called for desperate remedies. For the dawning and inescapable conclusion Tim had reached was that advertising only really works when people are afforded the opportunity to be neurotic. When a population is crammed together in tight

95

spaces, close enough to be horrified by each other's dandruff, halitosis, body odour and stomach noise, that's when you have a chance. In the small town of Taunsley, however, everybody appeared immune to advertising. Until some sort of disaster occurred, the contented and feckless were unlikely to be in the least bit self-obsessed or hung-up. There was, he felt, a shortage of material to work from. In London, there had been no such problem. Advertising executives inhabited the same pent-up world as the millions of punters around them. Neurosis was there in the office, just as it was on the tube, in the back of slow, grinding taxis, and crammed into loud, brightly lit bars. They saw what they perceived to be their public, and their public looked very much like them. Rarely if ever did they stop to think that the majority of the country didn't live in such claustrophobia.

But in a small town, Tim should have done his market research. This was the first rule. Know what the punters want. And he had ignored it at his peril. But where do you find statistics on the likelihood of an advertising business succeeding in a rural setting? Tim leaned back in his expensive and largely redundant executive chair. He knew what his dad would have said. 'Advertise your way out of trouble.' And this was precisely what he now intended to do.

Steak Out

Gary Shrubble slumped in the reclined front seat of his battered Ford Sierra and muttered to himself. He was reading a tatty piece of paper into his Dictaphone, his wet lips pressed into the microphone hole. He quoted the story with a clarity that belied an afternoon of concentrated drinking. 'Right, story one.

'Post Office Raider Foiled By Vigilant Staff
Police Constable Derek Wall described the incident to the court. He explained that John Matthews, 31, of Kerbside Villas, successfully robbed the nearby Bridgton post office, and made away with over six hundred pounds, mainly in loose change. Hampered by the sheer bulk of the money, Mr Matthews decided to return to the post office later and attempt to lodge the money in his own account. The cashier recognized his voice, as well as the suspiciously large number of coins, and called the police.

Mr Matthews was sentenced to three years.'

Taunsley's finest journalist coughed, lit a cigarette, coughed some more and scratched, readying his mind for the next story. Grin and bear it, he told himself, grimacing at his notepad. Just do the bread-and-butter stuff, keep things ticking over. And all the

97

time, month after month, year by year, work quietly on the one real story, the only one the town has ever needed to know. A whopper. The kind of scoop that makes the front page of daily nationals, wins awards for investigative journalism and cements careers. Gary Shrubble swigged from a can of vagrant-strength lager and swallowed the thick fluid. First the crap, though. He took a bite of a cold steak sandwich which seemed to be preserved in its congealed fat like a body frozen in ice and, finally prepared, began again, pressing Record on his Dictaphone.

'Cat Burglar Attacked By Cat

The trial of a Weston-Mare Sands man accused of breaking, entering and assaulting a household pet was yesterday adjourned for four weeks while a vet examines the animal in question. Before the adjournment, the court heard that Colin Didsbury, 36, of Frances Street, had stepped on the cat as he walked through the kitchen in the dark. The moggy, described as a prize-winning pure Siamese, then bit and scratched the defendant, causing him to cry out and wake the house-holders. In an unexpected development, Mr Didsbury said that he would be claiming damages of £100 for feline assault. The case will resume next month.'

Gary clicked the machine off and hunted around for the evidence that constituted the main story of the day. He thumbed through a pad of uninspiring notes before reaching the quote he had written down from the advertiser Tim Power. Picking up a grainy black and white photograph, he smiled to himself. Bingo. The story had just written itself. He was indeed a genius. He began to dictate the substance of his idea.

'Immigrant Crimewave Imminent
A gang of foreign criminal masterminds . . .

'Hold on,' he whispered, sobriety struggling through the alcohol. Ahead, in the dingy car park, a thick-set man with short legs was having difficulty levering himself into a Range Rover. Gary Shrubble switched tapes in his Dictaphone and noted the time. 'Seven forty-six. Mr Jenkins leaving his factory alone. Last person out. Carrying briefcase. Possibly pigskin.' He ducked down unnecessarily, the large vehicle exiting at the far end of the car park.

Gary Shrubble opened his door and squeezed himself out, wheezing as he did so. He unwrapped a small piece of towel in the spare wheel of the boot. Hidden inside was a hammer and a masterkey. Gary glanced around. He was too pissed to be nervous. He walked towards the door Mr Jenkins had just left. He had thirteen minutes. A security firm generally drove past for a third-gear inspection at eight o'clock. He inserted the key, turned it, and entered the premises. **Post Office Raider Foiled By Vigilant Staff. Cat Burglar Attacked By Cat.** Fucking amateurs, he slurred under his breath. He would show the hopeless criminals of Taunsley how to steal things. And not just flat-screen TVs or DVD players. He was after the truth. Of cover-ups, disappearances and massive wrong-doing. This, above all else, except uninterrupted drinking, is what he had become a journalist for.

Artist's Impression

Alistaire Smythe opened the *Taunsley Mercury* and almost gagged on his Cocopops. Expecting news of a daring early-hours raid on highly guarded office premises, he was instead confronted by the headline **Immigrant Crimewave Imminent**. Beneath it was a photo which had clearly been taken from CCTV footage in the near dark of early morning. The picture showed a suspicious man with swarthy skin and a ridiculous headscarf holding a brace of laptops. His first instinct had been to hurl racist insults at the ethnic in the picture, until this had come to a crashing halt under a weight of recognition. His mouth lolled open, and his head slumped closer to the article for a better look.

Next to the picture, Gary Shrubble's text offered little salvation.

A gang of foreign criminal masterminds, apparently headed by the ferocious man pictured (left), looks likely to subject Taunsley and surrounding regions to an onslaught of illegal activities. The break-in is already being linked to a similar escapade on the Taunsley Meadows Industrial Estate last week. The ruthless intruder, who stole an estimated 17 high-spec laptops worth over £40,000 from the *Mercury* offices, may well have been involved with narcotics at the time of the offence. According to Tim Power of Power Advertising, which was also targeted in the attack, 'The intruder was on drugs.' Meanwhile, the *Mercury* is offering a generous £25 for information leading to the capture of the potentially immigrant gang and the return of the 17 recently purchased, well-equipped and extremely high-specification computers.

Mute with fury, Ali tore the newspaper into inky pieces and scattered them around the room like dirty confetti. Then he spotted a recent edition of the *Taunsley Shopper*. This was the town's only other journalistic effort, a local freesheet that made the *Mercury* look like Pulitzer prize-winning reporting. The *Shopper* also featured the story, this time on page three. In place of the *Mercury*'s dubious photo was a large and mainly inaccurate artist's impression of the alleged thief. Drawn by possibly the world's worst portrait artist, the image appeared oddly familiar to Ali as he examined it in disbelief. In fact, the picture was familiar to a lot of people opening the *Shopper* on the same day. To avoid paying for photos, the *Shopper* often employed Eric Waters, who actually worked as a painter and decorator, to botch impressions of police suspects, drunk motorists and people appearing in court. And the reason his picture of Ali was recognizable was that, in common with all the portraits he painted, Eric specialized mainly in the famous, and generally adapted real people from the closest celebrity he could think of. Everyone unlucky enough to be touched by Eric's brush, from the dullest criminal to the most inebriated driver, therefore had a star-like quality. And for Ali – his teeth clenched so tight it hurt – this had been Yasser Arafat.

Ali threw the paper down in disgust. He felt sick. Defecation of character was one thing, but a racial slur was quite another. He stood up and paced round the room, spitting out Cocopops as he ranted and raved. First the fucking poodle attack and then this. If he ever met Gary Shrubble, there was going to be trouble. And as for the *Shopper*'s artist, the fucker would be painting with his left foot after Ali had finished with him.

Something occurred to Ali mid-tirade and he began to relax a little. There was one terrific bonus to the situation. No one was going to suspect him of the crime. He sat down again and resumed his breakfast. For once, the police weren't going to come around and drag him to a frankly unfair identity parade. He was underground, infiltrated, beyond suspicion. But just as Ali had begun to salvage some dignity from yet another dachshund's dinner of a criminal venture, his phone rang. The man who had paid him to raid the offices of Tim Power Advertising didn't sound as reconciled as he was.

'Where the fuck . . . are my files?' his voice screamed down the line.

'In the car park,' Ali answered meekly.

'All of them?'

'No. I think I got some of the ones you wanted.'

'And why the fuck . . . didn't you do the job . . . yourself?'

'What do—'

'Why get some foreign bloke . . . to do it, who probably couldn't . . . read a map. I mean, what the fuck . . . was I paying you for?'

Ali remained silent, fuming. He decided for a number of reasons not to mention that he was the man in the photo.

'I told you, get in there . . . do the job . . . and get the fuck out without being detected. That was the important thing . . . don't let anyone know . . . that any files have been nicked.'

'I was careful, like you said.'

'Careful? Fucking careful?' the man shrieked. 'I'd hate to see . . . you being negligent. I mean, what was I thinking . . . trusting a fucking amateur like you with . . . a professional operation?'

Ali swallowed some bitter-tasting pride. 'Next time, I'll do it right.'

'Next time? What next time? Unless you show . . . some serious initiative . . . we're finished. Put those files in the post. And you won't . . . be getting paid. Is that clear?'

'Yes,' Ali answered as the line was cut. He paced slowly around the room, kicking up strips of newspaper, each with random words and fragments of pictures. So it was initiative that he wanted. So be it. Ali stamped on a small piece of paper bearing the single word 'hospital'. Initiative was exactly what he was going to get.

RhylZig

In the absence of any better ideas, RhylZig became the working name of Product X, the lifestyle choice which no one in Taunsley would be able to live without. Or buy, for that matter. While it was by no means the greatest commercial label ever dreamt up, and was barely pronounceable even with practice, it certainly beat a few existing ones – muesli, Anusol and Volkswagen, for starters. Besides, it sounded foreign, which was a plus. It would feel like an invasion, Barry explained, something imported and exotic bursting into the town to threaten existing goods.

After the name, they were faced with the tricky business of imagery. Tim sat through several surreal meetings while Dave and Barry scribbled frantically on the office white board, desperately trying to conjure up the perfect representation of a non-existent item. In the end, they hit upon a winner. The obvious had been eluding them. What they really wanted, Dave explained, was two people walking hand in hand on a beach, waves crashing in the background, that sort of thing.

'And what about the logo?'

'Traditional font, nothing fancy. RhylZig has to be universal.'

'Slogan?'

Barry and Dave scratched their heads, Dave with slightly more success in terms of connecting with any hair. '**Simply the Best**,' the young assistant finally suggested.

Tim threw his pen at him. 'Barry? Any ideas?'

'I'm not very good at this sort of thing,' he conceded, 'but how about **RhylZig for Life**?'

'Not too disastrous.'

'Or **You can't beat that RhylZig feeling.**'

'Bit Coca-Cola, but reasonable. Dave?'

Dave cleared his throat impressively. '**RhylZig won't make you Real Sick**,' he proclaimed, before dodging another flying object.

Several hours later, with a few possibilities under their belts, the creative team of Power Advertising decamped to the pub to beer-storm some visuals. Financially, this was tricky. Photographers, models and locations added up to a lot of money. Taunsley wasn't particularly close to the coast, and, thanks to a distinct lack of raw material, didn't possess a model agency. Among the teatime Tetley drinkers a decision was finally made. The three of them would drive to the nearest beach in Barry's beloved people carrier, Dave would take the photos on the company's digital camera, and Tim would scour the town for a relatively presentable female to take along with them.

The following day, with variously low expectations, Tim, Dave and Barry drove to the dismal seaside town of Weston-Mare Sands. Also in the vehicle was a particularly unenthusiastic female in the form of Dr Ann Hillyard. For a month's free rent, she was going to be the female face of RhylZig, the face of bugger all, as she had pointed out. Barry was to be her co-star. Given that he was already in his late thirties, and that each child had added a further decade of greyness to his well-worn features, Tim's idea had been to leave the ad ambiguous. Barry and Ann, the RhylZig Couple, might just as well be father and daughter strolling down the beach in front of dramatic waves as two enraptured lovers.

Barry had planned the route in minute detail, sellotaping a list of directions to the dashboard. As a possibly poor omen, his on-board satellite navigation system had failed to locate the non-descript town of Weston-Mare Sands in its memory. He had therefore consulted a road atlas the previous evening, dodging flying food as he did so. With a piece of string and a ruler, he spent two hours meticulously calculating the shortest route for the forty-five-minute trip to the coast. Despite a build-up of macaroni cheese in the Sedgemouth area, and a flood of orange squash around North Wednesbury, he was eventually satisfied that he had designed the most efficient itinerary.

'So what have we got?' Tim asked as they eventually neared their destination. It was beginning to drizzle and his hopes weren't high. The town's only arcade was shut, which didn't inspire confidence. 'If it's going to interest everybody it can't be gender-specific, age-specific, demographically exclusive, socio-economically targeted or race-biased.'

'Ah,' Barry said from the driver's seat. 'Race. Bit of a problem.'

'How?' Dave asked.

'Fuck,' Tim exclaimed. 'You're right. Two white people is hardly going to engender cross-race support for the product.' He attempted to stretch, but found himself securely pinned in by his seatbelt. 'We need a couple to double its appeal. And, ideally, one of them should be something other than Caucasian, particularly if it's a foreign-sounding product.'

The four protagonists glanced at each other's pale faces. The plan, already shaky, was beginning to appear increasingly unlikely. 'But there's not exactly lots of black or Asian people living in Taunsley, Tim. Do we really need to be so multicultural?'

'The second law of advertising, Dave, states that you should always target, but never isolate.'

'Meaning?'

'Get as many punters as possible to buy your product.'

'And the first?'

Tim scratched his nose irritably. 'Never hire blokes called Dave.'

A small sliver of sun peered through a gap in the clouds and did its best to brighten proceedings. Faced with the all-consuming drabness of the town, however, it was up against tough opposition, and quickly retreated.

'I've had an idea,' Dave announced, as Barry parked the car in a space overlooking the muddy beach.

'Well, it'd better be a good one,' Tim replied, peering glumly out of the window, 'and let's face it, history is against you.' He unfastened his seatbelt. 'And as for waves crashing on the beach, the tide is about three fucking miles out.' He opened his door and jumped miserably out. 'Can't see any fucker being won over by the romance of a protracted stretch of mud.'

'Just wait till you hear my brainwave, boss,' Dave repeated, following Tim out of Barry's much-abused people carrier. 'But for it to work,' he said, bending down to pick up a small flat stone, 'we need to ring Flasher Simon.'

'Flasher Simon?'

'Simon Jasper. Mr Security. He might have some footage we can use.' Dave lobbed his pebble at the water and saw it land a couple of miles short. Despite its name, Weston-Mare Sands was famous for lacking any tangible beachage. The exotically grey mud of the shoreline eagerly gobbled the stone up and awaited more of Dave's wild inaccuracy. 'You know you always say **Become Your Product**?'

'Yes.'

'Well, what if someone else became our product? I mean, we'd have to add some hair and change a couple of other things, but I reckon it'd be OK.'

Tim strode on, tilted forwards into the wind, an unusual surge of optimism bringing him to life. Dave's idea was inspired. Sometimes, just sometimes, Dave was a star. And one other good thing had happened during the journey. They now had a slogan. And it was a killer.

Ten days later, residents of the insular town of Taunsley awoke on Saturday morning, their heads thick from drinking and fighting, to a sight that had eluded them for over twenty years. At prominent traffic-lights, junctions and roundabouts, on the sides of shops, next to bus shelters and on derelict buildings, a plethora of advertising hoardings had suddenly appeared. Varying in size from a small number of massive billboards to a larger profusion of modest poster-slots, all were blank, their brilliant whiteness shining out in silent promise. Local spray-can artists opened their eyes to the sincere belief that they had arrived in the promised land.

After lunch, Tim drove around the inner ring road and counted the number of opportunities open to him. All the major sites were being swarmed over by armies of bored youths, who spent the day soiling the hoardings with indecipherable graffiti. Soon the hoardings would be covered with a different kind of art. The carpenters had done a magnificent, if costly, job. Working through the night, they had set the scene for the big surprise. Also pulling an all-nighter, the bill posters, a firm from Brisdle who had been specially imported for the job, would be transforming the town in a couple of days. Taunsley, Tim had quickly found, was particularly low on bill posters. Again, persuading nine such men to travel the forty miles to Taunsley and work through the night had been a far from cheap enterprise. However, it would all be worth it. On Monday morning, the whole town was going to wake with one phrase on its lips. And, for once, that phrase wouldn't be, 'Where the hell are my underpants?'

Stretching Slightly

Rumours of the closure of Jenkins Meat Products first surfaced at the inaugural memorial service for Mayor Philip Blunt. It was a year to the day since the council leader had violently and prematurely died. Twenty or thirty downcast people filed into a small chapel around the corner from the town hall. On their way, they passed and ignored a plethora of brand new hoardings all screaming the promise of a brand new product. Amid the rabble quietly fidgeting in the heat were several members of the town council who had been forced to attend against their wishes, and assorted random Taunslians who felt obliged to make an appearance. The unspoken impression, especially among the Tory councillors, was that the death of Mayor Blunt had been no bad thing. Although by no means a Bolshevik, his control of the town's economy had bordered on the left wing. Speeches of variable accuracy and content began to stifle the positive thoughts of most of those gathered. Long descriptions of the mayor's mistrust of the commercial world, and in particular his dislike of advertising, aged the congregation considerably.

Mr Jenkins, porcine proprietor of Jenkins Meat Products and a vague associate of the late man, shuffled out to visit the toilets, glad of the chance to extend his chubby legs. He wiped a thin film of sweat from his forehead with a neatly folded handkerchief, and dabbed at his moustache, which had also become wet. Jenkins Meat Products were by some distance the biggest local employers, and had been for almost twenty years. Inside, as he attended to matters at hand, he was joined by a short, friendly-looking councillor, who casually asked him how business was. Many people asked this question on a daily basis, and Mr Jenkins was tired of answering it positively.

'Not so good,' Mr Jenkins whispered to his fellow urine contributor, staring into the harsh porcelain veneer. 'Not so good at all.'

The councillor, whose wife worked in the trotter-stripping section of the factory, broke Gents' etiquette by turning to face him. 'Why not?' he enquired with some concern.

'Because no bugger in the town is buying my meats any more.'

'And why do you think that is?'

'I don't know,' he answered, directing his voluminous flow onto a stack of toilet freshener cubes. 'But each year for the last decade sales have dwindled so badly it's barely worth keeping the bloody place open.' Mr Jenkins shook his member, which he'd been stretching slightly while he urinated. 'I'll tell you this, though,' he said, returning it to his trousers where it was free to shrivel to its normal size, 'the more I think about it, the more I reckon a move to another town would sort the business out.'

'Another town? But my wife . . .'

Mr Jenkins turned to the local government official while he washed his hands. 'Do you have any idea why I put so much of myself into Taunsley?'

111

'How do you mean?'

'The sacrifices I make? The hours? The effort? Do you know what I get back from all this?'

'Tell me.'

'It's not the money, the respect, the power.'

'No?'

'It's something much rarer, something far more valuable, something only ever understood by a small number of men. And something normal society can't even comprehend.'

'What, then?'

Mr Jenkins was flushed. Maybe he had said too much already. When he was angry, thoughts just flooded out of his mouth. He had to learn to be careful. So far, he was safe, but one day . . . He changed the subject. 'Your wife. She works for me, does she?'

'Half the town does.'

'And why does *she* think no one's buying Jenkins pork pies, or sausages, or Econoburgers?'

The man joined Mr Jenkins at the sink. 'You want the honest answer?' he asked, looking him in the eye.

'Might as well.'

'Because everybody knows what goes into them.'

'What?' Mr Jenkins thundered.

The councillor held his nerve. 'We've all heard the stories. Everybody knows someone who's worked for you.'

'What kind of stories?' Mr Jenkins demanded suspiciously.

'You know. The stuff that makes up your products. The eyelashes, the whiskers, the ground-up bone, the trotter parts, the sawdust, the nails, the fat, the hairs, the arseho—'

'OK.' Mr Jenkins raised a clammy hand. 'Spare

112

me the recipe. What the hell do people *think* pork sausages are made out of?'

'Pork?'

'*Pork*? What sort of a crazy idea is that?'

'And it's the pies as well. My wife says that they're a third gristle, a third fat, and she'd rather not know about the rest.'

Another sweat broke out across Mr Jenkins's face, this time an angry one. 'So that's what they think, is it? My meat products aren't good enough for them? Well, we'll see about that.' He finished drying his face and rumbled out of the toilets. 'We'll see about that,' he repeated, leaving the memorial service and heading for his car.

Inside the Gents', a toilet flushed and a man emerged from the cubicle. He was well dressed, with cropped grey hair and broad shoulders. He wore flat-soled shoes that slapped against the wet, tiled floor. The councillor noted with interest that he was missing an arm. He also noted an unpleasant air of menace suddenly in the small room, and left quickly, in a hurry to tell everyone he knew that the town's main employer was on the verge of closing down.

Washing his one hand in a skilful manoeuvre involving the use of his fingers and thumb, the grey-haired man smiled in the mirror. What he had just heard had made him very happy indeed.

The One Thing Your Life is Missing

Outside, the sun was doing its damnedest to warm the streets of Taunsley. It was a tough job, but its persistence was paying off. In his bedroom, Tim hugged the double duvet even closer to his fully clothed body and continued to shiver fiercely. He reached across in his prone position and touched the radiator, which was skin-damagingly hot. He briefly contemplated putting another jumper on, but dismissed the idea, appreciating that it would involve leaving the safety of his bedding for a few seconds. While his fever raged, the final slogan of RhylZig sliced in and out of his consciousness, the words appearing forwards and backwards, turning somersaults and endlessly repeating themselves. **The one thing your life is missing.** Even between bouts of excessive temperature the slogan refused to abate, and for this reason Tim knew he had a winner. **The one thing your life is missing.** It wasn't the catchiest motto Tim had ever spawned, and certainly wasn't a patch on **Lost in Mucus, Caught in a Hack**, but it did have one vital ingredient – it made you wonder. If you saw the billboard image fifty times a day, it would start to wear you down. **The one thing your life is**

missing. Probably, the first few times, you would walk past and take no notice, smiling, telling yourself you had everything you wanted. But then, seeing it time and time again, it would begin to permeate your consciousness. **The one thing your life is missing**. What is my life missing, you would ask hypothetically. If there was one single thing, not that there is, what would it be? The hook begins to bite. **The one thing your life is missing**. The product is mixed into your suppressed cravings. After all, a man is really two men – the man he is, and the man he wants to be. You speculate with successively more curiosity. And then the crucial point. **The one thing your life is missing**. You want to know. Not because you think this product will satisfy your unspoken longings, but because you need to know that it won't.

And then Tim began to fall into his own trap. **The one thing your life is missing**. What was his own existence lacking? He quickly realized there were a lot of things. A successful business. An available girl-friend. A cure for his alarmingly frequent headaches. **The one thing your life is missing**. But more than all this, a hole he had never been able to fill, something that picked at him still, day after day. **The one thing your life is missing**. A father. A normal father. One who kept his promises. One who didn't abandon his family in the quest for perfection at work. And one who hadn't unwittingly pushed his son into the world of advertising.

In the afternoon, and each subsequent day of his flu-addled odyssey, when he wasn't so hot that he felt cold, Tim rang Dave, keen to know how many enquiries the phone number on the posters had garnered. And then his eagerness rapidly ebbed and he would sink back to shivering and sweating at the same

115

time. Almost a week in, and nothing. Dave sounded oddly unaffected by it, and Tim started to feel he had overestimated the unfulfilled secret longings of the average Taunslian.

After work each day, Ann sat with him, and Tim began to notice that, bit by bit, she was picking herself to death. It was, he suspected, a hobby of hers. She attacked the broken skin which clung around her fingernails, and made a good job of ensuring it didn't stay there. If she peeled any more shreds away, the nails looked like they'd simply fall off. If it wasn't her hands, it was her eyebrows. She would fish for eyebrow hairs and yank them out one at a time, before bringing them back up to eye level for a sly examination. Occasionally, after a particularly successful night, her eyebrows would appear distinctly patchy, with gaps you could drive a make-up pencil through. In fact, if she wasn't attempting to ruin some part of her body, she didn't appear truly happy.

As she sat and picked, Ann gave him a run-down of the town news. The only story all week was the imminence of potential large-scale unemployment. Taunsley was unusually animated. People scurried about the place with worried expressions. The job centre reported its first ever queue. Mr Jenkins had refused to comment on the speculation that his factory was about to relocate, further fuelling the panic. There was even talk of encouraging the population to start eating Jenkins sausages again, but this quickly died down when someone pointed out that unemployment was one thing, but mass malnutrition quite another. Tim tried to take comfort in the fact that he wasn't likely to be the only unemployed person in the town, but it failed to cheer him, and he sank into a feverish depression.

At the weekend, when he was finally feeling strong enough to eat and his sheets no longer needed squeezing dry every couple of hours, Ann spent more time with him, nursing him back to health. It was an unselfish gesture and Tim greatly appreciated her efforts. If he did have a criticism, however, it concerned the actual quality of patient care provided by his housemate. Hot toddies, cold baths and litres of Pepto-Bismol were not, as far as Tim knew, good solutions for people with the flu. Indeed, by the close of the weekend, he was, he felt, regressing, and looked forward to returning to work in a couple of days in order to recuperate. Ann's unconventional approach to medicine was puzzling. He knew the health service was in a desperate way, but surely not this desperate. Still, Tim appreciated that junior doctors were unpractised and had probably learned nothing more useful at medical school than how to sleep with other doctors. Ann was also reluctant to talk about her work, which he found unusual. In his experience, women he had lived with generally devoted more time to talking about their day at work than they actually spent doing it. But any more of Ann's nursing and he would soon have to check into hospital himself.

The Meat is On

Derek Gribben opened a poorly addressed envelope
and flicked through the tattered pages within, which
had suffered on their way to him. He pictured the
papers skimming across a wet car park in the middle
of the night, and shook his head. Each was marked
with the words Power Advertising, and varied between costings of services and breakdowns of sales
targets. Among the stolen documents, four pages in
particular appealed to him. Beneath the letterhead,
several columns of numbers, headed with the words
JMP Sales, told the story he wanted to hear. There
was, he conceded, method in his madness after all.
First, recruitment of a borderline psychopath via the
Court News section of the *Taunsley Mercury*. Second,
persuading him to steal the figures upon which
all subsequent actions would be based. He stood up
and peered over the thin wall which separated him
from his secretary. Behind, and with her face pressed
unadvisedly close to a computer screen, Cathy
Dinsdale was playing Tetris. There was a quick rap
on the portable wall and Cathy pressed the Pause
button.

'What?' she asked truculently.

'Right,' Derek replied sharply. 'Get me the sales data

immediately before . . . and after . . . the month of August.'

Cathy sighed. 'Last summer?'

'Yes. And bring me . . . the exact point-of-purchase breakdowns.'

'All of them?'

'I want another look . . . at the figures.'

Cathy shrugged. 'If I must.'

It was true. Men were scared of him, knew what he could do, had heard the stories, stayed on his right side if they possibly could. But women in general, and Cathy Dinsdale in particular, seemed oblivious to these rules. Had his secretary been a man, he would have spent a lot of his time in the company of an emergency dentist. Cathy, however, continued alternately to ignore and insult him and he felt utterly unable to command any respect at all.

A couple of minutes later, Derek Gribben was in possession of the whole sorry story. Successive pieces of paper were picked up from the right with his single hand, scrutinized, and put down again on the left. There were times when a full complement of arms would have speeded up the bedlam he was about to unleash no end. Battling on with the wad of sheets, he compared his rough estimates with the actual numbers and gained a degree more confidence for his scheme. The six-week promotion had cost Jenkins Meat Products £4,742.13. There had been 112 radio slots of 20-seconds running time. During each slot, **The Meat is On** had been repeated six times. The name of JMP had been mentioned four times. Taunsley had therefore been subjected to several hundred repetitions of the product and the message. He rubbed his jaw slowly. A particularly damaged piece of paper was headed 'Net sales 2002/3'. He ran his eyes down to

the month of August. Tapping his calculator ferociously, he determined that **The Meat is On** campaign
coincided with an 11 per cent reduction in revenue for
Jenkins Meat Products compared with August 2001/2.
The fucker Jenkins had paid nearly five grand to lose
11 per cent of his net sales.

He turned to the folder Cathy had just dumped on
his desk and cross-referenced the JMP data against
his own. During August, he had seen a 13 per cent
increase in his own sales. It was undeniable. A direct
seesaw effect. Bad advertising not only harmed your
own business, it could actively benefit others. He gave
a face-contorting laugh. This was going to be the
lunacy which saw him through the troubled times
ahead.

Derek tried to remain calm. There was no point
getting carried away too soon. He had to be cold about
the whole thing. Criminal activities frequently got
themselves detected thanks to gung-ho tactics. While it
was true that you had to break a few heads to make an
omelette, and he now had the man to do this, you
didn't want to go around cracking skulls unnecessarily. Sometimes you had to be clear and focused on
your objectives. Under other circumstances, he would
have waded in, waved his twelve-bore around, maybe
broken a bone or two. But this time the strategy had to
be different. He would start with his brain rather than
his fist. And then, if it didn't go to plan, well, maybe
he would let his gun settle the argument after all. He
spent another few moments leaning back in his
chair, covering his face with his hand, thinking about
all the possibilities, looking for weaknesses. Shortly,
having considered all the angles, all the pitfalls, all
the dangers, he removed his hand and picked up the
phone. It was time to start the mayhem.

Exterior Changes

Simon Jasper peered out of his bedroom window at the love of his life. Parked quietly in the alleyway behind the house was his slowly decaying Vauxhall Nova. Despite obvious evidence to the contrary, the Nova was a Special Edition 'Celebration'. A celebration of what, exactly, Simon had been moved to ask when he first clapped eyes on it. Rust, maybe, or poor workmanship. However, things were now moving firmly in the right direction. Already, there were signs of improvement. The wheel arches were substantially wider than they had been. A sports aerial jutted proudly out of the roof, above the windscreen. Two of the side windows now had smoked glass and were impossible to see in through. While he yawned and stretched, his eyes wandered into the back yard. Below, his mother was hoovering the patio.

Simon dressed and headed downstairs. It was mid-afternoon, and he had four hours before Quayside Landings beckoned him again for another semi-nocturnal tour of duty. Before that, he had an appointment with Dr Ann Hillyard to discuss recent progress. He intended to spend the rest of his free time improving the car still further by fitting a new stereo. And not just any old stereo. This set of equipment, with its woofers, sub woofers, boot woofer, tweeters, amp, CD player, tuner and graphic equalizer had cost several times more than the Nova, and, he had it on good authority, would rattle living-room windows at fifty paces.

With the tantalizing promise of change, he began to install the individual components. While Simon had previously believed that having a loud car was about as useful as having a heavy boat, Maxx Power had urged him to make the transition. As far as he could see from reading about it, there should be an inverse relationship between the cost of the car and the power of its stereo. A crap, rusting Nova like his own should therefore have a hi-fi of stadium proportions. Further, the louder the equipment, he had been led to believe, the worse the music it should play. Hummable pop songs or pleasant acoustic ballads should be abandoned in favour of extended and repetitive out-pourings of ultra-low frequency vibration. When he heard such vehicles zooming down the High Street, it was almost as if they were being propelled merely by their bass lines. Given the dismal, rattling, elastic-band engine in his own car, this would be by no means unwelcome assistance. But changing the engine, Simon had firmly decided, was to be avoided at all costs. There was little to be gained from attempting to improve it, and a replacement unit was well beyond his means. Also off limits was the car's interior. By installing smoked glass all around, no one would be able to see inside anyway. So the resolution had therefore been made to customize the exterior of the car only, and to leave what was on the inside well alone. Apart, that was, from the stereo.

Later, as he ran a T-Cut cloth over the resprayed bodywork, he stopped at the driver's side of the car and frowned. If Robert Burns had an arachnid that climbed cave walls, Simon Jasper had a spider that lived in his car's wing mirror. Simon felt that while the Nova wasn't very fast, it certainly wasn't slow enough to catch insects. But the point was that this spider, like Robbie Burns's, was a tenacious little bugger. Every night it built a web, in the vain hope that flies would be attracted to the wing mirror of an ageing Vauxhall, and every morning the web fell apart. In between, it hid in the tiny crevice that surrounded the glass. Similarly, Simon would have to come out of his hiding place and fight to change his life, even if this meant doing so again and again. He had taken many knocks in his life and would have to take some more. Already, though, he had been partially cured of his insecurity. This had been a major start. But, as Dr Ann Hillyard frequently told him, they were a long way from normality.

He glanced at his mother, who was examining a hoover bag suspiciously. Staring up at the back of the house, he saw that it was a miserable building, which looked like it was waiting to die. Once, he had known how it felt. Now, however, he had a mission. The sooner he moved out the better. And when he had finished his quest for the perfect customized vehicle, he would start to seek some decent accommodation away from people who vacuumed the back yard. In a few short weeks, Simon Jasper was finally about to arrive. He grinned a toothy grin in the spider's mirror. And there was nothing Taunsley could do about it.

Snowball

Tim walked into the office with Wednesday morning and recent illness slouching through his veins. He mumbled the single word 'Coffee' to Dave, and slumped at his desk. In the car he had passed seventeen hoardings, all lit up with the promise of RhylZig now for over ten days. Although the RhylZig couple wasn't quite what he'd had in mind, Dave's idea had lent an undeniable charm to the doctored image. All in all, he told himself, he should be jumping up and down in anticipation. But Tim had learnt a long time ago that excitement was something best kept out of advertising. As soon as you expected results, they failed to materialize. Which is essentially what had happened. And having ploughed the last of his finances into Barry's scheme, the future was looking increasingly bleak.

Tim squinted across at Dave, wondering why he wasn't fixing the drink. There was something unusual about his deputy. He was sitting bolt upright in his chair, almost to attention, animation quivering across his features. Tim wondered fleetingly whether he'd sat on something.

'What?' he asked.

'The phone, boss.'

'What about it?'

'We've had some calls.'

'Yeah? I thought you said we hadn't had any.'

'We didn't last week. But we had two on Monday, and five yesterday.'

'Five? Jesus. That's a whole month's worth.'

'Yeah. And three today already.'

'Who's been calling?'

'Mixture. Some businesses, obviously feeling threatened, some punters being curious.'

'And what have they been—'

The phone rang. 'See,' Dave announced proudly.

'So are you going to answer it?' Dave was about to pick up the receiver but Tim stopped him. 'Actually, I'll tell you what – why don't you forward it to my phone, let me field it?' Dave pressed the requisite buttons and Tim's line lit up. 'Cheers,' he said. 'Right, here goes. Hello, Tim Power Advertising.'

'Hi, Tim. It's Mr Fellows here, of Fellows Motors, Simply the Best. I'm ringing about your adverts.'

Tim inhaled a nervous, excited breath. Barry's gamble was going to pay off. 'Ah, you've seen them? Pretty prominent—'

'This RhylZig,' he asked, cutting straight to the point, 'it is the *Fiat* RhylZig, isn't it?'

'Well—'

'Only when I came to see you recently, you told me I was the final garage you were going to represent. And now you're working for Fiat,' Mr Fellows shouted, rapidly gaining a momentum Tim was unable to interrupt. 'I see that as breach of contract, so I'm cancelling my agreement with you.'

'But—'

'And for your information,' Mr Fellows concluded, with a rising forcefulness in his voice, 'the Fiat RhylZig is a shite car.'

Mr Fellows slammed the phone down, and Tim lowered his receiver gently into its cradle. He glanced at Dave. 'Have they all been like that?' he asked.

'It's been varied,' his deputy answered.

'How do you mean?'

'Well, some people have—'

The phone rang again and Tim decided to find out for himself. This enquiry was in a slightly different vein, but was similarly confused. 'Could you tell me,' the caller asked, 'where I can buy some of your RhylZig?'

'It's not my—'

'Because I've heard it's good for headaches. Is this true?'

Tim shrugged. It was certainly beginning to make his own brain hurt. 'Yes,' he said, rubbing his face, 'you could say that.'

'But everywhere I've gone, none of the chemists seem to stock it. Can I buy it direct from you?'

'Unfortunately not,' Tim answered, pushing a fist into his cheek.

Between calls, Tim balanced his chair in a comfortable position and thought things through. After a week of utter disinterest, the adverts were beginning to encourage a few people to ring the office. On current evidence, this wasn't necessarily a good thing. He wondered why the lag had been so long. Picking up his daily copy of the *Taunsley Mercury*, the answer screamed out at him in the confusing headline **Pork Pie Porky Pies?** The text comprised largely pessimistic speculation about the future of Jenkins Meat Products.

While Mr Jenkins has refused to confirm or deny the rumoured 1100 job losses, one prominent local businessman who declined to be named was quoted as saying, 'It might all be porky pies designed to increase local interest in JMP. He's done worse in the past.'

So that was it, Tim frowned. The town was worried. People were anxious. The slogan was starting to eat into them. **The one thing your life is missing.** There was nothing like a little apprehension to stir up repressed longings. Bring along a potential panacea for all your problems, and the phone line was going to be busy.

There were seven further calls that day. Most of them fell into a profoundly confused category which could be described by any one of the following:

Caller: Is that RhylZig?

Caller: You can stick your adverts up your arse.

Caller: What is this Tim Powers stuff?

Caller: I want to cancel my account with you.

And, both disturbingly and confusingly:

Caller: RhylZig – you're a fucking Paki lover.

Verbal Abuse

Alistaire Smythe switched the phone off, satisfied with his work. That would teach RhylZig to come to his town and put up posters of white girls at the seaside cavorting with Asian gentlemen. He thought fleetingly about ringing one more time, but realized to his horror that he had just dialled without putting 1-4-1 before the number. If they entered 1-4-7-1 and passed his number to the police, he would be cautioned again for racial harassment. There was only one thing to do. He keyed in 1-4-1 and then pressed redial, hoping he wasn't too late. The phone was answered quickly.

'Hello, Power Advertising.'

Ali paused. Having covered his tracks, he should just hang up, but that felt rude. Maybe not as rude as shouting obscenities, but poor manners all the same. 'Er,' he said, appreciating that he was probably safe now, 'I was just . . .' Ali faltered. Think. Say something uncontroversial and switch the phone off. 'Er, interested in your product, RhylZig.'

The voice that replied was weary. 'What about it?'

'Where can I get some?' Ali answered meekly.

The receiver at the other end was suddenly slammed down and the line cut. Ali sat and glared at his own phone. Now that was downright fucking rude. Who did they think they were? Poncy advertisers. It might be time to visit Power Advertising again, and learn them some manners. Ali stood up and paced the room, his anger welling with each stride. Mixed-race advertising in a small town. It wasn't right. His size thirteens continued to worry the carpet. Liberal fuckers. And then something caught his eye. He stopped in front of the window. To make matters worse, one of the larger RhylZig posters faced almost directly into his living room. He drew back the net curtain and glared at it, feeling his muscles swell and his breathing quicken. They were taking the piss. They wanted you to ring them up, and when you did, even when it wasn't to racially harass them, they cut you off. Wankers. His mother entered the room, and Ali sat down hurriedly.

'Now, Alistaire,' she asked, 'are you using that phone again?'

'Sorry, mum,' he mumbled, 'just ringing a friend.'

'Not causing any trouble, I hope?'

'No.'

'Right. Well, how about a nice cup of tea?'

'Cheers.'

Ali examined the backs of his hands. Just below the knuckles, successive finger tops were tattooed. The left hand spelled out R-I-T-E and the right L-E-F-T as he clenched his fists together. These were the last self-administered tattoos Ali had indulged in, subsequently judging it safer to leave such matters to people who knew what they were doing. It wasn't that he wanted to live with his mum. Few self-respecting hard men should, he felt, share bungalows with their mothers. However, reluctant as they were to incarcerate him, the local magistrates court had made it a condition of numerous suspended sentences that he lived with his guardian. He was therefore stuck in a frustrating quandary. He could either be cooped up with his mother in relative comfort, or be locked up with fellow law-breakers in general discomfort. For the time being, he had settled for the easy option.

His mother returned to the kitchen and Ali stood up and walked to the window. The hoarding was even lit at night, the image burning through the darkness. As he began to wind himself up again by swearing at the massive picture bearing down on him, he noticed something about it he hadn't spotted before. Up to this point, he had merely taken in the fact that one of the people wasn't white. As with all foreigners, he saw no further than the colour of their skin. But tilting his head to one side, a dreadful conclusion seeped slowly through his senses to meet him. The ethnic looked familiar. More than that, he was positively identical. And the deeper he stared into the dusky face with its whitened teeth and modified hair, the more obvious the judgment became. The mother fuckers! he screamed, spinning wildly round and smashing the first thing in sight, which happened to be one of his mother's favourite vases. Who could have done this? What shitbag could have attacked him so publicly? Returning to the window and scowling up at the image, he was joined by his mother.

'What's all the commotion?' she asked quietly.

Ali slid the broken vase out of her sight. He reddened, almost quivering with rage.

'That nice coloured boy in the picture looks a bit like you, Alistaire,' his mother pointed out.

'A bit?' Ali grimaced. 'A . . . *bit*?'

'Such lovely skin. Takes me right back . . .' Deirdre Smythe shuffled out of the room, her mind wandering along an equally familiar journey.

Transfixed by the image, Ali was unable to avoid the

horrible truth of the matter. Even his mother had noticed. It was his own face staring across the street at him. Someone had taken the CCTV picture used by the *Mercury*, disguised it slightly and grafted it onto another person's body. And now Alistaire Smythe, committed racist, was the black face of RhylZig!

Ali sat down in shock and tried to repair his mother's ornament before she came back with his tea. He struggled to compute the implications. First, the *Taunsley Mercury* had recently launched a fair-minded campaign against illegal immigrants. Ali had written a letter of support, but that would have to bite the dust. In fact, given that the *Mercury*'s crusade was based firmly on the misapprehension that Ali himself was the town's sole illegal immigrant, it might even be better to make a stand against the crackdown. And if that didn't undermine him, then the information that he now wasn't just a foreign man implicated in a robbery, he was the Asian face of RhylZig, began to tear him to pieces. Ali's brain was on the verge of imploding. He wondered whether he ought to beat himself up and be done with it. Certainly, the evidence of his ethnicity seemed to be against him. Without trying to do anything more complicated than breaking into an office, he had become an enemy not just to the residents of Taunsley, but to himself.

Ali spotted a recent edition of the *Mercury* on his mum's coffee table and tore it open, scanning wildly for any further outrages. Inside was yet another full-page advert for RhylZig, which he ripped out, stamped on and then threw in the bin. Things were about to get worse, however. On page seven, a huge headline screamed, **Criminal Immigrant Poses For RhylZig**. Ali read the report, his lips moving in time with the news.

It appears that the actor used to promote RhylZig by local advertiser Power Advertising may be the same man who ransacked the *Mercury* offices three weeks ago. Staff at the paper have noted a strong level of similarity between security camera footage of the alleged asylum seeker and the male face of the as yet unidentified wonder product RhylZig. A spokesman for Power Advertising, David Manners, told us yesterday, 'I don't know anything about the story, and in no way have we grafted CCTV footage obtained from a friend onto the body of another actor to mock up the RhylZig picture. No way at all.'

Underneath the story, and the name Gary Shrubble, the paper had helpfully printed the two pictures side by side. Ali threw the paper down in disgust and returned to wearing out the carpet with his Dr Martens. He noticed a copy of the *Shopper*, but decided for mental health reasons not to open it. This was getting out of hand. And all blame pointed towards one building. The Quayside Landings. Specifically the journalists of the *Taunsley Mercury*, and, more importantly, Tim Power Advertising. It was time, he decided, to make a joint visit to discuss one or two issues with them.

Landlord and Lodger

In the afternoon, Tim Power scuttled through the corridors of Taunsley District Hospital, which managed to be both grimy and antiseptic at the same time. In his sweaty palm he gripped an Outpatients card for the ENT department. He was careful not to be recognized. Ann had reported seeing him a couple of weeks previously, and although he made a good fist of denying it, he felt this was a little too close for comfort. His ailment, of all ailments, must remain secret, even to his friends. Later, as he left the hospital after his appointment, he was equally vigilant to avoid detection. Maybe he was erring on the side of paranoia, but in a small town, it paid to be secretive.

The consultant had not brought good news. The tests, she told him, had failed to reveal any obvious causes, and hence any obvious cures. It was, she had opined with an almost dismissive shrug of her padded shoulders, just one of those things. Tim felt he could have received a similar level of medical expertise in the supermarket queue. When he reached the safety of the town centre, he checked his watch. Four thirty-five, and no real point in returning to work. Instead, he called in to the far more productive environment of a pub and sipped a couple of pints while reading the paper. Inside was an article on dangerous sports in New Zealand. He tried, and failed, to picture Zoe base-jumping or white-water rafting. Going to the shops without make-up was as close as she usually came to adventure. Lighting a cigarette, he wondered what *exactly* it was about Zoe that he missed so badly. Surely it was more than just her company and her sex, the latter of which, no matter how he attempted to ignore it, continued to gnaw away at him. Since late adolescence he seemed to have been in a perpetual relationship. With different girlfriends he had made various sacrifices in return for regular intercourse. Never had he been more than a month or two without it, and now he understood for the first time why it was so important to him. Sex simply pushed him close to the warmth of another human. It was as if in its absence he was cut off from the species, isolated, emotionally autistic, unable to interact. In short, coitus was humanity for Tim. Celibacy seemed to leave him increasingly tense and he saw his frequent headaches as a direct effect of this. Undoubtedly the period of disconnection was taking its toll. This was the gamble Zoe had instigated, and Tim felt a twinge of annoyance mingling with the alcohol. A year's separation was something most successful relationships never have to experience. As such it was an unfair test. And what was to say Zoe would come back at all, or, if she did, that she would be the same person who went away? Maybe twelve months of vastly different experiences would change them both so profoundly that they would no longer be compatible. He worried that sometimes if you pull things too far apart they change their shape and never fit properly back into place.

Tim finally sloped off home, continuing to miss and berate his absent girlfriend. Ann was already there.

She was in the kitchen and seemed to be engaged in a mammoth effort to involve every utensil known to man in the preparation of a single dish. Tim's stomach rumbled and murmured that it would also like feeding, and so he rescued the one remaining vessel from his lodger's attentions.

Ann watched him as he broke a handful of spaghetti into the pan, before adding water and encouraging it to boil by sitting on his arse and flicking through a magazine.

'Spaghetti tonight?' she asked.

Tim looked from pan to lodger. ''Fraid so,' he answered.

'And last night?'

'Yep.'

'And the night before.'

'Don't tell me you've spotted a trend?' Tim smiled.

Ann poured something into a pan, stirred it, decanted it into the blender, blended it, spooned it into a sieve, sieved it, put it under the grill, grilled it, and then tipped it into a mixing bowl. 'It's just that in the few weeks I've lived here,' she grunted, beating the mysterious mixture with a wooden spoon, 'I've noticed that you've eaten exactly the same meal every night.'

Tim continued to watch, fascinated and appalled in equal measure, as Ann soiled yet another saucepan. 'And?' he asked.

'Don't you ever get bored?'

'No,' Tim replied honestly.

'Or fed up?'

'No.'

'Or malnourished?'

'Ah,' Tim answered as Ann ladled her food into a bowl, which she then placed in the microwave, 'I have a neat trick to overcome the nutritional deficiencies of my cooking.' The spaghetti now ready, he drained it, stirred in three forkfuls of pesto, slopped it onto a plate and held a multivitamin capsule over the dish. It was Ann's turn to watch in horror as Tim opened the capsule and sprinkled it over his food. 'There,' he said proudly, 'no scurvy for me.'

'I wondered what garnish you've been using,' Ann muttered. 'Thought it was some sort of Parmesan cheese. But that vitamin stuff must taste horrible.'

Tim stopped. That hadn't been very bright. 'Can't really say it does,' he replied. 'No worse than pesto.'

'Anyway, I thought advertisers ate speciality products from remote regions of the world, washed down with twenty-quid bottles of wine.'

'Most of them do. Struggling propagandists in danger of going out of business, however, eat whatever they can.'

He took his plate into the living room and flicked the TV on. After several minutes of complicated kitchen noises and occasional swearing, Ann appeared, sweating lightly, and sat next to him. He risked a glance at her meal, which had shrunk considerably and seemed to have had the life heated, grilled, poached, flambéed, microwaved, sieved and beaten out of it. The thought of the sheer bulk of washing-up required made him nervous, and he resolved to quickly rinse his own pan and plate and stay the hell out of the kitchen. He was undeniably morose, and picked up the evening edition of the *Taunsley Mercury* he'd bought on the way home.

On page four of the paper was a headline which made him swear out loud. 'Stupid fuckers!' he shouted, before reading it again to make sure. **Just What Is RhylZig?** it asked. Beneath was another undemanding Gary Shrubble piece which attempted to catch the mood of the town, and had been written without inconveniencing anyone who knew anything about the subject at hand.

Inside sources suggest that RhylZig will hit Taunsley within the month. Meanwhile shopkeepers remain tight-lipped about the alleged **One Thing Your Life is Missing**, saying only that stocks will be severely limited. But RhylZig has already been heavily criticized in some quarters. Mr Fellows of Fellows Motors (Simply the Best) was yesterday quoted as saying, 'RhylZig is an entirely inferior product to, say, the Rover 200. And it's foreign muck as well.' And, in a related and ongoing story, the identity of the dark-skinned man in the advert still remains a mystery at the time of going to press.

Tim closed the paper in disbelief. A quarter-page article, and not a single mention of the bona fide product at hand – him. He picked up the *Shopper*, which had been rammed unwanted through his letter-box earlier that day. Inside was a similarly ambitious piece of reporting. **RhylZig Takes Town By Storm!** it announced. And instead of speculation so idle that it was virtually unconscious, as befitted the *Mercury*, the *Shopper* led with an artist's impression of RhylZig.

What was drawn encouraged a lot of examination. Even viewed from various angles and in several lighting conditions, the *Shopper*'s vision of RhylZig was ambiguous, to say the least. At its centre was a couple who were not dissimilar to Tim's mock-up and Ann. However, they weren't particularly similar either. Ann was oddly like Madonna during her brunette phase, while Tim's body and Alistaire Smythe's head looked disturbingly like Nasser Hussain. Surrounding them was a series of images which could have been just about anything, from cars to pharmaceuticals via cigarettes and bottles of spirits. At best, it was an unnerving montage. The caption below told the real story.

RhylZig, the product which is taking the town by storm, as envisaged by Eric Waters, the *Shopper*'s artist.

Where the *Shopper* had scored over the *Mercury*, though, was in its depth of probing. They had actually bothered to call Power Advertising. Tim read on in disbelief.

David Manners, Chief Executive Assistant Artistic and Creative Director at Tim Power Advertising, had the following comment. 'I'm not at liberty to say what RhylZig is, or when it's coming, only that it's not a publicity stunt for our agency. Certainly not. And you can quote me on that.'

Tim leant forwards and banged his aching head gently on the coffee table. Everyone had missed the point. He was about to go out of business.

Home Ergonomics

Barry Dinsdale walked swiftly to his car. In a single practised motion, he inserted the key in the lock and opened the door before sliding into the front seat, somehow still holding his keys. While the diesel engine warmed, he pulled the seatbelt across his chest, depressed the clutch and slid it into first gear. Then he started the car, dropped the handbrake and exited his parking space. Man and machine, that was the solution. Human harmony with metallic mechanism. And what a beautiful metallic mechanism, he sighed lovingly to himself as he exited the car park. He ran his fingers lightly around the steering wheel, caressing it like a slender pair of hips. This was his favourite place in the world.

He swept onto the ring road but quickly found himself behind a tractor. The vehicle was towing a trailer and was impossible to see past. Barry changed down to second and tutted. The journey home should only last eleven minutes. He had clocked it every day for a year and it rarely deviated from this time. The tractor seemed to be slowing, if anything, but to overtake would be to risk damaging his cherished car and that wasn't a risk he felt like taking. It saw enough battle action when his wife drove it. As he thought about Cathy, he shook his head slowly. The car's interior was blighted with a huge assortment of child- and wife-related clutter. She saw the vehicle as a dumping ground for domestic refuse that couldn't reasonably be squeezed into the house, while his children had seemingly been born without the tidy-up-after-yourself gene.

The tractor turned off, and Barry continued to ponder as he accelerated. He couldn't help but feel that while he devoted his days to the efficiency of others, at home things were going badly wrong. Despite enormous effort and numerous initiatives, his residence was still one of the least efficient places he had ever been. Lights were left on all night. Cathy seemed to visit the shops upwards of four times a day. Each of their six children attended a different school or nursery in a different area of the town, so that the school run was more of a marathon. His wife regularly drove to the gym to use a running machine. The kettle was habitually boiled dry. The toaster routinely burnt bread beyond recognition. To fit in around the children's tea time, his evening meal was usually reheated at least once. On other occasions it was simply scraped into the bin and Barry had to go out and forage for a takeaway. The toothpaste wasn't so much squeezed from the bottom towards the top as randomly mangled. Important items were frequently discarded and had to be bought again. As enterprises went, home was a mess.

While he didn't believe his wife was deliberately trying to undermine him, Barry imagined that there had to be more regimented women out there somewhere. These were the sort of wives who bought magazines stuffed with tips on saving money, organizing lives and balancing the needs of the household. Pulling into the drive, Barry made a big decision. It was time to bring his work home with him. There was little point lecturing people in factories all day about operator performance and standards of reasonable conduct, when his wife was clearly contravening all such principles at her leisure. A well-organized homestead meant an efficient family. And an efficient family meant a happy unit. Barry entered the house quietly and retreated to the bedroom, well away from his screaming brood.

Hiding from his progeny was becoming a habit of late. A reluctant conclusion had recently dawned on Barry. He wasn't proud of it, but was unable to escape its logic. Locking the door, he conceded that he had become afraid of his own children. He had woken up one weekend morning and the stark mathematics of the situation had slapped him in the face. As Sally, Peter, David, Harry, Sarah and Daniel stormed into the bedroom and jumped on his prone form, he realized he was utterly surrounded. Insidiously, and behind his back, the family had become too big. His offspring almost appeared to be reproducing of their own free will. Every time he looked, there seemed to be more of them.

'Couldn't we, you know, get rid of a few?' he'd asked his wife.

'Get rid? What are you talking about?'

'They've got us hemmed in. Everywhere I look they're huddled in groups, plotting things.'

'It's a bit late now. If you didn't want so many . . .'

'Look, I wasn't counting, I never really kept track. It's only when you see them all together. I mean, what if they mutiny?'

'Mutiny?'

'You know, rise up and oppress us. There's enough of them.'

'There's only six.'

'Exactly. And we're only two. They outnumber us three to one. I mean, we're not even fucking Catholics. We can actually use contraception. Think what a mess we'd be in if we had religion. And the sodding McGuigans at number eleven give *me* pitying looks. They've been playing rhythm roulette for donkey's years, and they've only got two kids. And what? You've been on the pill virtually since I met you. How did that work? Somewhere, Cathy, we've been ripped off.'

'So you're saying you don't want any more?' Cathy had asked, searching her husband's eyes.

'I'm saying there are times when I don't want the ones we've got.'

Cathy hadn't taken this well. In fairness, Barry blushed, it hadn't been a great thing to say. But now, rather than have them all adopted, he was going to do the next best thing. Barry spent every evening of the week feverishly reading books and writing notes, locked away from his ever-increasing family. From time to time he emerged, entered the kitchen or living room, took a couple of measurements and retreated again. He hummed a great deal as well, and annoyed his wife considerably with a vast array of uninspiring questions. What day did she wash the clothes? he asked. Every day, she replied. And what day was the big weekly shop? Most days, she answered. The bin men come when? he enquired. Fridays, she said, flicking channel and frowning. So what time do the kids get home? Depends, she murmured. And how often do you hoover? When I feel like it, she shrugged. After each inquest, Barry muttered to himself, scribbled a few notes and scuttled back to the bedroom. Cathy became increasingly apprehensive. Whatever her husband was

142

up to didn't sound like good news. She quietly braced herself for an onslaught.

At the end of the week, Cathy lay back on the sofa and revelled in the magical hour of eight thirty. The children, who had refused to get into the bath and then refused to get out, had been frogmarched to bed, where they spent half an hour complaining bitterly before promptly falling asleep. The house was silent except for a pacing noise coming from upstairs. This had been growing ever more urgent over the last few days, and Cathy chose to ignore it. Technically, it was Friday, which meant a trip to the gym. She inhaled the sweet fumes of her glass and swallowed some more wine. Sod it, she'd go tomorrow. Besides, the car wasn't driving well of late, possibly because she'd treated it to a couple of inadvertent gallons of petrol the previous week before realizing her mistake and topping it up with diesel. She imagined this wasn't a mix that would necessarily aid the overall driving experience. Also, she'd scraped it again, and this time accidentally. She made a policy decision not to tell Barry about either issue. Above her, the sound of footsteps became more insistent. Something was brewing.

She flicked the TV on and vainly searched for a programme worth viewing. A sitcom, ruthlessly purged of jokes, ground on to wild applause. Presently she heard Barry begin to descend the stairs. She sighed, anticipating another round of tedious questions about her domestic rituals, and increased the volume to hinder him as much as possible. When she glanced up, Barry was standing over her. He was dressed in the white coat he used at work and was holding a clipboard. A sprinkling of perspiration

143

clung to his forehead and there was a worrying intensity in his eyes. The words 'Oh fuck' lit up in her brain. She made a desperate attempt to distract him.

'You know,' she said, 'I've been meaning to say. My boss is behaving a bit weird.'

'Your boss *is* weird. But don't tell him I said that. Or anything else that I might or might not have said.'

'But I think Gribben's up to something.'

'Like what?'

'A vendetta. Or an attack.'

'Not on us, I hope?'

'Wouldn't have thought so.'

'Good. Anyway.' Barry cleared his throat. 'Cathy, as you may have noticed, I've been doing a bit of thinking about our domestic situation over the last few days,' he said. 'What I've decided is this: the house is being run very inefficiently.' He paused, waiting for a response. Cathy merely raised her eyebrows, scratched herself and swigged some more wine. 'So I've been performing some assessments of our current situation. I've examined working environment ergonomics, workload analysis, operator performance, behavioural expectations, cost-benefit assays, usability evaluations, systems requirements capture and interface motivation.'

Cathy rubbed her face irritably. 'And?'

'And we're failing to meet our targets in almost every area.'

'We?'

'You.'

'Right.'

'We all know that good task analysis makes for a happy household, so what I suggest is this. I've drawn up a timetable of activity, which I've cross-referenced against chores, people and responsibilities.' He held up a piece of paper which was decorated with a series of offputting flow diagrams. 'And this,' he continued, producing another sheet, 'is a list of the precise temporal-spatial interval at which each event fits into the general scheme.'

'Do you think it might be more efficient to use the English language occasionally?'

'It's simple. Look.' He pointed to a coloured line on a chart. 'The temporal-spatial interval intersects with rota A on Tuesday—'

'For fuck's sake, Barry,' Cathy interrupted, 'it's only a house.'

'But that's what they all say. It's only a biscuit factory, Mr Dinsdale. We only make paperclips, Barry. That's not the point.'

'Well, what is?'

'The house is a shambles. It's time to make some harsh decisions for the good of everybody. We're just not performing optimally.'

Cathy drained her glass and walked to the kitchen for another. On the way there she took the opportunity to scowl at her husband. Barry was the type of person you ended up with, she cursed. Few partners set their sights on a Barry. It was like a playground picking exercise. Barry was the one that teams argued about getting stuck with. No, *you* have him. No way, he's *yours*. But somebody always did. And in the end it had been Cathy. She accidentally overfilled her glass and some wine spilled onto the floor. There was no way she was going down without a fight. Stick that on your chart, she said under her breath, heading past Barry and back to the sofa.

Target Practice

A diminutive vehicle left a short secluded drive and headed onto the main road. Its headlights scanned the face of a borderline vagrant, who protected his eyes with the arm of a grubby overcoat. Dropping a can of cider, the man started his own car and followed through the outskirts of Taunsley. 'Come on, Gribben,' Gary Shrubble slurred to himself, struggling to keep up, 'let's see where you go at night.'

Gary held back as far as he could without losing his quarry. Gribben picked up speed through the empty roads and Taunsley's finest journalist accelerated along with him. The car ahead turned right at a roundabout and flashed through a red light. Gary Shrubble closed his eyes and did the same. He wondered idly whether he ought to put his seatbelt on, but decided against it. There were, he felt, certain advantages to having a serious car crash. With any luck, he might be able to trade a few of his organs in for new ones. An unsoiled liver would be of particular advantage. The odd kidney and bladder wouldn't go amiss either. Both cars careered through a further set of traffic lights with little regard for other road users. Wherever Derek Gribben was heading, Gary shrugged, he was eager to get there in a hurry. Street lights began to thin until they were in the hedged darkness of the countryside. The small car in front slowed on a long straight road which was barely wide enough for vehicles to pass, and Gary worried momentarily that he had been spotted. Gribben then turned left down an even tighter track. A sign lit up in Gary's headlights and he squinted. It read 'AJG Meat Suppliers'. Two hundred yards further along the road, Gribben's car pulled onto a small patch of gravel that served as a car park. Gary stopped and turned off his headlights. He swung out of the front seat and crept closer.

A security light came on as Derek Gribben left his tiny car and walked towards a low-rise warehouse crouching in the dark. Gary sniffed. They were in the middle of a farm. He could hear the odd guttural grunt and an occasional contemplative moo. There were no people around and they had long since passed the last house. Thirty yards away, Gary Shrubble watched Derek Gribben open a padlock and slide a door back. He then returned to his car. As he pulled out a large shotgun and what appeared to be a pistol, Gary suddenly felt the need to piss. He probably would have felt this anyway, on account of the four cans of journalist-strength cider he had consumed while waiting for Gribben to leave his house. However, the need was urgent, and Gary treated the hedge to an extended flow of watery urine.

Derek Gribben disappeared inside the building and, shaking his penis as he walked, Gary made his way nearer. Reaching a gap in the large double doors, he appreciated that the warehouse was refrigerated. Cold air sneaked out to mingle with the warmer summer air. Peering in, he was confronted by row after row of skeletal pig carcasses, hanging silently up, their skin and organs long since departed. Gribben was nowhere to be seen but he could hear his footsteps pacing up and down and from time to time saw a moist breath hanging in the frigid air. For a couple of moments there was silence and Gary endeavoured to place Gribben within the room. A few noises of metal against concrete echoed from the rear. Then a colossal bang rocked Gary back on his piss-stained shoes. He shook his head, ears ringing, and stared wildly around for the source of the noise. A sole carcass was swaying back and forth to the left, a head-sized hole apparent in its midriff. Gary's hands shook with something more than their usual tremor. Gribben came into view. He was carrying a shotgun in his right hand, resting it back against his shoulder like a cricketer coming out to bat. He examined what was left of the pig, running his fingers through the hole and out the other side. He smiled. Gary watched him lower the gun to the floor and, pushing it against his foot, break it open. In a complex and well-practised series of actions, Gribben replaced the spent cartridges and cocked the weapon once more. Gary wondered how the hell he was going to fire it with only one arm, but he had obviously developed a system. He brought the gun up to the horizontal and trapped its butt between his side and his elbow. Suitably anchored, he span around and discharged both barrels into another carcass, some ten yards away, firing from the hip and recoiling, just retaining his balance. Gary felt the urgent need to relieve himself again, but was too fascinated to leave. He studied the glee on Gribben's face as he admired his handiwork. Another pig, already denied a dignified end, was swinging in the air, all shattered bones and missing flesh.

Then Gribben changed tack. He pulled out a pistol and set about destroying what was left of the carcass.

With each deafening shot, another hole appeared. He was almost ecstatic, shouting and screaming with successive blasts. 'Jenkins, you fat cunt!' Bang. 'Power, you sucker!' Bang. 'Smythe, you fuckhead!' Bang. 'Cathy Dinsdale, you disrespectful bitch!' Bang. 'Shrubble, you pissed old hack.' Bang. On hearing his own name, Gary had an unnerving premonition of his own body hanging in a warehouse somewhere, being pumped full of bullets by an unhinged man with only one arm. He began to retreat, careful not to be spotted. Ignoring the fresh protests of his bladder, he jumped into his car. Gary reversed hastily down the lane, regularly clipping the hedge on alternate sides of the track, until he reached the road and was able to turn around. Only when he was safely back in the presence of houses and streets did he pause to urinate in a wide-necked bottle he kept in the glovebox for just such an emergency.

Perpetuating Mediocrity

Tim Power had once been told that he could sell windows to double-glazing salesmen. Now it looked like he might be fitting them.

When he had finished university in the early nineties, the new word on everyone's lips was communication. Systems were being developed. Faxes were flying around. Emails began to appear. Mobile phones materialized. Satellite dishes clung to the sides of houses, sucking in huge numbers of TV stations. Rumours surfaced of an interlinked telephone and computer network enveloping the planet like a web. There was a real feeling of the endless possibility of the exchange of ideas. What had attracted him towards the advertising industry was the opportunity to communicate with millions of people, to influence their interactions and to be influenced himself. More importantly, however, and the real clincher, had been the vain hope that through doing so he might finally understand what had taken his father away from him.

Tim began in graphics for magazines at a thriving Soho agency called A2Z Advertising. He carried out copywriting for small, unimportant half-page ads before progressing to full-page glossies. A couple of years later he was let loose on a few radio campaigns. Finally, he had a stab at TV. And that was where it had all gone wrong. Fatally, he had begun to understand too much.

A single conversation with a colleague at A2Z had brought things into sharp focus on a fuzzy afternoon, some time in the middle of his three disastrous campaigns. He had been fiddling with an expensive rollerball which had just fallen apart and showed few signs of being reparable. As he tried in vain to reunite the business end of the pen with its inky other, he felt a sudden surge of anger and banged his desk. Jeremy Croker, Assistant Executive Artistic Director, looked over at him.

'What's up?' he asked.

'My fucking pen's just fallen apart.'

'Yeah, mine too,' Jeremy said, examining a detached nib with interest. He was a year or two older than Tim and significantly more jaded. While Jeremy didn't actively have a drug habit, he was aspiring towards one, and spent a considerable proportion of his time vainly trying to find the right substance to become addicted to.

'But this is a Shafter 3000. It's meant to be the best there is.'

'That's what the shoutlines say.'

'Exactly!' Something that had been simmering for a long time was about to boil over. 'Don't you see the logic? Crap product? Spend more on advertising. That, in a nutshell, is our mantra.'

'So?' his workmate asked.

'So maybe this is all our own fault. Maybe all we're doing each day is perpetuating mediocrity, mediocrity which then comes home to roost. Because when I buy a product and find it's useless, I suffer as well.'

151

'That's why you're paid so handsomely. It means you don't have to buy awful products.'

'So you're saying that more expensive items are better.'

'Always. Except the Shafter 3000, of course.'

'And what about Zander?'

'What about it?' Jeremy asked, once again considering his narcotic situation. The trouble was, he couldn't yet afford to be addicted to cocaine. Lesser drugs were cheaper, but frustratingly less easy to become dependent upon.

'Let me remind you,' Tim said. 'We recommended the client that the reason Zander washing powder wasn't selling was because it was too cheap. People didn't trust the brand. So what did we do? We renamed it, doubled its price and it became the fourth best-selling detergent.'

'I'm sure you're going somewhere with this.'

'The reason it didn't sell wasn't its price. It was because it was shite at shifting dirt. Now it costs a packet, people buy it for status. The cost of a product isn't therefore a guarantee of its quality.'

'OK, what car do you drive?' Jeremy asked, shifting tack.

'Audi A6.'

'Good car?'

'I like it.'

'Cheap?'

'Not exactly.'

'And do you think a cheaper car, say a Nissan Micra, would be better?'

'No, but that isn't my—'

'You get what you pay for, by and large,' he said, leaning back in his chair, arms folded behind his head to reveal healthy patches of sweat. As his words came out, however, Jeremy appreciated that this probably wasn't true of drugs. Most of the time he didn't know what he was getting.

Tim stood up excitedly. 'But you don't. You get what you're told to pay for, and that's not always the same thing.'

'Sounds like it to me.'

'Look at this.' Tim picked a catalogue from his shelf and read a section out loud. 'The role of the market researcher at Universal Polling is to identify consumer wants and give our clients a comprehensive understanding of those wants and the best way to satisfy them. Specifically, we focus on the development of new product notions and creative communication concepts.' He shut the brochure.

'So?'

'It's bollocks. The role of market research isn't to find out what the public wants.'

'No?'

'No. It's to tell the consumer what they need. Not immediately, but when that data has been processed, you and me come up with bright ideas on how to turn around the existing crap product we've got so that it *appears* to be what Joe Public wants. Market research therefore doesn't tell us what will make the public happy. It tells us exactly what we can palm off on them.'

'Can't see the difference myself.'

'The difference is that we are busy perpetuating the mediocrity of products, while telling the consumer we're making their lives better.'

'And,' Jeremy added, grinning from ear to ear, 'making shedloads of cash.'

'This fucking rollerball-easy-write-continuous-action pen, for example,' Tim said, holding both ends in front of his eyes, 'just about sums it up.' He threw the useless item at the bin, and each bit missed, the continuous-action nib spilling a small puddle of ink over the carpet. 'Look, Jez, I've been thinking about a lot of things. Shit products proliferate because their manufacturers spend enough money on advertising. I can't help but feel, therefore, that advertising is simply holding society back. Let me sound a few ideas off you. Tell me if I'm going a bit daft.'

'I'll see what I can do.'

'Right.'

Tim stood up and began to pace the office with an intensity his colleague had rarely witnessed. 'The humble advert which once informed us is now there to confuse us,' he began. 'We don't know if we're coming or going. Does my kettle have limescale? Do I have dry skin or oily skin? Is my scalp flaky or normal? Are they fine wrinkle folds around my eyes or laughter lines? Can a man develop cellulite? Can a woman be prone to shaving rash? Does my breath smell? Am I prone to water retention? Do I constantly fluctuate somewhere between constipation and diarrhoea? Are my migraines simply tense nervous headaches? Do I need to filter out UV B as well as A? If so, is my cereal providing enough vitamin D? Can a suntan lotion really firm my skin? Do I have athlete's foot or do I just need to change my Odour-Eaters? Do scientists really stand around all day inspecting newly washed clothes? What product will clear up the rash given me by my new ultra-biological Zander washing powder? If smoking is making my teeth yellow, and coffee is staining them brown, and red wine is dying them black, will the blue stripe in my toothpaste really make them white again? And can chewing sugary gum actually improve my oral hygiene? In fact, what is oral hygiene?'

'You've got me.'

'Don't you see? The mouth is designed to be a thoroughly unhygienic place. Look, why has my cat wasted millions of years evolving into a ruthless hunter, only to be presented with seventeen different varieties of low-odour, low-mess dried meat pellets? What's the point in feeding your mutt sachets of gourmet food when we all know dogs will eat fucking anything, sick included? What's the difference between a deodorant and an antiperspirant, and how does this affect me? Can I honestly taste the extra milk in one brand of chocolate compared to another? How does thicker ketchup improve my life, when I can't get the stuff out of the container? What's so fucking difficult about taking two bottles into the shower? And can one shampoo really clean *and* condition my hair at the same time? Can I really eat myself thinner? Isn't that a bit like trying to drink myself drier? What's the point of cars designed to do 150, when I rarely get out of second gear in the traffic? Would a different manufacturer's sanitary towel really make me feel any freer?'

'Probably wouldn't do *you* many favours.'

'And what does a trombone-playing Morph look-a-like have to do with the taste of butter? Is my world in the least bit improved by any consumer durable I buy? Isn't Consumer Durable now an oxymoron, given that everything you buy is obsolete or fucked a year after you've bought it? Aren't we simply creating hunger, dangerous hunger? Those who can't resist it and can't pay take it anyway. And so the product you were told would solve your problems opens up a whole new set when someone mugs you for it.'

'I think you're getting a bit carried—'

Tim interrupted him, keen to maintain his momentum. 'And are we really all individuals, as we've been told for so long? If so, why do millions of us rush out to buy the same make of jeans, marketed with the slogan **Because no one tells me what to do**? Aren't we, as advertisers, simply laughing at society? Aren't we telling punters to **Go on, have another one**, and then showing them they're too fat for the beach with stuff like **Lose your excess baggage this summer**. Aren't we saying **You Are Unique**, and then persuading them all to buy the same car? Aren't we spending millions promoting products we tell them are **So Good They Advertise Themselves**?'

Jeremy yawned. 'All straightforward so far. So what's your point?'

'My point is that I don't mind the fact that the commercial world is one big fat conspiracy to take my money. What I do object to is being told that they are doing it for my own good. And not just mine. It's the planet as well. Tigers advertising jungle-raping petrol. Fishes promoting river-soiling diesel. Jaguars pushing wildlife-squashing cars. Eagles selling bird-swallowing jets. We really are shafting nature, and while we do it, making animals actually hasten their own demise.'

'Aw, they'll never find out. I won't tell them if you don't, comrade Power.'

'Look, I'm not against capitalism, it's just that it's beginning to fuck with my head. And I'm on the inside. That's what's so frightening. If I'm one of the evil peddlers of shoddy goods, and I'm getting fucked over, what about the poor sod in the street? And, more important, what about our families?'

'What about them?'

'Don't you see how they suffer?'

'Not really.'

'But they do,' Tim mumbled, sitting down and

holding his head in his hands. As he did so, his boss walked in.

'Tim,' he began ominously, 'time we had words.'

One advert, more than any other, summed up Tim's growing disillusionment. His second shot at the big time had involved a product called Aspirilligan. Through meticulously biased market research, a pharmaceutical company had identified a new human vanity issue. A deep-seated insecurity about foot appearance had been apparent among the hundreds of people queried. This was all well and good, but most toe issues were already covered. Athlete's foot, corns and verrucas were swimming in creams and powders. What had been needed was something else to capitalize on the fact that feet cooped up all day inside nylon socks mortify their owners when they appear in public. And by trawling the medical literature for rare and harmless conditions the manufacturers of Aspirilligan had come up trumps. Toenail fungus.

The aim had been to show enough doctored film of toenail fungus to lodge the ailment in the public's mind as foot enemy number one. And where better to start than the very place many insecurities begin – the locker room. Tim's ad had a simple theme and ran as follows:

Music: Shoo Wap Song by Cher.

Video: Two men playing squash. Cut to the swimming pool. One is still wearing his trainers. In the sauna, he is wearing his trainers. In the showers, he is still wearing his pumps.

V/O: DO *YOU* HAVE A SHOE FETISH?

Video: That night in his bedroom, the man climbs into bed. He is wearing shoes. His wife gives him a disapproving look.

V/O: LEAVE YOUR SHOES BEHIND WITH ASPIRILLIGAN.

Video: Close-up on a yellow toenail.

Video key (projected across toenail): Aspirilligan.

V/O: BECAUSE TOENAIL FUNGUS LOVES SHOE VERY MUCH.

The campaign, however, was never seen on TV. Test screenings had been poor, with significant numbers of people objecting to both the thought and the sight of toenail fungus. Certainly, showing close-range images of discoloured toes had put off even the hardiest of foot perverts. The promotion lost momentum and was eventually scrapped. One vestige remained, though. Tim began to worry about toenail fungus. And he had been forced to ask the question: before shooting the commercial, was he embarrassed by, or even aware of, unsightly toenail fungus? And then the next logical step. He contracted the disease. Despite being possibly the rarest syndrome available, he was convinced that he had it. Numerous specialists disagreed, and Tim marvelled at their lack of expertise. He bought multiple tins of Aspirilligan and bathed his feet in it at regular intervals, which did little to improve their appearance. Several weeks later, when the pretend fungus was beating an imaginary retreat, Tim began to wonder that if adverts were making him a hypochondriac, and he knew they were nonsense, what about the general population? How the hell were they faring when they were bombarded with the constant crap that Tim and his ilk foisted onto them?

Bit by bit, he was finally beginning to see how his father's job had undermined his family.

Bank Rupture

'Dave . . .'

'Yes?'

'It's crunch time. I'll be honest with you. We're in debt. The bank are calling today, and it's more than likely they'll close us down. I had to borrow five grand to keep us afloat and prop up the RhylZig campaign, but I haven't been able to repay anything. It isn't looking good.'

Dave didn't look good either. Tim realized that probably the only successful advertising he had managed since moving to Taunsley was selling Dave the dream of becoming an advertiser. For a moment he flushed with guilt. Personal failure hurt, but failing others brought out pangs of betrayal and embarrassment.

'Surely we can hang on for a bit?'

'Another client cancelled us today.'

'Who?'

'The Otteridge Butchers chain.'

'Shit.'

'Seems that rather than making businesses feel like they need to compete, we've merely upset our existing customers. And butchers are probably feeling the pinch if Jenkins Meat Products are on the verge of going under. That's what happens in a micro-economy. The big employer folds and everyone becomes nervous. And when companies are suffering, the first thing they do is cancel their advertising contracts.'

'But there must be something we can do?'

Tim shook his head. 'I'm skint. I've already lost all my savings. In fact, I might actually be bankrupt for all I know. I'm not sure how you tell.'

'Well, let's not answer the phone. Maybe we'll get some work before the bank tracks us down.'

'If we don't answer the phone,' Tim said, pointing out the obvious, 'we're not likely to be offered any work.'

'But we're getting twenty calls a day. The whole town wants to know about RhylZig.'

'Exactly! But they don't want to know about us. The entire population has got the wrong end of the fucking stick. We have,' he said quietly, 'created a monster.' Tim cradled his head in his hands. 'A teaser campaign which everybody took literally. A threat which businesses took too personally.' So this is what defeat feels like, he thought. Uncomfortable, upsetting, frustrating.

'OK, how about this, boss? I'll ring round people who expressed an interest in RhylZig, try to drum up some business.'

Dave's refusal to quit was touching, but far too late. The only decent thing to do, Tim appreciated, was to take him to the pub and buy him a few beers. 'Come on,' he said, 'let's go to the Goose. It's over.'

Dave stood up. He was pale. 'So this is it? No job tomorrow? Nothing to show for all my ideas? All that copywriting will end up in the shredder?'

'I'm afraid—' The phone rang, and Tim glanced helplessly at Dave. 'Come on,' he sighed, 'let's get out of here.'

'But don't you want to know . . .'

'No. Even if it's not the bank, it will be some poor misguided sod desperate for RhylZig. Turn the lights off and we'll go and get drunk.'

The phone continued to scream for attention. Dave was twitchy. 'Shouldn't we at least . . .'

'I don't want to hear the inevitable.'

Dave walked towards the phone.

'I'm warning you, leave it alone.'

'Or what? You'll sack me?' Dave picked the phone up in defiance. 'Power Advertising,' he answered, 'David Manners, Chief Advertising Executive speaking.'

Tim shook his head and wandered out of the office. To be closed down by a financial institution was one thing. To have the dignity to end proceedings yourself was quite another. After a substantial night of drinking, he would visit the bank in the morning and inform them that he was no longer trading.

Slowly descending the stairs, he tried to recall the few brief moments of triumph over the last seven months, the handful of successful campaigns he had been paid to do, the small number of slogans he had inflicted on the people of Taunsley. There was **Go to Work on a Leg** – the push for the local disability shop, which was having a special on artificial limbs, and sold four extra orthopaedic shoes in the month-long campaign. And who in the town could forget **Bernie Otteridge for a Firmer Sausage** – the now-cancelled butcher who reported a 15 per cent increase in sales, and a 200 per cent rise in innuendoes. Then there was **I Fought the Lawn (and the Lawn Won)**, for a large garden centre's turf sale. **The Meat is On** had been another good one, a vain attempt by Jenkins Meat Products to drum up some barbecue business and extend end-of-summer burger sales. In fact, **The Meat**

161

is On had been by far the largest campaign he had managed. It had everything – a willing client, media saturation and a cracking ad, with the word 'Meat' shouted over 'Heat' in the song 'The Heat Is On', and yet, the less said about the results the better. Still, there had been a few other victories. Of special interest was **Lost in Mucus, Caught in a Hack**, for BuyBulk Chemists, who had recently bought a job lot of Beecham's Powders. Tim reached the exit. Now, however, BuyBulk Chemists had also cancelled their contract. At the time, he had been particularly proud of **Lost in Mucus**. Taunsley Long Wave had even been broadcasting it, with Sister Sledge's classic hit over-dubbed with the word 'mucus' in place of 'music'. It had been so bad it was brilliant. But, multiple **Simply the Best**s aside, that was it.

In the pub, the jukebox was dormant. Tim walked over and punched in a few numbers. As he sat down, and Dave finally sauntered in, Tina Turner, singing the town's only fucking song, burst into life. If you can't beat them, Tim said miserably to himself, you might as well beat yourself up.

Dave stood expectantly in front of the table. He usually did this when he was about to pitch some of the worst ideas known to marketing. 'What?' Tim asked.

'A teaser campaign.'

'Oh come on,' Tim replied.

'I'm serious.'

Tim continued to shred his beer mat. 'Dave, please don't think me rude when I say I'd rather not spend the last afternoon of our joint employment discussing surreal and unlikely ad campaigns which will never see the light of day. But that's what I'm saying. So grab a beer and come and sit down.'

Dave remained where he was. Something wasn't right about him. He appeared to have been cogitating. 'I think we can buy some time. The phone call. Jenkins Meat Products want some more work doing.'

'From us?'

'No, from Saatchi and fucking Saatchi.'

Tim sat upright. 'So what exactly did he say, Mr Jenkins?'

'It wasn't him. It was his sales manager, Mr Rhinegold. Wants to commission some MR, maybe other stuff afterwards, depending.'

Tim glanced around the empty pub. A dangerous-looking man in the corner was mouthing the lyrics to the song. Two TV screens peered down from above the bar, a couple of soap actors silently shouting at each other. Another man stood in front of a fruit machine wordlessly inserting coins, the flashing lights reflected across his pale skin. He pressed the Hold buttons even though they weren't lit. 'It might be too late,' Tim sighed.

'Ring the bank. Tell them you've landed a new contract. Surely they'll extend the overdraft.'

'He didn't mention money at all?'

'No. But it's a start, until something bigger comes along.'

'Well, it'll have to be a fuck lot bigger than commissioning some market research. Mind you, after **The Meat is On**, it's a wonder that they're using us again. What happened to the sales woman we dealt with last time?'

'Said she's been moved sideways after the last campaign. Looks like she copped a lot of the blame.'

'Things must be desperate there,' Tim said guiltily, appreciating that at least part of the reason JMP were suffering poor sales had to be down to the previous summer's disastrous campaign. Maybe this was a last-gasp attempt to save themselves from going under.

'As you say, if all else fails, advertise yourself out of trouble.'

'Yeah. And look where that logic got *us*.'

'Still – what do you think, boss?'

Tim fiddled with the fragments of his beer mat. In a way, going out of business was going to be a blessed relief. As he peered up at Dave through the smoky pub air, he realized there was only one decision. 'Get us a drink, Dave,' he said. 'And then tell me exactly what this Mr Rhinegold is proposing.'

A Clinical Event

Something happened that neither Tim nor Ann had really anticipated. Tim had rung his housemate and suggested she meet him in town to celebrate their month-long stay of financial execution. Mainly, he needed extra company to dilute the over-enthusiastic presence of Dave. A polite congratulatory pint after work turned into a last orders frenzy, and Tim and Ann had staggered home from the pub together. In the living room, on the sofa, Tim's hand glanced Ann's leg, and it had started there, a slow, lingering kiss, an embrace, long squeezing sighs, touching and feeling, lips pressed hard, clothes coming undone, two hungry people fumbling their way upstairs.

Lying side by side on his lodger's bed, lit only by a street light, Tim absorbed the sheer magnificence of the partially undressed Ann. Her skin was surprisingly dark, and seemed to have a sheen to it which winked at him as she moved her willowy limbs. Her breasts were small and firm, her hips slender, her stomach taut. For women like Ann, clothes were crude distractions from the splendour beneath. He kissed her shoulder, neck, breast and mouth, tasting her very essence. Ann held him close to her, bony arms wrapped around him, and slowly began to run her fingers over his torso. She smiled and her eyes sparkled in the gloom.

'This is very bad,' she whispered.

'No. This is very good,' Tim said, cupping her left breast in his hand, his words short and clipped.

'What if, you know, things don't work out between us?'

'They will,' he answered, a heady mix of alcohol and desire surging through his veins.

'You sure?'

'Sure as I'll ever be.' He ran a finger down her spine and gently squeezed one of her cheeks. 'Sure as I'll ever be,' he repeated, lost in his lodger's sweet embrace. Ann pressed her lips against his and opened her mouth slightly.

After several minutes of frantic kissing and investigating each other's bodies, Tim's excited mind took stock of the situation. For the first time in over half a year, he actually felt close to someone. Ann's breasts were pushed so tightly against him that her heartbeat resonated through his chest. The heat of her living essence warmed his skin. He was being thawed gently from the outside, his soul slowly awaking from its torpor. Almost seven months without so much as brushing past someone, and now he was in bed with a beautiful female. For the moment, only one thing mattered, and that was long-denied pleasure.

Ann, too, was lost in a beautiful moment of inebriated desire. Recently, she had felt a growing and urgent need for sex. In the last few months before she left Pete they had barely slept together. Ann was low on confidence but high on longing. However, with the thought of her recently finished relationship, a tiny shaft of sobriety pierced the haze. Ann pulled her face away from Tim's.

166

'Look, Tim,' she whispered, holding him close, 'it's just . . .'

'What?' he asked, touching her flushed cheek.

'I mean, it's OK for me. But what about, you know . . .'

'Mmm?'

'Zoe.'

'Zoe?' It was Tim's turn for a prick of conscience. Zoe's face lit up before him and he frowned. Since returning from the pub he had suppressed Zoe's memory as a way of justifying his actions. It was as if by keeping her out of his head, his body was not being unfaithful to her. 'But . . .' He left the word hanging, a reminder that there was no excuse for what he was doing.

'And, I don't know, it's been a few weeks since I left Pete, but I guess, thinking about it, it still feels . . .'

'What?'

'Too soon.'

'Yeah?' Tim was aware of Ann edging slightly away from him. She was right. They were pissed but this was indefensible. Unless he acted now he was about to fail his relationship test with flying colours.

'So what do you suggest?'

'Maybe we ought to think first, before leaping into something we might regret.'

He ran a finger down the bridge of Ann's nose. 'That sounds a bit sensible.'

'Perhaps we should just kiss each other and say goodnight.'

'But . . .' Tim once again ran out of argument. An uncomfortable nervousness inside his gut told him that it was time to go. And so, with a long, lingering kiss which neither of them wanted to end, he climbed out of bed and made his way to his room. Ann and

Tim lay on their backs, awake, thinking, guilty, excited, just inches from each other.

In the dark, three thoughts tormented Tim. First, he hadn't had sex for seven months, and yet had just experienced half an hour of concentrated foreplay. He pictured a child's toy being wound up and wound up, only to be placed firmly back in its box. This could, he felt, be mentally damaging in the long run.

As sobriety began to gnaw away at him, a second issue gathered momentum. He came to appreciate that this state of affairs could be catastrophic, and not just in terms of testicular well-being. He had been semi-unfaithful to his girlfriend with a woman who shared his house. Things could go disastrously wrong. The enemy was within. Lovely though Ann was, she had the potential to destroy him. Zoe started to force her way once more into his consciousness. He pictured her sleeping alone, counting down the days until she saw him again, asking the all-important question: Did you pass the test?

Third, and away from the glaring issue of infidelity, another assumption about the medical profession was in danger of becoming well and truly shattered. As someone who had clearly spent many years studying anatomy, Ann's foreplay had contained as much awkward fumbling as any other sexual encounter. Although undoubtedly enjoyable, this had been a long way from the magnificently clinical event he had envisaged.

Closing his eyes, Tim grimaced slightly. Hormonal excesses, dubious medical care and partial infidelity. Things had just got complicated.

Intellectual Input

Mr Rhinegold was an unusual client. For a start, he was curiously reluctant to visit the offices of Power Advertising. Tim was hurt. The office might not be the greatest in the world, in Taunsley even, or in the building, in fact in the corridor, and certainly couldn't offer panoramic views across downtown Hong Kong, but Tim found this lack of interest in his workspace wounding. On the plus side, however, he would at least be kept well clear of Dave.

Glancing over at his assistant, Tim realized he had inflicted a long-term dilemma upon himself by his choice of workmate. With JMP's money about to trickle in, he could either sack Dave, live happily for a while but do lots of work, or retain Dave, live unhappily, do very little and make virtually no money. Although a simple choice in principle, there were other considerations. Without Dave, Tim Power Advertising comprised just Tim Power, which hardly inspired the impression of a thriving business. Besides, Dave performed all the duties which fell into the general category of Can't-Be-Arsed, such as photocopying, filing, manning the phones, making tea and banking rare cheques. And, Tim sighed with an attack of compassion, watching him writing and crossing out, he was a decent lad who needed a job.

After phoning the office the previous day, Mr Rhinegold faxed through a brief, as well as an invitation to invoice him for the market research when it was finished. This would enable Tim to pay Dave and keep the office ticking over for three or four weeks. Then all he needed was a couple of **Simply the Best**s, one or two **What More Can We Say?**s and the odd **It's the Natural Choice** and he would scrape into the month after next.

The brief itself, however, was far from straightforward. Tim read it carefully a couple of times before asking Dave for his intellectual input.

'So what do you think?' he asked when his colleague had spent some minutes gently mouthing the words to himself.

Dave paused, scratching his chin. After a few seconds, he ventured the considered opinion, 'Fucked if I know.'

'It's this bit that gets me,' Tim continued, trying not to be overwhelmed by his assistant's insight. '"It's not the product, it's the people. Rumours about what goes into JMP pies are strangling our local business, which accounts for most of our sales. Things are in danger of becoming untenable. I want you to commission market research to determine exactly what the population of Taunsley thinks about Jenkins Pork Pies. But do it quick. As soon as you possibly can. We need to know *now*."'

Dave offered another winning piece of awareness. 'So what, boss?'

'He doesn't actually mention any real advertising. Usually, as you may have noticed, we make most of our market research up in the pub. Then we spend the rest of the budget on ourselves, and a small bit on the actual ads. Mr Rhinegold here, on the other hand, wants to see signed MR forms from real people.' Tim grimaced. 'It's a fucking scandal. We're going to have to talk to members of the public.'

It was Dave's turn to wince. 'And by "we" you mean me, don't you?'

'Usually, Dave. But this time we're both in the shit. And if we want to survive for another few weeks, we'd better get it done quickly – otherwise we'll be out of business before we get paid.'

Two hours later, Dave had cobbled together a hasty working draft of the research form they were imminently about to inflict on Taunsley. He presented it to his boss, who remained calm, breathed deeply, bit savagely into the end of his biro, scratched his head, exhaled through the side of his mouth and quietly asked him to write something decent this time. After a further hour of frantic activity, Dave rushed over to Tim's desk and submitted a revised version. Tim closed his eyes, screwed his fingers into tight balls, clenched his teeth and said, 'Well done,' before spending the rest of the afternoon writing the bloody thing himself. And then, as he compiled a list of pork pie consumer preferences, he had an idea. There were opportunities here. Questions he needed to know the answers to. Things that bona fide market researchers wouldn't touch with a bargepole. Enquiries that might just solve all his domestic problems.

Questions and Answers

Having drawn up a suitable questionnaire, Tim printed off ten copies and admired his handiwork. While not the most conventional market research form ever written, it was certainly one of the more interesting. A number of moral and ethical dilemmas had been muddying Tim's waters since he had ended up in bed with Ann the previous night. For instance, had he actually been unfaithful to Zoe, given that fully penetrative sex hadn't taken place? A protracted naked fumble, as far as he was aware, was not technically the same thing as adultery. And should he ask his lodger to move out, now that they had managed to make life difficult for themselves? For her part, Ann had been aloof, leaving early for work. He had tried calling her mobile, but it was either switched off, or else she was declining to answer. Instead, should he ring Zoe, assuming he could narrow her progress down to a specific continent, and inform her of his indiscretion? The questionnaire would, he hoped, shed some light on these and other issues.

Tim handed Dave a sample form and asked him to speed-read it. He was expecting some fairly harsh cross-examination and sat up in his chair expectantly. The clock above Dave's desk monitored the passing minutes. This was a race for survival. Tim drummed his fingers on the table. Dave opened his mouth to speak but closed it again. A small spider began to construct a web between two leaves of the office's only plant. Finally, after an age of frowning, Dave cleared his throat. Tim blinked, eager to get the market research criteria sorted and onto the street.

'This MR thing,' Dave began hesitantly, 'are you sure it's wise?'

'How do you mean?'

'Well, just look at it.'

'Yes?'

'Some of the questions are a bit, well . . .'

'What?'

Dave read from the sheet. 'Take question two, for example. "Do you own your own house?"'

'Reasonable start.'

'Yeah, but the next one doesn't really seem relevant. "If so, would you ever consider renting out a room?" What's that got to do with pork pies?'

'Demographic profiling.'

'Right. And I suppose the next one, "If so, would you sleep with your lodger?" is also for demographic reasons?'

Tim shrugged. 'Possibly.'

'"And if you did, would you tell your girlfriend/ boyfriend?"'

'Moral outlining.'

Dave continued to quote from the questionnaire. '"If 'Yes', would you still tell your girlfriend/boyfriend if she/he was staying in Australia for another five months and was unlikely to find out?"'

'Ditto.'

Tim's assistant peered doubtfully over at him. '"What would you consider a reasonable length of

173

time after sleeping with your lodger until you asked them to leave? a) 1 week, b) 2 weeks, c) longer."'

'We are simply getting to know our customers.'

'Getting to know them? You're virtually taking them to pieces. I mean, get a load of the next one. "Or, given that your lodger was attractive and good company, would you place a greater emphasis on finishing your current relationship in order to be with them?" How well do you really want to know these people?'

'As it happens, not very well at all.'

'Look, I know I haven't worked in advertising long, but I just don't get it. Here's another question. "Do you consider the medical profession to be expert on intimate anatomy?" What has that got to do with meat products?'

'You've always got to think tangentially in this business, Dave.'

'Tangentially?'

'Outside the box.'

'Out of your head, more like.' Dave swigged his coffee using a style copied from police movies to show that he was firmly in charge of the cross-examination at hand. 'Well, the last query is the only one that really makes any sense. "Oh yes, and how much do you like Jenkins Pork Pies?"'

'Turn it over, there's one more on the back.'

Tim's faithful if somewhat puzzled deputy turned the page over, his interrogation losing momentum. '"How much does your lodger like Jenkins Pork Pies?"' he read, obviously nonplussed.

Investigating his executive paperweight, Tim was quiet for a few seconds. The item was pointless, mainly due to the general lack of commotion or activity in the room. His papers rarely moved anywhere except closer to the bin, and, on occasion, into the car park in the early hours. The paperweight was transparent and featured two small plastic dolphins bobbing in a blue viscous fluid. It was a miserable object. The dolphins, which seldom floated the right way up, appeared utterly trapped in an imitation glass world. He glanced up and stared out of the thick office window. The small part of Taunsley he could see bustled with activity and for a moment Tim felt hopelessly boxed in.

'You know, Dave,' he said, maintaining his gaze, 'it's very rare in life you get a chance to ask the questions you want to ask.'

'Yes, boss,' Dave answered, none the wiser for having done so.

'And when that chance comes along, you have to take it.'

Having been suitably enigmatic, Tim continued to peer out of the window while Dave mooched about, photocopying forms and attaching them to clipboards. He thought again about Ann. This was becoming a real problem. Although he felt awkward about the situation, there had been something deeply appealing about her. But theoretically, since he had been almost cohabiting with his errant girlfriend, who might or might not return, it wasn't a good idea to be unfaithful. Besides, while he clearly missed sex, this was obviously not the answer to all his problems. What he needed was advice. He had tried the usual routes, ringing three of his male friends from different parts of the country. Their recommendations had been identically useless. It was the sort of male advice he would gladly have given in return, the kind of heartfelt counsel which said: 'It's your life. I don't really care what you do. But if I did have a preference it would be for you to do something that will brighten my own existence up, possibly by providing some interesting gossip at a later stage.'

Tim was well aware that his friends wouldn't, in their wildest dreams, have undertaken the course of actions they had proposed. But that was the very point of male advice, as far as he could tell. It was vicarious. You were merely suggesting what you would like to have the nerve to do if you were caught up in your friend's problems.

The questionnaire he'd just drawn up, however, was a once in a lifetime chance to get unbiased wisdom from the general public. It would be a true vox pop on the subject of sleeping with your lodger, being unfaithful to your girlfriend and eating pork pies.

As Dave slouched out of the office with a wad of answer sheets to inflict on people making their way home from work, the phone rang, and Tim decided for once to answer it. Rather than another misguided RhylZig enquiry, it was a client he hadn't heard from for several months. As they chatted, another idea occurred to Tim. It wasn't just impartial advice which might see him through the tricky situation at home. Tactics were called for. And here was just the man to help him. Despite being far from the best plan he had ever come up with, he thought it was at least worth a go. After the call, Tim picked up the phone and dialled a number. After a brief conversation, he left the office satisfied.

Medical Negligence

Dr Ann Hillyard closed the door of her office and wished she could seal the words, images and bizarre behaviours of the day inside the room. Instead, most of these would follow her home, hang around the kitchen and insist on going to bed with her. Rarely was she able to lock her feelings away after she had walked out of work, and at night she was especially prone to sifting through the baggage of her job. Being alone made this problem even more acute. If she still had a partner, she could share the troubles of her day, a kind of confessional that passed the lunacy from her patients to her boyfriend, thereby cutting out the middle woman.

Now things were even worse. She had slept with her housemate. Ann cursed herself. With men, one of two things habitually happened. She met someone she liked but was forced to leave him because he eventually let her down. Or she met someone she liked who left her for reasons she never quite determined. Either way, she learned little, which was why she lacked confidence in her ability to love. And at this moment, she was particularly short of self-assurance. With the end of her long-term relationship, the support, the reliance and the care had also evaporated.

Which is why, paradoxically, she had occasionally found it easier to have a one-night stand when she already had a partner. Her debacle with Tim was symptomatic of the other side of this. Recently single, she was unhappy, and when she felt low, intimacy was a forced and panicky endeavour. In addition, her choice of profession was little help. As a trained psychologist, Ann knew more than could really be healthy about human behaviour, but very little of this knowledge permeated her everyday actions. She was the classic example of the dentist with bad teeth, the mechanic with a rusty car, the drugs counsellor with a crack habit. Ann's vast scientific wisdom, stored inside her own brain, was too remote to help her. While she catalogued the foibles of a thousand people, she was unable to pigeonhole herself. Her behaviour was beyond analysis, she had concluded a long time ago, because she was too caught up in it. And so, one more time, she had allowed things to become complicated, just when she had met someone she actually liked. Even if she summoned the self-belief to pursue a love affair with Tim, she would have to tell him that she had lied about being a doctor. Given that relationships are built on trust, and that she had essentially been untruthful to him from the first moment they had met, this hardly marked her out as good girlfriend material.

Leaving the Behavioural Studies building and making her way through the grim hospital site, Ann appreciated that the troubles she had at work were in danger of being surpassed by the ones she had created at home. Perhaps the time was right to leave Taunsley and find a post in a large teaching hospital or academic institute somewhere, to lose herself in her work and forget all about the opposite sex.

Ann's mobile rang and she answered it.

'Ann, it's Tim,' the voice said. 'Come to the pub.'

She had kept her phone off most of the day. They hadn't spoken since the early hours of the previous morning. Between patients, she had tried to think things through. 'What? Now?'

'On your way home. I'm heading there after work. And there's someone I'd like you to meet.'

'Who?' she demanded suspiciously.

'Surprise.'

'Seriously, who?'

'Just make your way there.'

Ann hesitated. She couldn't avoid her housemate indefinitely. Short of confidence and unenthused by the venue, she decided for once to face her demons. 'The usual?' she asked, sucking in a nervous breath.

'Yep. See you there. Bye.'

'Bye.'

Ann changed course and headed for the other side of town, flipping her phone shut as she did so. Last Call 0:21 Mins, the display informed her. That was the thing about mobile conversations, Ann frowned – they were quick. Even when you had a lot to get off your chest. The curious thing was, almost everybody owned one, and almost every owner used them often. The volume of telephone traffic was therefore vastly greater than ever before, and yet nothing more meaningful was being said. In fact, quite the opposite. Communications weren't helping us communicate, they were simply enabling us to talk more frequently about less important things. Issues weren't getting solved, meaningful debates weren't being settled, dialogues weren't opening up. Better facilities for interaction only left us with nothing to interact about, umming and ahhing on a crackly line. And all we really seemed to be saying to each other, she told herself, crossing

179

the road and slotting the phone into her bag, was, 'I'm going to be late,' 'Do you want chips for tea?' or 'I'll see you in the pub.'

Ann ran a hand through her hair, hoping she would appear fashionably tousled. It was a vain hope, based more on desperation than design. After a day spent dealing with behavioural delinquents, her curls were as frazzled as her brain. The pub, as she reached it twenty minutes later, appeared busy. Taunsley's pubs were always packed between five and seven until workers sloped off home to complain about their hectic days. She steadied her nerves and entered. Tim was at the bar.

'Hey, Dr Hillyard,' he said, greeting her with a semi-inebriated hug. Coming in from the cold, Ann would have been happy for the embrace to last a little longer. It was like a mini reunion, the first direct contact since they had been naked together. For an instant she imagined that maybe there could still be something between them. Tim, however, was intent on ordering the drinks. 'What can I get you?' he asked, stepping back from her outstretched arms.

'Something to erase my brain. Double G and T will do for a start.'

Tim ordered the drink and passed it to her. 'Here,' he said, 'go and sit down.'

'Where are you sitting?'

'Table by the window.'

'Who's the bloke?'

'I've brought a friend along to meet you.'

'Who is he?'

'A client of mine. Great guy. Dr Ashok Kumar.' Tim gave Ann a firm nudge in his direction. 'Just go and say hello.'

'Doctor?' Ann sensed a problem. 'What kind of doctor?'

'Same sort as you.'

'I doubt it,' Ann said quietly to herself, cursing her decision to come. And not just because Tim seemed evasive. More tangible trouble was brewing in the form of Dr Kumar, who stared over from the far side of the room.

'Go on,' Tim encouraged. 'Catch up with you when my drink arrives.'

Ann dragged her feet to the other side of the room, feeling distinctly set up. Her fingers were wet around the glass and she wondered whether this was sweat or gin. In the last twenty minutes she had experienced exasperation, depression, elation, possibility and now fear. This was going to be tricky. A real doctor was the last thing she needed. The situation was getting out of hand as it was. One small lie to get into decent rented accommodation and Ann was beginning to feel like she was walking slowly to her own slaughter. She made a mental note to finish her drink and leave. As long as she kept the conversation lighthearted and non-clinical, everything would be OK. And then she would move out of Tim's house and go and live abroad somewhere.

Dr Kumar stood up and offered his hand as she approached. 'Ashok Kumar,' he said, with a disturbingly frisky shake.

'Ann,' she replied, saying a quiet prayer and glancing over at Tim to see how long he'd be. 'Ann Hillyard.' A slight silence set in straightaway. Anything but medicine, Ann repeated over and over in her brain, desperately trying to summon something neutral to say. She met compulsive liars on an almost daily basis and here she was, as bad as any of them, and attempting to lie her way out of a sticky situation. Anything but medicine. Anything but medicine.

'So, Tim tells me you're a fellow medic,' Dr Kumar offered as an opening gambit.

Fuck. Here we go, Ann cringed. What was it she told her patients? Lying is the first act of self-abuse. 'Yes,' she replied.

'At the hospital?' He took a deep drag on his cigarette and necked a healthy quantity of lager. 'So what are you? Registrar? SPR?'

'Registrar.'

'Rotation?'

Fuck knows. Take a guess. 'Yes.'

'And what's your speciality?'

Taking an innocuous situation and making it into a disaster. Ann rubbed her face. Her hands were shaking slightly. Her own lack of poise was exaggerated by the real doctor's façade of composure. Think. Her department was next to Audiology. 'Audiology,' she said finally.

'Audiology?' Dr Kumar asked, a single eyebrow shooting upwards above his glasses. 'You mean ENT?'

ENT. Ears, nose, throat. That didn't sound too dangerous. What the hell. 'Yeah. ENT.' Ann sniffed her drink, and found some strength in the sharpness of the gin. 'But actually, Ashok, I hope you don't mind, after a busy day dealing with patients,' she began assertively, 'I have a strict rule. I prefer never ever to talk about—'

'You'll enjoy this one,' Dr Kumar said, drinking a shot of chaser. 'Had a chap in the other day, side of his face like a bloody basketball.' Tim joined them and Ann took a massive slug of her own drink. 'Didn't know what the hell it was. Only clue I had – he'd gone stone deaf. About the same time, this other chap comes in, and you'll never guess what he had?'

Tim and Dr Kumar both looked expectantly at Ann,

182

who agreed to herself that she *would* never guess. 'What?' she asked.

'Well, he had a scrotum torn in several places. Testicles virtually hanging out, they were. Turns out the two were lovers. He was an epileptic with a strong gag-reflex . . .'

'Right,' Ann said slowly.

'So obviously he had been, you know . . .'

Ann didn't know. 'Obviously.'

'When he'd had a seizure. And the other poor chap had grabbed a frying pan – must have been doing it in the kitchen – when his scrotum was about to be bitten off. Smashed him a forward drive to the temporo-mandibular joint, fracturing his orbital fossa, giving him a retro-orbital haematoma.' Dr Kumar drained his pint and chaser in a nice double action. 'And of course you know what the only cure for that is?'

'Drinks?' Ann blurted almost desperately, finishing her gin in one.

'Er no, I meant . . .'

Ann stood up. 'Lager and a chaser, is it?'

'I was just saying . . .'

'And a Stella for you, Tim?'

'Well . . .'

Ann made a dash for the bar to order the slowest round of drinks ever purchased.

Tim asked Dr Kumar what he thought.

'Not bad at all,' he replied. 'Bit skinny for my liking, but other than that, pretty tasty.'

'No, I mean about her medical abilities. As I told you, with the exception of your good self, she seems to be the worst doctor I've ever come across.'

'Tricky one. ENT isn't easy. Lots of buggering about with small fiddly things, if I remember rightly.'

'But did you ask her about it?'

183

'A bit,' Dr Kumar answered, lighting a new cigarette. 'And?'

He blew a large and satisfying stream of smoke out of the side of his mouth. 'Think you're barking up the wrong tree, Tim old mate. Medicine's a huge field. You can't know all of it. Look, I'm a GP. Take it from me, I know sod all about anything, except colds, rashes, fevers and piles. She's a specialist. Probably forgotten half her basic training.'

'But when I mentioned the word perineum in bed last night, she didn't know what it was.'

'Peri-what?'

'It's part of your—'

'Besides,' Dr Kumar answered, lazily flicking ash in the general direction of the ashtray, 'there's one sure-fire way to tell if she's a competent medic.'

Tim leaned forwards into the thick blanket of smoke that surrounded his friend. 'Yes?' he asked eagerly.

'Does she drink like a fish?' Tim and Dr Kumar glanced across at Ann, who was downing a large gin. As soon as she finished it, they clearly heard her ask for another one. 'You see,' Dr Kumar said, summing up his evidence, 'I've never met a woman who could drink like that who wasn't a good medic.'

Tim slumped back in his seat, the evidence circumstantial at best, while Dr Kumar bemoaned a medical negligence case gathering momentum against him. As Dr Kumar drank, smoked and cursed the sector of the general public unlucky enough to be counted among his patients, Tim watched Ann at the bar. The set-up had been a disaster. When Ashok had rung and suggested a drink, Tim grabbed the opportunity with curious and desperate hands. Ann's lack of medical and anatomical knowledge was perplexing. The best way of judging her proficiency, he had decided, was to have her interact with a fellow medic. Admittedly Dr Kumar was, by his own admission, a long way short of competence, which had compromised the scheme considerably. But he didn't know any other doctors and so he had been forced to make do.

An hour later, and six gins to the good, Ann left the pub with Tim in tow. Tim proposed, and Ann agreed, that they should maintain a distance from now on so that Tim wouldn't be unfaithful to his girlfriend and Ann could lick her post-boyfriend wounds. Ann also suggested that she start hunting for somewhere else to live, and Tim reluctantly accepted that he would soon be looking for another lodger. And this time, hopefully not one who would put his relationship in jeopardy. Walking into St Paul's Square, Ann felt disappointed and yet at the same time strangely rewarded. Her lips bent upwards and she shook her head slowly. Although it looked like she would soon be moving on, Dr Kumar had just offered her a job as a GP.

Inside, Tim sloped miserably up to the bathroom, where he noted that Ann had bought a new set of toiletries. He moved his own four lonely items further away from them. In his room, he lay on the bed, inches away from Ann, the TV muted. As he listened intently, he thought he heard her breathing, which did nothing to improve his desperation for her. Tim turned the lights out and sighed. In the corner, the television flashed away unseen, a myriad wasted images lighting up its screen.

In the early hours, a noise made Tim's heart race. Footsteps were padding across the floorboards towards him. Peering through the gloom, he could just discern a naked female figure. He remained silent, staring more intently. Ann was pulling the duvet back and

185

climbing into bed with him. Tim made an instant decision to sleep with his lodger. He wrapped an arm around her and sighed her name, gratefulness surging through him. If ever there was a woman to solve his problems it was his housemate. 'It's been a crazy twenty-four hours, Ann, and—'

The reply was not quite what he had expected. 'Who the fuck is Ann?'

There was something familiar about the voice. He struggled to wake up. It was almost . . .

'I said, who the fuck is Ann?'

He filtered through several options. She sounded like . . . but no, it was impossible.

'Well, are you gonna tell me?'

Tim sat bolt upright, realization suddenly upon him. 'I'm waiting.'

The shock sucked the air out of his lungs. He swallowed. Shit! 'Zoe!'

His long-lost girlfriend flicked on the light. 'G'day, boyfriend!' she said, grinning insanely in the painful brightness.

'G'day indeed,' he said. Zoe threw her arms around him and he did the same to her.

Whitened

'Surprised to see me, sport?' Zoe asked, her face awash with excitement.

'Fuck yes,' Tim answered, trying to sober up. He blinked rapidly, adjusting to the brightness. 'How come you're here?'

'Long story. Tell you later.'

'You weren't supposed to finish your trip for ages.'

'As I said, all in good time.'

Zoe released her grip slightly and Tim leant back, propped up on his elbows, desperately attempting to catch up with the situation. 'It's been an eternity,' he muttered, shaking his head.

'I know.'

'I can't believe you've returned to me, that you're actually in my bedroom.'

'Nor can I.' Zoe tugged gently at her earlobe. 'But I had to be with you.'

'Jesus. I still can't believe it.' No matter how much he shook his head, it still didn't make sense.

'A year was too long.'

'Tell me about it.'

'I don't know what I was thinking. Not one of my better ideas. So how've you been?' she asked, pulling herself further away to read his face.

'Good,' Tim lied. 'Very good.'

'And the house?'

'Fine.'

'The business?'

'Fair to middling.'

'Bonzer, mate,' Zoe replied. 'Really bonzer.'

Tim was taken aback. 'Jesus, Zo, you sound like an Aussie.'

'I *have* been living in Sydney for the last three weeks, you know.'

'Three whole weeks? Did they offer you citizenship?'

'No need to knock it, mate.'

'I was only joking,' Tim said, scratching his head.

After an uncomfortable lull, Zoe asked, 'Have you got any tinnies in?'

'Shouldn't you be sleeping?'

'I'm on Sydney time,' she explained.

Tim yawned, his body still dragging itself free from its torpor. Every time he closed his eyes he was plagued by images of what would have happened if Zoe had come back the previous night. 'I'm afraid I'm running on Taunsley meantime,' he muttered.

'Not that Sydney really sleeps . . .'

'Anyway, I don't mean this in the way it will come out, but how come you're here so soon? I thought you'd be another five months. What happened?'

'It all went a bit pear-shaped. Fell out with Liz. There was no point continuing alone, as I didn't have enough cash to go on by myself.'

'You didn't say anything in your postcards.'

'Happened so quickly. And I wanted to surprise you.' Zoe ran her fingers over some peeling skin on her forearm. 'Mind you, at least Liz didn't call me by the wrong name and then take the piss out of my accent.'

'Sorry about that. It's just such an incredible shock to see you.'

'So who is Ann?'

'Ann's the lodger. I thought . . .'

'She often gets into bed with you then?'

Tim remained quiet. Careful tactics were required. He monitored his elusive girlfriend out of the corner of his eye. Her face had browned a couple of shades and, seemingly to compensate, her hair had become a little lighter. She was no longer mousy, but wasn't fair either – she was inhabiting a limbo land between the two. The darkness of her skin made the whites of her eyes light up, and she had a new earring with a green stone at its centre. Other than that, she was the same Zoe who had left him seven months before. 'I was just having a weird dream, that's all.'

'So,' she said, letting the point go, 'did you miss me?'

Only enough to sleep with another woman, he told himself. 'Yes,' he answered slowly, 'yes, I did.'

'And did our relationship pass the test?' She stared intently at him. 'Is it important enough that you were willing to wait for me?'

He examined Zoe in more detail. As ever, a major dusting of make-up clung to her face and invaded the pores of her skin. Her eyes were heavily mascaraed, her eyebrows defined and tinted. All in all, he conceded, she looked good. But that was the thing about Zoe. She wasn't a beautiful woman, she just knew how to make the most of her assets. She was, he told himself staring into her eyes, a walking campaign for herself. And Tim had bought it completely. In the morning, with the make-up washed away and her hair left to its own devices, she would be plain again, a blank page on which to paint her looks. She smiled, whitened teeth beaming out at him, surrounded by lips that had been lightly glossed. He had a mental image of Zoe's rucksack with half of Boots in it. Belatedly, he appreciated where the extra bathroom cosmetics had come from. 'Of course,' he answered, 'of course.' And then he sat up and committed verbal suicide in order to change the subject. 'So,' he said, 'tell me *all* about your trip.'

Several hours later, as daylight was forcing its way through the gap where the curtains didn't quite meet, Zoe began to summarize the main points one more time. 'And then I met this great guy. And he bumped into someone from school – in the middle of Singapore – and we kind of hitched together. Then Liz wanted to do Japan and I was all for Thailand. So this other guy turns up with his girlfriend and they knew someone who had a sound system going. Turns out the brother of the DJ grew up only twenty miles away from the bloke we'd met in LA. And we were in the same row of the same plane, in the opposite direction, as he'd been just weeks before. Talk about a small world, mate. It's stranger than fiction when you think about it. And then I ended up hitching through the outback with this guy from Brisbane, you know, eating bush tucker, that sort of thing . . .' Towards getting-up time, Zoe ran out of steam and fell asleep with the desperation of the long-distance traveller. Tim got up and sat in the kitchen, slightly shell-shocked. This was, to say the least, unexpected. But what really affected him was the knowledge that while Zoe's return was exciting in the extreme, he was not in the least bit excited.

Shortly, Ann came downstairs and began to fix herself some breakfast. He watched her in silence. Unlike Zoe, Ann was pretty with or without make-up. In fact, as Tim thought about it, make-up, like clothes, only served to tarnish her beauty. She had yet to shower, and her cheeks were still pale and creased from hours of being pressed against the pillow. He fancied her eyes were slightly puffy from the previous night's gin. But all of this only served to highlight her splendour. He made himself a cup of tea and felt the steam on his face. Later, he heard Zoe, seemingly too disorientated to sleep for long, begin a lazy descent of the stairs. This was not good. Things could get out of hand.

Hot Hatch

'Ann Hillyard! What the hell are you doing here?'
    'Zoe! I didn't know you—'
    'Where're you living now?'
    'I'm living here.'
    'In Taunsley?'
    'I mean here.'
    'St Paul's Square?'
    'In this house.'
    '*Here* here?'
    'Right here.'
    'So *you're* the lodger?'
    'Yes.'
    'Bonzer!'
Ann's eyes darted quickly at Tim and then back to
Zoe. 'You could say that.'
    'You two know each other?' Tim asked, rocked by
the second revelation of the day.
    'Oh yes,' Ann replied. 'Although we've kind of lost
touch.'
    'But where have you been since uni?' Zoe asked.
    'Stayed in Brisdle for a few years, moved to the
dreaded Bridgton, then ended up in the town about
nine months ago.'
    'Why Taunsley?'

'Got a job at the hospital.'

'At the hospital? But weren't you studying—'

'Talking of which,' Ann interjected, suddenly aware of one potential difficulty with the current arrangement, 'I'd better go and get ready.'

'That's wild, you living here. When Tim said he was sharing with someone called Ann I didn't even give it a second thought. We'll catch up later. I've got a lot of experiences to share with you.'

Ann looked doubtful. Besides, she had a lot of experiences she would rather not divulge to Zoe.

Tim was curious, however. 'I'm sure you've got a couple of minutes before they'll actually sack you,' he said. 'So come on, how do you two know each other?'

'We were at uni together,' said Ann.

'I gathered that.'

'We met when we joined the same society – Target Club.'

'What the fuck was that?'

'Only the society run by the sexiest man on campus.'

'Guy Rogers!' Zoe exclaimed.

'Jesus, yes. And how.'

'I guess I thought it might be somewhere to meet blokes. I'd tried everything else.'

'And I'd come to the same damaging conclusion.'

'Trouble was they were all psychos who spent more time polishing their weapons than, well, you know . . .'

'So we were the only two girls, and almost all the men were too busy firing their air pistols at small pieces of paper to notice us. To tell the truth, we lost interest after the first term. Then I took up yoga, bending myself into all sorts of interesting positions . . .'

'And I got a boyfriend, to do that for me.'

Ann and Zoe laughed. 'Then what?' Tim asked, eager to know exactly how well the two knew each other and how this might affect the chances of his girlfriend detecting his indiscretion.

'We saw less and less of each other. Given that we were on different courses, we drifted apart. You know, like you do,' Zoe said, making eye contact with Ann.

'Until you find yourselves living together,' Ann smiled. 'But not for long. I've already given Tim my notice. Time to move on. And now that you're back, I'll start looking for a new place straight away. But first,' she continued, 'I'm about to be fired. I'd better get sorted. Catch you both later.'

Ann dashed upstairs and banged about from bedroom to bathroom and back again. Zoe wrapped her arms around Tim. 'So what are we going to do today?' she asked.

'I've got to go to work,' Tim answered, genuinely regretful after months of enforced celibacy. 'And I think you'd better get some sleep.' He carried his girlfriend upstairs and laid her on their bed. While he brushed his teeth, she fell asleep, murmuring the name Guy Rogers. He made the downstairs hallway just as Ann was closing the front door and shouted after her, 'Can I give you a lift?'

'I'm fine,' Ann answered.

'No, really,' Tim insisted. 'I think there's a couple of things we ought to get sorted.'

In the minimal Taunsley traffic, Tim watched as Ann turned the car's fan on full and directed it towards her face, flicking her hair in the hot air. 'Didn't have a chance to properly get ready,' she explained. 'Just wanted to bolt the hell away from the house.' Tim continued to monitor her. It was a beautiful image, long, wet, dark hair swimming around Ann's face, her fingers running through it to help it dry, the blower on full making her face slightly flushed. Advert-wise, it was perfect. **The New Fiat Pinto, More Than Just a Normal Hot Hatch . . .**

'Do you often use the car to dry your hair?' he asked, cutting through the town centre and towards the hospital.

'All the time. Generally when I'm driving.'

'You do this when you're in charge of a vehicle?'

'Only mainly at traffic lights. And roundabouts. And occasionally on the motorway.'

Another series of visions flittered around Tim's mind. 'Look, Ann,' he said, 'this is a weird situation, to say the least.'

'Drying my hair in your car?'

'You know what I mean.'

'Don't worry,' Ann replied, turning to face him. 'Just because Zoe and I once knew each other slightly doesn't mean I'm going to say anything to her. And if you give me two or three weeks I'll find somewhere else to live. We'll all get along fine and things will be OK. It's probably for the best.'

The rest of the journey was passed in silence. Tim dropped Ann off and headed for Quayside Landings, where things were no less vexing.

Mr Rhinegold, it turned out, was not amused. Having been faxed a copy of the overnight market research findings, he rang the office in a major state of agitation. While Tim had anticipated some flack for the unconventional approach, he hadn't expected quite the level of venom that was being spat in his direction.

'And what the fuck did most of these questions have . . . to do with Jenkins Pork Pies?' his client screamed into the receiver.

'They were, er, laying the context of the commercial narrative,' Tim replied.

195

'And just what the fuck is that supposed to mean?'

'It means, in order to sell something, you first have to know your customer.'

'And ten fucking questions relating to . . . fucking a house guest . . . helps you know what brand of pork pie they prefer?'

Tim blew some air out of the side of his mouth. 'In a way, yes,' he answered unconvincingly. 'And besides, we've got you this preliminary data in record time.'

'Well, I'm not fucking happy.'

'Look, with all due respect, Mr Rhinegold,' Tim said, trying to rescue the situation, 'you now know that the people of Taunsley quite like Jenkins Meat Products, that women find them particularly enticing, and that their lodgers, should they have one, find them equally appealing. Bingo. We target the female population and their lodgers with a series of high-profile—'

Tim didn't get the chance to continue his side of the argument. Mr Rhinegold slammed the phone down.

'Told you,' Dave grinned.

'What?' Tim asked.

'He's pissed off big-time.'

'Nonsense. He'll come round. Anyway, it was all worth it,' he said quietly, holding a pile of papers in front of him, drumming his fingers on the forty successfully completed questionnaires. He now had replies to the questions that even his friends wouldn't answer honestly. More than that, he had a growing and overwhelming sense of pride about the town he had recently called home. Inhabitants he had mistaken for being sub-Victorian had turned out to be closet bed-hopping liberals. For instance, 56 per cent of Taunsley believed that sleeping with a lodger was a good thing to do. And only a third suggested that subsequently telling your partner of the said indiscretion was a positive move. That proportion dropped to under 10 per cent if your partner lived overseas. And when it came to, 'What would you consider a reasonable length of time after sleeping with your lodger until you asked them to leave? a) 1 week, b) 2 weeks, c) longer', most of the town had plumped for c) longer. Tim was amazed. He also felt that he had reclaimed some moral high ground – after all, it is difficult to be truly amoral if the majority of the population agree with your actions. But it was the answer to the big question that really cheered and impressed him. When asked, 'Given that your lodger was attractive and good company, would you place a greater emphasis on finishing your current relationship in order to be with them?' a healthy majority of punters had suggested just that. Taunsley was, for once, on his side, even though now, with Zoe back, the situation was less clear-cut. 'Anyway, Dave,' he continued, 'where are the rest of the questionnaires? You've done, what, forty? We're still waiting for the other sixty.'

'But Mr Rhinegold—'

'It'll only take another couple of mornings to do the rest. Besides, I'm curious.'

Dave didn't appear particularly cheered. 'I'll get on to it,' he said sullenly. When Tim left the room, Dave picked up the phone, making sure his boss was out of earshot. 'Simon? It's Dave,' he whispered. 'Yeah. Listen, he wants some more of those fucking forms doing. How're you fixed? Sixty. Think you can manage? Right, I'll drop some round.' And with that, he picked up a bundle of empty forms and headed out of the office before Tim returned from scratching himself in the bathroom.

Life's Made Me Hard

Alistaire Smythe strode fiercely through the town centre towards Quayside Landings, the piercing sun screwing up his eyes, so that he appeared even angrier than he already was. Taunsley was suffering a protracted heatwave, which failed to improve his mood. Above almost everything, Ali hated summer.

Glancing in a shop window, Ali noticed to his dismay that he was already bronzing. With all the recent goings-on, he had forgotten to steal any sunblock. This was not good news. Examining his face in more detail, he was horrified to note that things had progressed beyond a mere suntan. Once more in his life, his genes had conspired to undermine him. He wasn't just slightly brown – he was fucking black! Ali dragged his eyes away from the window image and picked up his pace. Someone at the newspaper or the advertising office was going to pay for his humiliation.

However, before he had made any meaningful progress, he came to a sudden halt. A massive RhylZig poster was bearing down on him. As he stared in fury at the image, he appreciated that he was starting to resemble his dark alter ego. In fact, the poster appeared to be bleaching slightly in the summer brightness so that they were about to meet in the middle, in mixed-race no-man's land.

Ali glanced nervously around him, worrying suddenly that he was visible, even more so than usual. Here he was, a supposed illegal immigrant, effectively holding his own public identity parade. All it needed was one Taunsley resident to lift their sweaty gaze from the pavement and Ali was fucked. As he continued to glare at the picture, weighing up his options, he took a small amount of comfort from the fact that the body his face had been grafted onto was substantially different from his own – slimmer, shorter, and with no visible tattoos.

Resuming his quest for blood with increased vigour, Ali turned off the high street and cut through a small shopping centre. Quayside Landings was dead ahead. He passed a chip shop, and for a second his lust for violence mingled with the smell from within. Ali slowed and stopped, almost dribbling. Through the window he could just make out a large kebab rotating with teasing intent, juices gently oozing out, its shaven surface gleaming at him. He shook his head like a dog foaming at the jowls. The kebab was calling, and he placed his palms against the window, staring forlornly in. He gritted his teeth. Focus, he whispered under his breath. Avoid temptation, and focus. He would shift the desire for kebab meat into the desire for human flesh. Pulling himself away, he strode on with renewed vitality. One way or another he would have his satisfaction.

Two minutes later, he reached Quayside Landings and made his way to the back of the car park. Above him were the offices of the *Mercury*, where Gary Shrubble was doubtless perpetrating new outrages against him. Further down the corridor was Power

199

Advertising. Ali sat on a kerb, out of the sun, and tried to think through a plan of action. This was an unusual situation for him. Generally all his brutality had been random and spontaneous and all his breaking and entering performed at night. Also, he usually carried a knife, whereas today, due to a grave tactical oversight, he was unarmed. This fact only served to make the challenge ahead more exciting. A good old-fashioned kicking was what he'd been put on this earth to deliver, and that was what he was going to provide. But first, the ritual. He pulled a small mirror out of his inside pocket. Staring into it, he began to chant, quietly at first, but growing in volume and violence. 'Life's Made Me Hard.' He stood up, psyching himself into the mirror. 'Life's Made Me Hard,' he repeated, glancing up at the building. 'Life's Made Me Hard,' he shouted. In one of the windows was a RhylZig poster, in another, a banner for the *Mercury*. 'Life's Made Me Hard.' He was almost screaming. 'Life's Made Me Hard.' He slotted the mirror away and stomped towards the entrance. Ali clenched his fists. It was time to restore some dignity.

Desk Clutter

Returning from the toilet, Tim turned his attention to the impressive row of desk clutter in front of him. Nothing had fallen apart for several days. He ran his eyes over the highlights of the collection. On the far left was a large chrome pendulum device, which flipped itself over every few seconds in a very distracting way. Towards the centre of the assembly was his sellotaped set of clackers, which hovered between being kitsch and classic, depending on the day. Past the substantial dolphin paperweight was an admittedly pointless electric pencil sharpener. But the real pride of his enormous desk was the anthology of products he had advertised in one way or another over the years. There was the 1/16th scale car, courtesy of a magazine campaign for the revamped Renault Clio (**Clio Sets You Frio**). Next to that, a metal model aeroplane, from the slogan he developed for the low-cost airline Simple-Jet. **No Frills Flying, Low Bills Buying**. To the left was an empty tin of Aspirilligan (**Fungus Again? Use Aspirilligan**). In the middle were two smaller items. First, a silver throat lozenge mounted in a thick perspex case, which had been given to him before the now infamous **Pepsils Lozenges – They've Got What It Snakes** promotion.

Second, and also housed in a sturdy lump of plastic, a replica T-shirt with a small and at first sight potentially offensive logo. Tim decided it was best not to dwell on this item, and ran his eyes further right, to his favourite object, an ornamental paper knife of such proportions that he had never dared use it for its intended purpose. He might as well put his mail through a bacon slicer as attempt to open it with the sabre-esque object. He picked it up and felt its weight. It was unwieldy and off balance, most of its mass lurking in the ornate handle. As he put it down again, he recalled the minor campaign for a razor manufacturer that had resulted in the gift. **Wilmington Blade Shaves You Three Times as Fast with Smoothness to Match**. The blade, which was as blunt as Dave, was inscribed. Beneath lurked the ominous lettering 'Made in PR China'.

Tim was just about to dust a couple of the items when the door swung open. He glanced up from his collection. Dave had popped out clutching another wad of questionnaires to inconvenience the town's population with. Tim had been expecting a visit from a rather irate customer for some time now, and this man was nothing if not enraged. He stood up. 'Mr Rhinegold?' he asked, extending his hand. 'Maybe it's time we talked about those question—'

'I'm not Mr fucking Rhinegold,' the man replied viciously.

On closer inspection, Tim could see that he had been badly mistaken. The gentleman in question was by no means typical of the business community. As far as he could recall, people at the cutting edge of the commercial world – or even those eking out a living in Taunsley – didn't have shaven heads, large boots and tattoos. Staring more closely, Tim appreciated that he had seen the character who was rapidly advancing towards him before somewhere. And as the character with a maniacally contorted face and white-knuckle fists reached the end of the desk, it clicked. Here was the living face of RhylZig. **The one thing your life is missing.** Tim was suddenly nervous, his stomach unsettled. 'Are you Tim fucking Power?' the thug screamed.

'No,' Tim replied hastily.

RhylZig Man spent an embarrassingly long amount of time studying Tim's desk sign, which read, 'Tim Power, Chief Executive Officer, Tim Power Advertising'. Above, next to a board housing a multitude of cut-out headlines, was a mounted photograph of Tim accepting a minor award for his only TV campaign, with his name clearly typed beneath. Strewn across his desk were numerous business cards with Tim Power emblazoned on them. Tim glanced around appreciating that the evidence was mounting. 'I'm his broth—'

The man raised an enormous hand, which silenced Tim mid-excuse. Something had caught his eye on the noticeboard. Below **Pipe Smoker Sets Himself Alight**, the headline **Burglar Begs Police Protection From Poodle** stared out at him. The skinhead's complexion, already dark, reddened further.

'It was a fucking dachshund!' he screamed, swinging wildly around for something to damage Tim Power with. In front of him was a collection of apparently random, and predominantly sharp, bric-a-brac. Ali picked up a hefty frame, housing, for some reason, a silver throat sweet, and frisbee-ed it across the long desk, where it struck Tim squarely in the gut. He grabbed the clackers and similarly chucked them, ball-bearings detaching along the way, spreading out like scatterbomb shrapnel and catching Tim in a variety of locations at the same time. And then he really got stuck in. He picked up the chrome pendulum device, which looked for all its life like it had been designed for combat, and thrust it at Tim. The weighty metal arm flipped over just at the right moment, and Ali rejoiced as it caught his victim square on the forehead.

Penned into the corner of the office by an unstable psychopath raining a plethora of variously pointed and heavy items down on him, Tim took stock of the situation. Nosebleed-inducing pain was enveloping his brain. Several bruises were quickly breaking out under his skin and scalp where the clacker spheres had struck him. A dull throbbing ache marked the spot at which the perspex-encased throat lozenge had slammed into his stomach. Meanwhile, the Simple-Jet model aeroplane took flight and nosedived into his groin. As a scale Renault Clio whizzed distressingly close to his face, Tim came to see the central truth of what was going on. He was being attacked by his own products. The very commodities he had put his heart and soul into promoting were battering his body with increasing violence. After all he had done to develop their positioning statements, protect their brand health, define their trade essence, and this is how they thanked him. He glimpsed his favourite advertising motto over his attacker's shoulder. **Become Your Product**, it said. At this rate, he was in danger of doing just that. The tin of Aspirilligan ricocheted off a wall and clattered into his head. Tim recalled insisting the tin be flat and round, and now, as it turned out, easy to throw and painful to be hit by. Meeting after meeting on target audiences, essential messages and campaign tracking. And the only real question he should have been concentrating on was, 'How painful is it to be hit in the head by Product X?' And the answer, as it turned out, was, 'Pretty fucking painful.' In between volleys, he belatedly appreciated that even the cause of all this payback was a Frankensteinian creation of his own making. The Face of RhylZig, which was a particularly unfriendly face, resumed his battering. Tim watched him pick up the enormous paperknife. A slow greasy smile spread across Ali's features and he paused, savouring the moment of calm before the real attack began. Tim glanced forlornly at the phone, which was out of reach. He was trapped. There was no way of escape.

Ali felt the pleasing weight of the unusual object in his hands and began to advance around the table. Although the blade wasn't particularly sharp, it would certainly do some damage. Besides, a blunt knife was more fun sometimes, requiring a more sustained attack to inflict a real maiming.

Tim scanned wildly around for something to help his cause. Bending down, he picked up the frame that housed a replica piece of clothing, and which had earlier missed his head by inches. He gripped it like an inadequate shield.

The crazy man stepped closer until he was in range. '**Cola 3000 – the Taste of the Future**,' he recited out loud from a poster on Tim's wall. 'And do you want to know what your future is going to be like, you wanker?'

'No,' Tim replied.

'It's going to be short.' And with that, Ali lunged forwards with the **Wilmington Blade Shaves You Three Times as Fast with Smoothness to Match** commemorative paper knife, stabbing it into the frame Tim was desperately holding up. He withdrew and made another thrust. Again, Tim parried the blow, but noticed with dismay that the makeshift shield was falling apart. Ali tried his luck a third time and the perspex case developed a disturbing crack down its midline. Ali perceived this with apparent glee.

'So you think it's funny when someone's in the paper, do you, you cunt?'

Tim remained silent, transfixed by the weapon.

'Well, let's see how you like it. **Wanker Killed For Being A Wanker**. Yeah,' Ali guffawed, 'that'd do the trick. Might even go and do that Shrubble bastard next. I'm starting to enjoy myself.' He pulled the blade slowly and deliberately back, before plunging it viciously in Tim's direction. The shield bore the brunt and shattered. However, as it did so, the commemorative paper knife also collapsed. Tim appreciated with interest that it was essentially plastic with a thin metal coating, and that its weight had been provided by a number of tightly packed stones in the handle. Ali examined the splinters that had pierced his palm. A new anger welled within him. He picked up a chair and was about to beat Tim over the head with it when the office door swung open, and Dave and Simon rushed in carrying a wad of papers. Dave, with rare presence of mind, picked up the phone and dialled 999. Simon Jasper, who recognized Taunsley's most famous son from the first break-in, walked slowly and deliberately towards him.

Ali lowered the chair. He didn't much like the look of the security guard who was heading in his direction. It wasn't that he was in the least bit menacing or dangerous, just that there was a disturbing expression on his face. Simon stopped a couple of paces away. Grinning insanely, he undid his belt and dropped his trousers, which seemed to unsettle the intruder. Utterly perplexed, Ali turned to Tim, who also appeared fairly bemused. 'You'd better watch out, Power,' he shouted, a long, thick finger waving. 'I haven't finished with you yet.' And with that, he decided enough was enough, and that he could quite happily live without the presence of naked men or uniformed police.

Sex and Gymnicity

It was, Barry Dinsdale readily conceded, a mess of his own making, and, as such, was all the more depressing. He was both the architect and the victim of his downfall. The lose–lose situation he currently found himself in could be traced directly back to a few poorly chosen words the previous year.

The trouble was, after six children, Cathy had decided that enough was enough, and there was no point being slim if she was only going to swell up again sometime soon to accommodate a fresh foetus. She might as well remain on the large side and await the inevitable. The inevitable failed to materialize, however. And the reason for this was that, in her engorged state, Barry no longer felt sufficiently aroused to accidentally inseminate her. A status quo had thus been achieved. No slimming, no sex, no more children.

Such a blissful existence now taunted Barry with its memory. A fat contented wife was, as he had discovered over the last few months, far more fun than a skinny miserable one. And all it had taken was an unintentionally honest answer to a benign question, which had caught him unawares the previous winter. How after several years of perfectly successful marriage he had allowed honesty into the bedroom he would never know. But one night it sneaked in, and he was stuck with it now.

Aware that their reproductive organs were on the verge of wasting away and would need introductions and name tags to remember who they were and what they did for a living, Cathy had taken the initiative one evening while she undressed. 'Darling,' she began, 'I honestly can't remember the last time we had sex.'

'Ninety-four,' Barry had answered.

'I'm serious. Has something changed?'

Barry felt a shiver as a breeze entered the bedroom. At this moment, an evil wind of honesty slipped into his lungs and encouraged his mouth to betray a lifetime of creative falsehoods. Proper answer: 'It's me. I've just been tired for the last decade or so.' Suicidallystraightforwardanswer blurted out during a momentary lapse: 'It's just that when I met you, you were slim and attractive.'

'And now?' Cathy had asked incredulously, her eyes welling.

Proper answer: 'There's even more of you to love.' Suicidallystraightforwardanswer: 'You're large.'

'And attractive?'

Still, the malicious honesty refused to retreat. Proper answer: 'Of course you are.' Suicidallystraightforwardanswer: 'Not really,' he replied, ruining the course of his marriage for ever.

Cathy had not taken the news well. 'So you only want to fuck me if I'm thin?'

By now, a sense of self-preservation had kicked in. Barry's relationship emergency pilot had seized the controls. However, the crash was already happening. 'It's not that . . .'

'I mean, how fucking shallow. I have your children,

209

and when I've been through all the pain and misery, you no longer want to have me.'

What she said was true. Although he didn't like himself for it, those were the hard facts of the situation. He was shallow. He wanted his wife to look like most of the women you see on TV. But, with certain notable exceptions, she didn't. The emergency pilot ploughed on regardless. 'Of course I want you. I always . . .'

'Well, there're going to be some changes around here,' Cathy had answered ominously, pulling her dressing gown on, 'I can tell you.'

'Changes?' Barry had asked nervously. 'What sort of changes?'

'You'll see all right. In a few months' time, you're going to be begging me for sex.'

And, to be fair to his wife, he was. Almost constantly. Seven months of impressive dedication to the dual pastimes of not eating very much and going to the gym a lot had transformed Cathy into an altogether more attractive proposition. Which is where the problem lay.

Barry peered across the room from behind his newspaper. Cathy was bending over in a short tennis skirt. The tops of her thighs were brown and toned, her calves taut and defined. Although there was something distinctly unnatural about leching your own wife, Barry was fast becoming an expert in the art. Cathy straightened, and Barry felt a similar movement. She picked up her gym bag and walked towards him. He placed the newspaper firmly in his lap to hide the evidence of his arousal. Despite already knowing the answer to his question, Barry appreciated that he would be letting himself down badly if he didn't at least ask.

'How about giving the gym a miss tonight?' he said

hopefully. 'We could open a bottle, listen to some music, cuddle up on the sofa . . .'

'I'm having a sauna,' Cathy replied flatly. 'Because I need to unwind.'

'I could help you un—'

'Look, things are getting weird at work. Gribben's going downhill. He just sits there, having weird phone calls that don't make sense, typing out strange letters that he won't let me see, scowling at everyone and then disappearing for long stretches. Yesterday he opened a box of bullets and counted and recounted them in front of me.'

'But . . .'

'So I'm going to have a swim and a sauna to drown the scary thoughts I'm having at the moment.'

'Right,' Barry answered for about the sixtieth consecutive night. 'Well, I'll just sit here by myself then, shall I?'

Cathy headed for the door, a tight T-shirt moulding the shape of her breasts. 'You don't *have* to sit there, you know.'

'No?'

'You could get off your arse and do some press-ups or squats.' She pulled the door open. 'Only you're beginning to get a bit flabby.' She closed the door and Barry peered miserably down at his belly. He had, he readily appreciated, been thoroughly outflanked by his wife. While this was by no means unusual, he was stung by the irony of the situation. She was too obsessed with keeping her body in shape to want to share it with him. On the rare evenings that she wasn't in the gym, she would brush his clumsy advances away just as lightly as he had done when the situation had been reversed.

He stood up and headed to the kitchen for a beer. So

far there had been no good opportunities to initiate his efficiency directive. Barry had tried to broach the subject several times, only to be met by a wife who seemed to be perpetually about to go somewhere and do something strenuous. He pulled a can from the fridge and lined a glass up on the counter. Sliding a protractor off a nearby shelf, he held the glass at an angle of exactly 45 degrees and poured the mouth-wateringly cold lager into it, making sure to avoid unnecessary foaming. He decided he just needed to catch her at the right time. Licking his lips, Barry resolved to pick his moment. Then, and only then, when he had her undivided attention, would he be able to break the exact details of the new house order to her.

We Only Talk During the Adverts

Hiding in the bathroom, Tim hacked at his face with a razor. He scratched the graze on his cheek where the plastic-mounted throat lozenge had caught him. His shaving arm and forehead ached from the impact of the pendulous executive toy. Two raised bruises under his hairline throbbed with the memory of clacker bombardment. An open cut on his hand marked the spot where the paper knife had penetrated his make-shift shield. One of his testicles pulsated unpleasantly from time to time. An intense migraine was beginning to pierce every thought he had, although it would probably have done so whether he had been attacked or not. Very much distressed from being assaulted at work, he considered the problem he now found himself in at home. Over a few short days, he had come to realize that the woman he loved he no longer wanted, and the woman he wanted didn't love him. The woman who was living on the other side of the planet had returned, just as the one from the room next door was about to leave. To make matters worse, the two knew each other, increasing the potential for disaster. The balance of his life had shifted with disturbing speed.

While he had undoubtedly been lonely and

miserable during Zoe's absence, meeting Ann had shifted his perspective. He had often tried to picture what exactly it was about his girlfriend that he craved when she wasn't there. When he had lived in London and travelled to see her at weekends, time had always been precious. The moment was everything, and in between was just a vague sense of being deprived of something, which, he now appreciated, he may have mistaken for actual yearning. For the first time, with Zoe back and all the days in the world ahead of them, an aeon of togetherness opening up, the answer had suddenly crystallized. It was obvious to him that what he had missed about Zoe was that he missed her.

The razor stubbornly refused to slice through his stubble, its triple blades doing all they could to snag and tear each hair they descended upon. It was a far cry from the Wilmington Blade commercials, where square-jawed men shaved with lightning speed and accuracy, running the razor across their faces with reckless abandon. **The first blade shaves you close, the second blade shaves you closer, and the third blade takes your fucking skin off**. His relationship with Zoe had always been a long-distance one. Maybe now with no strings binding them across a divide, they would simply fall apart. Perhaps, he was forced to admit to himself, it had never been cut out for extended proximity. The longest period they had ever spent together was the five weeks when Tim first moved to Taunsley. But even that had been imbued with a sense of imminent departure, of being denied something other people took for granted. And now he had a sharp relief against which to evaluate the relative merits of long-term cohabitation with Zoe.

Between eye-watering scrapes of his face, Tim glanced around the bathroom with dismay. Vast shelves had now disappeared beneath the weight of Zoe and Ann's intermingled skincare products. Downstairs the washing machine appeared to be permanently stuck in a spin. Male lifestyle magazines were overwhelmed by their feminine counterparts, which encouraged equally unobtainable existences, and, perplexingly, also had pictures of semi-naked women. Washing-up was taken care of on an almost hourly basis. A mysterious board-like contraption appeared, onto which clothes were placed before having their creases removed with a hot, angular object. All in all it was an unsettling environment. Tim rinsed his razor under the hot tap, noting a thin redness appear in the water. He applied a layer of aftershave gel, designed to **Moisturize, Soothe and Replenish**, which stung the shit out of his skin.

Zoe was watching TV and shushed him as he came in and tried to say something. 'Wait till the break,' she said.

The art of conversation isn't dead, Tim shrugged, sitting beside her, it's just floundering in the gap between programmes. Commercial breaks have become conversation areas. Talking during a favourite sitcom or beloved soap is likely to be met with, at best, a series of grunts. He tried again. 'I just wanted to tell you some more about the attack, something which doesn't seem right.'

'Yeah, well, it won't be long till the adverts.'

'But the town's economy is—'

'Look, I'm trying to watch this. I've missed Pommie TV.'

'I'll wait for the break then, shall I?'

'Mmm.'

Tim gave in. The programme Zoe was watching featured a series of tigers trapped in zoos which had apparently stopped mating. Tim glanced at his girl-friend. Being cooped up in the same living space meant they had abandoned all sexual behaviour. Zoe scratched herself and reached for some more crisps. The vet had resorted to feeding male tigers Viagra in an effort to encourage them to reproduce. Ann came home and prowled about the kitchen. She looked as if she was about to go out somewhere. Tim ached to go with her. The adverts duly arrived and Zoe stood up and headed for the bathroom. Ann walked over to her landlord. She appeared to be unhappy about some-thing.

'I was asked some very interesting questions in town today,' she said.

'Oh yes? Who by?'

'Dave.'

Tim's heart sank. 'Right,' he answered, silently cursing his assistant.

'Things like, "If you slept with your lodger, how quickly would you ask them to leave?"'

'Well . . .'

'And, "Would you tell your girlfriend if she was on the other side of the world?"'

'I was trying to . . .'

'Shall I tell you how this looks to me?'

'Not good, I'd imagine,' said Tim.

'It looks like a coward's attempt to make a decision.'

'OK, what about question ten? "Given that your lodger is attractive and fun, should you just stay with her?"'

'What about it?'

Tim stared into the overwhelming promise of Ann's eyes. 'I'd begun to think . . .'

Zoe was descending the stairs.

'That maybe we . . .'

216

'Yes?'

'Had some sort of . . .'

'Yes?' Ann demanded impatiently.

Zoe was close to the bottom.

'Potential of becoming . . .'

'Get to the point.'

'Perhaps if you felt the same . . .'

'Tell me.'

'Are the impotent tigers back on?' Zoe called, stepping into the room. 'Only I was desperate for the dunny.'

Tim turned from Ann to his girlfriend and sighed. 'Oh yes,' he answered. 'They're back on all right.'

Copywriter's Block

Mr Rhinegold was in a more conciliatory mood and sounded as if he'd cooled off in the couple of days since Tim had last heard from him. Having faxed over a copy of the final market research findings, they were now in a position to consider the next step. If there was to be a next step.

'Look,' Mr Rhinegold said through the speakerphone, 'while the research you did wasn't ideally what JMP would have wanted, I think we know enough . . . to go ahead and ask you to pitch some ideas at us.'

'What did you have in mind?'

'I'll be straight with you – we're struggling. No one in the town's buying our products.' Mr Rhinegold ran his finger down a list of figures on a much crumpled piece of paper. 'Local sales account for over . . . 60 per cent of our business. At this rate things are unsustainable. What we need is a Taunsley campaign . . . to change our image. We want you to work more of your – ' Mr Rhinegold battled a badly timed coughing fit – 'magic.'

'And is it pork pies specifically?'

'We've decided to broaden this to all our products. So we're after a wide-ranging strategy.'

Tim jotted a few words down. Here were two businesses about to fail dismally, each utterly dependent on the other to sustain their livelihood. He saw for the first time the nature of their joint destiny. A good campaign and both would thrive. A bad one and they would be seeing each other in the job centre. 'Right,' he replied, 'I think we can come up with something. My assistant and I will get cracking on it straight away.'

'How quickly can you give us some possibilities?'

'Three or four days, tops.'

'Right, I'll wait to hear from you.'

'And you received the invoice?'

'Oh yes. I've passed it to Accounts. We generally settle within twenty-eight days.'

'Great. The sooner the better,' Tim replied almost desperately.

Ending the call, he examined the desk debris in front of him one more time. Everything was very nearly as it had been before the attack. Admittedly, the model aeroplane was missing a wing, the Renault Clio looked to have been in a bad frontal impact and the large ornamental knife would now struggle to open a wet paper bag, but the overall impression was reasonably pleasing. The phone rang again and he continued to stare at the motley collection. As the answering machine kicked in, he heard his own voice say, 'This is Tim Power at Power Advertising. We have no comment to make about RhylZig at this time. For all other enquiries please use our postal address.' The machine beeped, faint breathing just audible, and then the line went dead. In quick succession, the office received a second call, with a similar outcome. There were up to forty-five calls a day. The only fucking thing he had ever successfully advertised in Taunsley didn't even exist. Tim slumped in his chair and

219

wondered how he had got into such a mess. Staring at the mounted lozenge, he realized its roots lay firmly in London. Unlike his father, who had entered advertising to escape real life, Tim had been thrown firmly back in the opposite direction.

After a promising career spanning tens of minor and a few major campaigns, two adverts had sealed his fate. The first was a national campaign of well-placed magazine ads, escalator panels and hugely prominent posterboards. The product itself wasn't exactly Ferraris and helicopters, but there were possibilities. A well-known brand that was perennially popular, particularly in winter. Tim pitched a couple of ideas and was given the nod. Some four months later, therefore, he was extremely put out to discover that his apparently benign press campaign for menthol throat lozenges had raked in 146 objections to the Advertising Standards Authority.

There had been nothing inherently wrong with the advert itself. It featured a man driving a taxi. He had a boa constrictor curled around his neck, its jaws disengaged, about to swallow his head. The image was captioned, **Sore throat? Trouble swallowing?** Beneath the image lay the tag line, **Pepsils Lozenges – they've got what it snakes**.

The reason the ad became a personal disaster for Tim was a chain of events no one could possibly have predicted. Publication of the advert initially preceded but then coincided with widespread media coverage of the bizarre death of a celebrity chef. In a bid to branch out from butchering animals to studying them in their natural habitat, the chef had travelled to Africa with a film crew to record a live feature. At the appropriate time, the London studio, in concert with five million shocked viewers, watched in horror as a large snake dropped into shot and slowly proceeded to squeeze the corpulent chef to death. Although the picture had been cut after forty-five seconds or so, when the London director had begun to suspect that strangulation by snake wasn't in the script, the chef's muffled screams could still be clearly heard over the top of some desperate filling. Following this well-publicized event, Tim's advert began to appear a little unpleasant. On massive boards around the country, the image of a man slowly being asphyxiated by a python stared down at all and sundry, a grim reminder of recent events. In a polite letter, the ASA pointed out that while most complainants felt that one famous cook less wasn't necessarily a bad thing, it was distasteful to publish the advertisement in the light of the incident.

The blame for the second disaster lay closer to home than the ill-advised African adventure. The word within certain sectors of the advertising industry had been that Collected National United Trousers were about to rebrand. The company, now moderately successful in all areas of clothing, were concerned that their staid image and outdated name were holding them back from further sales opportunities. In essence, they explained, they were looking for a more cutting-edge profile to allow them to appeal to fashionable ABC1 youngsters with lots of cash. A team from A2Z Advertising pitched for the account and were offered the chance to earn unreasonably large amounts of money by making the same old designs appeal to a new generation of hapless punters. Tim was lead copywriter on the project and quickly began to work some of his magic by sitting in the pub all afternoon pretending to think. After three sobriety-free weeks, he had failed to summon a single idea. He came to a damaging conclusion – he was suffering copywriter's block.

The pressure was on at A2Z Advertising and was increasing all the time. The Owners were hassling the Senior Management, who were haranguing the Senior Accounts Director, who was bothering the Deputy Accounts Director, who was annoying the Accounts Supervisor, who was getting up the nose of the Executive Creative Director, who was nagging the Associate Creative Director, who was bugging the Graphic Designer, who was upsetting the Media Buyer, who was mithering the Chief Copywriter, who was gnawing away at Tim whenever he got the chance. And still nothing. Barren hour after barren hour with a biro in one hand and a beer in the other. Days frittered away just staring at the words of the product. And then, finally, late one afternoon, he saw it. Tim raced back to the office and summoned the creative team. In front of a hushed room, he drew out his vision on a white board.

'"Collected National United Trousers = c,n,u,t,"' he wrote.

A senior accounts manager was moved to ask, 'What the fuck?'

'Get them to register their new company name as "cnut",' Tim replied.

'And where the hell does that get us?'

'Let me tell you.' Tim knew he was onto a winner, and explained. And so it was that several weeks later, posters began appearing in selected magazines and on prominent hoardings. Invariably, the ads featured bored-looking teenagers in modish clothes, with tag lines such as **You'd be a cnut to buy from anyone else**, **Feel snug in a tight-fitting cnut**, and **All fashion is a load of cnut**.

The adverts drew massive amounts of publicity to

the products of Collected National United Trousers. It was deliberately provocative stuff. The only trouble was entirely the wrong sort of people were provoked. Already late with the adverts, and in the rush to promote cnut, several short cuts had been taken. None of the slogans had been run past Copy Advice. Focus groups had not been consulted to determine exactly how offensive the ads might be. The cnut team had not sought the counsel of the higher echelons of A2Z Advertising. Within weeks, the campaign had garnered a record 812 Advertising Standards Authority complaints. Tim's promotion won the coveted top slot in 2002's ten most offensive campaigns of the year. The ASA upheld the complaint and asked the advertisers to withdraw the advertisements. The campaign was dropped. cnut rebranded themselves as Collected National United Trousers and reported record losses. Teetering on the edge of financial ruin, the global company was snapped up by one of their rivals and promptly shut down, costing several hundred people their jobs. Tim, already notorious for the Pepsils Lozenges fiasco, appreciated his career was in severe jeopardy. He had been a big daft cnut. He was effectively dead in the water. What had started as a mission to understand corporate advertising had left him with just one choice. Slowly and unpleasantly, Taunsley began to rear its ugly head.

But, Tim smiled to himself, slowly rubbing his chin, before it had all gone wrong things had been good for a couple of years. He had been making progress with a highly successful foray into TV in the form of the well-known Boots campaign of 2001. It even spawned a catchphrase which lived on past the advert's shelflife to annoy right-minded people everywhere. Still now, in the odd pub or on the occasional factory floor, Late

enough for you? could be heard, regurgitated and used to fit any mediocre situation. Tim rummaged through the drawers of his desk before finding what he was hunting for. He took the video tape and slotted it into the office VCR, which sat on top of the office DVD and was hooked up to the office plasma screen TV. On reflection, he appreciated, the client entertainment package had been a poor investment. After a few seconds, his sole moment of triumph flickered into life. He sat back in his chair and tried not to get too depressed by his change of fortune. The first scene appeared as follows:

Video: It is late at night. We see three men head-on, seated. We are in an environment which appears to be medical in some way. The men are quite rough, stubbly types, possibly builders. There are occasional sideways glances between them.

Music: A tinny radio plays 'I'm Every Woman' in the background.

Speech: Man #1 to Man #2: 'What're you in for?'

Speech: Man #2, slightly embarrassed: 'Touch of cystitis. You?'

Speech: Man #1: 'Water retention. You know.'

Video: Both other men nod sympathetically.

Speech: We hear an educated female voice say: 'Katie Simpson?'
Still focused on the trio of builders. The middle man looks shiftily sideways, before saying: 'That's me,' and standing up.

Video: More head shots of the two remaining men.

The female voice pipes up again: 'Emily Green. Which one of you's Emily Green?'

Video: Man #3 nods to his co-conspirator and stands up. 'Wind,' he explains to the remaining man. We suddenly see that he is in a pharmacy. A clock behind him shows that it is just after midnight. He takes a small package bearing the Boots logo from the pharmacist.

Video key: **BOOTS 24 DISPENSING**

Video key: **FOR WHATEVER YOUR NEEDS**

Video: Man #3 walks outside after being handed the prescription and passes it to his wife through the car window. She is cradling a baby.

Speech: Mother: 'There you go, Emily,' she says tenderly, 'that should ease your wind.'

Video: The baby smiles a gummy grin.

Video key: **BOOTS 24 DISPENSING – LATE ENOUGH FOR YOU?**

The tape ended with the usual copyright information. Tim paused it, his name dancing between frames. He pressed Play and watched the cast list appear, there just for trade use and never normally seen by the public. As the names scrolled by, one caught his eye and he paused the video again. Brian Hawkins. 'Rough Builder #3'. While a clever ad campaign for Jenkins Meat Products could help his bankruptcy prospects, if ever there was a man to sort all his other problems out, it was Brian Hawkins.

225

Reference Manager

Barry Dinsdale stood before the bedroom mirror and examined his clothing from several angles, all of them bad. No matter what the lighting, or how he postured, the inescapable conclusion was that he had become a scruffy bugger.

It hadn't happened by design. Initially, Barry had developed a system, a two-tier strategy, which enabled efficient clothing usage. For work, he wore smart suits with sharp creases which screamed authority. At home, he entered the bear pit in shabbier, rougher outfits which tolerated stains well. But now, he was forced to accept, the lines had become blurred. In fact, more than this, they had become one and the same thing. It was difficult to tell whether he was dressed for work or for home as the general stainage was roughly equal no matter what he wore. Smarter items had been dragged into the domestic mayhem and were now as blemished as his Daddy Clothes. Once stylish ties had been grabbed by a succession of six tarnished pairs of hands. Previously acceptable suits had received multitudinous and copious doses of vomit. Formerly spotless shirts had fallen prey to flying items of food and chocolate handprints.

Cathy entered the bedroom and Barry half turned from the mirror to ask, 'How was work today?'

'The usual. Except he's freaking me out even more.'

'Hmm?'

'It's not every day you watch your boss sitting at his desk loading and unloading a gun.'

'Yeah,' Barry said distractedly, rummaging in a drawer.

'And he keeps a baseball bat and God knows what in his filing cabinet. He's getting more irrational by the day.'

'Hmm.'

'I tell you, work used to be the place I went to escape all the chaos at home. Now I'm glad to get back in one piece. Maybe the rumours about him are true.' She rubbed her face. 'I'm losing sleep over this.'

'Right.' Barry pulled a vest out and examined it suspiciously.

'But I can't exactly go to the police. What the hell am I going to do? I really am starting to get frightened.'

Barry opened another drawer and cursed. 'My green shirt,' he said. 'Where the hell has my green shirt gone?'

Cathy stood and glared at him for a second.

'What?' he enquired.

'It's in the wardrobe.'

Barry opened the door and pulled out his favourite top. Aware that Cathy was still glowering, he once again asked, 'What?'

'I've been trying to tell you something important, and all you can do is fail to find a piece of clothing.'

'I was listening. Derek Gribben—'

'Do you know the principal thing marriage has done to you?'

'Made me look like a tramp?' Barry answered hopefully.

227

'As well as stopping you listening, getting married has destroyed the part of your brain that deals with the day-to-day organization of life.'

'Meaning?'

'Meaning that rather than think, you ask. Rather than remember, you ask. Rather than look for your own fucking shirt, you ask. I've become some sort of glorified filing system for you.'

'I was only—'

'Last Saturday, you wanted me to tell you what size shoes you wear.'

'I'd forgotten.'

'It transpired recently that you have no idea where we keep our cutlery.'

'It's a big kitchen.'

'You barely know your own birthday without me telling you. I seem to exist merely as a source of reference.'

'Rubbish. I know lots of stuff,' Barry replied, rising to his own defence. 'Anyway,' he said, judging the time right to finally instigate his home-efficiency plan, 'I've been meaning to talk to you. I've drawn up—'

Cathy held up her hand. 'I want to put something to the test.'

'What?'

'Let's see how it works if things are reversed.'

Barry smiled, and quickly wished he hadn't. 'How do you mean?'

'Come on, what do you know about me? What do you really know about the woman you've shared your life with for the last ten years? Let's find out.'

'But my scheme . . . I've even drawn some graphs.'

'For a start, what size are my shoes?'

'Which ones?' Barry asked, playing for time.

'Any of them.'

'Seven?' he guessed.

Cathy picked up one of Barry's nearby clipboards and jotted something down. 'And how much do I weigh?'

Barry winced. This was a lose–lose situation. He speculated on the low side. 'Ten stone. Ish.'

Another hastily scribbled clipboard comment. 'Bra size?'

'Small?'

Cathy took a sharp breath. Barry knew that was going to cost dearly. 'I mean in numbers and letters.'

'What are you after, its fucking postcode?'

'You know what I mean.'

'OK. Thirty . . . six . . . C.'

'Date of birth?'

'July the twelfth.'

'Year?'

Barry attempted to work it out. '1964?'

'Dress size?'

'Fourteen?'

'Bastard,' Cathy replied under her breath. 'And which bedroom drawer do I keep my underwear in?'

'The underwear drawer?'

'Which is?'

'The top one?'

'Without looking, what colour are my eyes?'

'Bluey-greeny. With hazel bits.'

'Which colour, precisely?'

Barry racked his brains. This wasn't going well. 'I'd have said blue.'

Cathy scribbled irritably on her piece of paper. As she did so, something occurred to her. Another inequity, far greater than her husband's inability to remember small details about her life. And what was more, there was a simple way to tease it out of him.

She allowed her questions to change tack and began to set a trap. 'How many men have I slept with?' she asked.

'Eight, including me.'

'And who were they?'

'Starting from 1985, Collin Blakesford. Then the following year, there was Simon Philips and Geoff Barker . . .'

'Right. And how many times have I bumped the car bad enough to have it repaired?'

'Seven.'

'How much did it cost you when I had to surrender my Monsoon storecard four years ago?'

'Three hundred and ninety-two pounds, forty-two pence.'

'How long did it take to get my figure back after our first child?'

'Must have been ten and a half months.' Barry relaxed. These were easy. After a difficult start, he was going to cruise it.

'What's the average length of time I spend in the bath?'

'Forty-five minutes, give or take.'

'How many pairs of shoes do I own?'

'Must be at least twenty.'

'And lastly, and I want you to think clearly and honestly about this, what mark would you give me out of ten? You know, if you had to rate me as a woman, in terms of my appearance.'

Barry thought long and hard. Honesty was the key. She had said it herself. If Kylie was a ten, and Ann Widdecombe one, then it stood to reason that Cathy was somewhere in between. However, for the sake of not making a mistake he would have to hear about for the rest of his life, he decided to err on the side of caution. 'Seven,' he replied at last, relieved to have thought his answer through. And then, seeing the expression on his wife's face, he added proudly, 'and a half.'

Cathy was silent for a few seconds. On the clipboard, and on top of all the answers she had just scribbled down, she inscribed a large 7½ deep into the paper. She continued to hack the number into the surface. Barry sat and fidgeted. Finally, Cathy steadied herself and began. 'You have just proved a very important point to me,' she said.

'No problem,' Barry replied. 'Happy to help.'

'And that point is this: you don't know anything about me at all. In fact, the only things you do know are the ones which have in some way inconvenienced you or put your nose out of joint. The reason you remember them is because they are minor grievances. You see my breasts every day, and yet you couldn't size them to save your life. However, you have never met Collin Blakesford, Simon Philips or Geoff Barker, and I've probably only mentioned their names once, and you have this information etched on your mind for ever.'

'But they took your virginity!'

'They didn't all take it.'

'You know what I mean.'

'OK, the Monsoon storecard issue. Four years later, and you can recall the exact amount. Down to the nearest penny. The times I've pranged the car. The pairs of shoes I own.' Cathy's eyes moistened. 'But the colour of my eyes? They're green, by the way.' A tear fell onto the clipboard and she rubbed her face. 'To you, I'm a walking fucking encyclopaedia of trivial information about you that you can call on whenever you want. But me . . . I barely exist.' She blew her nose. 'So you can stick your ergonomics nonsense up your arse.'

'There's no need to get carried—'

'I'm going to my mum's.'

'But she won't have room for all the kids.'

'Precisely.'

'You don't mean . . .'

'Oh yes. You think you can run this house better than me. You want to install some sort of efficiency system. Well, let's see you try. I'll be back in a fortnight.'

Barry was suddenly pale. 'Not all six of them. Surely?'

'Uh-huh.'

'What about my job?'

'Tell them you're working from home. Which you are. And besides, you've always believed being a housewife is a soft option. So lounge around. Relax. Enjoy it.'

As the door slammed, Barry uttered the single word, 'Fuck.' He glanced up. One of the kids had ventured along the landing to see what all the commotion was about.

'What does "fuck" mean, Daddy?' she asked.

'It means I'm in severe trouble,' he answered.

From outside came the clear noise of Cathy crunching down the gravel drive and away from the house.

Slaughterhouse Pig

'OK, Dave, let's have it,' Tim sighed.

Dave had been slaving over the JMP account virtually non-stop for two days. Not for the first time in their working relationship, they were alarmingly short of good ideas. JMP wanted the proposals straight away and were insistent that the promotion start as soon as possible. 'You know,' he began, 'that you haven't always liked all of my brainwaves.'

'You could say that,' Tim replied.

'Well, you're going to love this one.'

'I'm willing to give it a go. I mean, we've got fuck all else.' Tim had been badly distracted from the business at hand. The last three nights had witnessed a series of abusive phone calls to his house. He had recognized the voice immediately. The skinhead had got hold of his home phone number. And if he had that, there was little doubt he also knew his address. The police had been of limited use, having been unable to track Alistaire Smythe down following the assault. 'So let's hear it,' he encouraged.

Dave tightened his tie and puffed out his chest. '**Slaughterhouse Pig!**'

'What?'

'**Slaughterhouse Pig!**' he exclaimed excitedly. 'We're going to humanize Jenkins Meat Products.'

'With a pig?'

'You know what I mean. **Slaughterhouse Pig** will be the face of the product, smiling out on posters, raising his trotter like he's giving the thumbs up. And there'll be a killer tag line.'

'Which is?'

'**You can be sure more of my flesh ends up in your pies.**'

'Hardly likely to convert any vegetarians.'

'That's not the point. The aim is to tell Taunsley that Jenkins Meat Products actually contain loads of meat. And who better to do that than a pig?'

'Well, it's a start, I suppose. Anything else?'

'Couple of other things. But nothing as good as **Slaughterhouse Pig**.'

'Go on. We're desperate here.'

'OK, people are worried about what goes into Jenkins pies, so we focus on the health issues. We show them that Jenkins Meat Products are as safe as houses.'

Tim raised his eyebrows. Dave was in danger of getting straight to the point of an advert. 'So what have you come up with?' he asked enthusiastically.

'**Jenkins Pies – Now With 50% Less Botulism Than Most Other Brands.**'

Tim's eagerness disappeared as foolishly as it had come. 'Jesus,' he sighed.

'Anyway, what about you?' Dave asked, a rising anger in his voice. 'Let's hear your bright ideas.'

'Look, I'm not saying mine are any better. I've been a bit busy for the last few days.' He yawned through lack of sleep. 'I had **You'll JMP For Joy With Our New Pies**. And then underneath, '**JMP Pies – now with 45% more pork goodness.**'

'OK, I suppose.' Dave shrugged, relishing his reversed role as critic.

'Or: **Pigs Might Pie**. And in small print: '**Despite what you've heard, JMP have more meat per pie than Top Class Pasties.**'

'Who's Top Class Pasties?'

'The only other manufacturer of low-grade meat products in the town. Run by a Mr Derek Gribben. I actually did some research. Turns out JMP have a rival. And while JMP's profits have been draining away, Top Class have been catching up. I thought we could try and have a dig at the opposition.'

'Makes sense. How about **Top Class Pasties Are Consistently Nasty**?'

'Reasonable, but there's a fine line between implying a competitor's brand is inferior and slagging them off publicly. Besides, there are laws against such things.'

'So what do you think, boss?'

'By my reckoning, we have three or four pitches. Mr Rhinegold wants to come over tomorrow and see mock-ups.'

'We're actually going to meet him?'

'Seems like it.'

'Right, I'll sketch some pigs in various poses.'

'Nice. And, Dave . . .'

'Boss?'

'This is important. We can't afford to balls it up.'

The next day, Tim and Dave met JMP's sales manager for the first time, and a very striking person he turned out to be. For a man of financial expertise, however, Tim couldn't help but feel that his commercial acuity left a lot to be desired. Certainly, Mr Rhinegold had shown negligible interest in both of Tim's ideas. **You'll JMP For Joy With Our New Pies** had been met only with a poorly suppressed yawn.

Pigs Might Pie had simply been frowned at. What was more disturbing was the eagerness he had displayed for Dave's proposals. Against his boss's wishes, Dave had prepared a mock-up of **Jenkins Pies – Now With 50% Less Botulism Than Most Other Brands**. What had really caught him though was **Slaughterhouse Pig**. He described the proposed campaign as an inspired moment in advertising.

Lighting up a cigarette and sighing out the smoke, Tim attempted to demonstrate the obvious problem with having a pig advertise itself. 'People will feel unnerved by it,' he explained, taking another drag. 'It would be like having a baby advertising baby-eating. The image of a pig actually asking you to boil it up and shove it in your mouth is too close to the bone in these supposedly enlightened times. If you'll pardon the . . .'

Mr Rhinegold had been sold, however. 'Nonsense,' he said. **'Slaughterhouse Pig** is what we're going to run with.'

'But . . .'

'And give me the slogan again,' he continued, smiling at Dave.

'You can be sure more of my flesh ends up in your pies.'

'Perfect!' Mr Rhinegold examined the artwork admiringly. 'When can we start?'

'A matter of days.'

Tim flicked the end of his cigarette impatiently. He decided to have one final attempt at talking Mr Rhinegold out of the course of action he seemed desperate to embark upon. 'Look, JMP sales are in trouble as it is. This was never a serious contender among our pitches, just there to show you how good the other ideas were in comparison.'

Mr Rhinegold held up his hand. 'Mr Power,' he

began, 'I've made my decision. I like the image – it speaks to the common man. If you want our business, I suggest you begin advertising . . . as soon as humanly possible. Make the pig a bit bigger, with less hair and we're on to a winner. But other than that, leave the artwork as it is – I like the rough, unfinished style.'

'But it's just a mock-up.'

'It's good enough. Time is of the essence. I remain confident that **Slaughterhouse Pig** is going . . . to for ever change the fortunes of Jenkins Meat Products.' He raised himself unsteadily to his feet and shook Dave's hand. 'For ever change our fortunes.'

Flower

Sally Dinsdale's two-year-old screams sliced through Barry's sleepy ears and pricked at his subconscious. He turned over and reached across to nudge his wife. Half comatose, he extended his arm further and further until it was hanging off the bed. And then he smiled and tried to return to his slumber. Cathy must be sorting it out. He wrapped the duvet tightly around himself and stretched.

However, a couple of minutes later Sally's dawn chorus had failed to subside. What was his wife doing, he wondered, slightly put out that his sleep was being disturbed. And then Peter, three, joined Sally in a duet of high-pitched whingeing. Soon after, there were two dull thuds on the bed as David and Harry, the twins of six, jumped up and down. 'Daddy! Daddy!' they shouted in unison.

Barry opened his eyes. In the doorway, Daniel, eight, and Sarah, nine, were loitering with intent.

'Where's Mummy?' Sarah asked.

'Mummy? She's . . .' Oh fuck, Barry said silently. She'd buggered off. 'She's gone away for a little while to see Grandma.' In the background, Sally and Peter were continuing to protest from the cages of their cots. Oh fuck, indeed. 'Daniel, go and get Sally and Peter out of their room,' he instructed, 'and bring them downstairs. The rest of you, get some clothes on and come to the kitchen.' That, Barry told himself, should buy some time.

As he descended the stairs with all the enthusiasm of a soon-to-be-executed man, he took in the enormity of the disaster that had befallen him. Six children. Six. Six mouths to fill, six sets of clothes to choose. Six double-rows of teeth to be cleaned, six faces to wash. Six pairs of shoelaces to be tied, six heads to be brushed. A school-run and nursery-dash of epic proportions. Lunches to be prepared. Washing. Cleaning. Nappies. Dinner money. Christ. This was worse than divorce – this was a fucking calamity! Barry put a big pan of porridge on and placed four slices of bread in the industrial toaster. He poured out a wide range of beverages and assembled a mountain of cutlery. How the hell did Cathy do it, he wondered, as the first of his offspring appeared and demanded their breakfast. Pretty soon, the whole massed ranks had made their way downstairs.

During breakfast, Barry felt the conversation was, if anything, a little one-sided.

Daddy, I don't like orange.

Shoe. Shoe.

Can Harry have his tea?

No.

Gaggy, birdie. Birdie. Birdie.

Daddy, why?

Daniel's socks. Don't want Daniel's socks.

Want backcurra.

Why?

Miss Greening says we've got to hold hands, Daddy.

No. No. No. No.

Birdie. Car. Brum brum.

Where's my drawings?

Why, Daddy?

Shoe. Shoe.

Because you can't.

Backcurra. Daddy, I want backcurra.

Mummy says it's not right to hold hands with boys.

Daddy, watch telly.

Birdie. Shoe. Brum brum.

Daddy, where's my drawings?

Telly. Telly. Telly.

No want orange. No want orange.

Book. Daddy, read book.

Need dinner money.

Shoe. Birdie. Shoe.

Amid the cacophony, Barry sat and thought how he had ended up in this mess. It had started eleven years ago. Before he met his wife, he had loved no one, and this sentiment had been ruthlessly reciprocated by the female population. And then he bumped into Cathy, and within months she was pregnant. When Sarah was born, she had opened him out like a flower. Suddenly, from being devoted to nobody, he was in love with two people. He was ecstatic. A year later, Daniel had arrived and his happiness was complete. He loved Cathy, Sarah and Daniel, and they loved him back.

Another three years down the line, however, Cathy had given birth to twins. This had been a difficult jump. Almost overnight they had doubled their offspring. And still they kept coming. Peter was soon followed by Sally. At this point Barry had slowly begun to feel swamped, and the feeling had perpetuated and intensified until he felt like he was vainly thrashing about in turbulent treacle, always one breath from drowning.

It wasn't that he didn't adore his children. Each of them had brought him untold pleasures of the kind you can't imagine from reading books or watching films. No one had told him how funny it would be, how many raucous belly laughs there were just being around the blameless purity of his offspring. There was a completeness to his heart which told him that previously, without really realizing it, he had always lacked something. But then he had stumbled across it, and in abundance. Maybe, if anything, he recognized looking around him, too much abundance. The trouble was that rather than having time to wallow in the parental payback of family, he was at the front line of almost permanent chaos. There was no time to appreciate his children's individual characters, to soak up their innocent beauty, to luxuriate in their innate depiction of everything that was right about the world. Instead, it was a domestic war zone of epic proportions. There was always something that needed cleaning, fixing, washing, scrubbing, ironing, drying, preparing or throwing away. They were constantly one step behind the pace of their offspring's hyperactivity. A buttered piece of toast flopped onto the floor, narrowly missing his sock, and a glop of porridge sailed through the air. It was time for action.

Barry was facing the biggest challenge of his professional career. He had always said that the house wasn't being run efficiently. Now here was his chance to put it right. It was time to go back to basics. While he stood up and attempted to iron a small yellow dress, he opened an ominously thick textbook entitled *Advanced Ergonomics*. As he read and ironed, doing both badly, he came to see that what was true of industry could also be true of the home. He just needed a system. The dress began to burn. Cathy would be overwhelmed with the changes he was going to implement. So much so, he hoped, she might even be willing to sleep with him.

An hour later, and with Sally, Peter, Harry, David, Daniel and Sarah loaded into the MPV, Barry began a mammoth expedition of child delivery to various nurseries, schools and playgroups in the area. En route, he explained that there were going to be some immediate changes in the way the house was run. First, all after-school activities would be ceasing. Second, no child was to come home for lunch, either alone or with friends. Third, no food was to be permitted in the car. And fourth, pocket money, where appropriate, was to be curtailed for two weeks with immediate effect. Sitting in front, Sarah, nine years old and of impending adolescence, took the news with greater affront than her younger siblings. 'You'll be telling me soon I can't use my mobile,' she complained.

Barry swung round to face her. 'You have a mobile?'

'Yes. But it's not a very good one. I want a Knockya 700 next. I saw one on the telly last night. And I need the new CD by Boys4Ever. And I'm running low on nail varnish.'

Barry stared grimly back at the road. She was turning into an adult like she was on fast forward. And, if he wasn't careful, he was about to miss her childhood. Stopping at a junction, he spotted two enormous posterboards bearing down on the traffic. One bore the airbrushed image of five asexual teenage boys who somehow appeared to have dodged the acne and grease that plagued their peers. Below, bold, thick words screamed, **Boys4Ever. Buy the new album Now!**

'Look, Daddy,' Sarah said excitedly. 'Boys4Ever.'

The lights remained defiantly red. Barry peered up at

the second image, hoping for a better omen. Behind, Harry followed his father's gaze and said, 'Pig. Pig. Pig.' His twin brother David started snorting. The poster featured a cartoon pig giving a caricatured thumbs up and winking. Beneath came the unpromising slogan, **You can be sure more of my flesh ends up in your pies**, and the name Jenkins Meat Products. As the recent calamity of RhylZig had proved, Barry knew precious little about commercial promotion. However, even to his unskilled eye, it was awful, amateurish and disturbing, the last thing in the world that would encourage anyone to buy low-grade processed-meat goods. Barry thought briefly about Tim Power. The lights flickered from amber to green and he pulled away, leaving the cartoon pig behind. He turned off the main road towards one of Taunsley's three junior schools, suffering a sudden pang of guilt. Despite his best efforts, and partly due to them, Tim was still obviously floundering. His efficiency directives had failed to alter the downwards spiral of his fortunes. He wondered if there was anything else he could possibly do. However, there was a time for sympathy. He had problems of his own. After dropping off his offspring he would begin to implement a set of procedures that would, he hoped, for ever maximize the potential of his household.

Smart Arse

Three days into the **Slaughterhouse Pig** campaign, Tim Power was very surprised to pick up the phone and have Mr Jenkins spend several minutes screaming into his ear. 'I mean, what gives you the fucking right to do this to me?' he shouted. Tim opened the office window, slightly bemused. Outside, the sound of a thousand strimmers buzzed the air. It was the first sunny day after a period of summer rain and Taunsley residents were rushing home early to ensure their lawns didn't show any signs of growth. 'I can't believe you'd treat me this way,' Mr Jenkins continued. 'People are laughing at me in the street. I'm going to be suing you the fuck out of existence.'

'I'm afraid fate has beaten you to it. Anyway,' Tim said, cutting to the chase, 'what do you mean? I know the campaign isn't exactly a success.'

'Isn't a success? I'm losing thousands a day. This is killing me.'

'I don't see why you're blaming me. I was only trying to help.'

'Help? I hope to fuck you never try to harm me,' Mr Jenkins yelled. 'Jesus. And what were you thinking? That this might be some sort of compensation for the disastrous **Meat is On** thing?'

'I'm sorry, I don't follow . . .'

'Your fucking posters are up everywhere I go. Please, get them down. Now. I'm about to go under.'

Below, Gary Shrubble, ace reporter, skulked out of the building. He walked as if his whole being was based around the cigarette he always carried, a cigarette that pointed firmly in the direction of a drinking venue, like a miniature divining rod seeking out alcohol. At the far end of the car park, the journalist unsteadily opened the door of a shabby vehicle and climbed in. Tim doubted he was about to do any strimming. 'I did attempt to warn you,' he explained quietly. 'I said I didn't think it was the right message to hit Taunsley with. I mean, if you anthropomorphize something you eat, it's beginning to verge on cannibalism.'

'What the fuck are you talking about?' – Tim held the phone a safe distance from his ear – 'And when did you warn me about anything?'

'Well, not you. Your sales manager.'

'Which sales manager?'

'Mr Rhinegold.'

'Who?'

'Your key accounts—'

'Brenda Davies is my sales manager. Always has been.'

A stab of panic pricked Tim's stomach. 'So Brenda is still your key accounts person?'

'Like I said.' Mr Jenkins was quiet for a few seconds. 'This Mr Rhinegold. What does he look like?'

'Tall.'

'And?'

'Well-built.'

'Anything else?' Mr Jenkins demanded impatiently.

'A bit unhinged.'

'Rhinegold. Rhinegold. That rings a bell somewhere. Rhinegold. Fuck! Please, no. Tell me, there's something else about him, isn't there?'

Tim walked over and closed the window, the strimmer symphony outside reaching a climax. At all costs, the Black and Decker screech seemed to be saying, maintain your control over nature. He racked his brains for the obvious characteristic he was missing. 'Oh yes,' he said, sitting down. 'And only one arm.'

There was a lengthy pause, during which Tim imagined Mr Jenkins swelling even further in size. 'That one-armed cunt Gribben!' he screamed.

'Gribben? Who's Gribben?'

'Rhinegold is Gribben. The same motherfucking person. Just using an alias.'

'Derek Gribben of Top Class Pasties?'

'One and the same. And you believed him when he said he was my financial director?'

'I had no reason not to,' Tim answered defensively. 'His letters were on JMP stationery.'

'Thieving bastard.'

'So he *doesn't* work for you?' Tim asked, his panic beginning to turn into a dull ache of premonition.

'Not any more.' Mr Jenkins whistled through his teeth. 'Jesus Christ.'

Tim suddenly understood why Mr Rhinegold had been so keen on **Slaughterhouse Pig** in the face of far more sensible approaches. And he quickly realized that he wasn't about to be paid by Mr Jenkins.

'OK, let's think about this. So we've both been duped. How quickly can you get those fucking posters down?'

'Couple of days,' Tim replied miserably.

'Well, that might be too late. The damage has been

246

done. I'm in trouble, and no one's buying my products. It's going to take a miracle to turn this one around.'

'I know what you mean,' Tim replied, glancing sadly about the office. 'I know exactly what you mean.'

After Mr Jenkins had ended the call with a final barrage of swearing, Tim sat and considered his options. He had been tricked, for reasons that were not exactly clear. His business was on the verge of collapse. Only one person could tell him what was going on. He picked up the phone and dialled Mr Rhinegold's number, asking for Derek Gribben. Understanding that the ruse had been discovered, Derek Gribben continued where Mr Jenkins had left off.

'You fucking say any fucking thing to anyone . . . and I'll have your arms broken. And your legs. Let's see you advertise . . . fuck all then.'

'Listen,' Tim said defiantly, 'what you've done is illegal. If you threaten me as well . . .'

'You think the police . . . will be remotely interested? You imagine Taunsley's constabulary . . . are big on prosecuting . . . false advertising? Let alone even knowing . . . what the fuck it is?'

'All the same.'

'Hear this, you yuppie twat . . . if you even think of doing anything . . . that will harm me or my interests . . . I will have you . . . severely done over. I've got just the man. He's gagging to . . . get hold of you. Knows where you live as well. One word from me . . . and you'll wish you never moved to Taunsley.'

'I do already,' Tim agreed.

'And I don't like . . . fucking smartarses. So as I say, you keep quiet . . . otherwise you'll be losing a lot of blood.'

'But I don't understand why you commissioned me. It cost you a lot of money.'

Down the line came the noise of unforced laughter. 'That's good. That's really good. You seriously think I'm going . . . to pay for that rubbish?'

'Look, we had an agreement. Forget about the other stuff, just send me the money. I'll keep quiet and we'll leave it at that.'

'Are you deaf as well . . . as stupid? If you want paying . . . send the bill to that fat cunt Jenkins.'

'But if you don't pay me, I'm out of business.'

Again, Mr Gribben's high-pitched laugh squealed down the line. 'Yeah? You and Jenkins! Two wankers with one fucking stone!'

'So let me get this straight. You did this solely to hurt JMP?'

'Hasn't he told you? I'm assuming you've already talked to him . . . because you're ringing me.'

'I did speak to him . . .'

'And he didn't tell you why?'

'No.'

There was more shrieking. 'Priceless. Fan-fucking . . . tastic.'

'Look, Mr Gribben, what's between you two is your own business. But as for me, I need paying. Please. Or else.'

'Or else what?'

'Or else I'll have to chat to my friend Gary Shrubble at the *Mercury*. See if he's interested in the story.'

There was a brief silence. Tim pictured Mr Gribben winding himself up for a final attack. Instead, his response was even and measured, and lacked its usual interrupted delivery. 'You contact Shrubble,' he said quietly, 'and my friend will be paying your house a visit. You and the two women I've seen you with. And my friend especially likes women, if you know what I mean. In fact, now you're here, I'm going to ring him anyway. Get him to come round. One night soon. Four, St Paul's Square, isn't it? Blue front door, flimsy back door? He'll be through that in a fucking flash. You won't even know he's inside till it's too late. So watch your back, Power,' he snorted, 'watch it well.'

And with that, Mr Gribben hung up, and Tim was left with a threat all the more worrying for its calm enunciation.

Stubble

Outside, Gary Shrubble finally got his car going. He had made a number of attempts to encourage the vehicle to move, all of which had been in some way flawed. First, he had wrestled the thing into gear, checked his mirrors and floored the accelerator, only to realize that he hadn't started the engine. Second, he had then forgotten to disengage the hand-brake, which had severely hampered his progress. Third, when all seemed to be going smoothly, he had reversed into a stationary car, courtesy of being in the wrong gear. At the fourth attempt, Gary made his way out of Quayside Landings and through the side streets of Taunsley, drifting occasionally across lanes. Two miles further, he reached the imposing factory gates of Jenkins Meat Products and parked with some difficulty in a cul-de-sac facing the large industrial complex. Rummaging around in the heavily stained glovebox, he retrieved a notepad, three whisky minia-tures, his omnipresent Dictaphone and an electric razor. Using the rear-view mirror, he ran the shaver over the puffy contours of his skin, whistling as he did so, the tremor in his hands encouraging him to miss whole tracts of stubble. Happy with the result, Gary opened a miniature and splashed it over his skin.

'Best aftershave there is,' he muttered, picking up his notebook.

Another series of local news stories awaited him. With all the enthusiasm of a blind man at a beauty pageant, he began to dictate.

'Right. Story One. **Doc In The Dock**. Dr Ashok Kumar of . . . wherever the fuck . . . is being prosecuted for failing to spot a near-fatal case of . . .'

Gary struggled to focus on the name of a rare syndrome he had scribbled on the back of his hand.

'Ashbrought . . . Askbinder . . . Asthbright . . . have to make the fucker up . . . *Ashbrighton* disease in a young woman from Netherton. Dr Kumar has refused to comment, except to say that "Medicine is a big thing and you can't know all of it." An independent medical tribunal will look into the claims. It seems that . . .'

Gary yawned and stretched. People were walking past his car. Glancing at the dashboard clock he realized he had been asleep. This was not unusual, particularly when compiling local stories. It was a quarter past six and a steady stream of relieved workers was filing out of the factory. Mr Jenkins didn't usually leave the site until around seven. Gary sat up and watched intently. From his position, he could just make out Jenkins's Range Rover at the far side of the car park. He opened a Top Class pasty and prepared himself for another low-nutrition meal. The pasty was chewy, stringy and noxious, but washed down with two whisky miniatures seemed to do the trick. Gary spent a number of minutes removing the crumbly debris of his food from the folds of his suit and placing them in the ashtray until a movement ahead caught his eye. Jenkins was struggling into his car, accompanied by three men. Even by the pork factory's low standards of personnel, these workers were meat packers of the roughest variety. The Range Rover sped towards the exit and Gary struggled to start his car. He was excited. Finally, Jenkins was panicking.

Staying a discreet distance behind, Gary followed the car to an industrial estate on the other side of town. Jenkins stopped in a lay-by and all four doors opened. It was approaching dusk and the men glanced round apprehensively at the rear of the vehicle. Jenkins said something to them and removed what looked like a couple of petrol cans, then they walked across a short stretch of broken tarmac towards a factory building. Gary noted with interest a huge sign that read 'Top Class Pasties Ltd'. His stomach rumbled uncomfortably, its contents nearing their spiritual home. He climbed stiffly out of his car and crept to a vantage point. Fifty yards away, one of the men picked up a brick and threw it at a window, which failed to break. There was much gesturing and discussion before another, larger stone was lobbed. A third lump of concrete winged through the air and similarly failed to worry the toughened glass. Finally, the largest meat packer picked up a metal pipe and javelined it at the window, breaking a reasonable hole. A small cheer went up, which was immediately quelled by Mr Jenkins. Gary struggled to contain himself. This was the big moment. Stake-out after stake-out and finally his hunch was paying off. Missing people, industrial accidents, commercial skulduggery . . . he searched for suitable phrases to pepper The Big Story with. Then he realized he had left his camera in the car. He scuttled back to his vehicle, a cigarette pointing the way, and ripped open the door. He froze. The alarm was screaming at him. He had left the fucker on. Headlines slipped off the page, print dissolved before his eyes. He desperately tried to focus on his key fob to find the button that switched it off. Seconds later, the first meat packer appeared. Gary Shrubble knew there was little point trying to escape. A second thug showed up. The alarm died. The final heavy arrived, followed slowly by Mr Jenkins himself, who was sweating from the short walk. Gary leant against the lumpen bodywork of his Sierra.

'Gary Shrubble,' Mr Jenkins began. 'So nice to see you. What brings you to a deserted factory site late in the evening?'

'Working on a story,' Gary slurred.

'What about?'

'An FSA man, a fat cunt, a trail of clues pointing in his direction.'

Mr Jenkins laughed, and his trio of gorillas guffawed as well. 'I think you've got the wrong end of the stick.'

'And how might that be?'

'What you mean is an FSA man, a *one-armed* cunt and a trail of clues . . .'

'Derek Gribben?'

'Why do you think we're here?'

'I was hoping to find out.'

'Look, sometimes you've got to take the law into your own hands. Sometimes, with someone like Gribben, you've got to come mob-handed. There's a lot you don't know about that fucker . . .'

'Oh, I know all about Derek Gribben.'

'I don't think you know everything.'

'The FSA man told me a few things before he left.'

'Yeah, well, did it ever cross your mind that he

253

might have been feeding you information that he had been paid to deliver?'

'How do you mean?'

'Figure it out. You're the journalist. Just remember that a lot of people are scared of Gribben and that he's got a lot to gain in a small town like this.'

Mr Jenkins turned away and his men followed him, slightly crestfallen that there was to be no beating.

Gary Shrubble stood and watched them go. They climbed back into the vehicle and left the site. The Big Story suddenly had another element.

Fury

At best, it was a ludicrous line-up. Four pale white males, who appeared suspiciously police-like, standing cither side of a huge tattooed man with short hair and olive skin. Simon Jasper and Tim Power had been encouraged into the bare magnolia room to stand just feet from the assembled ranks. This was the last thing Tim wanted to do. After Gribben's threats and the skinhead's attack he would have been happier not swapping air with the source of his recent fear. However, the police had finally apprehended their man, who had been hiding for some days in a garden shed, and were keen to have him identified and charged.

Simon was advised to take his time and, when he was certain, to leave the room. Outside, he would indicate his choice by silently circling a number on a notepad. Simon, however, had other ideas. Strong medication gushed through his veins, drowning such delicate considerations in its wake. He paced up and down, relishing the power of the situation. When the police had come to Quayside Landings, his description had resulted in Alistaire Smythe's capture. This was his baby. Four of the protagonists smiled back at him as he grinned along the line. The central suspect, however, was less enthusiastic. Simon paraded in front of the men time and time again, gaining confidence on each journey. He was beginning to enjoy himself. And with each pass of the main offender, he beamed a little more. Suddenly the duty sergeant appeared to lose patience.

'Have you made your choice?' he asked curtly.

Simon stopped in front of the tall thug.

'Yeah, it's the Asian gentleman here,' he said, pointing proudly ahead. 'He's the one.'

The man in question appeared to take this news badly. After some spirited swearing, he had to be restrained by his fellow suspects, all of whom, it turned out, had handcuffs in their possession. Tim monitored the large skinhead's progress and took a couple of steps back. The skinhead was busy shrugging off the considerable efforts of his co-suspects. Things were in danger of getting a little too interesting.

'Asian? Fucking Asian?' the man screamed, with two policemen each side failing to control their suspect. 'That's fucking offensive, that is. If I catch hold of you . . .'

'OK, Indian then,' Simon added, attempting to atone for what he believed to be disrespectful stereotyping. 'Or Pakistani.'

His efforts only seemed to encourage the man. Tim tugged his arm. 'I don't think he's . . .'

'I mean, no offence. You've got your culture and I've got mine. Just because you're black, or brown or whatever . . .'

'Si, shut the fuck up.'

'I'm only trying to placate him.'

Tim watched the skinhead bite one of the officers and headbutt another. He didn't appear particularly placated. In fact, it was time to make a rapid retreat. 'Let's get out of here,' he urged.

Alistaire Smythe lunged forwards, just a couple of feet away, almost foaming at the mouth in fury. He aimed a punch at Simon, which whooshed through the air, narrowly missing him. The coppers regrouped and grabbed a limb each. Ali growled and grunted, pulling policemen back and forth with every movement of his body. Hindered as he was, he started to tire, the four officers finally getting on top of things through their weight of numbers. As the dull ache of fatigue began to sap his fight, his ears caught the parting words of the security guard who had identified him.

'A disgrace to peace-loving Hindus, Sikhs and Muslims everywhere,' Simon said, leaving the room.

A new fight suddenly surged through Ali's bull-like body, a fresh burst of adrenaline washing away the fatigue. His fists started flailing with renewed enthusiasm, his head butted with increased eagerness and his jaws clamped with enhanced hunger. Within seconds the coppers were reeling away, bruised, broken or bitten. Ali sensed victory and leapt over the counter and sprinted out of the door. There were just two more small problems to deal with. And the wankers couldn't have got far.

Herding Cats

Sprinting through the grounds of the nearby Taunsley District Hospital, Tim began to regret attending the identity parade. It had been an act of solidarity with the previously insecure security guard. Now it appeared an act of dangerous folly. The skinhead was almost upon him, snarling and growling as he hunted down his prey. They tore through a car park and Tim knew his minutes were numbered.

From the moment he left the police station, a series of dots were beginning to join themselves into a line of motive. He had often lacked moments of clarity in his life and could now see that the answer was simple. Persuade a rabid lunatic to chase you through the streets and your mind suddenly becomes focused on the bigger picture. The Pork War of 1995 to 1997, the deaths . . . it was all beginning to gel as his lungs gasped for air. Missing people, huge machines with teeth of steel, corruption, the stench of something even more rotten than pork pies, the shattering of an uneasy truce, random beatings and intimidation, threats and counter-threats, an entire economy ankledeep in porcine blood. Derek Gribben being Mr Rhinegold. Mr Jenkins as the rival manufacturer. Gary Shrubble's obsession with Jenkins Meat Products. Alistaire

Smythe working for Gribben. And now the skinhead was literally breathing down his neck. Gripped by panic, Tim's brain continued to assimilate recently learnt facts as if his life depended upon it. The town's dubious events had lain dormant for over six years, an itchy purple scar on Taunsley's belly. People had quietly forgotten and busied themselves with their families and jobs. But now it was happening again. The town was, he finally concluded, about to experience Pork War Two. And Tim Power, doing all he could to avoid hospitalization, in the middle of a hospital, was, in a way that he couldn't quite grasp, exactly at the centre of it.

On the far side of the site, Shamus Farley was busy scything through sticky tarmac with a pneumatic drill. The ageing road digger was operating without ear protection and was steadily going deaf. One floor above, patients in the Auditory Department were having difficulty hearing their test noises above the din. A nurse in Audiology spotted a number on Shamus's van and dialled it. Shamus continued to drill, his entire body shaking, and his mobile phone, which was set to vibrate, went unanswered. The nurse sighed and hung up. Regrettably, there was no easy way for Shamus to know he'd been called. If he programmed the phone to vibrate, he couldn't feel it even when he rested because his body still quivered. If he set it to ring, he couldn't hear it when he drilled, or when he didn't, due to the buzzing in his ears. So Shamus drilled on regardless, becoming ever more deaf. The hard of hearing remained even harder of hearing. In the middle distance, a smartly suited man was sprinting in his direction. Behind, an ominously excited skinhead pursued him, and appeared to be gaining.

As they came closer, Shamus bent down to pick

something out of his trench, and cursed. There were, he had discovered, two main problems with holes. First, the volume of the stuff you removed always seemed to be greater than the size of the crater you had dug. Second, holes were self-filling. You only had to turn your back on one for a matter of seconds and it would already be stuffing itself full again with dirt or tarmac or gravel or crisp packets. Yes, digging ditches was as pointless as herding cats. You were always working against the laws of nature, fighting gravity, opening ground which preferred to be shut. He shook his head, clinging grimly to the pneumatic tool, leaning on it, his arms straight, the handle tucked up under his stomach, and disrupted another stretch of tarmac. He knew he couldn't do this job for much longer. As well as the prevailing tide of holes always flowing against him, his approaching deafness was making work increasingly difficult. These days his boss simply pointed at the drill and then at the patch of ground which needed digging. Besides, there was a new crop of drillers eager to take his place, with larger beerguts and more daring bum-cleavage. All in all, Shamus knew his days were numbered.

Alistaire Smythe was gaining on the advert ponce in front. Another hundred yards and he would have him. And then let him try and look so smug. They rounded a corner. He could almost reach the cunt. Fingertips, that was all. A few more paces and he would be able to grip the back of his neck. They dodged in and out of food trolleys and wheelchairs. He stretched his long arm as far as it would reach and leant forwards, still sprinting flat out. The smug bastard was floundering. This time, he would inflict a proper beating. It was all over. And then he was even further forwards. Too far forwards. The ground pounced up to meet his face. A

260

scraping, jarring sensation consumed his nose. Lightness and darkness swapped places. Images exploded behind his eyes. His head came to a rapid stop and his neck jolted. Palms became raw sources of pain and gravel. Areas of skin were burning. He lifted his face up and groaned, soreness and frustration assaulting him with similar success.

Shamus dragged his drill to a new position and tugged at the thick rubber hose that pushed high-pressure air through his tool. It was caught on something and he cursed. This was his manacle, the umbilical cord which kept him perpetually within ten yards of the generator's heavy diesel fumes. In this way, he felt unendingly tethered to a defeating piece of machinery. He pulled again, to no avail, and glanced back at the hole he had just been excavating with some irritation. The fucker was full again. Not with tarmac or earth or gravel or crisp packets, but with skinhead. And a strangely brown one at that. The man appeared to have tripped over the drill pipe and was now sitting on it, slowly shaking his head. This was an entirely new branch of the theory to deal with, the third bugger about holes. Occasionally, very occasionally, they filled themselves with large tattooed people. Down the road, the smartly dressed man was making a swift getaway. He rounded a corner and disappeared from sight.

Shamus walked along his hose to the point at which it was snagged. 'Do-you-speak-the-English?' he asked the foreign-looking man slowly.

The skinhead stood up, dusted himself down and appeared to take the nature of the enquiry badly. A punch was thrown, and then another. Soon after, a shocked eyewitness dialled 999, and an ambulance was scrambled to clean up the carnage.

261

Driller Killer

The ambulance driver was getting nowhere fast. In fairness, the scene that greeted him after he had raced over from Bridgton Infirmary, some six miles away, was one of unusual chaos. The clammy tarmac glistened with blood. Taunsley District Hospital didn't have a Casualty department, as an efficiency measure that regularly failed to impress anyone from the town who injured themselves. His patient, therefore, had been forced to endure twenty minutes of obvious agony surrounded by indifferent members of the medical profession while the driver negotiated his way through the ring-road traffic. He tried again.

'So tell me what happened.'

'What?' Shamus asked, rubbing his jaw.

'What happened?'

'What happened?'

'Yes.' There was blood everywhere.

'To who?'

'To you.'

'Me?'

'Yes. Look,' the ambulance man said, changing tack, 'have you seen the toes?'

'Whose clothes?'

'The *toes*. I've had a report about some toes.'

'Oh yes. The toes. They're in the hole.'

'Which hole?'

Shamus turned and pointed to the trench he had just dug. This was just one more thing that apparently clogged his holes up. 'There,' he said.

The ambulance driver followed a fresh splattering of red which led away from the trench. 'And I was told there were two of you. Where's the other man?' he shouted.

'Dunno.' Shamus shrugged, his shoulders aching. 'Ran off when he heard the siren.'

'Christ.' Bridgton was bad, but Taunsley . . . At least in his home town they had the decency to hang around and get stitched back together. Things were getting out of hand. The paramedic walked back to his cab and picked up the radio. This was a job for the police. Fifteen minutes of uninspiring conversation with the deaf driller, and a policeman sauntered up to the scene.

'I've come about the fracas,' he said.

'Well, we seem to have lost the main protagonist. And he seems to have lost some toes.'

'*Toes*?' the constable asked, understanding arriving late.

'Toes,' the medic replied.

'What the fuck sort of . . . Listen, Mr Farley,' he began, addressing Shamus, 'would you mind telling us what the hell has been going on here?'

'Where?'

'Here. What happened?'

Shamus glanced around. The sun was glaring with rare intensity. His eyes were no longer vibrating. A small amount of hearing was possible between the numbing waves of ringing that habitually plagued his ears. His jaw clicked uncomfortably when he opened

263

and closed it and his shoulder felt like it might be damaged in some way. It had all been so fast. One moment, weighing up the philosophy of holes. The next, being assaulted by a swarthy skinhead. The policeman was staring at him, a curious expression frozen on his clean-shaven face. 'Well,' he began, 'it was like this.'

Pneumatic Ease

Fleeing the scene as rapidly as he could, Alistaire Smythe was once again forced to curse his luck. Whereas beating up an elderly road worker was well within his abilities under normal circumstances, fate had conspired to make things difficult for him. What made events worse was the fact that proceedings had turned sour at the very moment he was about to inflict a monumental beating on the advertiser who had been the cause of all his recent misfortune. He was ten, maybe only five, paces from catching him by the scruff of the expensive-suited neck. He could smell his after-shave, almost taste his panic. And then Ali had gone and fallen in a fucking hole.

As he left the hospital site, he slowed for a moment to consider his options. He was in a great deal of discomfort, which was becoming more acute by the second. However, it wasn't wise to hang around. The best thing, he decided in between paralysing spasms of pain, was to retreat home and try to stem the bleeding there. With every difficult pace, he came to see that the whole mess his life was in was the fault of one person – a Greek waiter on the island of Kos. This would be, as actors said, his motivation. Peering down at his boots, he was rocked by a jolt of nausea, and resolved not to look in that direction again. Hobbling on, Ali added the road driller to his mental list of legitimate future targets. Tim Power. Gary Shrubble. Simon Jasper. And now the bastard driller. He tried to relive the events and work through the cause of the current state of affairs.

Everything had started so encouragingly. Picking himself out of the hole, he had planned to quickly deal with the driller, before once again pursuing the advert wanker. He swung a promising right, followed by a speculative left, both blows catching the man squarely. So far, so good. And then the old fucker had put his head down and run at him. Catching Ali entirely unawares and off balance, he had toppled into the hole for a second time. Before he had had a chance to inflict another killer one-two on the Irish fucker, he heard a disturbingly loud noise, which was worryingly close. Lifting his head, he saw that his luck was out. The road digger was coming towards him, waving his pneumatic drill round like a motorized scythe. Closest to him were Ali's size thirteens, sticking invitingly out of the trench. He had managed to snatch one leg back into the safety of the hole, but that was all. And then the man, with a sadistic grin on his face born from a lifetime of frustrating manual labour, a fizzy drink that had been shaken every day for forty years, ploughed the drill into his foot. Machinery that was designed to damage layers of tarmac pounded through Ali's steel toecaps with apparent glee. His toes, next in line, were shredded with pneumatic ease. As far as Ali could see, he had lost at least two of them, maybe three. But there had been no time to stand around counting missing appendages. The short stocky motherfucker was coming at him again. Ali had pulled himself up, judged it better not to try to throw an off-balance

266

punch, and hobbled away as fast as his broken foot would allow.

Alistaire Smythe leaned against a wall and considered his narrowing options. His energy was draining from fighting coppers and losing digits. The police would be looking for him, so home was out. There was no way he was going to hide out in a garden shed again. He was leaking blood at a distressing rate. With any luck they might be able to stitch most of the parts of him back together. He turned around and staggered back towards the scene of the amputations. As he did so, he made a policy decision. Although Gribben had been calling the shots until now, Ali was going to seize control of the situation. Gribben's greedy plans could go fuck themselves. He was going to devote himself to Tim Power's suffering. As soon as he was reunited with his toes, he was going to treat him to a severe kicking. Then he would really get started. But first things first. He was on the point of collapse, and leaving blood like a Hansel and Gretel trail for the cops to follow. A passer-by watched as the dark skinhead went suddenly pale. She phoned for an ambulance. Somewhere in not so nearby Bridgton, another ambulance was persuaded to battle several miles in his direction.

Merchant of Menace

Everyone knows one dodgy geezer. No matter how educated you are, how far removed from the inevitable violence of life, there is at least one person you know who fits this description. Even self-employed advertising executives.

Tim was unsettled. He had narrowly escaped another beating. The business was finally about to go under. He had become caught up in a vendetta between two unsavoury businessmen, one of whom had threatened to break into his house and attack the two women he lived with. There was only one person who could help him now. For when you are threatened with fire, as the man says, it is wise to fight it with fire.

Tim knew Brian. They had met just before the shooting of the Boots 24 Hours campaign. The casting director, had he not shaved it off to appear fashionable, would have been tearing his hair out as filming was about to begin. They were one builder short. Nowhere on the books of local casting agencies was there anyone remotely real-life enough to play the part of Rough Builder #3. Rough Builders #1 and 2 were already stretching the point, having cancelled minor roles in *The Merchant of Venice* at Stratford to cash in on a lucrative advert. What the campaign lacked, the shaven-headed casting director readily acknowledged, was authenticity.

Tim had come up with the goods. Before heading for the set, he had been forced to show a workman around his flat. Various jobs needed sorting on behalf of the landlord. Brian was one of the ropiest-looking characters he had ever met. He had been about to collect some of the flat's more expensive property before making a quick getaway in his van, but Tim had stopped him. 'Have you ever acted?' he enquired.

'As what?' Brian asked, surreptitiously replacing a camera and a Walkman.

'As anything.'

'Receiver of stolen goods, once.'

'No, I mean like on TV.'

Brian was unsure whether to punch the swanky suit in front of him, but his curiosity had been aroused. 'Why?'

Tim explained, and took Brian to the set, where the casting director felt so threatened that he immediately signed him up. Brian turned out to be as naturally dodgy in front of a camera as he was away from one, and thoroughly outshone his fellow Shakespearean actors. For a few glorious weeks, Brian was on TV up to five times a day, and was forced to stop robbing houses on account of being too recognizable. The repeat fees more than made up for it, however.

It had been a couple of years, but Tim picked up the phone and dialled Brian's mobile. Brian answered. In the background was the unmistakable sound of poorly planned building activity. 'Yeah,' he grouched.

'Brian? It's Tim Power – you know, from the Boots—'

'Tim, you old cunt! How're you doing?'

'Good. And you?'

'Can't grumble.'

'Look, Brian, there's something I need you to do for me.'

'Another advert?' Brian asked eagerly.

'No. Something a bit more, well . . . Can we meet up and talk about it?'

'Course. No problem. When?'

'Tomorrow?'

'Definitely can't do tomorrow.'

'I'll make it worth your while.'

'Not a chance.'

'Oh, go on.'

'OK then. Tomorrow it is.'

Of Brian's most glaringly obvious faults, by far the most debilitating was his ease of suggestion. Part of the reason Brian had never progressed further than his dual enterprises of building and stealing while building was the sheer ease with which people were able to manipulate him. After only ten or so minutes in his company, even the least perceptive of house-holders would detect a certain vulnerability about him absent from the rest of the building industry. For a man who wouldn't break sweat tearing you limb from limb, this was indeed a handicap. Canny homeowners who chatted with Brian while he botched menial repairs usually managed to get the work done for virtually nothing. Except, that is, for the cameras, watches and jewellery he stole while they were making him cups of tea and planning how to use his suggestibility to their advantage. In the end, things often worked out fairly even.

It was Brian's pliable nature that had made him such a convincing actor. He had believed the lines, lived the part, done exactly what was required of him, with no tantrums, no in-fighting and no quibbling. His Shakespearean colleagues had been appalled. With such an unprofessional attitude, they agreed with some satisfaction, his acting career would go nowhere. And they were right, and, as they thought about it, mighty glad there hadn't actually been any tantrums or in-fighting, because Brian was not a man two highly trained thespians necessarily wanted to come to blows with.

The following morning, Tim made his way to London. Nothing happened during the night, but he had spent the hours nervously pacing about, a hammer in one hand and a screwdriver in the other. He was ready for an attack at any moment. The journey was only two hours but felt longer. It had been a few months, the first time he had returned. He had to act quickly. If Gribben's threat was real, a large skinhead who had already assaulted him once was about to do so again. When he found him, Brian was ruining a job on a three-storey terrace in Islington.

'So what can I do you for?' he asked. Brian wasn't overly tall, but what he lacked in height he more than made up for in width. His dark hair was short and dense and grew with unsettling vigour. His nose was on the squashed side, and what little of his brow poked from under his impenetrable hair jutted vertically up, giving the impression of an ideal head-butting implement.

'I'm in trouble.'

'How do you mean?'

'A psycho is on his way to hurt me. He's started to ring my house at night, threatening to break in and attack me and the two girls I live with.'

'Two? Lucky bastard.'

'It's not quite like that.'

'Do you think either of them would, you know . . . with me?'

271

'No.'

'Right. So what about the cops?'

'Same old story. Won't do anything till he does something.'

'And what do you want me to do?'

'Scare him.'

'Bit of a ponce, is he?' Brian queried, scratching his stubble like he was considering the answer to a difficult question.

'No, that's the problem. He's a big bloke who enjoys fighting.'

'I'm beginning to like him.'

'Well, for a few quid, do you think you might dislike him?'

'How much?'

'Hundred a day. Plus travel expenses.' Tim suddenly remembered Brian's weakness for persuasion. 'I mean fifty. I'm a bit broke. What d'you think?'

'Fifty quid, eh? Call it seventy-five.'

'OK, how about fifty-five?'

'Seventy.'

'Fifty-five.'

'Sixty-five.'

'Fifty-five.'

'Sixty.'

'Fifty-five.'

'Right, fifty-five. Deal.'

Tim watched Brian glance at his Guccimarni watch and lick his lips. He made a mental note to hide it from him.

'So when do you want this geezer sorted?'

'Now.'

'I can't leave the site.'

'You have to.'

Brian glanced around. 'OK. But let's have a couple of

pints on the way to the station. I know this fucking great pub where you can open the back of the fruit machine with a screwdriver.'

Tim once again looked at his watch. While it didn't work, it was highly fashionable and difficult not to check on a regular basis through force of habit. He guessed it was about 2.30 p.m. 'OK,' he said reluctantly, 'but only a couple.'

'Fine.' Brian picked up a short metal bar and tucked it inside his jacket.

'Now promise me you're not going to get pissed.'

'Like you said, we'll just have a couple.'

'Right. We have to remain focused. We've got a fight on our hands. Any night now a large psychopath is going to break into my house.' Tim walked into the street to hail a cab. 'And when he does, he won't know what the hell has hit him.'

Sheep in Wolf's Clothing

Simon Jasper stood back and admired his handiwork. The transformation was almost complete. Virtually the entire exterior of the car had been altered. The paintwork was fluorescent blue, from its original off-white with a hint of rust. A hefty spoiler had been welded onto the roof just before the precipitous downwards slope of the hatchback. The wheels were now alloy, the tyres fat and slick. The bonnet had a bulge in it, where an unwieldy engine block might have resided if Simon had chosen to insert one. The windows were dark and menacing. The Sports Silencer peeked out of the back, under the enlarged bumper. The standard numberplates had been replaced by ones with lettering which leant slightly to one side, encouraging the impression of speed. Flared wheel arches and a less than subtle body kit made the car six inches wider than it was before. Across the top of the windscreen a sticker optimistically proclaimed 'MOTORSPORT'. The wipers now matched the Nova's pearlescent blue. The whole car had been lowered by four inches so that it sat taut and squat, close to the road, and even closer to speed bumps. All in all, it looked the business. Already, with his stereo thumping out repetitive bass lines, he was getting what he believed to be envious looks in the High Street. Several cars had even attempted to drag-race him at traffic lights, which Simon had been forced to duck out of for obvious performance-related issues. Indeed, if the car did have one residual weakness, it was that the 948cc motor was unlikely to provoke much interest from the town's single speed camera. Still, he stuck to his guns. This was all about transformation, about change, about influencing the way people saw him. No longer was he an insecure security guard. He was a man with the meanest-looking car in Taunsley.

With each new day, Simon had taken one more step towards rehabilitation. He had worked feverishly, day and night. The car-park lights at Quayside Landings were bright enough to see him through until the morning, when he drove his beloved vehicle home, slept a little and resumed the delirious activity. While he polished and painted, his mother continued to steam-clean the front steps, dust the front door and scrub the windows. He would watch her, caught in the reflective paintwork, once again running her Dyson over the patio. Had they possessed a lawn, he felt sure she would have hoovered that as well. From time to time, Simon would yawn, stretch and take a break, heading into the house for refreshment. Inside was a total mess. Nothing was ever thrown away. Bags of shopping sat on the kitchen counter unemptied and simply eaten out of. Boxes of junk lounged around everywhere. Not a single surface was left untouched by clutter. And yet his mother, dressed always in her neatest clothes, continued to polish the outside as if her life depended upon it.

At school, his mother's behaviour had cost him the chance of making any real friends. Classmates came round just the once, and after that were strangely elusive. He was the weird one, by virtue of the sort of house his mum kept. His father left when he was young, and so there was little possibility of changing her ways. She scrubbed and scrubbed the exterior, while the interior rotted away.

With the car virtually complete, Simon leant proudly against the driver's door and took stock of the situation. His life savings had been swallowed up in the project, but the results were self-evident. The Vauxhall Nova now looked pleasingly evil. And not only was it an object of brutal beauty, it had also recently saved him from a thorough kicking. After the police line-up he had been able to sprint for his car and, at the second or third attempt, start the engine and pull away from danger, with the psycho who had broken into Quayside Landings switching his attention to Tim Power instead. As he thought about it, pausing to scrape what looked like birdshit off one of the door panels, he recalled that although he had been glad to escape, the drawback was the alarmingly sluggish performance of the car. Indeed, this seemed to be rapidly deteriorating, which was glaringly apparent when he'd had to take such rapid evasive action. The trouble was that the ageing Nova was now weighed down by the numerous additions he had made to its original spec. Sturdy wedges of plastic had been bolted onto it. Huge fat tyres tormented the engine. The stereo didn't help either, the boot full of an immense bass bin and the bonnet housing an amp that would have embarrassed many nightclubs. But other than this small concern, things were improving by the day. He was flashing less, his medication had been reduced and still he was happy. Dr Ann Hillyard had been amazed and wrote copious notes about his revolution. She asked probing questions, ones which he now felt fully able to answer. He hadn't exposed himself to her or anyone else in several weeks. All in all, he felt, life was getting better, both for Simon and for the females of Taunsley.

Ali's Angels

Zoe was the first to wake. She heard the creak of a door. Someone sounded to be staggering around. She groped about for the phone. It was downstairs. Drawers were being tried, heavy footsteps banging and scraping. She reached under her bed, took out a small box and left her room.

Ann heard her door open. A figure stood over her. An outstretched arm held something. She strained to see, frozen in terror. In the half light she saw that it was a gun. A hand was placed firmly over her mouth. She tried to scream, but the hand pressed harder. And then the intruder spoke. 'We've got company,' Zoe whispered, releasing her grip. 'You still got your target pistol?'

'You bet. No ammo though.'

'Me neither. Still, get the gun.'

'Who is it?'

'Fuck knows. But they're inside.'

Ann grabbed her weapon from the top of the wardrobe. 'What now?'

The stairs were being climbed. Slow thuds of badly disguised progress. 'Put the bedside light on. Place a towel at the bottom of the door.'

Ann did as she was told. Zoe blinked and stared

frantically around. 'You got some of those blusher-ball things?' she asked urgently.

'On the dresser.'

Footsteps were creaking down the hallway. They were slow and uneven. Zoe heard her door being tried. Her breathing became erratic. She grabbed a handful of the small, solid make-up spheres and passed half to Ann. 'Load,' she instructed. Both women poured several tiny spheres into the holding compartments of their high-power air pistols.

'I'll take the left,' Ann said, wiping nervous sweat from her forehead. 'You keep him busy. I'll try to get down to the phone.'

'What if there's more than one?'

'Keep firing. Remember sexy Guy Rogers's advice – Target the Torso.'

The bathroom door was opened and then closed again. 'Look, Ann, in case this goes badly wrong . . .'

'Yes?'

The handle began to turn. 'I know about you and Tim,' Zoe whispered tersely.

Ann was silent, fixated on the door. It was last-confession-before-dying time. 'We almost slept together,' she muttered. 'Sorry.' The door opened gradually. 'It only happened once. But I think we've got more important issues.'

Ann managed an edgy half-smile in Zoe's direction, which was not reciprocated. A long arm appeared through the aperture, holding a substantial knife. The door was flung open. A large psychotic man filled the exit. Ann took a step backwards into the shadows, seconds from hysteria. The psycho lunged forwards.

'Where the fuck is that cunt Powers?' Alistaire Smythe shouted, lumbering towards them.

'Not here,' came the reply from the two females in front of him, cowering in the darkness.

'I can see that. Now where the fuck is he?'

'London,' one of them answered. 'And he'll be back any minute with help.'

'Help?'

'A big bloke he knows. Really hard . . .' The tanned blonde dried up.

'A builder who's been in adverts . . .' The brunette similarly ran out of steam.

'Adverts?' Ali screamed. 'Adverts? *I've* been in adverts. Why the fuck do you think I'm here?'

'They really will be in the house any minute.'

'So maybe we'll just wait for him.' Ali closed the door, and kept his knife pointing forwards. 'Got me a nice couple of hostages. Should be interesting. So which one of you is his bitch?'

'Bitch?'

'Slag. Woman. *Girl* – ' Ali contorted his face to give a mock politically correct expression – *'friend.'*

The two women glanced at each other, and Ali wondered whether Power was banging both of them. Another injustice shuddered through his body and his desire for retaliation surged once more. A poofter in a suit had two women, while he had none. He limped forwards, newly reacquainted toes fighting to be free from their stitches again. As he peered down at his swollen foot, loosely wrapped in an enormous wad of bandages, yet more fury spurred him on. He had lost nearly three pints of blood because of that fucking road driller. His only hope was that whatever donor had replaced it was white. Staring at the frightened females ahead, Ali gained a desire for revenge against all his present misadventure. He had never stabbed a woman before. 'I've changed my mind,' he said, thoughts spilling out of his mouth. 'Maybe we won't wait for you to be rescued. I've had some bad luck, and you two are going to have some of your own.' The women stood defiantly still, three or four paces away. 'It's time to show Tim Power some of his own medicine.'

The penultimate step towards his quarry was an unexpectedly painful one for Ali. Although all paces had been painful to some degree since his tangle with the pneumatic drill, this stride was especially excruciating. He stopped. His chest was stinging, and his hand felt like it had been lacerated. And then his thigh was on fire. He peered through the gloom, perplexed. The women seemed to be holding something. As his arm suffered a similarly agonizing scald, he belatedly saw that they were brandishing what looked like guns. 'Shit!' he screamed, as his knee was hit. He didn't know what they were firing. Despite smelling good and leaving an orangey-pink stain, it sure hurt, like a miniature paintball hitting home. Bending down to examine the latest wound in more detail, Ali was aware of two shadowy forms darting past him, one on either side. The door was thrown open, and he spun around and hobbled after them. The girls reached the stairs and launched themselves down, pausing only to turn and fire. Halfway down the stairs after them he heard their voices in the kitchen.

'About that Tim thing,' one of them said.

'We'll sort it out later,' the other replied.

'Anyway, nice shooting.'

'Not so bad yourself.'

'We need dried peas, lentils, anything.'

'Multivitamins?'

'Be the healthiest thing that motherfucker has tasted for a long time.'

Ali reached the door, and listened for a second more in a vain attempt to discover just what the fuck was going on.

'Do they fit?'

'Lentils are best. Here. Quick. He's coming. Remember your target practice. Let's aim a bit higher.'

Ali didn't like the sound of the last bit. He thundered into the kitchen, knife outstretched, a number of bruises already breaking out over his body. The lights were fully on and for the first time he managed a good look at the duo and their weapons. At best, they were air pistols. That would be no match for a combat knife. Once more, he advanced towards them, and once more he provoked a volley of whizzing pellets, some of which hit home while others bounced off walls. A dried lentil hit Ali straight on the nose, feeling like someone had driven a nail into it. Another one caught him on the chin and made him scream. The bitches were going for his face. He was thwacked in the groin, a single testicle bearing the brunt. Ali began to back away. Still the onslaught continued. Shielding his face, he noted between his fingers that they appeared to be actively enjoying themselves. They were leaping around like in the movies, keeping each other covered, jumping out from behind kitchen cupboards, one of them firing in quick and painful succession while the other reloaded. Still more missiles hit home, the air alive with hissing objects that carried the punch of vicious kidney jabs.

And then he heard the blonde say, 'How's your aim?'

'Pretty good,' the dark-haired one replied.

'Aim for his foot then.'

Ali attempted to retreat still further, but was too late. Two surprisingly effective thwacks banged against his tender foot, doing all they could to rip out his stitches. He began to regret escaping from the hospital so soon. Ali had no idea how long reattached toes took to heal, but guessed it was longer than a couple of days. As a fighting force, he realized he was severely compromised. He turned and staggered into the living room. The light-haired woman sprinted to the left, her accomplice to the right. Caught in the middle, he came to an unsteady halt. Cowering slightly, he tried to sum up his options. There was no way through to the front door. The women seemed intent on inflicting more pain. His only chance, Ali decided, was to try and talk his way out of the mess he was in, and then overpower them. 'Look,' he began, 'it's not you I'm after, it's that wanker Power. No disrespect to which one of you's his—'

'I want you to answer carefully,' the brunette said, interrupting him, her pistol pointing at Ali's still stinging groin.

'Yes?'

'How did you refer to us just earlier?'

'Bitches,' Ali swore, encouraging the slap of two more bruising shots.

'And would you like to rephrase that?'

He paused, watching them reload, shovelling what looked like dried peas into their weapons. In the corner of the room, an object called out to him in his hour of need. Always when he was at a low ebb, the same thing happened. Among several bottles, one marked 'Ouzo' had caught his attention. For a second, he smelt the sickly aniseed odour and felt its taste counterpart on his tongue. If there was one thing he craved at this moment, it was Ouzo. But there was little chance of that now, and he grew suddenly angry again from the injustice of the situation. 'No,' he said, in a defiantly suicidal last stand, gaining strength from the spirit, 'you're still bitches.'

As Ali entered possibly the most uncomfortable two minutes of his life, encounters with psychopathic road diggers aside, he spied the phone on the other side of the room, and made a one-legged sprint for it. Protecting himself as best he could, he dialled 999 and asked for the police. 'Two crazed lesbians <ow!> are shooting at me,' he screamed. 'Er, four <fuck!> St Paul's Square. Alistaire <shit!> Nikolaos Smythe <bitch!>. Get here fast <fuck!>. They're armed and dangerous. Hurry <ouch!> before they kill me <shit!>.'

Replacing the receiver, Ali was aware that the shoot-. ing had stopped for a second. He stole a glance at his throbbing hand. There was a dent in the surface of his knuckle and a couple of layers of skin had been removed. It was the same for his other hand, deep tissue bruises already budding in his flesh. The wounds over his body hurt like hell. Running his eyes from left to right across the room, he saw that the dark- and light-haired women were pointing their weapons at him and smiling.

'You know, that blusher really suits him.'

'How are we for ammo?'

'About two stone of dried peas left, couple of bags of lentils, a few multivitamins. Enough to keep him here for a few more days.'

The blonde examined her gun with pride. 'I had no idea just how versatile and powerful these things were.'

Ali was forced to agree. He counted seconds, willing the police to arrive. This was an unusual state of affairs, to say the least. Generally, they turned up without his intervention. He wondered what the fuck was keeping them.

*   *   *

On the other side of Taunsley, an atmosphere of excitement rarely witnessed among its officers was threatening to spill over in the police station. Despite the best wishes of a few of the more cavalier constables, gun crime was non-existent in the town. That was, until now. All three of Taunsley's police cars were scrambled. While there wasn't an armed response team, what there was, and in abundance, was desperation for the kind of action generally witnessed on TV and in films. Canisters of mace, extendable truncheons, pepper spray, rubber batons and even the odd knuckleduster were hastily assembled. Hurtling through Taunsley's slumbering streets, cornering on two wheels, the cars screeched to a dramatic halt in St Paul's Square. There was a mad dash out, each policeman eager to be number one into the line of fire. Gun-toting lesbians were something all of them sincerely hoped to witness at first hand.

The most senior figure among them, Sergeant Michael Flitcroft, stopped in front of the garden gate and raised his right arm. Crouching down, he brought his excitable troop to something approaching order.

'Right, lads,' he said quietly, 'let's get things sorted. No need to get too carried away. On my signal I'm taking a run at the door. Is that clear?'

There were a few crestfallen faces.

'Maybe I should be first in,' a young-looking copper suggested hopefully.

'And why would that be, Rory?'

'I've seen a lot of videos about this.'

'*Videos*?'

'You know, lesbians with guns, that sort of thing. What you've got to do is—'

'Sarge, I've seen them as well.'

'And me.'

'We all have. Remember that one with the two birds out of—'

'These wouldn't be *illegal* videos, would they, by any chance?' their superior officer asked sternly.

Taunsley's lower ranks were unusually quiet. None of the constables met Sergeant Flitcroft's eye.

'Sarge?'

'Yes?'

'If you wrestle one of those lesbians to the ground, and you need a hand with the other, give me a shout.'

'Or me, Sarge,' another constable piped up.

'There will be no wrestling of lesbians to the ground. Not unless I say so. OK?'

The mob shook their heads, each one deciding to disobey this order if the opportunity arose.

'Right,' Sergeant Flitcroft announced, opening the gate slightly, 'let's do this thing.' It was many years since he had seen active service. But this was too good to miss. With a mounting nervousness, he stood up and sprinted towards the house, screaming as he did so. In the very act of readying himself to kick the front door in, however, Michael Flitcroft came to a sudden halt. The door was opening. Through it came a six-foot-four skinhead, virtually in tears. He was covered in what appeared to be make-up of some sort. And rather than evade arrest, the man slumped down on his knees and begged protection from the lunatics inside. Almost immediately, two female forms appeared, dropping their weapons onto the front lawn. An audible sigh of disappointment heaved through the assembled ranks of policemen in the square. While the duo may well have been armed, they certainly weren't the all-action lesbians most of them had optimistically imagined. Knuckledusters fell quietly on the lawn and rubber batons were discreetly put away. A few officers turned and walked back to their cars silently cursing. One of them made a mental note to destroy several of his more dubious videos – after, that was, a final ceremonial viewing.

Hitched

Tim returned the next day with Brian, who was understandably upset to learn that he wouldn't be partaking in any violence. Worse, he was unable to spot anything worth stealing. Two drinks in London had turned into a typical Brian onslaught and they had ended up missing the last train. Tim had frantically called home for an hour and a half but the line had been engaged.

'But I'm all keyed up,' Brian complained, scuffing a shoe along the pavement outside Tim's house.

Tim paid him as promised and dropped him back at the station to await a train that would actually stop in Taunsley. Generally, locomotives tended to pass straight through, almost seeming to accelerate on their approach, making certain they cleared the town even if they ran out of fuel. Eventually, a train dared to linger and he bade Brian a glum farewell. When Tim arrived back at the house, expecting high spirits and further tales of daring escapades, there was a distinctly uncomfortable atmosphere awaiting him.

'What?' he asked, as lodger and girlfriend sat in stony silence.

Ann refused to look at him, preferring instead to examine her fingers for fresh skin to massacre.

'I think you'd better come up to our room,' Zoe said. Tim shrugged and trudged up the stairs a pace behind her. Inside, the cross-examination began in earnest. He sat on the edge of the bed, while Zoe stood, leaning back, her elbows on the windowsill. 'Were you unfaithful to me while I was away?' she asked quietly. She was flushed, trembling slightly. Her eyes darted back and forth, probing Tim's features, already suspecting the worst.

By the hurt in her face, Tim knew better than to try to bullshit her. 'Sort of,' he replied softly.

'Sort of?' Her tone was angry and vulnerable at the same time.

'Well, you know, some kissing, but no actual sleeping.'

Zoe's eyes watered almost instantly. She wiped a tear away with the back of her hand. 'And was this someone I know?'

Tim quickly appreciated that Zoe had insider knowledge. These weren't random enquiries. But to tell the truth would mean a colossally complicated domestic situation. And things were bad enough as they were. He remained silent, squirming, embarrassed, guilty.

'Like someone we live with?'

She knew. The very thing he'd feared had happened. Ann had told Zoe. 'Yes,' he acknowledged sadly. 'Although . . .'

'But how could you sleep with her? She was my friend.'

'I didn't realize that at the time.'

'So that makes it OK?'

He scratched the back of his head like he'd suddenly been stung. A pain was beginning to develop. 'Nothing makes it OK. I'm really very sorry. It was just one of those things. And it wasn't even as if we did much. Just some light fumbling . . .'

'What?'

'Nothing.' Several hundred excuses and reasons flashed through Tim's mind, none of which could help him now. 'But, Zoe, I don't know what to say apart from sorry.'

Zoe stared out of the window, noiselessly crying. After a tense couple of minutes, she said, 'When I came home, I asked you if our relationship had passed the test. And you said yes. So your definition of a successful separation is fucking my friend behind my back and then lying about it?'

He didn't answer. His girlfriend sniffled, and with each involuntarily sharp intake of breath and subsequent sigh, Tim's remorse deepened. He felt the grim certainty of a new headache settling in for a long visit. As his life went from bad to worse, these were becoming increasingly more pronounced, and the gap between the departure of old discomfort and the arrival of fresh shorter and shorter. His left eye flickered. This was the first warning. Soon after, the right followed. His field of vision shrank to a crescent-shaped patch of light. A dull ache seeped forwards from the rear of his skull, gaining in intensity until it grasped his frontal lobes, squeezing them tight. He pictured a cold metal hand inside, slowly folding its fingers to form a fist, his grey matter compressed in the palm, fingers releasing slightly and then clutching, releasing and clutching, tighter each time.

'So I guess we found our answer. If we aren't strong enough apart, we're not strong enough together.'

'I'm not sure . . .'

'And if you can't manage a few short months away from me without looking for – ' Zoe met his eye – '*sex* somewhere else, then we've been wasting our time for the last three years.'

Tim's migraine started to reach its peak, the fist pummelling the inside of his skull. Blood pounded through his temple, as loud as the roar of crashing waves. He sat still, debilitated, consumed, trapped. Even moving his head forwards a fraction gave the impression that his brain was plummeting towards the ground, about to impact on the pavement. As he spoke, his words sounded distant and removed, uttered by someone else. Listening was even more difficult. Tim's concentration was almost entirely consumed by the pain. However, he realized that his hurt was mirrored by that of his girlfriend. 'I thought we'd manage,' he uttered slowly. 'I really did. I knew my feelings for you were strong enough. But don't forget you were the one who went away. A long period apart is never going to be easy. You placed that strain on us. If you'd remained here like we'd planned, nothing like this would have happened.'

'So you're blaming me for your infidelity?' Zoe shouted, blowing her nose raucously on an already damp ball of tissue. 'Well, I'm glad we found out sooner rather than later that if an opportunity did arise you would jump into bed with it.' She fell on the duvet and started to weep uncontrollably. Tim watched the side of her face through his distorted vision, amazed at how plain a pretty female could look when she cried. It was a wonder that nature didn't compensate somehow, making women more attractive when they were upset so that men might feel even more helpless than they did already. He was paralysed with guilt, indecision and numbness. His head was almost unbearable. And still she sobbed, her back heaving every few seconds as fresh torment racked her body. Tim remained rooted to the spot, staring at the carpet, no idea how to react. After an eternity, Zoe's sobs

291

slowed and she blew her nose less frequently. She pushed herself up and began to speak. 'Actually, there's something I should tell you.' She turned to face him, make-up slowly sliding down her face on the back of swollen tears. 'Since we're being frank with each other.'

'Yes?'

'That Aussie bloke I told you about that I hitched with?'

Tim struggled to recall the details among the overwhelming buzzing in his brain. 'Mmm,' he answered slowly.

'I suppose, knowing what I know now, I don't feel as bad at just spitting it out. Look, the reason I cut my trip short was that, well . . .'

'What?'

She began to cry again. 'I ended up having a fling with him.'

'You did what?'

'The guilt killed me. Liz was furious and made me feel worse. I came home because . . .' Zoe was verging on the hysterical.

'Why?' Tim asked dejectedly.

'I was ashamed of what I had done just because I was away from you.' Tim walked over and held her stiffly. 'The great irony is that it took going away from you to find out what we had. I mean, part of my mission was to put some distance between us . . .'

'Too much distance, maybe.'

'To see just how much I loved you, whether this was the one, if I was willing to spend the rest of my life with you living in Taunsley. And yet even in that time, as I realized that, yes, I did want to be with you, I started a relationship with someone else. Bit of a fucker, really.'

'You could say that,' Tim mumbled. He hugged Zoe so hard that she exuded tears. Each time he gripped her, more water appeared in her eyes. In the end he was afraid to grip her so tightly for fear of precipitating any more moisture.

'I guess we failed the test,' Zoe sobbed.

'I guess so,' Tim mumbled. He kissed her cheek again. And in that moment, when his lips touched the powdered surface of Zoe's skin, a decision was made.

Fish and Sea Drive

Cathy Dinsdale strode into the house, nervous, excited, angry, forgiving, hopeful, a jumble of conflicting emotions buzzing around her body. Two weeks was a long time to be without her children, but to be without Barry hadn't proved too difficult. She was an hour early, unable to stay away any longer. She had made her point and there was little to be gained from stretching it out. As she stood in the living room and dropped her bags, it was quickly apparent to her that things had changed. She had been expecting to witness something approaching *The Lord of the Flies*. Instead, it was like *The Sound of Music*'s Von Trapp family in reverse. For a start, all her children were wearing the same colour clothes – a sort of off-white that aspired towards greyness but didn't quite make it. Added to this, when each of them turned around to greet her, she saw that they had numbers on their front and back. While they were far from being unkempt, kemptness too was a fair distance away. The living room had also changed. Its surfaces were festooned with pieces of paper. She walked forwards and read one of them. 'Day Six, Group 2, Offspring 1 and 5, Rota 3b; Homework 17:30–18:45. Chores Category Blue, 18:50–19:15.' Perplexed, Cathy hugged the nearest child to hand and asked her what had been going on.

'Daddy's fish and sea drive,' she answered.

'What?'

'Fish and sea drive,' she repeated.

Cathy looked around for anyone over the age of six. Sarah, who was sporting the number four, stepped forwards. 'We've been running the house like a sick kittie, Daddy says. So we've got to make it better.'

'I can see that,' her mother replied. 'And you don't seem to be wearing any lipstick.'

'Daddy says I'm too young.'

'He's got a point, I suppose. Look, don't tell anyone I'm here. Just have your breakfast like normal. And especially don't mention to Daddy that I'm back.' And so, instead of hugging all of her children in turn, Cathy wedged herself behind the open door of the lounge and watched events through the gap of the frame. Barry was out of sight and evidently hadn't heard her come in. When she was sure he was in the kitchen, she addressed the fruits of her overactive looms in a whisper. 'Now, everyone, let's play a little game. I want you to have your food like you have been with Daddy. Pretend I'm not here. OK?'

There were a couple of nods from the older ones, and the odd chorus of 'Mummy' from Sally and Peter, which quickly died down as order was re-established. Cathy, her eye pressed to the crack, watched as her offspring ate in relative silence. Every five minutes, a timer went off somewhere, and one of them would stand glumly up and trot upstairs to the bathroom. Presently, they would return, the alarm would go off again, and the next one would similarly go for a wash. In the meantime, and hidden from her line of view, Barry served toast and cereal, which was passed in a clockwise direction around the table. Cathy had never encountered such silence. Aside from Sally and Peter, who almost constantly pointed at inanimate objects and provided occasionally accurate descriptions, there was a pervading atmosphere of hushed murmuring. Older children helped feed younger ones. Harry was clearly on mop duty, as every time something was spilled he leapt up and rubbed it deeper into whichever unlucky surface it had hit. Daniel was helping to put Peter's shoes on. David dutifully held Sally's bottle upright. Barry emerged, and Cathy could just make out part of his face as he stood at the head of the table and made an announcement.

'Now, as you know, it's weekday six, so rota three-b applies. Sarah and Daniel, you may take your lunch money out of the kitty.'

'Kitty. Meeow. Kitty,' Peter said.

'Also, the Blue timetable applies to tonight's pick-up times. Failure to be punctual will mean you walk home.'

Cathy glanced at Sally, who could barely totter, and raised her eyebrow through the crack in the door.

'Those of you who haven't brushed your teeth, please do so now. You may use the bath, the kitchen sink and the bathroom sink. The others, pack your school bags and prepare to assemble in the hall.'

'Mummy. Mummy,' Peter recited.

'Your mummy will be back later, as I said. And while we're on the subject of your mother, when she does return, I want you to tell her what great fun you've been having with your daddy. OK?'

Cathy noticed a distinct lack of enthusiasm. Somewhere a timer went off again. 'Right,' Barry said, 'rear-seat passengers, you may begin boarding. Daniel, take Sally to Car Seat One. Sarah, take—'

296

'Peter to Booster Seat Two. Yes, I know, Dad.'

'Right. Good.' Barry ticked a piece of paper somewhere partially out of view. 'Forty-seven minutes,' he mumbled to himself. 'Two minutes quicker than yesterday.'

Cathy remained hidden until all her offspring had walked out to the car. As Barry performed his final checks on the house and stuffed a dirty bib down the back of the sofa, she caught his attention. He was shocked to see her, to say the least.

'Cathy!' he exclaimed. 'How long . . .'

She pushed the door fully open and stood in front of him. 'Drop them off,' she said, 'and then come straight back here. It's time we had a few words.'

Taste

Tim leaned against the kitchen counter watching Ann. Her dark brown hair was pulled back and tied up, a couple of errant strands constantly worrying her eyes. She wasn't classically beautiful, but there was an undeniable grace and poise about her. She was one of those women whom just walking past feels like an honour, to look at an indefinable pleasure. Her eyes were a no-man's land between green and hazel, her lips thin and mischievous. She had a distracting way of showing her belly, which was gently swollen with unspoken promise. He drank in her magnificence. Feeling the weight of Tim's gaze, Ann turned to him.

'Pesto again?' she asked.

'Uh-huh.'

'I mean, without wanting to sound critical, you're still eating the same thing every day.'

'True,' Tim replied, preoccupied.

'And that vitamin thing.'

'What?'

'Why don't you just swallow them with water like everybody else?'

'I prefer it this way.'

'But it must taste horrible.'

'I wouldn't know.'

'What do you mean?'

Tim paused, the vitamin capsule open in two halves, powder cascading gently out of one onto his spaghetti. 'It doesn't seem to matter now that I'm out of business,' he said. 'The reason I do this is that I've lost my sense of taste.'

Ann ran her eyes around the kitchen. 'I guess some people might think so, but . . .'

'No, I mean my actual sense of being able to taste things. And I'm not too hot on smells either.'

This would explain a great deal, Ann thought to herself. 'Hence you only have four toiletry products.'

'That's down to an entirely different affliction,' he replied.

'Which one?'

'Being a man.'

'But how did you lose your taste and smell?'

Tim explained what he knew. It began very quickly, coinciding with the end of a prolonged and unpleasant cold two weeks after he moved to Taunsley. As the germs eventually left his body in an outpouring of phlegm and an avalanche of sneezes, one part of Tim's normal function failed to return. His nose was struggling to detect even the most obvious of odours. Three weeks later and Tim still couldn't smell anything. Worse than this, tasting had also become a bit of a non-event. Not wanting to inconvenience a doctor with the fact that two of his five senses had ceased to be, Tim spent the next month desperately trying to provoke his taste buds and nose hairs with a variety of increasingly pungent substances. He ate Stilton, fish, curries and peppers. He sniffed coffee, creosote, socks and armpits (his own, mainly). Then the acid test. He cooked an entire meal comprised of items he couldn't bear. He began with anchovies, pickled gherkins and lard. Barely a grimace passed his lips. For main course, he rustled up a beetroot, tripe and liver casserole. He helped himself to seconds. To end with, the pièce de résistance – gooseberries and lychees in a Danish blue cheese sauce. He licked his spoon clean. And despite feeling spectacularly off-colour for several days, Tim believed that he had proved the principle beyond reasonable and medical doubt – he was truly taste-disadvantaged. Eventually conceding that there might be something wrong, he went to see a doctor. The GP referred him to a consultant, who assigned him to a specialist, who directed him to an ENT waiting list at Taunsley District Hospital. Five months later, he was still waiting for a diagnosis, stuck in a tasteless world which failed to excite his nose.

In the meantime, Tim had devised a series of procedures to meet the challenges of his new circumstances. He came to see that his predicament was by no means debilitating, and in many ways could actually be advantageous. With only three senses to offend, life was considerably more bearable. Taunsley tasted better and smelt fresher than it otherwise might have done. And for a man with limited abilities and even lower enthusiasm in the kitchen, it was a positive godsend.

While it was easy to adapt his life in the kitchen, other issues were less straightforward. The sense of smell, he came to appreciate, wasn't just an inconvenience, but was there for a reason. It told you when your breath was dangerous, when your underpants needed washing and when your body odour was going critical. Without such safety checks, Tim had been forced to enhance his personal hygiene levels, just when he should have been easing off in the absence of his girlfriend, who was too far away to smell him accurately. He had thus implemented several changes to his routine. He showered every morning, applied a thick layer of deodorant to his body, gargled with mouthwash to protect his breath and wore clean underpants each day. Although these actions were far from onerous, and indeed probably what most people did anyway, the irony of increased cleanliness at a time of enforced bachelordom hadn't raised his spirits.

'But why so secretive about it all?' Ann asked, assembling a multitude of ingredients for another mammoth cooking experience.

'See it from my side. The only advertiser in town, and it gets out that I've got no sense of taste. How could I advertise sausages, pasties, pork pies, beef-burgers or black puddings when everyone knows I can't taste or smell anything?'

'Bit of a problem.'

'It's just a word, taste, but the implications in a business like this, well, I thought they'd be catastrophic. As it turns out, it probably hasn't made the faintest difference.'

Creaking sounds of movement came from upstairs. Zoe was in the bathroom, pacing around. Tim wasn't at all relaxed. In fact, he was on edge. Certain issues needed to be broached, difficult subjects discussed. He walked into the lounge and sat down, and Ann followed him. Since the previous day's break-in and subsequent confessions, an uneasy truce had been established at number four, St Paul's Square. Zoe had been elusive, and had taken some time to visit her uncle Barry. She had returned with tales of domestic bedlam and household anarchy. Ann had also made herself scarce, and Tim had so far been unable to tell her what was on his mind. He turned the TV on, and Ann perched on the other sofa while her pan of water boiled.

As Tim fiddled with the VCR remote control, he decided to take the plunge. At best, he had a few short minutes while Zoe applied yet another layer of make-up. The moment he resolved to open his heart to Ann, anxiety twisted inside him and a blush of heat spread across his face. He sighed a long breath, the emptiness in his chest making his heart beat harder. 'You know, Ann, I finally figured it out,' he said, unable to make eye contact.

'What?' she asked.

'The one thing your life is missing . . .'

'And what is it?'

'The thing you are always striving for.'

'Which is?'

Tim hunted for the start of a programme he had taped. 'It all depends on how happy you are.'

'If you're miserable?'

'Could be anything.'

'And if you're blissful?'

'It's likely to be more of what you already have.'

'Yeah?'

'And if you have to think long and hard about the answer, then the answer is "nothing".'

'And what do you have that you want more of?' Ann asked.

Tim pressed Play and turned to Ann. 'The one thing I want more of is you.'

'I see,' Ann replied, quickly looking away.

'What do you think?'

Ann's gaze focused resolutely on the TV. 'I don't know,' she said.

'Well, what's on your mind?'

'We haven't exactly got off to a good start. And living here is freaking me out.'

'Tell me about it.'

'And I've found a temporary place to stay.'

On screen, an advert showed a happy family of lovable rogues seated around a suburban dining table, bickering over whose turn it was for the gravy. 'Fucking Poxo cubes,' Tim cursed bitterly. 'Where?' he asked, averting his eyes.

'The other side of the hospital. In a funny way, I'll be sorry to leave the house. I kind of fell in love with it when I first saw it.'

Tim glanced around the room, only able to spot its faults. Ownership was like that. When something belonged to you, the bad points were glaringly obvious. Someone else's effects, however, were faultless and perfect, mainly because you didn't have to live with them every day. The same was undeniably true of Ann. Because he couldn't have her she appeared unblemished and flawless. Perhaps if he ever did possess her he would begin to notice her shortcomings. At this moment in time, he conceded, dejectedly scanning the backs of his hands, he would give anything to be close enough to Ann to get to know her problems. But it was evident that she would miss the property more than the landlord.

'And when—'

'There's something else as well.'

'Yes?' Tim asked, dismayed.

'I've got a job interview.'

'For what?'

'The post of . . . senior registrar.'

Tim hunted for the fast-forward button. The slogan **Poxo – Cubes of Pork Goodness** flashed up, pasted over the grinning family. Above all adverts, Tim hated the seemingly relentless Poxo campaigns. For reasons he understood more clearly than he would own up to, they undermined him ruthlessly. 'Whereabouts?'

'Newcastle.'

'Newcastle? But that's miles . . .'

'I know,' Ann said quietly, raising her eyebrows. 'It's only an interview. I probably won't get it.'

'Look, Ann,' Tim began, sounding unusually impassioned, 'I understand this is a difficult question, and it's killing me to ask it, but what do you feel about me? I've told you what I want.'

The creak of movement shifted above them as Zoe sounded to be leaving the bathroom. 'I don't know, Tim. I really don't know. You're a nice guy and everything. It's just . . .'

'What?'

'This job thing. It's taking you apart. You've lost all your savings, and maybe, I don't know if I should say this . . .'

'Go on,' Tim said flatly. 'Give it to me straight, doc.'

'You seem to have lost your direction in life. Almost like you've come to a full stop.'

Tim pressed Play, now that the ads had been zoomed through. 'More a semi-colon, I'd have—'

'But you know what happened before I moved in. The boyfriend I left behind?'

'Pete?'

'A loser. Even by Taunsley's standards. He bummed money off me, did nothing but lounge around all day cursing his luck. Now I'm not saying you're like that, but . . .'

'What?'

'I'm nervous. I need someone I can rely on, who's financially independent, who won't take me to the cleaners again. I'm sorry, Tim.'

304

The two sat in silence, as Zoe came nearer and nearer. The word Poxo repeated itself endlessly, a grey hopelessness seeping through Tim's mind. It felt like his skull was pushing inwards, the letters squeezing his cortex. Zoe appeared, freshly made up, carrying a cup of coffee with her. Ann stood up and walked into the hallway and out of the house, her pan of water boiling pointlessly in the kitchen.

Zoe sat down, careful not to occupy the space recently vacated by Ann. She noted the air of intimacy in the living room, and sighed. Tim gazed sorrowfully at the carpet. Zoe broke the ensuing silence. She didn't appear too upset about the sudden distance between them, which now felt greater and less surmountable than when she was on the far side of the world. In fact, as he thought about it, there was almost a tangible essence of relief about her. 'One thing remains,' she said. 'What about the product?'

'Which one?'

'RhylZig.'

'What about it?'

'Look, how many calls are you getting?'

'Dunno. The answering machine stops at fifty messages.'

'I was talking to Uncle Barry earlier. He said that people are still baying for it. He reckons you've got to give them something.'

'You mean actually come up with a product?'

'Exactly.'

'Another Barry Dinsdale short cut to ruin,' he sighed. 'Besides, all the product ideas me and Dave have had turned out to be disasters.'

'Like what?'

'There was Dave's **Bachelor Pads**.'

'Which were?'

305

'Drinkers' Diapers. You know, so you didn't have to keep going to the Gents' when you were out drinking.'

'Right. Any others?'

'Self-lighting cigarettes.'

'Uh-huh.'

'A quadruple-blade shaver.'

'Mmm.'

'Breath fresheners for dogs.'

'I see.'

'A sports bra for fat blokes who jog.'

'Useful.'

'Pooper scooper for goldfish.'

'Oh.'

'One-size-fits-all shoes.'

'How did they work?'

'Don't ask.'

'That's it?'

'Lots of things with pointless internet connections, like toasters and wrist watches.'

'Hardly likely to solve your problems.'

'Yeah,' Tim answered. It was going to take more than an internet toaster that ordered more bread to solve the mess of his life. He had sunk his life savings into a failed business venture, messed up a perfectly good relationship and would have to start looking for somewhere else to live. His quest for understanding had truly undone him. He had no job, and as an alleged full stop was not good boyfriend material. Ann, who was soon to be moving away, would take with her just about the only hope he had in his life.

In the early hours, on the sofa, Tim heard Ann enter the house. Minutes later, she left again. By the sounds of her laboured activity, she was carrying a suit-case. Awake and alone, he was struck down by an all-consuming hunger. He had an overwhelming desire for a bacon sandwich. Comfort food was rarely more keenly needed. He stumbled into the kitchen and assembled all of the required ingredients except the bacon. Swearing bitterly, he realized that they were out of the stuff. Even meat products were deserting him. While he could simply have eaten some bread, as his taste buds would hardly have noticed the difference, there was something haunting about the remembered flavour of bacon. He wondered whether his lack of taste made the longing all the more acute, a sensation locked away somewhere in his brain, pure and unsullied by the toothpaste in his mouth or the slightly damp odour of the room. He gave up and sat miserably down on the sofa. And then, as his useless taste buds continued to salivate, he had an idea, the sort of revelation which might just change his future.

Showdown

Derek Gribben turned the wheel of his Smart car and indicated at the same time. This was the one vehicle he could easily drive, automatic as it was, and with power-steering so light he could steer using the fingers of his only hand. The sole alternative, when he had looked into it, was one of those glorified motorized wheelchairs employed by pensioners to annoy both pedestrians and road users alike. Also of benefit, the Smart car was cheap, economical and great around town. Parking was easy and service intervals were long. If he had one criticism, however, it was that other local hardmen rarely resorted to such miniature modes of transport. The unwritten rule seemed to be that the more dangerous you were, the larger your automobile had to be to reflect this. His fellow tyrants drove unwieldy Granadas, long Mercedes and wide BMWs, not 600cc dwarf cars. As he headed along the end of Taunsley's main high street, he kept his head bowed slightly, in the hope that no one he knew would see him.

Towards the outskirts, where Taunsley petered out into flat, soggy fields, Derek turned right onto a factory site and continued past several large machinery plants. The steel and concrete buildings resembled a smaller

version of the Jenkins Meat Products site. An unpleasant memory stirred as he jarred over the uneven
tarmac in his diminutive vehicle. Derek had once been
the head foreman in the Pork Retrieval sector of the
JMP factory. The manufacturing works had numerous
divisions and functions, from Cattle Slaughter to
Beefburger Processing, past Spare Rib Extraction and
Pasty Assembly. It had been Derek's job to supervise
daily running of the sausage component of JMP's
operations. As such, he managed 120 staff at various
stages of disillusionment about the food industry. Pig
heads went in at one end in large wheelbarrows, and
sausages came out of the other in small packets. In
between the two states of affairs lay a host of processes
most carnivores could happily live without seeing in
action. Part of the work was manual, with over
forty people carving swathes of flesh away from pig
skulls, but the majority was performed by vast
shredders, which consumed tendons, bones, gristle,
sawdust and occasional pieces of meat, spitting out a
veiny substance which eventually became the sausage.

He turned onto a paved road which was showing
signs of wear and tear. Ahead was a sign that read
'Top Class Pasties'. He slowed as he entered the empty
car park and then drove out the other side, past a
single-storey building marked 'Top Class Pasties Headquarters'. The road worsened considerably and Derek
found himself on the receiving end of the car's scaled-
down suspension. The surface was obviously being
repaired. He drove by an ageing road digger who was
leaning against his drill, smoking a fag. He watched
as the man plucked his mobile phone from his belt,
held it against his ear, shook the phone, examined its
display, held it to his ear again, shook it again, before
shrugging and attaching it back to his belt. The driller

finished his cigarette and bent down by the hole he was making. Pulling out what looked like a crisp packet, the workman appeared to curse before resuming his attack on the road.

Thirty yards further, Derek arrived at the predetermined spot. The site was an abandoned industrial unit, vigorous weeds reclaiming the land that was once theirs. He brought the tiny vehicle to a grateful halt and drummed his fingers on the dashboard, appreciating that he was early. He scratched his stump, which was close to his shoulder, and another unpleasant memory jogged. The whole reason he was here today. The single event that had cost him his dignity. The time had arrived for payback.

In his mirror, Derek spotted a car picking its way through the industrial estate. As it drew closer, he noted that Jenkins was alone. Unlike him, Mr Jenkins had opted in means of transport for size, comfort and environmental damage. The overgrown Range Rover purred up to meet him. Derek appreciated that with a little careless parking the fucker could run his car over quite easily. He opened his door and walked towards a stack of burning pallets. Staring into their simultaneous promise and threat, he reminded himself why he was here again. Six years previously, while attempting to mince a spinal column, one of the shredders had become unexpectedly jammed. While he had isolated the power and attempted to fix it, the machine had rattled into life and taken his arm. And he still wasn't sure that it was an accident.

There was a scuffing of footsteps behind. Without removing his gaze from the fire, he appreciated that Mr Jenkins was standing beside him. Above the crackle of the glowing wood Derek could just detect his laboured breathing. So, Jenkins wanted to negotiate. Well, bring it on. Let him have his fun. And then the real business could begin.

'You've got something I want,' Mr Jenkins wheezed after a few moments.

'I know.'

'Rhinegold. That was original.'

'Thought you'd like it.'

'Ruination was the word you used last time you insisted on a meeting. Well, you nearly ruined me, Gribben, but you failed.'

'Not by very much.'

Mr Jenkins snorted. 'I've had worse.'

'Only once.'

'I seem to remember that was your doing as well.'

'What the Food Standards man found he would have discovered anyway. You cut corners and you were going to be investigated.'

'Yeah, but with a nod and a wink from a greedy fucker on the inside, I was about to be closed down. Still, you got your comeuppance.'

'Oh I certainly did. And with the . . . fucking machine off, there was no way . . . it could have been an accident.'

'So you're blaming me for the power surge, are you?'

Derek Gribben rocked back on his shoes. The old cunt was attempting to wind him up. He let it pass. He had to be in control. Retribution was a cold business. The fire in front of him was truly mesmerizing. 'This time . . . I don't want to ruin you,' he said quietly.

'No?'

'I came close enough . . . to see you sweat. Your piggy face squealing . . . with panic. Running round town, ripping down . . . posters. Your own face staring back at you . . . telling everybody **You can be sure more of my flesh** . . . **ends up in your pies**, well, that

311

just about sums . . . it up. Only it wasn't your flesh, was it? It was mine.'

'For fuck's sake. Look, just name your price . . .'

'Can't bear to hear it, can you? In fact, you can't even . . . stand to look at my arm.'

'I can hardly look at a missing limb.'

Derek swallowed the anger flaring in his gut and seething through his body. Still he was trying to rile him. On other days, he would have run to his car and got his gun. But today, bitter though it tasted, it was worth gulping down the bile. He would have his moment.

Mr Jenkins's eyes bored into the flames. He changed direction. 'Look, we're here to do business. I want to buy your factory. I need room to develop a new product. But first I want to see the goods.'

Derek Gribben turned and walked away from the fire. Behind him came the sounds of unhurried progress. In the background, behind Top Class Pasties, he heard the intermittent clatter of a pneumatic drill. He approached the nearest factory door, took out an unwieldy bundle of keys and unlocked it. Inside he flicked a large panel of switches, which encouraged row after row of neon tubes to stutter into action. The factory was roughly thirty metres long. Its air was loaded with an unsettling mix of raw meat and disinfectant. Almost all metal surfaces were covered with a sheen of dried blood. He sat down at a table and ran a finger along it, his nail gathering some indeterminate matter which was once alive, running, grunting, feeling and breathing. Out of the corner of his eye, he saw Mr Jenkins pace up and down, inspecting machinery, trying out the cold room, testing the weight of ceiling hooks. He climbed a gantry, puffing up the thin steel ladder as if he was soloing up a rock face. It was five or six metres. At the top, he looked finished, leaning against the guard rail. Derek finally had him where he wanted him.

Rushing to the ladder, his single arm gripping a rung, his body readjusting then his arm gripping another, he was up in seconds. Mr Jenkins was breathing heavily. Almost bent double. The large mouth of the shredder gaped hungrily. A need in Derek tore itself open, the poison bursting out. Six years of disability. Putting up with life instead of living it. He stepped back two paces before launching himself. Mr Jenkins lurched forwards under the momentum. He pushed a hand out to grab the safety rail but missed it. He was aware of a disturbing loss of contact with any surface. And then he landed with a hollow crash two metres down in the machine itself. The interior was slippery with pig fat and sloped steeply towards a rusty set of blades.

'Fuck, no!' he screamed.

'Fuck, yes!' Derek Gribben shrieked back, glancing at the control panel. Beneath the manufacturer's nameplate, which read 'Rhinegold Shredders', the Go switch was a circular green button with a metal surround. Next to it, a key poked out at a position marked 'Off'. A quarter turn was all that was needed for it to reach 'On'.

Mr Jenkins scrambled frantically inside the shredder, trying vainly to get up the side of the holding bay like a startled spider fleeing rising bathwater. The closer to the top he pushed himself, the more severe the angle and the less grip he found. Derek watched him gleefully. He had the fucker. There was, he felt, some poetic justice in the current situation, which he felt he ought to share.

'Do you know how much . . . this hurt?' he shouted, pointing to his stump. 'Still hurts?'

'Please!' Mr Jenkins begged. 'Please. Anything.'

'Do you know how sick I felt knowing that . . . it was out there?'

'I've got money. Whatever you want.'

'It wasn't the pain. It was the sickness. You and your fucking greed!' Several years of misery were boiling over. 'OK, maybe I did alert the FSA. I took that decision. But the decision . . . you took – you cunt!'

Mr Jenkins was perched one thick leg either side of the chute that led to blades he had seen once too often ripping pig heads apart. 'It's the past,' he said, through deep, uncomfortable breaths. 'The fucking past.'

'And would you recall . . . the batch? Would you, fuck!'

'Look, it would have ruined my reputation.' He lost balance and slid towards the blades before managing to wedge himself above them again. He was acutely conscious that he could only hold on so long. And if they were turned on, the vibration within the chute would make that virtually impossible.

'People ate it! People ate my fucking arm!' Derek screamed. 'My fingers, my bones, my tendons, my hairs, my nails, my muscles . . . Half of the town . . . are fucking cannibals!'

'Don't exaggerate,' Mr Jenkins wheezed. 'They only ate a tiny bit of you.'

'A tiny bit?' Derek spun wildly round and reached for the key. With a firm and rapid twist, he switched the Rhinegold shredder from Off to On. 'That was my whole fucking arm!'

'I mean each,' he panted. 'But please, I beg you . . .'

'And I'll tell you . . . another thing. That was the only fucking piece of proper meat . . . to ever end up in one of your sausages.' He peered down at Mr Jenkins, who was nearing exhaustion. He saw only a porcine head, though, with small cold eyes.

'But I paid you off. Gave you a tidy lump sum. Money you invested and used to buy this place, to start a rival business. You didn't go unrewarded for your loyalty. Now I'll even buy it back from you. Name your price.'

'Loyalty? Do you think I wanted . . . to be loyal to the man who had . . . taken my arm and allowed it to be eaten . . . by his customers? I took your money because . . . there was little else a one-armed man . . . could do, you fat fucker.'

'Please, Derek,' Mr Jenkins pleaded. 'Not like this. I can't hold on.'

'Shame,' Mr Gribben said calmly.

'Look, there's a new product in the pipeline. Power, the advertiser, came up with it. Going to be massive. I'll cut you in . . .'

'What is it?'

'RhylZig.'

'RhylZig? The fake campaign? Come on, you can do better . . . than that.' Derek's hand reached towards the green Go button. 'Might even get a few . . . celebratory pasties out of you . . .' He caressed the switch.

'Look, have it your way, we'll negotiate. Fifty–fifty. How about it? You've won, you got what you wanted – you've muscled into my business. Now, let me out.'

'I don't think so. I'm taking you *and* your business, Jenkins. From now on, there's only . . . going to be one meat producer in this town.'

The fight to stay above the blades was dying in Mr Jenkins. He changed tack. The psychological advantage still lay, he believed, with him. 'You haven't got the bottle, Gribben. To kill someone. Sure you can

315

make pasties, poor ones at that, but to kill me? Not a chance.'

Derek let him have his say. It was only fair. Last rites or something. Truly he was about to discover what revenge really felt like. Spurious advertising campaigns had been fun, but had only gone so far. The ads had nearly ruined Jenkins, but not quite. This, however, was the real deal. Plan B, as it were. While his former boss continued to goad him, he thought briefly about how he would dispose of the cunt's Range Rover. One of his contacts would take it, no questions asked, and ship it off abroad. That would make him a good twenty grand or so. Besides, there was likely to be precious little forensic evidence by the time he'd baked a few pies. He wondered briefly how it would feel to have your whole body shredded. He could testify that one arm ripped off was fairly unpleasant. But the whole lot? He smiled. The whole lot indeed.

'Finished?' he asked.

Mr Jenkins was flushed and sweating, unsteady on his feet, his suit coated in grease. 'No, I'm just—'

And Derek Gribben pushed the Go button firmly with his thumb.

Mound

Deirdre Smythe sat alone in her front room. Pouring herself a cup of weak tea which she further embellished with a vast quantity of milk and four sugars, she settled back in her armchair and sighed. She would certainly miss Alistaire. Two years had seemed a bit harsh, but as the judge explained, there was no place for such behaviour in today's society. In fact, he had gone on to press the point. 'What has made you think this way?' the judge had repeatedly asked her son. Deirdre gazed through her immaculate net curtains at the bleached RhylZig poster across the street. She saw herself thirty-three years earlier, climbing the steps of a plane, sticky hot air invading her loose clothing. In the hazy whiteness of her curtains, she watched the single key day in her life play back in a series of documentary images.

A substantially younger Deirdre Smythe shuffled onto the flightdeck of a DC10. Her face told a tale of hurt. She knew that Nikolaos would have left Departures already, oblivious to her suffering. In fact, rather than return to his home town, she appreciated that he had probably made his way straight to Arrivals to await the next batch of pale foreigners hoping to darken themselves for a couple of weeks. Turning

317

sideways to let a stewardess past, she frowned, wondering whether he had a sign to hold up reading 'English Hearts Broken Here.' Or, given his shaky grasp of the language, 'Engleesh 'arts ees broked ere.' And another smaller sign beneath reading, 'Init?'

Deirdre's eyes were wet. As she sat down in her cramped seat with its rough upholstery, she visibly smarted from the rejection. Nikolaos could barely have made his lack of interest in her more obvious. Peering through the small perspex window she saw her three suitcases, housing almost all her worldly possessions, being manhandled into the hold by a couple of men who had all the exuberance of abattoir workers. The piercing sun attacked her face and made her squint. Her eyes showed signs of overflowing. Even when she'd told him she was carrying his child, he had shrugged and looked around, indifference drooping out of the ends of his moustache. But I'm twelve weeks gone, she had pleaded as they reached the airport, rubbing a desperate hand over her belly. Deirdre, he'd replied, eet ees not mine. You must to go 'ome. And that had been that. Nikolaos had shrugged again, turned and sauntered away, heading back to his summer life of serving, bemoaning and shagging tourists in equal measure.

Deirdre had made a decision there and then. Pulling her seatbelt tight over the small mound growing inside, she vowed to keep the child. She would bring it up as best she could. Her family would help. She would manage. Taunsley might not be the best place in the world, but people would pitch in. They would survive. And she would make sure her child never trusted a foreign man the way she had.

The reverie faded and Deirdre took another sip of lukewarm tea. Just like the young version of herself, her eyes were moist. As she returned her attention to Alistaire, she worried that maybe she had been a little too successful. Rather than simply mistrusting people of other cultures, her son actively sought them out and attacked them. There was a fine line, she felt, and Alistaire had certainly put his size thirteens across it. Still, at least in prison he would finally stay out of trouble for a while. Maybe he would take up a correspondence course or learn a trade and pass his time constructively. They say that idle hands do the devil's work, she reflected, dunking a digestive into her drink. The main thing she hoped, sighing quietly to herself, was that he wouldn't spend all his time sitting around on his backside.

Incarceration

Alistaire Smythe was offered a chair but declined to sit down. Although he had spent most of the day on his feet learning how to brick a wall, the very last thing he wanted to do was to park his arse. And even though one of his feet was heavily strapped and excruciating to place anywhere near the ground, he was still happier in the upright position. In fact, he had hardly been seated for the last week, preferring to transfer his weight from good foot to newly reconstructed foot, discomfort rife through his body. And more acute in certain areas than others.

Picking up a copy of the *Brisdle Echo*, he leafed through it, looking for anything that would take his mind off the considerable discomfort he was feeling. On page two was a big news story he already knew in great detail. The successful capture and prosecution of Brisdle's most prominent Yardie gang. He studied the depressing details regardless. Fourteen members, wanted for everything from drug smuggling to murder, had been infiltrated, ensnared and incarcerated. He looked at their arrest photos, and their cold eyes gaped at him in return. Ali glanced up from his paper and scanned the confined communal area of Block C. Fourteen black faces stared back at him, and he gulped quietly.

It was true to say that the Yardies hadn't taken to Ali particularly well. While they weren't the friendliest group of people he had ever met, they had been especially unreceptive to Ali's attempts at civility. And although several of them were awaiting dispersal to other centres, he felt that he had already suffered more than enough for one lifetime. Even if only half of them remained, the situation was going to be acutely challenging. Ali dropped the *Echo* and rummaged around on the table for something else to read. Among the many papers provided by guards eager to demonstrate to inmates what they were missing out on, Ali spotted a week-old *Taunsley Mercury*. While there were plenty of other regional newspapers, this was the first publication from his home town he had seen since his incarceration. He leafed through expectantly, hoping to read about someone he knew. Several pages in, he stopped and gawped at an article occupying the County Court News section. With dismay, he saw his photograph and noted the dreaded name of Gary Shrubble. This could only mean bad things. Slowly, he mouthed the words and attempted to digest the exact implications.

One Man Crimewave Overpowered By Ladies And Lentils

A Taunsley man wanted for assaulting several police officers, resisting arrest and breaking and entering was last night beginning a lengthy prison sentence. Alistaire Nikolaos Smythe, of Meadows Estate, was taken into custody by two young women a fortnight ago following a lengthy struggle. A number of recent incidents have ensured that Mr Smythe has become something of a town legend, and with his recent County Court appearances, his popularity is set to travel further.

Taunsley Magistrates Court heard that Mr Smythe, 33, had

gained access to the property on St Paul's Square, Taunsley, in the early hours. Once inside, the two women, Ann Hillyard, 31, and Zoe Joseph, 29, fired dried peas and lentils at the robber, using low-calibre air pistols, forcing him to phone the police for protection. According to police reports, it seems that Mr Smythe was experimenting with make-up at the time, and was covered in what appeared to be blusher when the constabulary finally apprehended him. This is the second such incident in a number of weeks for Mr Smythe, who was previously set upon by a puppy at a different address, and also called for police intervention.

In an interesting twist to the story, Mr Smythe was, it emerged yesterday, the advertising face of the product RhylZig, which was conceived and is about to be manufactured in the town. Also in court, Mr Smythe admitted to breaking into the headquarters of the *Mercury* last month and stealing computer equipment worth in excess of £40,000. The *Mercury* further understands that Mr Smythe, who lost a number of toes in an incident several weeks ago, has attempted to launch a prosecution of his own, alleging that his feet were damaged deliberately by an elderly pneumatic driller.

Following Mr Smythe's successful conviction, however, the Magistrates Court has asked us to point out that we were mistaken in our belief that the computer thefts had been carried out by someone of foreign extraction. The *Mercury* would therefore like to make the following statement:

'Given it now appears that Mr Smythe is at least partially Caucasian, the *Taunsley Mercury* unreservedly apologizes to all unwanted immigrants, illegal foreign beggars and un-welcome no-gooders who should be living elsewhere.'

Ali threw the paper down in fury. Gary fucking Shrubble had stiffed him again. He looked up, anxious not to draw any further attention to himself. He had attracted quite enough interest for one week. The most obvious thing about Stretham Prison, he'd seen when he arrived from the police holding area, was its ethnic diversity. Certainly, had the prison been located in Taunsley, things would have been very different. But Taunsley didn't have a jail. The nearest major detention centre was in the city of Brisdle. And Brisdle had turned out to be quite unlike his home town. He had quickly learned that prisons in large populations were disproportionately black. And that was even before a Yardie gang had decided en masse to pop in for a while.

Of course, there had been a time when Ali imagined being locked up had a lot going for it. He could see now that he had been badly wrong. Painfully wrong. On the outside, he was a big, intimidating man. In a place like this, however, he was nothing special. Inmates who had violated, manslaughtered and murdered their way through society surrounded him everywhere he went. They spent several hours a day lifting weights and building their bodies. Some of them were huge. From the far side of the common room, two of the largest Rastafarians winked at him, and Ali winced again. There was no doubt that they could be friendly if they wanted. It was just that, if he had a complaint, when they did they were a little too friendly. The more solidly built of the two held his pool cue in a manner which managed to be simultaneously menacing and suggestive. For the thousandth time since his recent captivity, Ali regretted the majority of the tattoos that festooned his body. Of particular lament were two prominent images administered by a sympathetically prejudiced local artist. He had been asked many searching questions about these two by the fourteen-strong Yardie gang.

Not the sort of gentle enquiry he might have envisaged, but a far more probing and penetrating approach. Ali winced one more time recalling the last interrogation a couple of days previously.

'Painful?' he had been asked mockingly, mid-stroke. 'How about I take your little mind off it?' And then a fellow inmate had stamped on Ali's bad foot. Stitched together toes took the brunt of the force and seemed to separate slightly again. But this was nothing compared to the pain he felt elsewhere.

'And this tattoo of Hitler,' another gang member said. 'What do you think it's going to take to put a smile on his face?'

'Fucked if I know,' Ali grunted through clenched jaws. From the kitchens he could just smell dinner being abused, a familiar odour seeping under the door of his cell. Kebabs. Ali's mind had tried to shut itself off, to journey elsewhere, away from the pain.

As Ali continued to stand quietly in a corner of the communal lounge, he shivered, recalling the events of the last few days. The kebabs had turned out half decent, which had been a bonus. One of the chefs was a Cypriot called Andreas, whom Ali had struck up a bit of a bond with. Although slightly dark, he was a top bloke. In between involuntary buggerings, Ali had played a bit of pool with Andreas and they had chatted about the outside. All in all, Ali thought, sloping off to confine himself to his cell before he was molested again, there was hope yet. But if his recent experiences had taught him one thing, it was that a small amount of breaking and entering could result in a lot of illegal entry.

Disconnection

Barry Dinsdale strode in from work and threw open the living-room door. Dropping the MPV keys on a table, he quickly took stock of the situation. It was chaos. Sheer chaos. Noisy, vigorous chaos, a cacophony of laughter and screams, a blur of colours that shook the room and threatened its furniture. He kicked off his shoes and removed his jacket, slowly sitting down on the sofa to avoid crushing any of his offspring. So this was what life felt like in its pure and unadulterated form. He smiled as a missile narrowly missed his head. A hand reached across and yanked his tie. Beneath, the twins were knotting his shoelaces together. He stood up, made an act of tripping over and rolled around on the carpet with as many of his children who felt like a wrestle. While they were all comparatively little, cumulatively their mass almost overwhelmed him. Almost. But those days had passed, he said to himself, standing up and roaring, a son under one arm, a daughter under the other. It was time to be a big man in a big family. He winked at Cathy, limping through the room, dragging a leg which David had grimly wrapped himself around. He was going to immerse himself in the exuberant energy of his household. In short, Barry had resolved over the last few days, he was going to have fun.

His change of heart wasn't solely from spending more time with his children, however. Something much deeper and more tumultuous had happened, an experience that would live with him for ever. He had recently spent two weeks in abject terror. Looking after six kids for a fortnight had so thoroughly scared the shit out of him that he would never take his wife for granted again. He roared like a caveman and beat his chest. From now on, he was going to be like one of those dads you saw in TV adverts.

Idly wondering what to cook for tea, Cathy watched her husband with a newfound interest. While going away had turned her into a nervous wreck, it seemed to have done Barry the world of good. Something had changed in him. Maybe he'd come to see exactly what he had. Life was like that. Shake all its pieces up and they would often land in different places and establish themselves from new footholds. As he continued to lurch across the living room with all six sons and daughters now clinging to him like monkeys, she noticed a strength about him which hadn't been evident before. For a fleeting moment she felt physically attracted to him, and a couple of sexual positions flitted behind her eyes.

'Test me again,' he said later, while they padded around the bedroom maintaining a careful distance, the children already in bed. Since Cathy's return, they were yet to make love. Although they had become civil, almost respectful of one another, they had steadfastly avoided the issue of sex. Barry felt that a barrier had been removed, but was petrified of initiating any physical contact in case his wife rejected him. He tried another tack. 'Go on, ask me.'

'What?'

'All those questions that I couldn't answer before you went away. I've been doing some remembering. You've become my specialist subject.'

'How do you mean?'

'Like your shoe size. Five. And your eyes. Green and bewitching. Dress size. Ten. Date of birth . . .'

'OK, Barry, just come to bed.'

'Go on, test me. The important details that got lost in the mess of our life, I've recalled them. I've looked at photos, talked to your friends, read my diaries of the early days. So ask me anything.'

'Anything?'

Barry slid into bed, careful not to get too close. 'Fire away.'

Cathy moved her body subtly nearer to her husband. 'What . . .' she began.

'Yes?'

She wrapped her arms around him. 'Is . . .'

'Yes?'

She kissed him. 'My . . .'

'What?'

'Favourite . . .'

He felt her kiss his ear. 'Mmm?'

'Ever . . .'

'Yes?'

'Sexual?'

'Aha.'

'Position?'

Barry treated it as a rhetorical question. The truth was, he could no longer remember, it had been so long. 'Come here,' he whispered, deciding to bluff it, 'and I'll show you.'

Afterwards, as they lay on their backs in the semi-dark, smiling, Barry said, 'I've been doing some

327

thinking. Why stop at six?'

'What do you mean?'

'Maybe we should have another child.'

Cathy hugged him close to her and kissed him passionately on the mouth. 'Not a fucking chance,' she whispered.

'No?'

'No. I want you to go and see Doctor Kumar in the morning.'

'What for?'

'There's a vital piece of your machinery which needs disconnecting.'

Barry grinned to himself. It really had come to something when the thought of having a vasectomy cheered you up. But he'd gladly have his whole appendage removed rather than lose his wife. Before she had left, he might as well not have had one anyway. But now things looked rosier. He kissed Cathy on her still-flushed cheek. Very rosy indeed.

RhylZig

RhylZig hit the streets on a quiet Wednesday morning. It was to pigs what Bovril was to cows. RhylZig used porcine detritus that even JMP had previously shied away from. It was marketed as **The Bacon Sandwich in a Jar** and came in two flavours – Ketchup and Brown Sauce. The infrastructure was already in place. Adverts around the town had been screaming its promise for weeks. Taunsley had been crying out for RhylZig. Speculation had reached fever pitch. Power Advertising had been dogged by a phone call roughly every twelve minutes for longer than Tim and Dave cared to remember. RhylZig became the fastest food-stuff ever to go from inception to production in the town.

When the identity of the wonder product was finally revealed, the population of Taunsley was not overtly disappointed. While Tim was happy to concede that a bacon sandwich spread was probably not **The one thing your life is missing**, it was at least a start. And the town agreed. RhylZig flew off the shelves. It also didn't matter if they soon tired of the substance. A second wave had already been planned and was undergoing extensive taste testing. Phase Two was RhylZig's logical cousin: **The Sausage Sandwich in a**

Jar, which would come in three flavours – Ketchup, Brown Sauce and Mustard.

In the first week, Jenkins Meat Products shifted enough RhylZig to stave off bankruptcy for a couple of months. In the second, they were forced to take on new staff. In the third, Mr Jenkins was talking share options with Tim. In the fourth, JMP's turnaround had perked the town's economy up so much that people were happy to return the favour and bulk-buy RhylZig. And in the fifth, Mr Jenkins opened up a new factory division within an enormous old warehouse on the industrial unit.

But something else began to happen. Slowly, the craze spread to nearby Bridgton, which lapped up RhylZig as if its sleepy life depended on it. And then Burnbridge, followed by Weston-Mare on Sands. Pretty soon, even Brisdle had heard about **The Bacon Sandwich in a Jar**. It became a student classic – slightly naff, but undeniably convenient. It was the Pot Noodle of bread snacks. And the students from Brisdle took it home with them to Sheffield, Manchester, Dublin, Leeds, Birmingham, Cardiff, London, Belfast, Glasgow, Edinburgh, wherever their parents lived. They introduced it to their friends and families and began to stock up for the holidays. The number of calls to the RhylZig hotline, which dipped when Taunsley's curiosity had been satiated, rocketed up again, and Tim was forced to buy another answering machine. Maybe it had been a mistake printing Power Advertising's number on the side of the jar, but at least his name was spreading across the country. Slowly but very surely RhylZig began to become a phenomenon. Mr Jenkins found a national supplier who pushed its availability further and wider. Within a few short weeks, RhylZig was universal. It was at this point that

Tim judged the time was right to go to London. He made a couple of phone enquiries and talked to some of his ex-colleagues. He even sought the opinion of Jeremy from A2Z Advertising, who finally seemed to have fulfilled his wish of substance dependency. On a cloudy Tuesday morning he packed several items into an overnight bag. The name of Power Advertising was in the public domain, in their fridges and on their shelves. 'There's something I need to do,' he explained to Zoe. Although he had moved out three weeks previously and was living in a poky one-bedroomed flat, he had popped round to collect some more of his possessions.

'Suit yourself,' she replied curtly.

'Now that I've made a success of the company in Taunsley, London beckons. A few meetings, that sort of thing. By tomorrow evening, you'll be looking at a very different man.'

'I don't really want to be looking at you at all,' she replied. 'And the sooner you move the rest of your stuff out, the better.'

'I'll pick it up when I get back.'

'Right. It'll be in the spare room.'

'But, Zoe,' Tim said, his eyes glistening with expectation, needing to tell someone, even his ex-girlfriend, 'all of my working life has been leading up to this. This is the dream that kept me going when **Simply the Best** was the only slogan in town. I have to do this.'

'Whatever,' Zoe shrugged.

Tim was distracted, obsessed. 'Can you give me a lift to the station?' he asked. 'There's a train to London in half an hour with only one change. I know it's a lot to ask.'

Zoe shrugged again. 'Only if you agree to definitely move your stuff.'

'Oh, I'll be moving it OK,' Tim answered. 'Moving it well away.'

On the train, Tim fluked a cluster of four empty seats with a table and set about his idea with grim determination. He pulled out a packet of Nurofen Extras and swallowed three tablets. Despite exceeding the stated dose, another migraine was growing inside him and showed no signs of easing. His eyes flickered, announcing the arrival of imminent agony. His brain, for about the fifth time in as many days, felt compressed and crushed. In fact, it was fast becoming the mother of all headaches, and Tim had a fair idea that the Nurofen wouldn't touch it. Despite the pain, however, he forced himself to focus. This was going to be the most important pitch of his life. He scribbled frantically on numerous pieces of paper, refusing to allow his narrowing vision to throw him off course. As the train rattled towards London, things slowly began to take shape. A theme, a plan of action, an overall objective. He worked with an intensity that had been distinctly lacking over the previous few months. Every second was ploughed into the mission. Countryside ambled past unseen. In stark contrast to his mode of transport, an impressive momentum began to build.

Examining a wad of forms an hour into the journey, a thought distracted him. Recalling the town's unexpectedly liberal opinions on infidelity and pork pies, he appreciated that the most important deduction to be made from all the many questionnaires he had designed during his career was this: market research is virtually the same process as falling in love. The mechanics are frighteningly similar. Mate selection and marketing follow the same basic principles.

Summing people up for relationships is like ticking boxes on high street forms.

In those weeks when you skirt gently around your new partner, you are observing and learning. Innocent questions hide serious issues. You get to find out what sort of a person your potential mate is, what their needs are, how you might be able to satisfy their desires, whether they will be able to meet your requirements. Criteria are discussed and the outcomes noted. Tick enough boxes and a course of action is instigated. Fail to provide satisfactory answers and the product is rejected.

And both mate selection and marketing are also about advertising. While you censor each other and make your minds up, you vigorously promote your good sides. Faults and weaknesses are glossed over. You look your best, make an effort, sell yourself, just as you would if you were canvassing opinion on a new product. From this, it was a short jump to the plan of action he was about to unleash.

He watched cars on a parallel motorway, some of them travelling faster than the train, others more slowly. Their motion made his head throb even more acutely. A scruffy man opposite was squeezing a tube of RhylZig onto a cracker. Tim smiled, half grimace, half satisfaction. The papers on the table reminded him that he had to concentrate on the current venture. A good advertising campaign, like the one he was about to mastermind, required several classic elements. There were locations to scout, materials to be designed and manufactured, people to coordinate, props to assemble, budgets to be calculated, actors to hire, dialogue to write. While he'd had some ideas about content, certain rules and formats had to be adhered to, whatever you advertised. A simple message with clear copy. A creative hook. Layers that overlapped but still remained discrete. Coordination of the audio and the visual. He would have to make the viewers feel like they were participating. He would force them to think through the power of market research. Unsettle them. Involve them. Make them laugh, make them cry, whatever he had to do to touch an emotion he could hang his product on.

Most of all, though, Tim wanted them to think. That was the important thing.

Proactive Upward Thinking

In plush Soho Square offices, the senior board of Fakenham, Morgan and Sterner Advertising chatted nervously among themselves. They had all battled through London rush-hour traffic to be here on time. It was a day when all possible sky colours appeared in the same horizon, from promising blues through passive greys to ominous blacks. At the head of the low-slung, mammothly expensive table, Miles Sterner ran his frequently manicured fingers over two days' worth of stubble. A change in fortunes was desperately called for. The company's share price was on a daily roller coaster and he had seen his own stake-holding fluctuate between millionaire status and bankruptcy in a single morning. In truth, he had given up looking. It was bad for his health. Besides, all they really needed was a good, high-profile media campaign or two and they were back on track. And here, any second, was the brightest young thing in modern advertising. A complete maverick, by all accounts, but the hottest ticket in the business. Miles Sterner had the full backing of the board to break the already fragile bank to get their man.

Miles glanced from his watch to the boardroom clock and frowned. The fucking thing was losing again. He asked the nearest executive to him for the right time, and then fiddled unsuccessfully with the adjustment bevel – which looked exquisite but wouldn't, for the life of it, do anything – before accepting defeat. Just where is this fucking marketing genius? he asked out loud. The board took sideways glances at each other, fidgeted with their papers and scratched themselves. Do we have a mobile number for him? he demanded. No one seemed to know. Playing hard to get, Miles muttered under his breath. A clever bugger. Just what they needed. And then the door swung open, and their saviour stood before them.

Maverick didn't do him justice. Clothes like that were so avant-garde they almost looked unfashionable. Here was a man who clearly pushed convention to its limits. Miles Sterner faked a smile, stood up and walked over to him, his glorious hands outstretched.

'How was your journey?' he enquired.

'Oh, not too bad.'

'And where are you located at the moment?'

'Taunsley.'

'Taunsley? Where the fu— where exactly is that?'

'About eighty miles in the direction of Brisdle.'

'Great. Right. Sit down. I want you to meet the board. But first, I want to express what I think we all feel – tremendous admiration for your work. RhylZig was a stroke of genius. Utter genius. And it's that kind of proactively upward thinking that we want you to provide for us here at Fakenham, Morgan and Sterner. We want you, and your incredible brain, to transform this multinational company.'

Taunsley's finest executive advertiser ran his eyes around the room. Twelve beaming faces shone out at him, twelve eager hands ready to be shaken, twelve wealthy people all wanting his services. The central table was glass and so shiny he could see his face in it. He caught sight of his reflection and ran a hand through his thick hair. Dave couldn't help grinning as his mirror image adjusted its tie in unison. He had arrived. A few bullshitted conversations, a wildly inaccurate CV circulated to some top agencies and here he was. About to work for a proper company, one that would make Power Advertising look like the amateurish affair it undoubtedly was. Just as long as Tim Power himself didn't find out.

'So, David, one of the first things we should talk about is the package,' Miles purred, winking conspiratorially.

'Which package?' Dave asked, peering at the table, expecting to see some sort of parcel.

'Your package.'

'I didn't bring a . . .'

'Because, well, let me lay our cards on the table, so to speak. What do you want? How much are you prepared to let your services go for? What was your last salary?'

'I was on four fifty an h—'

'Four fifty? That's a hell of a . . .' Miles took in the sheer hunger of the board. 'I mean, I think we can match that.'

'Great.'

'Four hundred and fifty thousand it is, then. If that's OK with you?'

'Well, I wasn't expecting . . .' Dave began, genuinely shocked.

'Tell you what, we'll call it half a mill.' Miles Sterner smiled despite the colossal sum of money. 'What do you say?' Once again, he extended his hand. 'Do we have a deal?'

Dave took stock for a second. Advertising seemed

337

quite a good career if you put your mind to it. And it was true what they said. London folk did seem to earn huge salaries. Still, if that was the way it was, who was he to argue. For five hundred thousand pounds a year, he would gladly eat broken glass. 'I should say that I've got a lot of ideas,' he said. 'The Polish town of Danzig, for example. A couple walking on a beach. You know that song by The Nolans? "I'm In The Mood For—"'

Miles cut him off. 'You see, everybody, ideas already! This is exactly what we need. Now, do we have a deal, or do we have a deal?'

Dave shook the strangely feminine hand in front of him. 'Oh yes,' he replied, adjusting the nylon tie that was half throttling him. 'We have a deal.'

Parting Shot

With no boot to speak of, Derek Gribben was forced to place all of his equipment on the front seat of his tiny car. While it was OK to carry whatever he wanted in full visibility at night, in broad daylight such endeavours made him nervous. He thrust his pistol into the microscopic glovebox and laid his loaded twelve-bore down on the floor behind the two seats. The rest of his luggage was crammed into whichever spaces came to hand.

As far as Derek could discern, several months of planning and coercion had all been ruined by one idiot. Had he been a gambler, he would have bet money that if his masterplan was going to come a cropper, it would have been through Alistaire Smythe fucking something up. Although Ali had gone off at a tangent, becoming obsessed with the advertiser Tim Power, Derek's ultimate downfall had not come through this route, however.

Into the passenger footwell of the Smart car Derek wedged a sports bag. This was stuffed with cash. He had sold the premises of Top Class Pasties to a re-development company who wanted to create a park and build executive town houses around it. The factory was to be demolished in a matter of days. Although

Derek had let the land go cheaply, he knew that time was of the essence and he had to grab what he could and get the fuck out. When the quarter of a million pounds had been electronically transferred into his bank account, Derek had withdrawn it all and everything else he had besides. All together, he had amassed nearly four hundred thousand pounds. The frantic financial activities of the last few weeks had been undertaken very quietly. No one was aware of his parting shot. Even now, workers at Top Class Pasties were churning out more dismal foodstuffs on the Saturday morning shift, not knowing that their employment had effectively ended already. On Monday, the bulldozers would be moving in. He pictured Cathy Dinsdale and smiled. He was finally repaying her lack of respect.

Since he had unsuccessfully tried to mince Mr Jenkins, Gribben had put his mind entirely to the act of vengeance he was about to perpetrate. There had been a ferocity about his planning that had kept people even further away from him than usual. The only man who had not maintained a careful distance was the ever-thirsty journalist Gary Shrubble. Derek was acutely conscious that the *Mercury* man had been following him for almost a year now. He had even been there on several of his practice shootings at the slaughter warehouse. Derek smiled to himself for the first time in weeks. He had put on quite a show for him. Not that Shrubble had done anything about it. He would, Derek appreciated, never amount to much. Despite tagging him doggedly, day in, day out, Shrubble was still ignorant about the actual goings-on of recent months. Locking his front door for the last time, Gribben acknowledged that only two men knew the truth. And soon, he vowed through a nervous grin, only one would.

Passing a rabble of workmen by the side of the road, Gribben began to seethe once more. The timewasters were leaning on shovels, smoking fags and reading newspapers. The whole reason he was leaving Taunsley was down to a fucking useless road digger. For the only time in his life he had had Mr Jenkins exactly where he wanted him. He had listened patiently to his pleading and bullying and then had decided that enough was enough. The control panel of the Rhinegold shredder had been lit up like a fucking Christmas tree. Right until the moment he had pressed the Go switch. Then there was nothing. The factory lights died, and with them, his moment of victory ebbed away.

Derek cut through Taunsley's roughest estate and made for the centre of town. He was excited and chewed the life out of three sticks of gum. Thinking about the task at hand he once again pictured Jenkins, trapped in the shredder, helplessly scrabbling about. As he had frantically pumped the Go button, Derek had initially suspected that a fuse must have blown. He had traced his way down to the fusebox, but none of the switches had tripped. He checked whether it was a power cut, but outside lights could clearly be seen in the windows of nearby offices. And then he had spotted an ageing pneumatic driller examining a cable in the ditch he had been digging. The fucker had been repairing the road and Derek had driven past him on his way in. He spent a couple of minutes calmly deciding who to kill first. And then, racing back into the factory, Derek discovered that Mr Jenkins had managed to climb out of the Rhinegold and escape. He was nowhere to be seen. Behind him he heard his Range Rover skidding out of the car park.

It was difficult not to be furious with the way things had turned out, and yet Derek was well aware that at crucial moments like this anger could only hinder him. He had to concentrate. Mr Jenkins, he knew for a fact, always lounged around in his town apartment on Saturday mornings. This was his one chance. The door to his flat was in a back street, which would mean very few witnesses. Derek edged his car into a queue of traffic heading for the main road through town. He could be in and out in a matter of seconds. And while the fat cunt lay bleeding to death into his thick carpet, Gribben would be on his way out of the centre, away for ever. Victory would ultimately be his. By virtue of surviving, he would have won the second great Pork War of Taunsley.

Mind Games

Ann Hillyard closed the door of her new office and wished she could seal inside a whole new rainbow of problems she would rather not have heard about. Instead she would take them home with her to the small terrace she had recently moved into. There, she would attempt to grill, poach, heat and microwave the fuck out of them. Then, if the last six weeks were anything to go by, she would pour herself a generous gin and a stingy tonic, and pass the evening silently absorbing the TV's outpourings until she felt normal again.

It was dark by the time she reached the house. Autumn was closing in, daylight insidiously leaking away each night. In another month or so it would be pitch black by four thirty and almost the entire day would be spent under bulbs or striplights. She didn't think about Taunsley much now. Things had happened so quickly. Finishing 'Car Customization as a Substitute for Personal Transformation', the paper she had written on Simon Jasper. Its acceptance by an American journal dealing with personality research and drug side effects. A faxed offer of a job interview in Newcastle from one of the journal's reviewers. An awkward interrogation by the Psychology Department panel. The award of a three-year fixed-contract post.

The rapid exit to Newcastle from a situation that had become untenable in a town that had grown un-inhabitable.

Sometimes quick solutions were the answer, sharp separations, clean wounds with no lingering infection. As Ann poured herself a drink and entered the kitchen, she told herself that she preferred it like that. The doctor lie had been firmly buried in the south-west of England among people she didn't know any more. And if she ever changed her mind, she knew where Taunsley was. She was in control. Not, she readily admitted, pulling a stack of pans out of a cupboard, that that was always a good thing.

Later, on the sofa, with her legs folded under her and a plate balanced on her lap, Ann saw her first RhylZig commercial on TV. She stopped chewing for the entire duration. An article she had read in the paper a few days ago about the RhylZig phenomenon had mentioned Tim Power as the creative force behind its marketing. The television advert featured a montage of pleasing images, people from multiple socio-economic groups, families linked by their enjoyment of **The Bacon Sandwich in a Jar**. It was classy and professional. Seemingly every possible advertising cliché had been thrown in. But, Ann readily appre-ciated, they weren't aiming to target ABC1s. They wanted it to be universal. And the commercial was nothing if not wide in its appeal. Whatever your status or outlook, this was the sort of thirty-second headfuck that messed with your mind. You knew you would want whatever they were selling. In fact, it was one of those sales messages where buying the product became a payback for the sheer entertainment value of the TV. Over the pictures was a thumping soundtrack, sung, if Ann was not mistaken, by Tina Turner. The final slogan, which was superimposed over a grandma and her grandchild both grinning insanely as they bit into a RhylZig sandwich, was **RhylZig – Simply the Best**. She chewed again, picturing Tim directing the ad, inserting his one joke against advertising. She wondered, her mouth salivating slightly with the thought of bacon, if this meant that in the world of advertising he had finally arrived.

At work the next day, a new procession of border-line insanity filed into her office one by one to discuss behavioural changes linked to prescribed medicines. The department, which was attached to a large teaching hospital, was active in cataloguing and in-vestigating pharmaceutical-induced psychological shifts. Under the auspices of the universally respected Professor James Adu, the division was becoming a renowned national centre and Ann felt pleased that having served her apprenticeship in small towns in the south-west she had graduated to such a place. It had been worth the gamble of relocation. Professor Adu, however, was notorious for playing mind games within his department. It was his way, she had been assured by her colleagues, of keeping staff on their toes. So far Ann had seen little evidence of this, but as her first and second patients of the day came in wearing very similar badges with strange lettering she began to feel that the test had just begun. Her first subject was a compulsive liar.

'Let me have a look at your badge,' Ann asked at the end of her note-taking.

'I'm not wearing one,' the patient replied.

'It seems to say "Totylim". What is that exactly?'

'It means that I'm a member of the secret services,' the compulsive liar replied proudly.

'Does it?'

'No. Yes. I don't know.'

'Where did you get it?'

'I won it. Was given it. Inherited it as a family heirloom.'

Ann dismissed him and ushered the next one in. The woman, who was experiencing narcoleptic attacks in response to a blood pressure treatment, was similarly unhelpful.

'Your badge seems to say "Mily Tot".'

'I suppose it does.'

'So where did you get it? Mrs Goodwin? Mrs Goodwin?' But Mrs Goodwin had fallen asleep.

The third patient was wearing a similar badge with similarly impenetrable words. This time, she made a little more progress. 'Where did you get the badge?' Ann asked, slightly spooked.

'Outside. A nurse is distributing them at the hospital entrance.'

After work, Ann left her office considerably more nonplussed than usual. A whole day's worth of subjects, all of whom wore similar badges with bizarre wordings. Had they started to fuck with her head? she wondered. Psychologists fucking with the minds of other psychologists? Was the division finally setting her some sort of covert test of her reasoning powers? Heading onto the street, Ann resolved to think about it over a gin or two. Maybe she should start encouraging her patients to wear badges of their own just to muddy the waters a bit. As she reached the bus stop, she was approached by a middle-aged woman in disablingly thick glasses.

'Excuse me, pet,' the woman began, 'are you waiting for a bus?'

Ann glanced up at the bus shelter, the sign perched above it reading 'Bus Stop', the yellow lines on the road enclosing the words 'Buses Only'. No, she was waiting for the fucking opera to start. 'Yes,' she answered doubtfully.

'Great. Would you mind filling out a questionnaire until it comes?'

Shit. She hadn't seen that one coming. She was stuck, unable to pretend to be in a rush to get somewhere. Ann shrugged. 'Sure.'

'Right,' the woman began. 'This is a lifestyle survey we're carrying out for a new product.'

'Great,' Ann replied, vainly hoping a bus would appear. Preferably one that would mount the kerb and run over the market researcher. Getting caught like this was the street equivalent of having the Jehovahs show up at your house.

'The questions are fairly straightforward, although a few of them are, well – ' she glanced myopically around – 'a little unconventional. You know how these lifestyle things are. Anyway, here goes. You ready?'

'As I'll ever be.'

'Right. Question One. What do you consider the most important thing in life? Work? Love? Or money?'

Ann shook her head slowly. 'I've got to pick one?'

'That's the idea. All the questions require a single response.'

'OK.' The word 'love' screamed inside her head. 'Let's say work,' she said.

'Two. What do you think the point of modern existence is?'

'The point? I don't know. To live a decent, contented life?'

'So, contentment?'

'Whatever.'

'And what makes you happiest?'

'What are the options?'

'You tell me.'

'You just want a single answer again?'

'That's the idea.'

Ann monitored the road in near desperation. The number 63 was supposed to come every ten minutes. After a day of probing others, she was finding the questions surprisingly taxing and irrelevant. What was most important in her life? What was the point of it all? What did truly make her happy? 'A happy medium of love, money and work.'

'You've got to choose one thing.'

Again, the word 'love' lit up, but in the light of her recent success within the field of employment, Ann responded, 'Work.'

'What is the single most important quality you look for in a partner?'

Broad shoulders. Thick arms. Nice bum. The lack of a genetic disposition to leach money. 'That chemical thing that there's no name for.' Ann smiled. The interrogation was over. A bus was approaching. 'I'm sorry,' she said, 'but I've got to go. Good luck with your survey.' She stuck her arm out and the bus sailed on past, oblivious. On the verge of rage, she noticed two things about the vehicle. First, it was empty, and second, it had a large advert on the side, featuring a face that appeared familiar. There hadn't been time to study it properly, however. The pollster cleared her throat.

'"That chemical thing", you said.'

Ann frowned, resigned to waiting another ten minutes. 'You know, love at first smell. When you meet someone and their skin is like heaven. You can't sense it exactly, it's just that when you breathe in, something gets sucked inside which excites you.'

'Can I put smell?'

'That's not exactly what I meant, but what the hell.'

'Five. Would you rather have a good job but a lousy relationship or a lousy job and a good relationship?'

'I honestly don't know. A good relationship can solve many problems, but a crap job can make you miserable.'

'So?'

'OK. For the sake of this questionnaire, let's say a good job but a lousy relationship.'

'Fine. Six. You attempt to have sex with someone but it doesn't quite work out. What would you do?'

Ann smiled. Another bus was approaching. 'That's one I'd prefer not to answer,' she said. 'And besides, here's my lift home, finally.' She watched as the bus slowed, indicated and then speeded up again. Ann stood with her mouth open. The bus was empty. She got a better look at the picture on the side, but still not enough for full recognition.

'So what would you do, pet?' the woman asked again.

'What?'

'If you attempted to have sex with someone but it didn't quite work out. What would you do?'

Ann's patience waned. 'That's none of your business.'

'OK, how about question eight. Have you moved location in the last year?'

'Yes.'

'In which case, would you rank new friends as more or less important to you than old friends?'

'Where the hell are these questions coming from?'

'Do you ever think about the ones you leave behind?'

'Which ones?'

Something had changed in the market researcher. She was rattling questions off with no desire to hear a response as if she was stuck on fast forward. 'Do you ever feel that daily life occasionally ruins everything? Have you ever met someone who under different circumstances would have been a life-mate? Why do we allow petty inconveniences and awkwardness to interfere with the important issues? When the right bus comes along, do we know it's the one we want?' The pollster glanced up and down the road nervously. 'Er, when the right bus comes along, do we know it's the one we want?'

Ann felt things were going a bit strange. She had the uncomfortable sensation that she was being asked a specific set of questions for a reason. 'You've just asked me that.'

The woman appeared anxious. 'I'm sorry, pet. Er, let me think . . .'

The picture on the bus suddenly crystallized in Ann's brain. Seeing it flash past had been like subliminal advertising. And then she realized what her patients had been trying to tell her with their badges. She wasn't being tested by devious professors. She monitored the road, guessing what was coming next. Sure enough, the same bus appeared, and this time it came to a halt. On the side, she could clearly see now, was a full-sized picture of Tim Power's face. Above it read, **The One Thing Your Life is Missing**. She reluctantly climbed on. The market researcher followed her. The lower deck was empty and so she ascended the stairs. At the front, facing forwards, was Tim. Ann sat down next to him.

'Are you deliberately trying to mess with my mind?' she asked.

'Yes,' Tim replied quietly. 'So where do you live?'

Ann told him and he shouted the address down to the driver, who pulled away from the stop.

Headfuck

While the bus took corners impossibly wide, Tim and Ann chatted.

'Look, I see enough fuck-ups, enough compulsive liars, enough mid-life crises, enough career problems,' Ann said. 'It's not that I look for success in a man – I just look for lack of failure. This is important to me.'

'My days of failure are over.'

'And how do you work that out?'

'I'm no longer working in advertising. I had one last campaign, which went well, and now I've packed it up.'

'So what was the last campaign?'

'You.'

'And you think it worked?'

'We shall see. But I've made you think about a few issues, exposed you to the product, that sort of thing.'

'There was a RhylZig ad on TV yesterday. Did you direct it?'

'Me? Hell, no. I had nothing to do with it.'

'But this was your big chance! Your wonder product! This is what you'd been aiming for all this time.'

'No. What I was aiming for was a soul. Communication. Touching people. Meaning. Substance. And, more than anything, understanding. Adverts I can take

351

or leave.' Tim scratched the back of his head, a sharp jab of pain prompting him to open up. 'You see, my dad was Ronnie Power.'

'Who?'

'You know, the man who created the Poxo family.'

'The Poxo family on TV? He was an advertiser?'

'Oh yes. '

'You're using the past tense. Is he . . .'

Tim twitched. 'No, he's alive. But he walked out on us when I was twelve.'

'How come?'

'That's the thing. He creates the most successful family in advertising history, twenty-five years and still going strong, grinning merrily around the dinner table, pouring Poxo over everything in sight, and at home, a total fucking disaster. A nervous wreck. Didn't even have the decency to run off with another woman. Just couldn't handle having a wife and kids. Said the strain was too much. And every day writing lines for perfect housewives to parrot to perfect husbands.'

'Do you see him?'

'Never. Mum hears the odd report of his whereabouts, what he's up to. But he made such a dismal job of being a father that apparently he can't face seeing me or my sister. And every time I see a fucking Poxo cube, or a Poxo advert, I see his hassled face, frowning down at me, saying, "Some day, I'll come back for you."' Tim rubbed his aching forehead. 'But he never did.'

'So you went into advertising . . .'

'I suppose I wanted to know what it was that took my father away.'

'And?'

'I'm not sure I ever found out. Things got complicated. I even made a mess of my fictional worlds.'

'Now what?'

'I've dissolved the business.'

'You got rid of the company?'

'Yep. Went to London to see my accountant. He sorted it out.'

'Tim Power Advertising is no longer a viable concern?'

'Never was. But I've decided to move on. Stop wasting my life trying to understand my dad's world.'

'So what's Dave going to do?'

'Dunno. He's buggered off somewhere.'

'And what about Tim Power himself – is he still a going concern?'

Tim turned to face her. 'Very much so,' he replied. 'Look, I've paid my debts off, I have my savings restored and I'm thinking about buying a house.'

'A house? Where?'

'Wherever.'

'And what do you mean you've got your savings back?'

'This ex-advertiser in front of you owns a stake in RhylZig. The fastest-growing junk food product for a decade. Can't even taste it myself. But not to put too fine a point on it, things are looking up.'

'What about Zoe?'

'I moved out soon after you did. Events reached a stalemate. It turns out that she had been seeing someone in Australia. She had a couple of calls at ridiculous hours of the night and I assumed they were still in touch. Normally I would have been distraught. But what upset me more was you leaving.'

'How did you find out where I worked?'

'Wasn't that difficult. I knew which city, guessed some sort of hospital department, did a lot of ringing around. And here I am.'

'And here you are.'

'Look, I had to win you over the only way I knew how – by advertising myself to you.'

'You could just have phoned.'

'That wouldn't have been any fun. I've had a great time playing at being a proper advertiser. Putting lines in people's mouths, making badges . . .'

'Totylim – **The One Thing Your Life is Missing**.'

'Getting posters made, hiring props, auditioning actors.'

'The pollster?'

'And the nurse handing out the badges. And writing MR questions, of course. Which reminds me. Let's get to know the real Ann Hillyard.' He stood up, disappeared downstairs and returned with a piece of paper. 'You know the one thing I've learned from an obsession with market research is that there are two ways people answer. They either give outrageously honest responses, admitting things they would never even tell their partners. Or else they lie, and give the answers they think they should give.' He raised his eyebrows at Ann. 'There seems to be a discrepancy between the people we are in surveys and the people we are in real life. In hypothetical situations, we are saints. In actual conditions we are sinners. And nowhere, Dr Hillyard, is this more apparent than in the minefield of human relationships. Question three, for example.'

'What about it?'

He read Ann's response. 'Work doesn't make you happy. Not truly, smiling-in-the-dark, warm-inside happy.'

'Maybe not.'

'Ann . . .' He closed his eyes. The narrow confines of his vision had shrunk to pinpricks. The throb in his

354

head was so loud he couldn't hear anything above it. There was a roar in his ears. The bus went round a corner, and Tim went with it.

'What?' Ann laughed, as Tim keeled over and slumped into the aisle, where he lay on his side. 'Tim. Stop fucking around. You've made your point.' He failed to move. She shook him. 'Look, enough stunts for one day. Maybe you're not a failure any more. Just get up and we'll talk about it. I'm not promising anything, OK? It's going to take more than a cheesy ad campaign to change my mind about you.' She shook him again, more firmly this time.

Tim twitched and opened his eyes. 'Ann. Help me. I'm . . .'

'Shit.'

He didn't look good.

His eyelids drooped.

His skin suddenly had a tinge of blue.

She jabbed him in the side. He whispered the words, 'You've got to help me,' gripping her hand. Ann screamed. The bus stopped and the driver ran upstairs, followed quickly by the pollster.

'What's the matter with him?' the driver shouted, staring down at the prone form in the aisle.

'I don't know.'

'But you're a doctor, right?' the pollster said, pointing to Ann's ID badge.

'Well . . .'

'I don't think he's breathing.'

'Maybe a heart attack?' the driver guessed.

'Quick, doc. What're we going to do?'

Ann remained frozen. It had finally come home to roost. A small lie that seemed destined to follow her to her grave. If she'd had the courage, she could have admitted to it. But no, here she was, about to face her own personal nightmare. Tim's clammy fingers held fast around Ann's hand.

'Doc?'

'Come on. Do something.'

Ann looked up, sheer fear galvanizing her into action. 'Where's the nearest Casualty department?'

'The General. Two miles.'

'Right. Get downstairs and drive there,' she said to the driver. 'Put your hazard lights on. Here . . .' she said, gesturing to the market researcher.

'Jean.'

'Give me your coat.' Still holding Tim's hand, she draped the garment over him. As they ground towards Casualty, Ann took out her mobile phone and dialled 999. 'We're heading for the Newcastle General in a bus,' she told the operator. 'Thirty-two-year-old male, unconscious. ETA 10 to 15 minutes.' The traffic was virtually seized, and they were making very slow progress. Ann looked up. The inaccurately titled rush-hour was in full effect. Pedestrians were keeping up with the bus. She started to panic. There was no chance of getting Tim down the stairs, even if there was a quicker way to Casualty. Calling an ambulance probably wouldn't help him. She tried to clear her mind. There was a lot she had learnt while living with Tim. His apparent hypochondria had forced her to. She had read textbooks on medicine, physiology and anatomy. In between his descriptions of multiple symptoms she had pored over reference books, scrutinizing potential causes, readying herself for any future cross-examinations. She ran over his indications, desperately trying to separate the facts from the chaff. Frequent headaches. No sense of taste or smell. Loss of visual field. Sudden unconsciousness. She glanced up. They were barely moving. The driver was frantically sounding his horn, but the road was solid in both directions. Tim was still out. She shook him, and he murmured something before relapsing again. At this rate it would take half an hour. Ann opened her handbag. It was time for action. She pulled out a half-empty bottle of mineral water. Fishing more deeply in her bag, she extracted a small brown container and poured a couple of tablets into her palm. Rolling Tim from the recovery position and onto his back, she pushed his jaws apart. Then she placed the pills as far into his throat as possible and tipped some water in. Tim swallowed involuntarily and then coughed. Ann peered into his mouth. The tablets were gone. She was far from superstitious, but as she rolled him onto his side Ann crossed her fingers. She hoped to fuck she was right. The next fifteen minutes were as agonizing as any she had ever known. The bus suddenly gained some momentum and Ann appreciated that they were finally in the hospital grounds. Soon there were shouts. Two paramedics appeared on the top deck with a doctor behind. They were followed by the driver and the market researcher. The lead paramedic asked Ann some perfunctory questions, before setting up a drip and taking a blood sample from a canula inserted into the back of Tim's hand.

'Can you hear me?'

'His name is Tim.'

'Tim.' The medic pulled open Tim's eyelids and shone a small torch into each pupil. 'Has he been drinking? Is he on medication?'

'Just non-steroidal anti-inflammatories.'

'What for?'

'Headaches. He's been having them for three or four months.'

'Any drug use? Heroin? Cocaine?'

'Don't know. But he works in advertising.'

The doctor raised his eyebrows. 'Cocaine then,' he said. 'Anyway, looks like an ischemic attack, maybe a stroke. We'd better assess him for anticoagulants.'

'No need.'

'What?'

'I've given him two aspirin.'

'How long ago?'

'Twenty minutes.'

'Are you a doctor?'

Ann paused for a second, trying not to meet the eye of the bus driver or the pollster. 'No,' she said firmly.

'Then why?'

'Obvious. Headaches, loss of taste and smell, blacking out. Classic pre-stroke ischemic attack.'

'Aspirin? For Christ's sake. What were you thinking?'

'But I'd read . . .'

'Depends entirely on whether he's a bleeder or a clotter.' The medic turned to one of his colleagues. 'Ring MRI, tell them we want an immediate scan. Get a stretcher we can take down the stairs. See if there's a bed in ITU.' Tim's eyes flickered. 'In fact, let's just lift him. We need to MRI him *now*!'

Scrambled

Simon Jasper cruised proudly down Taunsley's high street accompanied by 395 watts of ruinous bass and five grudging watts of treble. At this volume, supermarket windows rattled. Saturday shoppers turned their heads and opened their mouths, their chests suddenly pounding, and Simon was glad he couldn't hear what they said. He guessed it wasn't good. But that wasn't the point. He was being noticed. His car was fast becoming a legend in the town. At the end of the road, he nursed The Beast around a miniroundabout and treated pedestrians, most of whom had only just recovered their hearing and breathing from the first pass, to another dose of audio mayhem.

In the front pocket of his jeans was the forty quid Dave had recently sent him. A couple of months earlier, Dave had been understandably reluctant to ask the general population what they felt about lodgers and pork pies. In exchange for cash, Simon had therefore ticked random boxes at will. He heard that Tim Power had been pleased with the answers, so Simon imagined he must have done something right. While it didn't make a lot of sense that an advertiser should be happy to receive a selection of arbitrary responses to surreal questions, Simon had taken the money gratefully and thought no more about it. Besides, today he had a mission. Cruising up and down the town centre was just the warm-up. Nearby Bridgton was hosting a customization competition. Simon had entered, and having spent the day on extra-anal preparation, sniffed a potential victory. This would be the vindication of months of obsessive improvement. He would be acknowledged, coveted, envied. He would have arrived. He beeped his air horn at an unusually attractive Taunsley female and tweaked the stereo even louder for added ear damage. Road works lay ahead and Simon changed down to accelerate past them before the oncoming traffic.

Travelling fast in the opposite direction, Derek Gribben gripped the steering wheel of his Smart car with his one hand. He glanced up. Above the shops that lined the high street, Mr Jenkins owned a luxury two-storey Georgian apartment. Derek slowed slightly, looking for the entrance to the side street that housed Mr Jenkins's front door. Out of the corner of his eye, the dull metal of the shotgun brooded with silent intent. And then, just as he was about to pull over on the left, a man in front forced him into a sudden change of plan. Derek edged closer to the oncoming traffic and floored the accelerator. The engine picked up and his car gathered momentum.

In a coned-off ditch thirty yards ahead, Shamus Farley, despondent road digger, rested against his equipment and examined his handiwork, casting his proud eyes over the trench he was excavating. Nothing at all was clogging it up. Noticeable by their absence were crisp packets, gravel, skinheads and power cables. The latter had caused him a lot of unrest lately. While repairing a road near Top Class Pasties he had inadvertently drilled through a thick flex of the high-voltage variety. Electricity had immediately disappeared from the industrial estate and Shamus had left soon after, judging it best to keep the matter quiet. Feasting his eyes on the emptiness of his trench, Shamus realized with a start that it was Saturday and that time-and-a-half applied. He surreptitiously began kicking soil back into the hole just to slow things down a bit.

Derek Gribben's speedo nudged forty-five miles an hour. He overtook a knackered Sierra on the wrong side. First the road digger, and then he would go and deal with Jenkins. Two cunts in one day. Just twenty more yards and he would run the fucker over. He took aim.

Above, Mr Jenkins felt his windows resonate in time with a frankly unnerving bass line coming from the street. He hummed his way towards the fridge, lighting the hob as he passed, removed three packets of sausages and nudged the door shut with his considerable backside. The frying pan sizzled and Mr Jenkins salivated. These were the best sausages JMP had ever made. Three Special Editions, vintage productions. The only trouble was that he had almost exhausted the consignments. He was down to just a handful of packets. This was beginning to gnaw away at him from time to time. Obtaining another supply would not be easy. He read and re-read the labels, whistling, his mouth wet with anticipation. Pulling two sausages out, he snipped the twisted skin that linked them, dropped the delicacies into the pan and lowered the heat, careful not to overcook them.

Below, Gary Shrubble also approached the roadworks in the opposite direction to Simon Jasper. He was driving wildly, aiming his car desperately between the pavement and oncoming traffic. A small car, which appeared to be travelling even more erratically than he was, overtook him and he treated it to some liberal swearing. Despite several hours of concentrated drinking, Gary was nervous and excited, animated in a way that had rarely been witnessed before. In one hand, his Dictaphone absorbed another alcohol-rich outpouring. This was different from the usual local trivia, however. Finally, after months of research, the pieces had come together. This was his moment, and he knew it. The Big Story was complete. 'Headline. **Gotcha!**' he exclaimed excitedly. 'First column text. The Mercury can finally reveal that Jenkins Meat Products, who announced eighty new jobs yesterday, are behind a series of macabre events in the town over the last six years. In a violent series of beatings and brutality, involving coercion, threatening . . . shit.' Gary Shrubble tried to change gear and dictate at the same time. At this rate, he was going to miss the copy deadline for the Sunday Mercury. Just three fewer pints and he would have been OK. His obsession was about to become reality, but only if he filed the story in the next fifteen minutes. Otherwise it would have to wait until after the weekend, and there was no telling what might transpire in the meantime. ' . . . behaviour and the disappearance of key witnesses and public servants, Taunsley's only serious newspaper has uncovered evidence of . . . goings-on involving extortion, corruption – ' Gary struggled to read a word he had scribbled on the back of his hand – 'and, most seriously . . . oh fuck.' The small car, which he thought he recognized, suddenly braked and swerved in front of him, slewing across the road and causing him to frantically turn the wheel. He began to skid and lose control, bald tyres doing little to hamper his progress.

Shamus heard a noise and ceased work. How his ruined ears had picked it out was something he would always ponder. Turning round, he saw a miniature car ploughing towards him. Its driver appeared to be actively aiming for him, his clenched teeth clearly visible through the windscreen. Shamus jumped smartly out of the way and stepped back a couple of paces as the car zoomed by, inches from him.

Simon saw the car late. It had just missed an ageing road worker, who had leapt suddenly out of its path. Simon had about half a second to decide. A quarter of a second in, he floored the accelerator and threw The Beast towards the centre of the road. There was just enough room. He could get past the Smart car before the battered Ford Sierra coming in the opposite direction. It would be a tight squeeze. However, as he forced the pedal into the rusty floor of the car, the engine choked and spluttered and then died completely. He freewheeled forwards, momentum ebbing. The oncoming car was travelling erratically. Simon flung the wheel back to the left. The skidding Sierra hurried forwards to meet him. Simon breathed in. There was enough space. And then the extended spoiler and body kit smashed into the side of the oncoming car. Simon was flung forwards and his head rushed to meet the metal sports steering wheel he had recently installed.

Above the spitting of his frying pan, Mr Jenkins heard a commotion in the street. Peering through the kitchen window, his nose pressed hard against the glass, he saw something that gave him an enormous shot of satisfaction. He made a quick phone call and turned off the hob.

Gary Shrubble staggered from the wreck of his car. He was several times over the limit and two thoughts came to him simultaneously. First, he was sincerely desperate to evade arrest. A driving ban would halt his career, just as it was about to explode into the big time. Second, he was anxious to avert an appearance in the Court News section of his own newspaper. More importantly, he was keen to ensure the *Shopper* didn't get an opportunity to report the incident. He shuddered as he made his way along the unsteady pavement. The fuckers would type it with hard-ons. Still in shock, he pictured the editorial.

Shrubble In A Muddle

Turps-nudging journalist Gary Shrubble was last night beginning a custodial sentence for causing injury through reckless driving. According to eyewitnesses, the *Taunsley Mercury*'s main feature writer had been drinking heavily for around two and a half decades before the accident. It appears that at the time he had been in a hurry to file a story about a missing gerbil for the award-dodging *Mercury*.

And then below,

The forlorn Gary Shrubble, as pictured by the *Shopper*'s court artist Eric Waters.

He quickened his step and turned a corner, away from the high street and its gathering commotion. A siren began to pierce his crashing hangover. Given that he had abandoned his car at the scene, the police would soon be looking for him. Gary deemed it best to disappear for a few hours, sober up beyond breathalyser recognition and then claim some sort of amnesia. The story would have to wait a few days. As he scurried along the side road a smart front door opened in front of him and the town's leading impresario stepped out.

'Gary Shrubble,' Mr Jenkins said, 'what a pleasant surprise.'

'Can't talk,' Gary mumbled.

'Why not?'

'I've got to get away for a bit.'

'Really? Maybe I can help. Besides, I've been meaning to talk to you about a few things.'

Mr Jenkins pulled the door shut and pressed his key fob. A large car on the other side of the road flashed its lights at him. He assisted Gary Shrubble across the road. They left the scene at speed, screeching tyres burning up the tarmac.

Unperpetuating the Mediocrity of Products

Tim Power scanned the faces in front of him. He had lost another major function. This was becoming a little disconcerting. First smell, then taste, and now speech. At this rate, he would be better off in a coma.

The earliest sensation he had was one of numbness, in his mouth, his throat and down the left side of his body. He was utterly unable to form words. It was as if he had awoken into a world that could manage quite happily without his input.

In hospital, Ann had a rare opportunity to tell him exactly what had happened without interruption. She told him that he had suffered a small stroke. She neglected to mention that the aspirins could either have saved him from brain damage or have caused significant injury depending on whether his ischemic attack was due to a blood clot or internal bleeding. Although her prompt action had probably helped minimize the problem, she could just as well have inflicted serious permanent harm. She said that while strokes are more common in older people, a worrying number of those under forty succumb, and that the odds of having one are much higher in smokers and drinkers with poor diets who don't exercise. Another potential contributory factor, she explained, raising her eyebrows at him, was previous cocaine use. Tim scrawled the words 'Only three times, with A2Z colleague Jeremy' on his pad. Ann appeared puzzled, but let it go.

Tim was admitted to the Newcastle District Stroke Centre. This was a regional facility with a good record in rehabilitation. Ann accompanied him, but not without first admitting to her utter lack of medical qualifications.

'I'm sorry to tell you this,' she said as she helped wheel Tim along a brisk hospital corridor, 'but I'm afraid I lied to you all along about being a doctor.'

Tim drew a shaky question mark on his pad, which Ann read over his shoulder.

'I thought it might impress you, you know, help me get the room.'

He was still for a few seconds, considering the information, before writing, 'Was crying out for anyone to move in.'

'I didn't know that. And those patients who came to see me at the hospital were all under my psychological appraisal. I wasn't seeing them for, you know, clinical reasons. I know I've been stupid. It's one of those things, I suppose. I fell in love with the house when I saw it. Then I couldn't face telling you the truth. I was weak, and I'm still hugely embarrassed.'

There was a lull. Tim was a sick man. Besides, half-written, half-spoken conversations were awkward and one-sided, with little natural flow possible. By the time Tim had replied, Ann had already thought of something else to say.

The Stroke Centre proved to be an unbearably cheerful affair. Ann visited him most evenings. Her prediction that his life was a virtual full stop became

367

unerringly accurate. His progress was monitored daily. He was given routine tasks to perform in the way of therapy. The specialist advised that a further stroke was possible and so he was placed under careful observation until he was fit to visit the centre as a day patient. Time slouched past with a defeating lack of urgency. Visitors came and went again, never really knowing what to say for the best. His mother dropped in regularly, despite the long round-trip. And then one day a man entered whom Tim half-recognized. Pulling up a chair, he said, 'Saw your ads. Not bad.'

Tim's brain, already treacly, was slow to react. But when it did, he sat bolt upright. His eyes widened in disbelief. And then he suddenly reached for his pad. 'They're not mine,' he wrote frantically. 'I don't believe in creating fictional families.'

'I see.'

'While letting your own one fall apart.'

'Right.'

'So why did you never come back for me?'

He was an old man who hadn't aged well. Two decades had taken their toll. There was kindness and playfulness in his eyes, but also a mildly haunted look. 'I don't know. I moved on. I . . . look, I'm not proud of what I did, but at the time it was vital.'

'Vital?'

'For me.'

Tim stabbed his pen into the word vital. Children are vital. Parenting is vital. Twenty years of hurt tightened his throat. He tried to swallow, but couldn't. With all his pride, he defied his eyes to water.

'Look, what if, after everything, you discover that the real world is just too *difficult*? That nothing goes quite how you plan it? That you have no control? That . . . I don't know . . . the only option is to retreat?'

Tim drew a question mark, forcing his biro deep into the page.

The man fidgeted with his glasses, taking them off, cleaning them and slotting them back on. 'Come on, your mum must have told you how difficult I found it. And it wasn't that I was escaping into my career – it was the job that started to unpin me. By spending my time with fictional families I began to question the nature of human relationships. I came to see just how far we were from where we should have been. I didn't care about selling anything, I just wanted to explore how things could be if we got to write the rules again. You know . . .'

Tim had anticipated this moment of reconciliation since he was twelve, had rehearsed pages of dialogue, had imagined a multitude of accusations, but now that it was here he was mute. Even before the stroke, he appreciated that he would have struggled. There really wasn't as much to say as he had imagined. His father had left, Tim had chased after him in the only way he knew how – by following the same career – and now they were together again. For his own part, his father was uncomfortable and fidgety and looked like he wanted to leave. He stood up.

'Well, I wanted to make sure you were OK,' he muttered, pushing his glasses up his nose.

Tim stared into his pad, lost, unable to capture his feelings with a blue plastic ballpoint. 'Promise that you will come back some time,' he wrote, eventually. 'When I'm better.'

'I'll come back. This time I'll come back.'

As his father's footsteps echoed away, Tim glanced miserably through the window. Across the hospital site, people were going about their business, endlessly chasing their tails, scurrying like beetles. This, he

369

appreciated, was what the world was like. Circles within circles. Striving to earn, to buy, to use, to waste. Running in any direction that seemed right. For the first time, he could see that the many market-research campaigns he had instigated during his career had ultimately told him nothing about humanity. The seemingly random responses, the utter lack of coherency. Twenty-seven per cent of men, he had learnt, would rather attend a world-cup final than witness their child being born. And 18 per cent of females rank intimate hygiene above further education in a partner. And 21 per cent of drivers have a secret pet name for their car. And 52 per cent think that scientific advances will harm society more than help it. And 33 per cent of smokers believe that smoking isn't dangerous. And 48 per cent of both sexes have been unfaithful at some point. And 82 per cent of people trust their partners implicitly. And only 83 per cent of newlyweds truly expect their marriage to last. And 41 per cent of people can't spell commitment. And 74 per cent of adults are currently in relationships, and of these 73 per cent are sexually fulfilled. And 18 per cent of wage earners prefer not to make any provision for the future. And 71 per cent do not believe the government when it says something is safe. And the three most common sources of anxiety in life are money (33 per cent), family (21 per cent) and work (19 per cent). And 12 per cent of married men and women have seen a therapist. And 36 per cent of those polled grew up outside the 'normal' nuclear family. And so on, the whole population being no more categorizable than a million wrong-number phone conversations, and the advertiser's nuclear family looking distinctly unnatural. And how much of our behaviour, Tim wondered, can be traced directly back to someone's desire to make money? How many of our suspicions? How many of our affectations? How many of our obsessions? How many malnourished souls are desperately buying multivitamins to replace the nutrients stripped from their highly processed dinners? He saw that he had fallen into the trap as well. Inventing one more junk food to send our hyperactive kids obese and our obese kids hyperactive. And as if to compensate, Tim's own body had fallen apart just when the nation began ramming RhylZig down their nutrient-starved throats.

'Dribbling again?' a nurse asked on her way past. 'Must be the thought of all that lovely RhylZig.'

Tim continued to gaze out of the window, mesmerized, wiping saliva from the corner of his unbalanced mouth. Life was precious, miraculous. No one ever gained lifelong enrichment from buying a consumer durable. Being a commercial success didn't mean anything. He thought about a lot of things. There was little else he could do.

And then, as he watched his father pick his way through the car park, he decided once and for all what he was going to do with his life.

Journalistic Principles

'I just wanted to clear a few things up,' Mr Jenkins explained, nursing his car across the broken surface of the factory car park. Although it was designed for far more onerous driving conditions, Mr Jenkins was firmly in love with his vehicle, and treated it with a respect wholly absent from his dealings with livestock.

'I'm listening,' Gary Shrubble answered slowly. He'd banged his head in the accident and was rapidly sobering up.

'You've been following me around for a number of months now, turning up at the most unexpected places, frankly being a pain in the arse.' He turned an unnerving grin on his passenger. 'But that's your job, right?'

'Something like that.'

'Now the police are currently looking for you in respect of a drink-driving incident. I'm looking after you, therefore I'm breaking the law as well. You see what I'm saying? You give a bit of trust, you get a bit. I'm helping you, and I want you to help me.'

'What with?'

'If I tell you my side of the story, I want to make a bargain with you.' Mr Jenkins stopped the car and climbed out. It was cold and beginning to darken, winter biting and tormenting the industrial grounds.

'What sort of bargain?'

'Something I think will interest you. Come with me and I'll show you.' The reporter and factory owner made their way through the bustling site of JMP until they reached a depressingly modern warehouse. Inside, Mr Jenkins flicked a bank of switches and a multitude of neon strips blinked into life. The building was empty apart from some shiny new machinery and gleaming work surfaces. 'We're going to be making a new product in here soon,' Mr Jenkins said, licking the moisture from his moustache. Despite the cold, he seemed to ooze a perpetual oily sweat.

'Which one?'

'RhylZig Two. **The Sausage Sandwich in a Jar.** Another of Tim Power's inventions.'

Gary Shrubble stopped walking and propped himself up against a table. 'Come on, Jenkins,' he rasped, 'what's this all about?'

'I don't think you're going to go to the police now. You're in enough trouble as it is.'

'So?'

'So maybe we can have a chat. Man to man.'

'I'm listening.'

'I want to make you an offer.'

'Yes?'

'To become an integral part of Jenkins Meat Products.'

'How?'

'I need your input.'

'I still don't see . . .'

'I want you to get involved with our products. Very involved. Working from the inside. But first I think it's only fair that all issues are resolved. I'm interested in what you know, and what you think you know. When

373

we've got things straight between us, maybe we can get down to business. So, let's start with some basics. Trevor Bayliss, the Food Standards Agency man. What do you think happened to him?'

'He was either frightened off, or worse.'

Mr Jenkins smiled. 'Worse.'

'Meaning what, exactly?'

'Just, well . . .' He glanced at the enormous Rhinegolds at the end of the room. 'You know, dealt with.'

Gary Shrubble straightened. He had been right. The story was going to be huge. 'And Mayor Blunt?'

'Met a very sharp end.'

'And then Gribben. You stitched the town up between you.'

'After they stitched him back together, we decided that I would control ninety per cent of the town's meat business and he could have what was left. Things calmed down after that. You see, what you probably don't appreciate is that Gribben was trying to bring me down from the inside while he was working for me. He tipped off the FSA man, who began to cause a lot of problems. Even the fucking mayor got involved. So I had them all dealt with. I gave Gribben a generous sum of money to compensate him for his injuries, on the express condition that he stayed the hell away from JMP. He used the cash to set up Top Class Pasties.'

'And then what?'

'A few years later he got greedy. He began to notice that I was having commercial difficulties and tried to force me out of business with a series of unfortunate adverts. Nearly did, as well.' Mr Jenkins sat down on a table. 'And then he turned nastier.'

'When I followed you to his factory, one of your men broke a window. What were you up to?'

'I was going to burn the fucker's buildings down.'

'OK, so I'd figured most of that out.'

'Even the mayor?'

'I had a suspicion.'

Mr Jenkins stroked his moustache pensively. 'Maybe you're sharper than I gave you credit for.'

'You never know. So what can I do for you?'

'Pull the story.'

'What story?'

'The one you're working on.'

'Let's say I do. What's in it for me?'

'It's not just a question of what's in it for you – it's what's in it for everybody. Things are going well. Unimaginably well. The town is beginning to boom again. RhylZig is becoming huge – we're starting to get foreign orders. Already we're working flat out seven days a week. **The Sausage Sandwich in a Jar** is on its way. People will want to come and live in the town again. Property prices will soar. Unemployment will soon be a thing of the past. JMP are going to start investing in schools and worthy schemes. And, to answer your question, we're going to be pouring so much money into advertising that I'm thinking of buying the *Mercury*.'

'Buying the paper?'

'Why not? More people mean larger newspaper sales. In fact, I'm considering taking over the *Shopper* and closing it down. How about that? Of course, I'd need to install a new editor of the *Mercury*, someone I could trust to run the paper right. Someone with a lot of experience . . .'

Gary licked his dry lips. 'No more crap local stories?'

'As the place where RhylZig was born, we'd be looking to extend our horizons.'

'And pay?'

Mr Jenkins produced a cheque book from the inside pocket of his suit jacket. 'Consider this three months' advance wages.'

Gary took the cheque, swaying uneasily and considering his options. Some people were dead or missing. His Big Story wouldn't bring them back. In fact, all he had really hoped was that it would elevate him above the filth of local reporting. Which is what it had done, indirectly. He squinted at the sum of money involved. Fifteen grand. Almost a year's salary at present. While Gary was by no means a crusader for the truth, he did have some journalistic principles. The main one of which was being open to bribery where at all possible. He pocketed the cheque and shook Mr Jenkins's outstretched hand.

'So you'll pull the story?'

'No problem. Haven't even finished it yet.'

'Not finished?' Mr Jenkins took out his mobile phone and entered a number. 'That is good news.'

Two large meat packers quickly appeared, one from each end of the factory. Mr Jenkins stepped back from the journalist. One was carrying what looked like a cattle prod. The other pressed a button close to one of the enormous shredders, and the machine shuddered into action. As the larger meat packer approached him, Gary Shrubble had an uncomfortable premonition of extreme pain.

Later that evening in his substantial town apartment, Mr Jenkins melted a small knob of butter in a saucepan. Above his hob was a glossy mounted poster. It had come from the TV ads for RhylZig. The slogan was taken from a catchy Tina Turner song with an undeniably pleasing beat. He couldn't help but grin. Although there had been no need for immediate panic, his stocks had nonetheless been running low. He took his old vintages from the fridge and lined them up next to the new one. Now he would be fine for a long time. And then, who knew? Maybe another local gangster of a foreman might try to attack him. Maybe another mayor who had stifled commerce in the town would pay an uninvited visit to the factory late one night. Maybe another FSA man would come and poke around in the factory. Maybe another journalist would take it upon himself to investigate for several years without actually writing a story. But that wouldn't need to happen for a while.

Examining his bounty, he was particularly fond of the Gribben vintage. The fucker had tried to ruin him and had failed. He congratulated himself and felt a rumble in his considerable belly. Mr Jenkins feasted his eyes, running them from Gribben's Special Batch past Mayor Blunt's Limited Edition, to the FSA Flavour Sensation. And then there was the newest addition. Shrubble's Sizzlers. He grinned again. There was a sort of brutal beauty to it all. Gary Shrubble had been chewed up and spat out by his one Big Story. A manufacturer had devoured the truth. It was an evolutionary step forwards in business theory. Also, a greedy foreman had been disarmed, as it were, a mayor intent on restraining free enterprise had been consumed, and someone concerned with pork pie content had become just that. You could try to fuck with the commercial world, but it always won in the end. Nothing, Mr Jenkins laughed, could ever halt the process of capitalism. And if something did get in its way, then it was the job of every right-minded industrialist to mince it up and consume it. Maybe, Mr Jenkins was well aware, he took this a little too literally. But once you had a taste for such things, it was hard to let go.

He dropped a Shrubble's Sizzler into the pan. The skin crackled and spat and the sausage whined in complaint. He pierced it with a fork and a slight aroma of whisky escaped. Stroking his moustache, he prepared to taste the flavour of victory.

Mr Jenkins glanced up at the glossy poster once more. Of his four limited edition batches, this one promised to be simply the best. Better than anyone, he told himself, anyone I've ever ate.

Epilogue

Derek Gribben was eventually cut free from the wreckage of his car, which had embedded itself neatly in a trench dug by Shamus Farley, the man he had been trying to run down at the time. In the accident, Derek was unfortunate enough to lose his other arm. Several of Derek's possessions were retrieved from the scene, including a holdall full of money, which he was allowed to keep, and two guns, which he wasn't, and which wouldn't now have been much use to him anyway. He served three months in prison for firearms offences, where he was roundly bullied by psychopaths of equal standing and extra limbs. As his only line of attack, Derek Gribben developed an uncanny ability in the art of headbutting. On his release, Derek was moved to a council facility for disabled ex-prisoners, where he learnt to feed himself with his feet.

Mr Jenkins was charged with four counts of murder. Most of the evidence was discovered on a grubby Dictaphone found by police on the dashboard of Gary Shrubble's Sierra. A search of the journalist's desk revealed photographs, documents and other evidence relating to a series of serious crimes dating back eight years. Mr Jenkins later escaped on a technicality, however, due to the disappearance of a key witness. No one in the town ate sausages for more than a month. Jenkins became a reclusive millionaire, continuing to oversee the campaign for RhylZig world domination from the seclusion of his country house.

Gary Shrubble was awarded the town's first posthumous medal for journalism. At a moving ceremony, he was also charged posthumously with drink-driving. His empty coffin was cremated in front of a small number of mourners, principal among whom were local publicans and off-licence managers.

Simon Jasper left the security profession with the rare distinction of not stealing anything during his tenure. He joined a local garage and became a competent mechanic. By learning the most highly prized skill in automotive engineering – overcharging – he was soon able to earn enough money to move out of his mother's house. During his rehabilitation, he came to see that customization wasn't always the solution to life's problems. Perhaps, even in our image-driven world, he belatedly appreciated, it isn't enough to simply change the appearance of something.

David Manners, regarded by many in the world of London advertising as an avant-garde genius, oversaw a succession of variously disastrous TV campaigns. Of particular note was the launch of **Bachelor Pads** on an unsuspecting population. On the strength of this, he returned to Taunsley after three years and reopened Power Advertising under the company name Manners Merchandising. Business was brisk and Dave soon found himself gluing **Simply the Best** to whatever came his way. No one seemed to complain.

Alistaire Smythe served eighteen painful months and never returned to Taunsley. He journeyed to Kos and tracked his father down. Ali was the third illegitimate son to come knocking on the old man's door. Nicolaos ran a tourist fish and chip business near the beach of Kos town. Appreciating that options were narrowing in England, Ali decided to settle in Kos, where he was roundly and frequently abused by drunken English tourists for being Greek.

Barry and Cathy Dinsdale struggled vainly on, considerably hampered by the efforts of their six offspring. Cathy, who had lost her job as Derek Gribben's secretary when Top Class Pasties was sold to a development company, devoted her time instead to domestic engineering. Barry began writing a book on household efficiency, which he later abandoned due to flagging enthusiasm.

Ann Hillyard, supported by her partner's substantial commercial income, returned to university to read medicine as a mature student. She eventually discovered how to distinguish meningitis from a washing-powder allergy, and how to differentiate an ischemic attack from a full-blown stroke. As a general practitioner, however, she came to see some years later that the general public was far more disturbed than her mental patients had ever been, and that fixing bodies was only slightly less fraught than fixing minds.

After rehabilitation and recovery, Tim Power set up a one-man think-tank dedicated to Unperpetuating Mediocrity. Based initially in the clutter of sheds at the bottom of Ann's garden, he invested some of the considerable money flowing in from RhylZig to the invention of non-mediocre products. Tim's mission became the undoing of the misapprehensions he had foisted on people at various stages of his career. Among a range of products designed to help the population and make their lives better, Tim patented an early-warning stroke detector, a range of ergonomic office furniture and a continuous action pen that couldn't be broken into pieces no matter how hard you tried. The most successful idea perpetrated by Power Industries, however, was the rebranding of all vitamins as E numbers and their surreptitious insertion into junk foods. Childhood obesity and malnutrition dropped by over a third in the coming years as additive-addicted youngsters gobbled up foodstuffs they heartily believed to be bad for them. Even RhylZig became, if not entirely healthy, then substantially less damaging than it had previously been. With the aid of his father, Poxo cubes also benefited from this course of action. Tim Power eventually became famous as a maverick inventor, and one who left marketing to people who claimed to know what they were doing.

THE END

BIG SPENDER

John McCabe

'ONE OF THE TEN MEN MAKING THE NOVEL WORTH
READING AGAIN'
Arena

A novel about money, love and amusing industrial accidents.

When miser *par excellence* Norbert Flint dies in a bizarre
road accident, he leaves behind only his masterpiece of
financial parsimony, *First out of the Taxi, Last to the Bar*. His
nephew, Jake Cooper, nine-fingered safety inspector and
connoisseur of hazard-prevention videos, finds it and
starts taking its wisdom to heart.

But for a man who urges safety in all things, Jake has a
curiously dangerous past which is starting to invade his
present in the most alarming way. Unless he takes some
serious risks, he's about to lose another finger. Not only that,
he's getting suspicious about his uncle's demise.

And just when Jake believes life can't get any more
treacherous, he meets a woman who shows him that the most
hazardous thing we are ever likely to do is fall in love . . .

'MCCABE'S WRITING IS ORIGINAL, ENTERTAINING
AND COMPELLING'
The Times

'ONE OF THE FUNNIEST NOVELS YOU'RE EVER LIKELY
TO READ'
Birmingham Post

'WITTY AND INCISIVE ABOUT THE PREOCCUPATIONS
OF MODERN LIFE'
Observer

0 552 99968 7

BLACK SWAN

A SELECTED LIST OF FINE WRITING
AVAILABLE FROM BLACK SWAN

77083	3	**I'M A BELIEVER**	*Jessica Adams*	£6.99
77084	1	**COOL FOR CATS**	*Jessica Adams*	£6.99
99900	8	**THE HOLE**	*Guy Burt*	£6.99
99532	0	**SOPHIE**	*Guy Burt*	£5.99
99854	0	**LESSONS FOR A SUNDAY FATHER**	*Claire Calman*	£5.99
77097	3	**I LIKE IT LIKE THAT**	*Claire Calman*	£6.99
99945	8	**DEAD FAMOUS**	*Ben Elton*	£6.99
99995	4	**HIGH SOCIETY**	*Ben Elton*	£6.99
99847	8	**WHAT WE DID ON OUR HOLIDAY**	*John Harding*	£6.99
99966	0	**WHILE THE SUN SHINES**	*John Harding*	£6.99
77164	3	**MANEATER**	*Gigi Levangie*	£6.99
99874	5	**PAPER**	*John McCabe*	£6.99
99873	7	**SNAKESKIN**	*John McCabe*	£6.99
99984	9	**STICKLEBACK**	*John McCabe*	£6.99
99968	7	**BIG SPENDER**	*John McCabe*	£6.99
99907	5	**DUBLIN**	*Sean Moncrieff*	£6.99
99849	4	**THIS IS YOUR LIFE**	*John O'Farrell*	£6.99
99938	5	**PERFECT DAY**	*Imogen Parker*	£6.99
99939	3	**MY SECRET LOVER**	*Imogen Parker*	£6.99
77095	7	**LONDON IRISH**	*Zane Radcliffe*	£6.99
77096	5	**BIG JESSIE**	*Zane Radcliffe*	£6.99
99645	9	**THE WRONG BOY**	*Willy Russell*	£6.99
99952	0	**LIFE ISN'T ALL HA HA HEE HEE**	*Meera Syal*	£6.99
99902	4	**TO BE SOMEONE**	*Louise Voss*	£6.99
99903	2	**ARE YOU MY MOTHER?**	*Louise Voss*	£6.99
99639	4	**THE TENNIS PARTY**	*Madeleinc Wickham*	£5.99
99769	2	**THE WEDDING GIRL**	*Madeleine Wickham*	£6.99